Praise for

Queen of the Underworld

"Mesmerizing . . . The wizardry of this novel is its pitch-perfect rendition of what it was like to be a true solo artist, a female of ambition coming out of 1950s America."

—*The Boston Globe*

"[Queen of the Underworld] crackles with energy. . . . The pleasures of *Queen of the Underworld* are not thematic but visceral . . . just what you would expect and a good deal more."

—*The Seattle Times*

"Gail Godwin's new coming-of-age tale is filled with rich, romantic detail of a city on the cusp of enormous change."

—*The Miami Herald*

"*Queen of the Underworld* shows a delicious, unrestrained exuberance for the marrow of life. Character virtues and foibles appear in Technicolor detail; plot turns are sensational."

—*The Globe and Mail*

"Captivating . . . [The characters] are memorable and multi-faceted. . . . Sensitive and sharp portrayals of lives in flux."

—*Winston-Salem Journal*

"[*Queen of the Underworld* has] a gravity that isn't matched by many contemporary tales of young women striving to excel in their careers and their love lives."

—*Rocky Mountain News*

"A beautifully realized world . . . lively, often amusing, and filled with rich historical detail."

—*The Indianapolis Star*

"Well-drawn backgrounds, vibrant characters and delicious detail . . . vivid and juicy."

—*San Antonio Express News*

"*Queen of the Underworld* will be a delight to Godwin's many admirers for whom *The Odd Woman* and *A Mother and Two Daughters* remain luminous in memory, like old, dear friends. Here is the irresistibly readable Godwin voice, tender and sardonic, warmly romantic and unflinchingly funny. Godwin's new heroine, Emma Gant, is as alive on the page as any 'fictitious' character has a right to be, and when Emma takes leave of us, as she does in the startling ending of *Queen of the Underworld*, we miss her and can't help but hope that her adventures in Florida at the time of the Cuban revolution will be continued."

—JOYCE CAROL OATES

"Gail Godwin's excellent new novel seems to me to be a muted tragedy about a soul inside the body of a modern woman navigating through the terra incognita of modern times."

—KURT VONNEGUT

"Here is a wonderfully engaging story that explores the growth of a young woman beginning her career as a journalist. The inner workings of Emma's life are gracefully presented and marvelously mingled with the workings of the outer world; the combination provides a universe in which the reader is glad to reside."

—ELIZABETH STROUT

Queen of the Underworld

Queen of
the
Underworld

A Novel

Gail Godwin

BALLANTINE BOOKS

NEW YORK

2007 Ballantine Books Trade Paperback Edition

Copyright © 2006 by Gail Godwin
Reading group guide copyright © 2007 by Random House, Inc.

Published in the United States by Ballantine Books, an imprint of The Random House
Publishing Group, a division of Random House, Inc., New York.

BALLANTINE and colophon are registered trademarks of Random House, Inc.
READER'S CIRCLE and colophon are trademarks of Random House, Inc.

Originally published in hardcover in the United States by Random House, an imprint
of The Random House Publishing Group, a division of Random House, Inc., in 2006.

ISBN 978-0-345-48319-5

LIBRARY OF CONGRESS CATALOGING-IN-PUBLICATION DATA
Godwin, Gail.
Queen of the underworld : a novel / Gail Godwin.
p. cm.
ISBN 978-0-345-48319-5
I. Young women—Fiction.   2. Women journalists—Fiction.
3. Miami (Fla.)—Fiction.   I. Title.

PS3557.O315Q44 2006
813'.54—dc22
2005048592

Printed in the United States of America

www.thereaderscircle.com

2 4 6 8 9 7 5 3 1

Book design by Lovedog Studio

This novel is dedicated to the exiles,
wherever you are now

Part One

Caminante, no hay camino,
se hace camino al andar.

Wayfarer, there is no road,
you make the road as you go.

—Antonio Machado,
Proverbios y Cantares, 34

1.

NOW I HAD GRADUATED on this bright June Saturday in 1959 and few were the obstacles left between me and my getaway train to Miami—obstacles that nevertheless must be cunningly surmounted.

"Emma, you ride in front with Earl," said Mother, as expected. "I'll sit in back and reminisce a little more about *my* time here in Paradise."

"Oh?" challenged Earl. "What does that make the rest of your life, then, a comedown?"

"The rest of my life is still in progress," Mother lightly countered, making room for herself among my college leftovers that were going back to the mountains with them. "Ask me again in thirty or forty years."

We began the winding descent out of Chapel Hill as, seven years earlier, the three of us, with my mother's new husband at the wheel, had begun another descent into a new life. Only this time, they would be dropping me off within the hour at the Seaboard Station in Raleigh. My journey as part of this family unit would soon be at an end. Happily, my train to Miami left at one fifteen, so a farewell lunch had been out of the question, a circumstance diminishing that much further the chance of a last-minute blowup with Earl.

But still I was on my guard, for already he was making those engorged throat noises that preceded a sermon. I did not dare glance back at Mother for fear of catching her eye. An exchanged look of sympathy or, God forbid, a mutual smirk might still explode everything sky-high, as it had done plenty of times before. My job was to look respectfully attentive without rising to his bait. I folded my hands in my lap and faced front, focusing on the road ahead. Windows on both sides were open to let in the breeze, and the capricious little *whomp-whomp*s of hot air provided a divertimento against Earl's opening sally and helped me keep my own counsel.

Sacrifices had been made. If I would ever stop to think about other people. Empathy and gratitude not my strong suits. Had never known what it was to apply myself on a daily basis. Hadn't been required of me. Had been raised to think that the world revolved around me and that I could coast along without making much of an effort. Not completely my fault. Had been indulged too much for my own good by teachers as well as family. But now I was going into the real world where I would have to knuckle under and deliver the goods like everybody else.

"Though why you should choose to go off half-cocked to a place like Miami remains a mystery to your mother and me. Your dean told us the *Charlotte Observer* wanted you, but he said you'd had your heart set on Miami ever since you went down for that interview at Christmas. I said, well, we were the last to know she went to Miami for Christmas. She told *us* she was staying in the dorm to catch up on her work. We didn't learn the truth till February."

Damn and blast you, I thought. You have a single conversation with my dean, who adores me, and you make me out a liar.

"I didn't want to say anything to anyone until I knew I had the job," I cautiously replied.

"I told the dean, she doesn't even *know* anybody in Miami—"

I don't know anybody in Charlotte, either, I refrained from saying.

"She knows Tess," put in Mother from the backseat. Tess was her old college roommate from Converse. "Tess will be meeting her train tomorrow morning."

"So why didn't she stay with *Tess* at Christmas, when she went down for that interview?" His voice had edged up a decibel.

"Well, I guess she wanted to stay with someone else at Christmas," Mother neutrally suggested.

Of course I had told them, after the fact, with whom I'd stayed. Or rather I had presented an acceptable configuration of the way in which this family I had worked for last summer had offered me hospitality. Not that any configuration of the Nightingales would ever be acceptable to Earl.

"Well, I guess there's just no accounting for some people's taste, but to *move* down there to be with that tribe . . ." Menacing pause before the refrain: "When her dean said the *Charlotte Observer* would have taken her."

The voice rolled on, but so, I congratulated myself, did the car. Every mile we achieved was one mile nearer to my release. We had not veered off the road or had a flat tire and nobody had backhanded me to start a black eye for my first day at work.

Think of it as a scene early in a novel, I told myself: The stepfather picks one last fight with the daughter who has not appreciated him. The mother in the backseat, wedged among her daughter's boxes, knees tucked under her like a college girl, is forgiving of the wild little breezes that mess up her hairdo because they mute his voice. There will be plenty more of it to listen to on their long drive back to the mountains. Whose novel was this going to be? Not the stepfather's; the writer might never grow the empathy for that one. Not the mother's, either, though it catches in the daughter's throat to see the youthful way the older woman is clasping her knees, wrapped in her own memories of Chapel Hill, when she still expected to get everything she wanted. If it was going to be the daughter's, there would be some choked-back sobs in the mother's embrace at the train station, one last stoic offering of the daughter's mouth for the imposition of the stepfather's kiss, and then they would be gone on the next page.

When, as a last-minute taunt, Earl, in the act of setting down my suitcases inside my roomette, asked if I thought I had "money to burn" for this exclusive little compartment with its own washroom and pull-down bed, I suppressed the perfect comeback that it was indeed a "burnt offering" of my graduation monies to thank the gods for my escape from him. At long last I had learned that it was never too late for a black eye when saying goodbye to certain people.

————

ALONE IN my luxury cubicle, I relaxed for the first time in months, allowing the train's diesel engine to take over the job of getting me to my destination. Woods pinked with afternoon June light alternated with tobacco fields and tin-roofed drying barns. As we shot through a dreary little hamlet, a character offered herself for my perusal: a girl born and raised in this flyblown place who had dreams of going somewhere and one day wakes up on her deathbed, a forgotten old maid who has never left town, and hears this very train hurtle by. She feels the diesel cry in the marrow of her bones and in her last conscious moment believes she is aboard. She savors all the sweetness of having gotten out, and she expires with a rapturous smile on her face for no one to see but the undertaker.

Could such a woman still exist in the late nineteen-fifties, even in rural North Carolina? Why not? Maybe I would write this existential pastorale with its O. Henry–ish ending in the evenings when I got home from my newspaper job. It was the sort of thing that might get me published in a literary quarterly, especially one of the Southern ones, which abounded in stories about trains passing and nothing much ever happening at home. My plan was to become a crack journalist in the daytime, building my worldly experience and gaining fluency through the practice of writing to meet deadlines. Then, in the evening and on weekends, I would slip across the border into fiction, searching for characters interesting and strong enough to live out my keenest questions. My journalism would support me until I became a famous novelist. Perhaps I would become a famous journalist on the side, if I could manage both.

I began to lower myself into the environs of the old maid's unlived life until I started feeling queasy. Despite my desperate desire to be published, I knew this was a warning signal to get out of there. Letting yourself be trapped in the wrong story was another way of succumbing to usurpation. Goodbye, old girl, someone else will have to tell your boring tale.

I took first call for the dining car and sat down to a spotless white tablecloth and a red rosebud in a silver vase. Perfect icons for my new beginning. Like an antidote to my ditched character back in the roomette, a smart, suntanned woman in an Army officer's uniform slowly materialized through the haze of my nearsightedness. Her gaze lit on me, she murmured something to the waiter, and the next thing I knew she was asking if she might join me.

"Please do." I heard myself switching into my well-brought-up mode, even though I had been counting on dining alone and savoring my getaway some more.

Her brass name tag read "Major E. J. Marjac." She introduced herself as Erna Marjac. When I said "Emma Gant," she remarked on the similarity of our first names, which would have annoyed me had she not had such a warm smile (and beautiful teeth in the bargain) and had she not looked so straightforwardly charmed by the prospect of having dinner with me. By the time she had ordered from the menu, without the usual female shilly-shallying, I knew I envied her self-command and I resolved to use this opportunity to further my development.

She asked where I was headed, and I said I was going to Miami to be a reporter on the *Miami Star*.

"Really? You seem so young. I thought you were a student."

"I was until noon today. I just graduated from the university at Chapel Hill."

She laughed, exposing the beautiful teeth again. "You aren't wasting any time, are you? We ought to celebrate. May I treat you to some wine, Emma?"

"Thank you, that would be nice."

Major Marjac signaled the waiter. "What would you like?"

"Oh, whatever you're ordering will be fine." Having grown up in beer-and-bourbon land, I hadn't a clue.

"Well, since we're both having red meat, a half bottle of this Côte du Rhône will go down well. If we'd chosen the chicken, I would have suggested the Blue Nun."

My first lesson in wines.

She told me she'd just completed a very successful recruiting tour and was heading for some R & R with a friend in Pensacola before reporting back to duty at Fort McClellan in Alabama.

"What do you do on a recruiting tour?"

"I show a film about the opportunities the Army offers to women today and then I have interviews the rest of the day. I'm very good at assessing character and signing up the best ones, but this time I broke my own record. Thirty-seven young women from fifteen states will be reporting for duty at Fort McClellan by the end of the month."

I might have been number thirty-eight, I thought, had I not had my hiring letter from the managing editor of the *Miami Star* tucked in my purse. But then, of course, I wouldn't have been on this train.

Major Marjac's character-assessing gaze gave me a stamp of approval. "You're fortunate, Emma, you started ahead of the game. But for many young women, we offer the only hope of independence."

Over wine and dinner she told me stuff about code breaking and weaponry, and about the physical ordeals the new recruits would undergo: gas chambers and such. I strained hard to retain everything in case I decided at some future point to write a story about a girl in her last year of high school, desperate to escape her circumstances: she passes this window with a sign, ARMY RECRUITING WOMEN TODAY, and inside is handsome Major Marjac with her welcoming smile.

When we said goodbye—she would be getting off at Jacksonville before dawn—the major gave me her card.

"Slip this into your wallet, Emma. If things don't meet your expectations at the *Star*, drop me a line. With your college degree you could go straight into officers' training."

I asked the porter to make up my roomette for sleeping and was in bed before dark, swaying with the train's motion, mellow from Major Marjac's Côte du Rhône. When I was in my pajamas, I raised the shade again so I could get the maximum benefit from the experience, lying straight as a mummy in my little coffin-bed of rebirth, hurtling through one town after another where people steeped like old tea bags in their humdrum lives, speeding farther away by the minute from Earl-dom and all the other bottlenecks I had narrowly squeezed through.

It both gratified and goaded me that I had come across to an observant recruiter as one of those sleek, fortunate ones who "started ahead of the game." Wasn't that the image that I had cultivated? Yet, when so much lay hidden, I got no credit for my struggle, did I? When Major Marjac had proudly confided, "Weaponry is opening up to women in an unprecedented way," I couldn't help inventorying my own arsenal to date, the weapons best suited to my personality under duress: guile, subterfuge, goal-oriented politeness, teeth-gritting staying power, and the ability, when necessary, to shut down my heart. Forces had been mobilizing inside me for the past eleven years to do battle with anything or anybody who might try to usurp me for their own purposes again.

"Usurp" had become my adversarial verb of choice ever since I had seized upon it from a History of Tudor England course to trounce my archenemy, the dean of women, in my *Daily Tar Heel* column. ("With her latest Victorian edict, Dean Carmody has, quite simply, usurped the rights of every Carolina coed.") After that column, perfect strangers would call out familiarly as I crossed the campus: "Hey, Emma! Anybody been usurping you lately?" I delighted in the powers of the Fourth Estate. My twice-weekly column, "Carolina Carousel," carried a mug shot of me with flying hair, cagey side glance, and my best don't-mess-with-me smirk.

And the more I meditated on it, the more the "usurp" word compounded in personal meanings. Not just kingdoms and crowns got usurped. A person's unique and untransferable self could, at any time, be diminished, annexed, or altogether extinguished by alien forces. My soon-to-be twenty-two years on this earth had been an obstacle course mined with potential or actual usurpers.

Since day one, it seemed, I had been confronted by them in one form or another. After my alcoholic father crashed his car fatally into a tree on the day of my birth, Mother's Alabama cousin, a childless woman married to a rich man, tried to annex me. The offer included my widowed mother, but my grandmother Loney was not part of the package—the cousin thought Loney was "too undemonstrative"—and so Mother had to decline.

Next came a string of suitors who were willing to take on a little girl to get the attractive, sexy mother, but not willing to take on the grandmother, so once again I was spared. Next came World War II, four years during which my mother's job as a reporter on the *Mountain City Citizen* sufficiently engaged her libido. She covered the Veterans Hospital overflowing with wounded soldiers straight from the battlefront, interviewed visiting celebrities, reviewed books, and even contributed the occasional seasonal poem. But then the war ended and the men came home and wanted their jobs back and three of them wanted my mother. She chose the one my grandmother and I liked least, an oversensitive bully who brought to the match his overflowing trousseau of sermons and insecurities. After great storms of tears and reproaches between the women, my grandmother was left behind in our old apartment and I found myself part of a new family in a worse apartment on the other side of town, with new rules to follow and new things to worry about.

Earl immediately began his campaign to remove me from my "snobbish" grandmother's influence altogether. It took three years for him to get us out of Mountain City, but at last he succeeded, which meant plucking me out of my beloved St. Clothilde's, to which I had won a full high school scholarship the year before. Thus at the end of ninth grade, when I was going on fifteen, we packed up and drove out of our mountains, to begin our strange migrant years of "transferring" up and down the East Coast, gradually adding more human beings to our family mix, while Earl discovered, or his bosses discovered for him, that he was temperamentally unsuited to a career in chain store management.

In those gypsy years of Earl's and Mother's, I felt like someone kidnapped from my rightful environment and tethered to a caravan of someone else's descent.

In my last year at St. Clothilde's, when our ninth grade had been immersed in *David Copperfield*, Sister Elise, a svelte, scholarly young nun recently transferred from Boston, read us a letter the adult Dickens had written to a friend, describing his terrible experience of being sent to work in a blacking factory at age twelve. It was for less than a year, while his family was bankrupt and living in debtors' prison, but, Sister Elise informed us in her Back Bay accent, it left a scar ("skaah") on Dickens forever, even after he had become rich and world famous and was surrounded by an adoring family of his own. No words could express, Dickens had written to his friend, the secret agony of his young soul as he sank into this low life, pasting labels onto blacking bottles for six shillings a month in a rat-infested warehouse with urchin boys who mockingly called him "the little gentleman." Snatched from his studies with an Oxford tutor, obliged to pawn all his books (*The Arabian Nights*, his favorite eighteenth-century novels), the young Dickens felt his early hopes of growing up to be a distinguished and learned person crushed in his breast. All that he had learned and thought and delighted in was passing away from him day by day. His whole nature, he wrote to the friend who, Sister Elise told us, was to become his first biographer, had been so penetrated with grief and humiliation that even now he often forgot in his dreams that he had escaped it all and was famous, caressed, and happy.

Now I, too, knew that constant sinking feeling of losing ground. Each day seemed to put more distance between me and where I thought I should be by this time, had Earl not entered our lives. Had I stayed on at smart, rigorous St. Clothilde's, I would be polishing my already sterling record to a high sheen and—as many of my classmates would go on to do—would graduate with a nice bouquet of scholarship offers from top colleges, including Sister Elise's own Radcliffe. Whereas, tethered to Earl's itinerant career, I had to start all over again each year in a new high school (once I did two schools in a single year), make my qualities known as quickly as possible, and pray I could claw my way into a college, any college, somehow. Very early on in our life together, Earl had announced that even if he could afford to send me, which he certainly *couldn't*, he wouldn't, because his own parents, who *could* have afforded it, hadn't offered to send *him*.

His backhandings and beatings and sneaky nocturnal raids on my person accrued with my advancing teens. Like the slave owners in the not-so-distant past, he unctuously assumed it was his right to do as he pleased with the flesh under his care. No season went by without a bruise on my face for "answering back." I grew accustomed to awakening in the dark to find him kneeling beside my bed, engaged in one of his proprietary gropes beneath my nightgown. If I cried out, he would shush me sanctimoniously. Did I want to wake the baby, the babies? I'd been moaning in my sleep again, he said, and he'd only come to check.

During my last year of high school I wrote a masterful begging letter to Mother's rich cousin in Alabama, the one who had wanted to annex me and Mother, and she agreed to pay for one semester at a time at a junior college for girls in Raleigh. If I kept up my grades, there would be another semester, "but after two years, darling, you're on your own." The implication being that two years would give any diligent girl time to either win a scholarship to the state university or find a husband to support her. Already at seventeen the rich cousin had snared her future millionaire, as she had more than once pointed out.

I had no difficulty making the grades at the junior college and winning a scholarship to the journalism school at Chapel Hill, but that still left the summers to get through. I had to make money to cover expenses, and the job had to be somewhere that provided room and board so I could avoid Earl's nightly prowls. The first summer, I lifeguarded at a girls' camp; the second, I waited tables at a plush resort in Blowing Rock. The final summer, between my junior and senior years, I waited tables at the Nightingale Inn, a Jewish family hotel thirty miles from Mountain City. By this time, Earl and Mother were back in Mountain City, Earl having gone into the construction business with his father. And since their little house was now burgeoning with offspring, I was allowed to sleep unmolested across town beside Loney, the "snobbish" grandmother, in her lavender-scented four-poster bed when I "came home" to visit my family during college breaks.

And that, Major Marjac, is the behind-the-scenes résumé of the young woman you met on the train who "started ahead of the game."

———

As I stepped down onto the platform of the Miami depot, there was Tess, who had been my mother's college roommate at Converse until Tess dropped out her freshman year to go home to Florida and become Miss Miami Beach. The last time I had seen Tess was when I was seven and she came to stay with us in Mountain City to recuperate from ruining her life. I was surprised to see she was the same platinum-blond goddess I remembered. In a recent letter to Mother she had announced that her looks were completely gone and she was saving for a face-lift. But why was she wearing her white uniform and stockings and nurse's shoes on Sunday? She gathered me to her bosom like her own lost child and lavished effusions against my cheek in a whispery little-girl voice totally incongruous with her adult beauty.

"Emma, sweet, you're here at last! Even prettier than the picture your mother sent, which she didn't need to. I would have recognized you anywhere. Your 'Emma-ness' is exactly the same."

Though Tess tended to flatter everybody, her remark gave me a jolt of elation. I made up my mind to adopt this concept of "Emma-ness" as a talisman against those loss-of-self times that flattened me. She still wore Joy, the perfume her husband had chosen for her. What did she have to do without in order to buy it for herself now?

We tussled over who would carry the heaviest of my suitcases. She prevailed, and dragged her way fetchingly ahead of me to a baby blue Cadillac DeVille. She had not lost her slim, curvaceous figure, my mother would be glad to hear. Or would she?

"You have to be wary of this humidity, Emma, until your blood has a chance to thin. Also, we've been having this spate of damp weather, which doesn't help, either." Tess was puffing by the time she allowed me to help her heft the big suitcase into a carpeted trunk that could have held three more sets of luggage. "This is Hector's new car. He insisted I take it to meet you."

"How generous of him." On leaving the train, I hadn't noticed the humidity, but as soon as Tess drew my attention to it I could feel it sapping my energy.

After ruining her life, Tess had gone to vocational college and was now nurse-assistant to Dr. Hector Rodriguez, a dental surgeon in Coral Gables.

"Oh, Hector is the most generous man in the world. His patients call him Doctor Magnánimo. He's always giving things away and he'll see you on the weekend if you're in pain, which is why I have to head back to the office after we get you settled at your hotel. He's starting a root canal this afternoon for a man who's in agony."

"Doctor Magnánimo," I echoed, trying to copy the sexy way she lightly tongued the back of her front teeth for the first *n*.

"See, Emma, you sound like a natural already! So many of their words are the same as ours, only with this little extra flourish on the end. You'll pick up Spanish in no time in Miami." (Tess pronounced it "My-AM-uh.") "There are lots of Cubans and more coming over all the time, professional, well-bred people like Hector and his wife, Asunción, although they left a while ago to get away from Batista. The ones arriving now are coming because Fidel has let them down. But you know all about that, you're going to be a reporter on the *Star*."

"As soon as they wrote to say I had the job, I subscribed to the paper. I've been reading it cover to cover since February, everything from Castro's land grabs to the big Miami society weddings."

Damn, blast, shit, hell, Emma. Why didn't you stop at Castro? But Tess neither flinched nor looked sad, as though she didn't recall herself being the star of one of those big society weddings. Her perfect Grecian profile went right on smiling as she steered serenely down a wide avenue, the skirt of her crisp uniform tugged up to reveal her shapely white-stockinged thighs.

"Hector said you must be just phenomenally smart, to land a job like this right out of college. Everybody wants to be a reporter for the *Star*. I said yes, you were, just like your mamma. I can't wait for you to meet Hector. And Asunción, too, of course."

"Well, I don't know about phenomenally," I said. The way she had dutifully tacked on Asunción made me ponder whether Doctor Magnánimo might be more to her than just a generous boss.

But mostly I was occupied with keeping myself intact in this new environment. My guerrilla antennae were on full alert, sensing new threats and opportunities pulsing at me as we skimmed along streets lined with palm trees and sea grapes and modest pastel bungalows with those slatted glass windows that keep the heat and rain out. In this tropical city I would have to wear lighter clothes; more of my body would be on display for new critics as well as new potential gropers. There would be levels of sophistication to tap into without revealing my ignorance, levels far more demanding than Major Marjac asking me about wine. There would be new brands of wickedness undreamed of by someone arriving overnight from a sheltered Southern university existence. And usurpers a million times subtler and smoother than Earl.

"I think you're going to like your hotel," Tess was saying. "It has a pool and it's only a few blocks from Miami Avenue. You'll be able to walk to work in your heels. We were able to get you the special monthly rate because the manager, Alex de Costa, is Hector's patient. Alex was being groomed to take over his grandfather's hotel in Havana, but when things got shaky down there, the grandfather had the foresight to sell out in time and buy the Julia Tuttle here. It was a little run-down, but he's renovated it in the European style. Hector says it's exactly like a good family hotel in Madrid or Barcelona now."

"Should I know who Julia Tuttle is?"

"The Mother of Miami? You certainly should! She made Henry Flagler bring the railroad here from Jacksonville. When everything north of Miami froze, she sent him a box with an orange blossom from her tree, and that convinced him. Your hotel stands on the land where her old home was. Granny sewed for Julia and her daughter, you know. Mother remembers Granny altering a whole bunch of Julia's gowns for Miss Fannie right after Julia dropped dead. Poor Julia, she was only forty-eight. I'll be, well, close to that next year, but don't you dare tell a soul. Granny always said Julia worked too hard on her dream and it killed her. Miami was just a swamp full of Seminoles and alligators before Julia came down here on a barge after her husband's death, with all her furniture and sil-

ver from Ohio. She had this dream of creating a beautiful subtropical resort, and she made it happen, though she doesn't get nearly enough credit
for it nowadays."

Tess didn't resent other people's accomplishments or good fortune,
even with her own life so compromised. I was sure that in her place I
would have become bitter or crazy. Here she was working on Sunday in
a white uniform for a Cuban dentist when she had once traveled by private yacht. She had not seen her high-school-age son since he was fifteen
months old. The first thing I planned to do when I got to the *Star* was to
look up Tess in the newspaper's morgue. Not even Mother knew the
whole story, and I had promised I would find out what I could.

My first impression of the Julia Tuttle was a letdown, followed by a
distinct relief that I could just be myself here. Based on my furtive
Christmas stay at the Kenilworth over on the Beach, paid for by someone
else, I had expected more glitter and swank in a Miami hotel, even the
kind I could afford. Tess was the only platinum blonde in sight, and there
was none of that high-gloss decor or those snooty personnel strutting
around to make you feel unstylish. A black man in a striped bib apron
whom Tess addressed as Clarence loaded my suitcases onto a trolley. The
only other visible staff member was a morose-looking desk clerk in a
pleated shirt worn outside the pants and a few strips of hair plastered
over his bald pate. His countenance brightened when Tess introduced us,
and the next thing I knew he was handing me three letters, including one
from Mother and one from Loney.

When I saw the creamy unstamped third envelope with its elegant red
logo in the upper left corner, my heart sustained an electric surge, even
though I would have been furious had that exact envelope not been waiting for me. I slipped it quickly beneath the others as Tess was conversing
with the desk clerk in her sensual, tongue-tripping Spanish, which made
her seem like a different version of herself. She switched back into English while discussing my arrangements.

"Is Alex here, Luís? I'd like him to meet Emma." To me she said,
"That's the manager I was telling you about."

"No, *señora*, is his bridge game Sunday afternoon."

"Oh, of course, it's Sunday, isn't it? I'm confused because we're work-ing today, Doctor Hector is starting a root canal for a patient in pain."

As we crossed the Mediterranean-tiled lobby where Clarence waited with my bags by the elevator, an arresting family tableau caught my eye. A pretty woman wearing a pillbox hat with veil and a stylish traveling suit was reading aloud to a little girl who sat beside her on a love seat flanked by potted palms and surrounded by a stockade of matching suitcases. The girl supported two solemn-faced porcelain dolls on her lap in the laissez-faire way a loving mother might balance two well-behaved off-spring who could be depended on to stay put. The aloof faces of all three seemed to be equally riveted on the woman's sprightly reading— "*a la tarde . . . los niños saltaban . . . Platero . . . giraba sobre sus patas*"—and I was elated that merely in passing I could understand enough phrases ("in the afternoon . . . the children were jumping . . . Platero . . . spun on his hooves") to recognize Juan Ramón Jiménez's tale of his pet don-key, *Platero and I*, which we'd studied in our first semester of college Spanish. Close by them stood a strikingly handsome man in wilted white linen, frowning and looking slightly beside himself as he ticked off items on a list with a silver pencil. Meanwhile, a chauffeur carried in more lug-gage to add to the pile already surrounding them.

"Ah, God, here come some more," Tess murmured angrily as we passed. "If Fidel doesn't stop breaking his promises, he's going to wake up one morning and find all the good people gone."

My room was on the fifth floor of the twelve-story Julia Tuttle, and Tess, having sent Clarence away with a folded bill before I could get my purse unzipped, proceeded to check out my closet, drawers, and bath-room. I went first thing to the window above the air conditioner to see what I would be looking out on for the next few months. It wasn't the ocean view, which the front rooms had, but the vista was agreeable and in its way less lonely. The Miami River, with its drawbridge and boat traf-fic, was to my left, the hotel's Olympic-size pool, surrounded by blue-and-white-striped cabanas, gleamed invitingly below, and to the right was a portion of Miami skyline, including, Tess proudly pointed out, as though she had put it there herself, the top of the *Star* building, where I would start work tomorrow.

Tess explained that patients sometimes had adverse reactions, and she had to remain at the office until they felt well enough to travel, so she couldn't be with me my first evening. She named the eating places in walking distance, a White Castle and a Howard Johnson's, and we made plans to have dinner the next evening.

"And tomorrow night, we'll really celebrate," she promised as she headed gaily off to the root canal.

I had concealed my relief, satisfying her that I welcomed an early night in order to be fresh for the job tomorrow. As soon as I had assured myself of that third letter in the packet Luís handed over, I had begun worrying what lie to tell Tess, who had no idea I knew a soul but her in Miami.

As soon as I was alone, I threw myself on the bed and opened the creamy unstamped envelope with its Bal Harbour address.

Will call for you at your hotel at 7 p.m.
Paul

Then I flew into action, unpacking my bags and lining the drawers and shelves with the sheets of lavender-scented paper supplied by my grandmother. Loney had sent them, along with six pairs of stockings and a new Vanity Fair slip, for my graduation, from which "her heart" had kept her home. Which was true in the equivocal sense that she stayed behind with her mild angina to take care of my three little half siblings so Mother and Earl would be free to enjoy the trip alone.

After arranging my things in their Loneyed nests, I plugged up the tub, ran it half full of hot water, hung tomorrow's work outfit and tonight's dress on the shower-curtain rod, and shut them up in the bathroom to steam out the wrinkles. I then flopped back down on the bed to read my other letters.

Loney, who did not think of herself as a writer, had come through with her usual page-and-a-half nosegay of faith, hope, and unconditional love, with one of her observant sprigs of advice thrown in, like a florist's free fern.

. . . If you'll just remember, Emma, that you can't be everybody at once, you'll do fine.

My mother, whose thwarted desire was to have her writing talents recognized by the world, had gone all out with a four-page single-spaced masterpiece typed on Corrasable Bond, written and mailed the Monday before my graduation so it would be sure to be here to greet me. It was both an idyllic recounting of our best times together, mostly from the pre-Earl period, and her triumphal prophecy of my eventual success in garnering the laurels that had eluded her. She did not relay any news or anecdotes about my little half siblings. This was strictly a mother-daughter valedictory. Just skimming it elicited tears; it had probably, I thought, made the writer weep while typing it. To confront it sentence by sentence, which I postponed doing, would bring guilt and sorrow. She was the wounded comrade I had to leave behind in the cross fire of her conflicted destiny.

I returned to the note that had been hand-delivered to the Julia Tuttle, rereading and savoring it. I allowed myself to be the person who had pulled out a fresh sheet of club stationery from his desk drawer over in Bal Harbour and scrawled this ultrarestrained welcome. I imagined the images going through his head as he anticipated our reunion tonight, until the power of my own imagination brought on a little shudder of rapture. Whereupon I returned the note to its envelope and tucked it midway into the new "Go, Tar Heels!" spiral-bound notebook, which was to be the first of my Miami journals. I still had the rest of the afternoon to get through. Perhaps I would sample the pool.

2.

T ESS HAD SAID THAT Miami was having a spate of rainy weather, and sure enough, by midafternoon on Sunday, the day of my arrival, when I had just about motivated myself to try the Julia Tuttle's Olympic-size pool, the skies opened and I felt reprieved. I had nothing except a raincoat to wear over my bathing suit, an ancient but flattering long-waisted racer from my swim-team days at St. Clothilde's, and I was shy about crossing the lobby of what aspired to be a European-style family hotel without the proper attire.

Now I could wash my hair and fuss with it at leisure and continue to do what I liked doing best anyway: lying in bed reading or writing. I decided not to venture out to the White Castle; even one of their bitty burgers might take the edge off my evening appetite. Paul was always asking me was I hungry, and he was so pleased when I said yes. He equated youth with being hungry all the time (and with being able to eat vast amounts without getting fat), so he expected it of me.

The clanging of the drawbridge sent me scurrying for my distance glasses and then back to the window to see what manner of craft would be passing through its portals. If it was a yacht, I would be a success in my career and my love life; if a sailboat with a tall mast, I would have a pleasant workmanlike life but be unremembered after my death; if some dreary drudge of a vessel, I was slated for abject failure and loneliness, starting immediately.

It was a yacht, a fairly big one named *Dixie Naiad,* with three middle-aged people, two men and a woman, in skimpy bathing suits that would have been obscene without their tans. They wore big-brimmed yellow rain hats. I could feel how the downpour gave them a thrill of empowerment, like having a playful servant-god overturning buckets on their sleek brown bodies when they were all but naked anyway. I could hear the loud hollow rain plops as they would sound from inside the hats, and yet their hairdos would still be in place for dinner. They could no longer eat anything they wanted but were making a pretty good effort to keep in shape, considering they probably docked at a five-star restaurant every night. A married couple and a friend? The husband's friend or brother? The wife's secret lover? All we knew about Tess's calamity was that she had fallen in love with her husband's much-younger brother. If she had been more cunning, would she now be aboard her husband's yacht, with the young brother along for the ride and still in the picture, all three keeping their secrets to themselves under their matching rain hats?

Now they were waving to someone on shore, or else just generally waving, as the passing privileged tend to do, whenever envious peons might be looking on. If that striking Cuban family I'd seen in the lobby happened to be looking out at this same view from their room, their hearts could well be aching for some lovely yacht of their own left behind in Cuba. Or maybe they had come over in it, and were expecting, like so many others, that Fidel would bite the dust any minute, so they could go back and reclaim their usurped lives. Yes, amigos, wave and pass through, the Cuban father or mother might be saying inwardly in Spanish to the *Dixie Naiad* crew, you never know what turn of fortune waits to capsize *you* round the next bend.

Patas were the feet of an animal; *pies* the feet of people. The Cuban woman had been reading the little girl *Platero and I,* and I had recognized it! My mother had once worn a pillbox hat with a veil like that. How could I have been so stupid as to have sent my Spanish-English dictionary back to Mountain City?

I washed my hair and set it on rollers to get the curl out of it so I could loop it into the sleek French twist Paul liked. I then settled back onto propped-up pillows in my Julia Tuttle bed, which was an old-fashioned double—in other words, hardly more than a single—with a real head-board and footboard. All the furniture in this room could have come straight from my grandmother's. Whatever "renovations" the owner had carried out must have applied only to the bigger rooms or those over-looking the bay, though my light blue walls did have the look and the smell of a recent paint job.

I flipped to the back pages of the "Go, Tar Heels!" notebook and re-viewed the notes I'd been collecting on recent top stories in the *Miami Star.* I don't know quite what I expected, my first day of work: some sort of quiz, perhaps.

Name the most important news developments of international significance in the last three months.

Well, of course, everyone knows the Reds want us out of West Berlin and they're threatening to spoil the Geneva Conference; and Castro's "Robin Hood" land grabs continue to bring joy to the peasants and fury to the likes of Arthur Vining Davis; and Venezuela and all sorts of other people are arming Nicaraguan rebels. And on the home front Eleanor Roosevelt in her syndicated column, "My Day," scolds Washington for its lack of both imagination and breadth of world vision and declares herself frustrated by the Democratic congressional leaders' "want of comprehension about the real needs of the world." And Governor Earl Long of Louisiana, shouting hog calls and obscenities, is committed, re-leased, and returned to the mental hospital.

Also, I was hoarding for the opportune moment of newsroom repar-tee an AP wire story buried inside the June 1 *Miami Star* about Castro's plans to tax the society pages in Havana's newspapers: $1 per item, $1 per adjective, $5 for each square inch of photograph of a person men-tioned in a story, and $100 for each title of nobility of a Cuban national mentioned in a story.

I could hear myself remarking casually to a fellow reporter, perhaps to the city editor himself, "Better watch my adjectives, Castro's charging a dollar apiece for them now."

After reviewing these notes, I flipped back to the pristine first page of the notebook, which had been awaiting this moment, and entered the date, time, and place of composition, including my room number, 510. After announcing my arrival in Miami, I listed a few impressions, including Tess's continued good looks and the elegant displaced Cuban family in the lobby, and gave myself a pep talk about what I intended to accomplish at the *Star.*

I then switched over into my Paul-cryptography, worked out over the past year of our secret liaison, so that should these or any similar jottings fall into an interloper's hands, he or she would assume that the diarist was deliberately switching from reportage into the continuation of a fantasy romance between a distinguished alien from another world and the young protégée he has been sent to protect and instruct so that she can fulfill her destiny.

In this installment, the young woman is anticipating a reunion with her alien guardian-lover and, in her impatience to be joined with him after a separation of six months, frequently crosses the line into purple prose. The interloper could either hop aboard the passion train or watch it go by and scoff, "What a caprice! Of course, this could never happen in real life."

As I expected, Paul called from the house phone in the lobby at exactly seven, and I gathered up my raincoat and purse and went down.

He was in on the secret of my extreme nearsightedness and had positioned himself near the elevator so I would see him without having to gawk, but not close enough so I would collide with him when I stepped out.

I walked toward the dark blur in evening suit and tie, savoring his gradual materialization from elegant shadow into my fully focused Paul Nightingale with his tawny skin, Saracen features, impeccably barbered salt-and-pepper hair, and the four slashes of wrinkles—two horizontal, two vertical, like the beginning of a tic-tac-toe game—in the middle of his forehead. Finally the little gold tie pin, his logo, took on its familiar nightingale shape at about the same time his special cologne kicked in, and, though he was practicing his usual custody of the eyes, I felt the pulse-quickening jolt of being desired in all my details.

We were being noticed by the few others in the lobby. A group of men in those pleated smocklike shirts that I would learn to call guayaberas played dominoes at a table in the corner while listening to a Spanish-language station on their transistor radio. Behind the front desk where morose Luís had been stationed earlier, a square-chinned young man in blazer and someplace's school tie sat on a high stool reading a hardcover book. He looked up and gave us a polite nod as we went by. Paul nodded in return.

I saw us through their eyes: a suave Jewish man somewhere in his for-ties, and a queenly young woman in a well-fitting black dress with dark blond hair coiled up and away from her neck. Father and daughter? Too different in coloration, unless she's an adopted daughter. But there's a charged reticence between them that isn't at all familial. They could be two spies on a joint mission; but most likely, in this setting, she's his young mistress.

"IT'S BEEN a long time since Christmas." Paul's first words once we were alone in the car.

"It sure has."

"You're looking extremely well."

"So are you."

"Thank you, we try. You hungry?"

"I've been saving up all day."

"In that case, should we zip straight up Biscayne and cross over at Broad Causeway? That's the fastest."

"No, let's go the slow way, beside the ocean. I prefer to spin out my pleasures when I know they're finally in reach."

He laughed softly and reached over to cover my hand with his, the first time he had touched me since Christmas. His cologne, concocted for him by his aunt Stella, who had a thriving custom-perfume business on Miami Beach, enfolded me with its many associations dating back to last summer when I began waiting tables at the Nightingale Inn and realized I was falling in love with the owner.

Though it was drizzling and almost dusk, I could make out the bobbing lights of ships in their sea-lanes and they convinced me I was finally here, with both the job and the man I most desired.

"Now this was your aunt who fixed you up at the Julia Tuttle?"

"No, my mother's college roommate, but I guess Tess is the nearest thing I've got to an aunt."

"The one who works for the Cuban dentist. That figures."

"Why? Is there something wrong with the hotel?"

"On the contrary. How much are they charging you?"

"A hundred and three dollars a month."

"And the *Star's* starting you off at what, two hundred? You should be able to make it. With a few devoted friends feeding you regularly. No, her Cuban connection got you a good deal is all I meant. If you think Jews are notorious for sticking together, wait till you get to know some Cubans. That was your manager on the desk, Alex de Costa."

"That boy with the book? But he's so young!"

"A kid like you. Fresh out of Harvard, with some degree that has nothing to do with business. International Literature, something like that. The grandfather is Cuban-American, a real estate baron. The Julia Tuttle's just a handy sideline of his."

"For *what?*"

"His Coral Gables empire. All these exiles are going to be either renting or buying homes, depending on which way the wind blows down in Castro-land. The ones who weren't able to bring out their money, he lets them run up a tab at Julia's. Like the old company store. Whether they go back or stay, they'll be beholden."

"Do you know this grandfather de Costa?"

"His name's Prieto, Prieto y Portes in full. When you get to work tomorrow, have some savvy person escort you through the maze of Cuban monickers. All the surnames and compound names, it's a wild ride. The mother's name usually gets tacked on at the end. No, I've never met Prieto, he stays mostly out of the picture up in Palm Beach, but all of us in the tourist trade get the scuttlebutt. During the season when we're open, young Alex slips over to Nightingale's whenever he can and has a quiet game of cards upstairs."

"You *know* him?"

"He's a paid-up member of my club."

"But you two barely nodded to each other!"

"He needs his hideaway same as everyone else."

The parade of beachfront hotels soon began, starting with the old three- and four-story stucco dowagers with their wraparound corners accented in neon colors, where Paul had first washed dishes, then waited tables, in the pre–World War II years when he couldn't aspire to managerial positions in those restricted establishments. In those days, there were still signs saying "No Dogs or Jews" on Miami Beach lawns.

Then past the Blue Flamingo Apartments for retirees, formerly the Army-requisitioned Blue Flamingo Hotel managed by Corporal Paul Nightingale for the duration of the war (a satisfied general staying overnight had told Paul he had a rare gift for hospitality), and on into the neon sparkle of Collins Avenue where, after being demobilized, Paul had worked his way up through the management levels of ever newer—and now unrestricted—hotels, perfecting the art of treating tourists like millionaires for two weeks, until he decided to start his own nightclub where locals like himself could feel pampered and welcome.

Then came the taller sweeping curves of the debutante edifices with their movie-set interiors and cutthroat competition. The owner of the Fontainebleau, Paul had told me, had built a fourteen-story addition to shut out the afternoon sun from the rival Eden Roc's cabana next door.

And then on north into Paul's territory, where stretches of lonely beach could still be glimpsed between the most recently constructed hotels.

"So, what's your pleasure, darling?" Paul inquired as we entered Bal Harbour. "Should we repeat our Christmas routine or head straight for the Ivanhoe? It depends on how hungry you are."

"Let's keep our traditions intact and go to the Americana bar first."

"Their dry martinis won't knock you out after your long day?"

"My 'long day' has mostly been spent resting up for you on my bed at the Julia Tuttle after a good night's sleep on the train."

Before Paul, I would never have admitted such a thing to a man I cared about.

"Tell me something, Emma." On the rare occasion when he used my name, it still sent a jolt through my system.

"What?"

"How is it you're always better than I remember?"

"WE'LL START with two dry Beefeaters straight up with a twist, and then in ten minutes if you'd bring us two shrimp cocktails."

"Certainly, sir."

You could tell from the way Paul placed orders that he was imagining ahead for both of you just when you'd be ready for what. Ten minutes would be exactly the right amount of time for two or three slow sips of gin to dilate our receptor channels and enhance the savoring of our reunion. How I loved our preliminaries in these dark tropical spaces with their fantasy settings: a ship, an island, a medieval castle, even the inside of an airplane.

Paul nudged a flat silver case from an inside pocket, narrowing his eyes at a waiter as he flicked it open. Only when he was coaxing a cigarette from the case with exaggerated slowness did the waiter dart forward with a lighter.

"Three out of ten?" I suggested as soon as the waiter was out of earshot.

"Nope, he should have jumped the moment he saw the case. But we'll give him your three because he recognized his mistake and because I'm happy tonight."

A stickler for anticipating his guests' needs, Paul was merciless with his staff at both his establishments, the Nightingale Inn in North Carolina and P. Nightingale's, his club in Bal Harbour.

In my first week of waiting tables at the Inn last summer, Paul suddenly appeared beside me as I was complacently folding napkins at my station for the next meal.

"The garbage on the Cohen table is piling up," my boss coldly murmured.

I then saw to my alarm that all four Cohens had their knives and forks aligned down the centers of their entrée plates, on which there were hardly any remains, certainly nothing big enough to qualify as "garbage." But there was a stone in my chest as I cleared away their dishes. The friendly Cohens seemed not to have noticed my lapse, chattering on throughout the removals and sending me amused, affectionate smiles. The first night of their stay I had won their hearts by being the good-natured goy-butt of their joke. Mr. Cohen, the father, had asked me to see if the chef had any of that "good kosher ham," and I had dashed off to the kitchen and learned what was what. "Chef's fresh out of kosher ham tonight, sir," I came back to report, keeping the chef's annoyed outburst to myself, "but the brisket of beef comes highly recommended."

The stone lay on my heart for the remainder of the evening, because it was the first time my boss, with whom I was already in love, had found fault with me.

"I'M PUTTING in an upstairs kitchen at the club," Paul reported as we sliced into our medium-rare New York strip sirloins in the Knight Room at the Ivanhoe.

"For your private use?"

"That's what it says on the building permit. No need to raise the commissioners' hackles. My cardplayers tend to get hungry at three in the morning. Next season I'll be able to provide them with a short-order menu and a cook on call, just like the country clubs."

Beach gambling had been wiped out by Kefauver, Paul had explained to me, but Nightingale's was just as much a private club as the Surf, Bath, Indian Creek, or La Gorce, and if some dues-paying members wanted to get together in an upstairs room for a party of high-stakes bridge or poker, it was going to be harder to put the finger on them than on guests paying calls on a bookie in a hotel room.

"It'll mean frequent commutes over the summer. I'll be flying up to Carolina tomorrow to help Bev and Aunt Stella open the Inn, but I plan to be back here by Thursday evening to celebrate your birthday."

"That would be wonderful, but—"

"You've made other plans."

"No, but, I mean, won't it seem odd? Fly up there on Monday and leave again on Thursday?"

"Why? I've got to keep an eye on my contractor."

"But won't you be missed?"

"I flatter myself to believe I'd be more missed here."

That was the closest we came to "discussing our situation." Paul was my first married man as well as my first Jewish man; he was also twenty years older, and I took my etiquette cues from him. From the beginning, he had included his wife, Bev, in our conversations: Bev had said this, Bev had done that, though never anything about their private life. After a while it felt to me that the three of us made up a sort of unusual family, although Bev didn't know about this family. Meanwhile, she was joint owner of the Inn in Carolina and of P. Nightingale's in Bal Harbour. She had shared Paul's life for almost as long as I had been in this world.

I had gotten to know and admire her myself last summer after she had recovered from her hysterectomy in Miami and returned to the Nightingale Inn. When Paul brought her back from the airport and she emerged from the station wagon with her cloud of smoky-platinum hair, I thought of Kim Novak in *Vertigo*, but up close Bev was a smaller, finer-boned creature, and her speech was quick and mocking, a total opposite to the dreamy Novak style. Her feet were so sexy and perfect they drove me to despair, making me want to hide my own and at the same time labor over them after waitressing hours with creams and pumice stones and the exact shade of frosted rose polish she used. Now in her forties, she still modeled clothes in the seasonal fashion shows at Burdines, where Paul, in Army uniform, had first seen her behind the counter when buying a piece of costume jewelry for his mother's birthday in 1942.

One day soon after her return, Bev had plucked Lucy, another wait-ress, and me aside as we were pigeon-toeing (Lucy) and slouch-sashaying (I) through the lobby of the Inn and dryly proclaimed, "Girls, it's time somebody taught you to walk." Right there on the spot she drilled us in tilting our pelvises upward, throwing our insteps out ahead of us, and al-lowing our arms to swing loosely at our sides. When she was satisfied with her handiwork, she sent for Paul and made us walk back and forth in front of him. He smiled obliquely down at the floor (he and I had become lovers by then) and said, "You've gilded the lilies, Bev."

I'd be setting up for the next meal at the Inn, remembering and antici-pating his embraces, then I'd look out the window and see porcelain-perfect Bev in one of her gossamer dresses, gliding around the pool area in spaghetti-strap sandals, bestowing her daily dose of glamour on her guests. Or I'd be serving the two of them at the owners' table, overhear-ing her crisp patter of mockery—she loved putting Paul down and it seemed to amuse him—and I'd be dumbfounded that this suave, reserved man was willing to risk exposure for such an unfinished piece of work as me. Yet the secret I hoarded, rushing back and forth from my cabin in my drip-dry uniform and stodgy nurse's shoes, paradoxically filled me with a delicious sense of youthful superiority over them both.

Paul was proud of his club on the Beach as much for the symbolic evo-lution of its site as for what he had made of it. He'd bought it for cash in 1951. ("You were just starting high school," he remarked, as always fondly incorporating my past into his.) It was a Spanish-style villa on the northern tip of Bal Harbour, its front entrance across the street from the ocean, its courtyard facing in toward the bay.

The builder had been a speculator, hoping to cash in on what, before World War II, had been covenanted as an exclusive planned community, with limited commercial activity: "for Caucasians only, no lot to be sold to anyone having more than one quarter Hebrew or Syrian blood."

But when the builder finished the first villa in 1947, nobody wanted to buy it. Hotels were springing up all around—so much for the "limited commercial activity"—and the new ordinances forbade covenants from containing such restrictive language anymore. Several minor embassies in turn had leased the villa, but no legation had ever moved in. After the builder defaulted on his loan, Paul bought the villa from the bank at auction.

During the war ("You'd just started to grade school") the long swath of undeveloped oceanfront had been the Army Air Corps's rifle range.

"You'd see the boys lying single file all along the empty beach, aiming at targets set up along an embankment. No hotels in sight then, no Kenilworth-by-the-Sea, no Ivanhoe, no Americana. Clark Gable lay on his belly on the sand firing out to sea with the rest of them. Without his famous moustache; the Army shaved it off. He trained for the officers' corps here, you know. Later we had a prisoner-of-war camp on the bay side, mostly Germans captured in the North African campaign. If the barracks were still standing, you could look out and see them from my card rooms upstairs. The prisoners did street repairs along Collins Avenue.

"One afternoon my mother came out of her beauty shop and this POW remarked on her hairdo in German, not expecting her to understand. It was complimentary, but a little too familiar, she said, so she answered him back in his own language and did it take the wind out of *his* sails."

"I don't understand. Why wouldn't he have been pleased?"

"Because her German was High German and his was Low. It was a class thing. He wouldn't have dared to address her on the street if they'd been back in Leipzig."

"I feel so abysmally ignorant sometimes."

"Not ignorant, just insulated. It's natural, you're an American."

"But so are you."

"By birth, yes, but when you're an only child raised by a mother who recites poetry to herself in French or German and speaks Yiddish on the phone with her friends, and cooks and furnishes the apartment like she's still back in the Old Country, you're a different breed of American."

Tonight Paul drove past the darkened front of P. Nightingale's, past the tall, wrought-iron gate with its portals topped with golden birds whose eyes glowed red at night during the winter season.

We went around on a side street to the bay entrance. He clicked a hand gadget and the villa's rear gates floated open, then swung shut behind us as soon as we were inside the courtyard.

"Magic," I said.

"You never seen one of these before? All the Mafia have them down here now."

He came around to open my door, old-fashioned-gent style, and I sat with my hands folded on my lap, the agreeable anticipation of getting everything I wanted rising in me, and relished my alien man gliding around to release me into the dark compound of his kingdom.

"Welcome to my private entrance. It's a different world on the bay side, isn't it? Especially out of season with no one else around."

"On this side it's like, I don't know, an ambassador's villa by the sea."

"Watch out, this girl's a writer. Shall we take a look at the ambassador's hideaway upstairs?"

I'd been upstairs when I came at Christmastime for my interview at the *Miami Star*, but I'd gone up from the club side, accompanied by Bev alone, who'd been giving me a tour of the card rooms with their green baize tabletops and wet bars, and the roulette wheel hidden behind a big painting of a fox hunt in the largest room.

"As far as I'm concerned, this part of the operation we could do without," Bev had said, marching me along snappily. We were both wearing spike-heeled sandals from her closet; she'd vetoed my college-girl pumps as "too old-maidish" and run-down at the heels. "Paul and I don't get paid extra for the risks and all the *tsuris* so our members can feel they've got the best of La Gorce *and* Vegas, but it's all part of Paul's hospitality *shtick*. He wants to make it up to them for all those nasty signs they had to bicycle past in their childhoods."

"Are the members all Jewish?"

"Oh no, we've got our noble smattering of goyim. Mostly friends of other members or dice-rollers who dig our wall setup"—flipping her frosted nails airily toward the painting—"our dear down-home foxhunting scene from the old shtetl."

It always struck me as funny that Bev, of the goyim herself, liberally decorated her remarks with expressions taken from Yiddish, whereas Paul hardly ever availed himself of that colorful lexicon.

I'd briefly looked in on Paul's bedroom at Christmastime, with commentary by Bev: "He stays overnight when the card rooms are busy. Sometimes there's an argument and he has to provide his calming influence. I offered to fix the room nicely for him, but he preferred hand-me-downs from Aunt Stella."

Last December, Paul had put me up at the Kenilworth, where I paid my own bill—with his money. He visited me in the afternoons and then "officially" picked me up around eight in the evening for dinner and dancing at the club with him and Bev and sometimes Aunt Stella, who would wear one of her ancient Chanel suits from when she worked for Guerlain in Paris in the thirties.

By the time we arrived, Nightingale's would be in full swing with the charcoal smells, the dance band, the stand-up comedians making jokes against themselves (a perplexing new brand of humor for me), the noisy exchanges between tables. The members were friends who'd grown up together on the Beach, had gone to the same high school, belonged to the same synagogue, did business with one another all week, and most of them old enough to remember bicycling past those notices on the lawns, the word "Restricted" on the marquees of hotels, the signs in the windows of a certain rooming house on the causeway—EVERY ROOM WITH A VIEW WITHOUT A JEW—that the landlord took down only after convoys of American soldiers began to use that route and military headquarters complained.

Bev suspected nothing. She considered me her ingénue, ever since she'd taught me how to walk properly. She knew—indeed, had suggested it herself—that Paul drove me back to college at the end of the summer while she and Stella stayed behind to close the Inn. When I came to Miami last Christmas for my interview at the *Star*, she, along with Paul and Aunt Stella, had had her fingers crossed that I would get this coveted job. She also believed that, though Paul got me a special rate, I was paying my own hotel bill with Christmas money from a rich aunt in Alabama.

There was one close call when Paul and I were in bed in my room at the Kenilworth and she phoned up from the lobby to announce she had come to take me shopping. That was the day we bought the low-cut black dress I was wearing tonight. It was expensive and she wanted to pay half.

"Oh, Bev, I couldn't," I said, admiring myself in the three-way mirror.

"Okay, go ahead. Deny me my *nakhes*."

"What are 'knockas'?"

"Yiddish for the satisfaction parents get when their child does well."

"But I haven't done well yet."

"Emma, you're a work of art in that dress. And you're going to be a college graduate in six months. The world is yours. Won't you let me put my money on it?"

"Well, thank you, if you're sure." Our eyes met in the mirror and it struck me that in this dress and with our pink-and-white complexions and look-alike French twists we could pass as relatives. Not mother and daughter: though Bev was old enough to be my mother, she simply didn't come across as motherly. She'd told me once, with no sign of regret in her voice, that she couldn't have children even before the hysterectomy, and nothing more was said. Perhaps my older, glamorous, more worldly-wise sister, then? Or, I remember fantasizing this as our eyes met in the mirror, a pair of courtesans, the younger in training to the older, both under the care of the same protector.

PAUL HAD a fetish about cleanliness, intensified, he thought, by Aunt Stella's stories about never being able to get clean enough in the French internment camp before she got her visa to come and live with him and his mother in Florida. Paul's first lover's compliment to me, as we lay coiled around each other, had been that I smelled clean all over.

"You'd be surprised how many women neglect their hygiene," he confided dismally. "I'm talking about fastidious, well-groomed women who need two hours to make up their faces before anyone's allowed to see them. Their oversight is just a fact of life, I guess, but it makes *him* wither right up. None of my family were practicing Jews, but there's something to be said for those ritual baths couples take separately before having sex on the weekends."

Because Loney had often hinted to me that lack of attention to "down there" could lead to loathsome disorders, I had from an early age been scrupulous about my nether regions. But after Paul's first compliment, I became overenthusiastic and burnt my insides once or twice with strong douches I bought at the drugstore.

"I think you'll find everything you need in the bathroom," Paul said when we were inside his bedroom at the club. "You're welcome to my dressing gown, it's on the hook inside the door."

On our quick Christmas tour of Paul's quarters at P. Nightingale's, Bev hadn't included the bathroom, and I was surprised by its sleek fixtures and thick towels. I had been imagining something more like the camplike facilities in the cabin Paul had let me use last summer when I was working at the Nightingale Inn.

I toed off my shoes, folded my dress on the cushioned wicker bench, tucking stockings and underwear out of sight, and turned on both sink faucets medium force and refreshed my hygiene, although I'd gone over myself thoroughly back at the Julia Tuttle. I then briskly rubbed down my whole body to give it a glow and dropped the towel into the wicker hamper. I undid my French twist and laid the hairpins on the marble counter, being sure to remove all stray hairs so Paul wouldn't be put off by any untidiness if he had to use the bathroom. I examined the figure in the mirror. I was well proportioned and several boyfriends had told me I looked best in the altogether.

Paul was waiting for me under the covers. "That robe suits you. I'll make you a present of it."

"What will you wear, then?"

"I'll get another one. We can be twins."

I slid in beside him. When our bodies touched he gave a little gasp.

His body was years younger than his face. There was something touchingly boyish about it. Slim and rather soft-muscled, much paler than his face and neck, with just a few sprigs of curly hairs in the middle of the chest, none of them gone gray like on his head.

"Oh," he shuddered, slipping inside me in one smooth motion.

The blackout curtains that covered all the upstairs bay-side windows of the club were drawn in this room also. "No need for things to look too busy up here," Bev had commented during our Christmas tour of Paul's quarters. "It's nobody's business outside how many card rooms are in use, or whether the owner is sleeping over or not."

Paul's green-shaded desk lamp cast us in a flattering underwatery light: two enfolded creatures in their passion aquarium.

"We're plugged in again," said Paul.

"Yes."

It really was like being recharged, and I could feel the same current going through him. Joining with Paul was a planet away from my previous experiences with men. Connecting with him always made me feel fortified rather than raided. He really *was* my alien lover, from a place where lovemaking was practiced as a precise and artful mutual refueling. Each time I came away sharper and stronger and he came away happier.

But tonight, as he separated from me, I felt bereft and started to cry.

I don't know which of us was more surprised. For a whole year we had been cunningly building toward living in the same city, and here I was sobbing as though we were about to say goodbye forever.

"Hey, kid, what's going on here?"

"I suddenly had this feeling I'm going to lose you."

"Because I have to go away for three days? I told you I'll be back for your birthday."

"It isn't that."

"Then what? You were never like this when we had to say goodbye for much longer periods of time."

"I don't know what, but when we separated just now I had this awful feeling, it was so strange, I'd get dressed and you'd drive me back to the hotel and tomorrow I'd go out into a different world and we'd never be as close again."

He had been poised above me in an awkward half push-up, but now he pulled me to him and turned us sideways so I lay sobbing into the armpit of the shoulder that supported me.

With his free hand he covered us up with a sheet and then gently traced his fingers up and down my spine.

"You *are* going out into a different world tomorrow," he said in a gentle, fatherly voice, which only set me off again. "It's what you've been working for all these years, and look what you've already accomplished. You're not even twenty-two yet, not until Thursday. When I was your age, I was night clerk at the Miramar, which didn't even have its own postcard. I was a skinny little Jew boy with no college who still lived at home with his mother and had no idea what he was good for. And look at you. Educated, talented, and determined. You know what you want and you're already good at it. You got here on your own steam, and tomorrow your rise to fame and fortune begins. No, I mean it. I trust my instincts and my instincts tell me you're gonna make it, regardless of setbacks."

He continued to run his fingers softly up and down my spine, as though he were annointing my backbone with his faith in me.

"I'll never forget you stepping down from that bus last June. Jesus Christ, here I'd come to pick up the fresh, appealing college girl I'd hired the day before in Mountain City, and out comes . . . Well, you were a pretty grim sight with that shiner."

"Tell me the truth, now, you wanted to send me back, didn't you?"

We had been through this before, but I always looked forward to his answer.

"Never considered it. My heart went out to you. Especially when I asked you how you got it and you stuck out your chin and said, 'Oh, saying goodbye to my stepfather.' Without a trace of self-pity, almost with, well, humor. This is one spunky kid, I thought. But what was I going to do with you in the meantime? I couldn't take you up to the Inn and introduce you to the others, have you wait tables, like that."

"So you took me to your hideaway cabin instead. And sent Aunt Stella down to minister to me with her wet leaves and magic potions."

"And you were on the job within the week, and everybody at the Inn fell in love with you."

"But *you* didn't fall in love with me until I asked you to return my book to the library in Mountain City and bring me volume two."

"Nope, not even then."

We'd been down this road before, too, but it was a cherished part of our storytelling ritual.

"But you said that was when things changed."

"When I hid you away in the cabin and told everyone you'd come down with a bad cold, I already knew I wanted to protect you. Then when I returned your *Confessions of Felix Krull, Confidence Man (The Early Years)* and told the librarian you wanted the next volume, and she said the author had died before he got a chance to write it, I thought, how am I going to tell her? She'll be so disappointed. A smart college kid like her and she didn't know he died before he wrote volume two! I asked the librarian if she had anything else by Mann you might not have read, and she looked up his other books and said your name wasn't on the card in back of the stories—so I checked them out for you. And then, when I got back to the Inn and told you there was no second volume, you looked kind of deflated, but you recovered yourself and said, 'Well, that just means I'll have to imagine the second volume for myself.' And when I handed over the stories, I could see immediately that you'd read them, but you pretended you hadn't, to save my feelings, and that's when something shifted—"

At this juncture, as always, he picked up my right hand and placed it on his bare chest, over his heart. "In here."

HE RETURNED me the quick way, crossing onto the mainland at Broad Causeway and heading straight down Biscayne Boulevard. But instead of following the boulevard all the way to the riverfront entrance to the Julia Tuttle, he turned right into Flagler Street and drove slowly down two blocks of darkened storefronts to the only lit-up building in sight. The way it was positioned, on the corner of Flagler and Miami Avenue, made it look like the prow of an ocean liner bearing down on us, with *"The Miami Star"* glowing aloft in red neon letters. In some of the yellow squares of the wraparound second-floor windows you could see human shadows moving about the newsroom.

But there was more to come. With his typical acumen for planning the next treat, Paul had got us here just in time for the first edition's press run. He activated the button to let down the window on my side, then switched off the ignition and let the close, balmy night invade the air-conditioned darkness of the car. As though we were royalty and the performance could now begin, a bell went off inside the tall ground-floor windows. Men wearing hats made out of newspaper moved among the big presses—some were up on the catwalks—and the huge press cylinders began to roll, slowly picking up speed to the chop-chop of the folder knives. The folder spewed forth the first complete paper; the foreman gave it a fast page-through to make sure the plates were installed in the right order, then gave the high sign for the presses to accelerate to full speed. The chop of the folder knives got faster and faster until it merged with the roar of the presses into a frenzied blur of sound. There was something erotic about a press run, with its increasing tempo of excitement, its acceleration toward full speed and no return.

"Seventy thousand newspapers an hour," crooned Paul softly, his hand lightly cupping my knee. "Just think, by this time tomorrow your byline may be hitting the streets seventy thousand times."

3.

I SUPPOSE I EXPECTED more fuss when I stepped off the elevator into the noisy *Star* newsroom on Monday morning. Nobody even looked up. Men with rolled-up shirtsleeves assaulted typewriters, smoke rising above their heads. The pervasive odors were of tobacco, coffee, and the pulp copy paper Mother in her reporting days used to bring home from the *Mountain City Citizen* for me to scribble on. Segregated inside a glass cubicle, some middle-aged women in colorful dresses were clustered over fashion layout pages or prancing around in high heels or clacking out copy. All of them were puffing like dragons as well. A lanky, deeply tanned one with close-cropped silver curls caught my eye and smiled. I smiled back coolly and proceeded on to the managing editor's corner. My acceptance letter had said "general assignment reporter" and I had no intention of getting corralled into the women's department.

At least Lib, the managing editor's secretary, who guarded his office, was expecting me. I had made sure to write down her name after my Christmas interview. She said Mr. Feeney would be out to welcome me shortly. She asked me what I thought so far of the South Florida weather, and before I could answer said not to judge it by all the rain we'd been having, meanwhile giving me the female-to-female once-over and appearing satisfied with my neat French twist and forest green shirtwaist. ("Dark dress, hair out of face, and *stockings*, no matter how hot"—my grandmother Loney's career-dressing advice.) Lib herself wore a navy dress with a white collar, and her black hair was smartly sheared at earlobe level.

Supertall Mr. Feeney bounded out in his shirtsleeves and with an avuncular bow escorted me into his office. He was a gent, from the category of men I knew how to handle best. Gents tended to idealize bright young women and tried to smooth their way, shielding them from unpleasantness and strife whenever possible.

Since my Christmas visit, another executive desk facing Mr. Feeney's had been moved into his office, making the room look cramped. A solid, dark-haired figure in an uncannily white shirt was in the act of rising from this desk.

"Emma, this is my new assistant managing editor, Lou Norbright." That he presented the assistant manager to *me* indicated that Mr. Feeney was indeed of the old school. A lady ranked higher than her corporate superior. Then, in typical self-effacing-gent style, Feeney went on to praise us to each other as if that were his only role in life.

"Lou here came to us six years ago, Emma, all the way from North Platte, Nebraska, as a general assignment reporter for the *Star*, and before we knew it he was running the city desk, and now here he is, my second-in-command. All of which is to say, Emma"—another bow—"the *Star* encourages rising stars, if that doesn't sound too corny."

He then rattled off my glories to the new assistant managing editor. "Emma won her J-school's most prized scholarship and she had her own column in the *Daily Tar Heel*. A real crackerjack of a column, too, timely, lively, subjects resourcefully handled, witty, very witty. Her dean sent me samples. He and I were Nieman Fellows at Harvard together."

Lou Norbright heard out Feeney's encomium to me with the same smiling attention with which he had received his own. He was *gleamingly* at attention, you might say. His glasses gleamed, his coal-bright eyes behind the silver rims gleamed, his uncannily white shirt gleamed, his black-and-silver-striped necktie gleamed, his teeth gleamed. A thin edging of gold between his top left canine and the adjoining premolar completed the overall gleaming effect.

I couldn't place him in any of my male categories; he seemed neither gent, mentor, obstacle, adversary, sexual attractant, useful stepping-stone, buddy-cohort, nor anything potentially personal. He was more like an emblem or an idea, but I wasn't sure of what. He appeared perfectly cordial toward me, yet he conveyed, almost viscerally, a withholding of judgment that had the effect of shrinking my confidence. It was as if I could read his subliminal reservations in the gleaming mirror of his surfaces. What if Mr. Feeney and Dean Ligon had *not* been Nieman Fellows together? What if Dean Ligon had not been so obviously disposed in my favor? What if Paul had not talked me into traveling to Miami for the Christmas interview "because you come across so well in person." Where would my bare talents alone have gotten me at this early stage if Dean Ligon, Mr. Feeney, and Paul Nightingale had not been the sort of mentor-gents won over by young women like myself?

"Lou will show you around the newsroom," Mr. Feeney was saying, "and then we're going to start you right in at the city desk." He gave another courtly dip in my direction. "Just like the proverbial little duck being thrown into the water, if that's not too corny."

Lou Norbright seemed to glide along beside me rather than walk in ordinary human steps. "So, Emma," he said, "how are you finding our Miami weather?" The bright eyes behind the gleaming glasses appeared to expect something more "in-depth" than the conventional reply and so I allowed as how I found it a little harder to breathe in Miami. "The humidity, I guess, or my blood needs to thin. Did *you* find that when you first came down here from Nebraska?"

He flashed the gold-edged canine at me and looked as though I had just confirmed his private assessment of me. "No, I can't say that I did," he remarked cheerfully.

I was introduced first to Pat and Ed on the copydesk, both of whom wore green visors just like in newspaper movies. Though they both laid down their pencils from their respective slashings of triple-spaced copy and gave me friendly welcomes and appreciative male glances, I was enough under Lou Norbright's confidence-leaching spell to imagine them foreseeing exactly the kinds of trifles and inadequacies they would soon be slashing out of my prose.

Next I met Bert, a soft-voiced, cherub-faced man who doubled as book editor and religion editor; he said to let him know if I wanted to review any new books for him.

"Perhaps later, when she's settled in," Norbright smilingly answered for me.

Next came a disheveled reporter with wild eyebrows and a crooked red bow tie, Dave Bisbee, who cocked his head impudently up at Norbright from an appallingly messy desk and invited me to "bug" him with any questions I was afraid to bother the "brass" with.

"We'll all try to give Emma the benefit of our best guidance, Dave," Lou Norbright suavely countered.

At her own corner desk, guarded by a large basket-shaped straw pocketbook with fake cherries on it, presided the woman reporter I already considered my rival because of her frequent sensational front-page stories: Joelle Cutter-Crane.

"Nice twist on the Jiménez stash, Joelle," Norbright complimented her. "Readers have been calling in to comment. I'd like you to meet Emma Gant from North Carolina; she'll be joining us in the newsroom."

It hadn't escaped my notice that Norbright had presented me to everybody rather than the other way round.

"I'm honored to meet you," I told the small, brittle-featured woman with scarlet nails and a marcelled hairstyle and hair color similar to Tess's. "I've been admiring your stories ever since I began subscribing to the *Star* in February."

"How do you do?" said Joelle Cutter-Crane, barely glancing at me. She fixed Norbright with a hard, lipsticked smile. "It was my idea, not the copydesk's, I want you to know, Lou, to give all that equipment in dictator Jiménez's custom-built Cadillac—the machine gun and grenade racks as well as the luxury items—a box of its own."

"Ah, Joelle, don't we give you enough credit as it is?" Norbright teased.

As we continued on our rounds he said, "Joelle's the ribbon on our package and we try to keep her happy. The team concept of newspapering is completely beyond her." As he seemed too calculated a type to indulge in gossip merely for its own pleasures, I concluded he was giving me a token of his own "guidance." The only trouble was, I couldn't tell from his tone whether he was saying it was better to be a ribbon or a team player.

Next stop was the morgue, the library in newspaper offices where you looked up the people and events you wanted to know about and the stories of yesterday you needed for background. The stories were stored in open cardboard file boxes containing alphabetically labeled envelopes stuffed with all the paper's clippings on that topic. Tess's sad story from the forties was lying there right now in an envelope bearing her ex-husband's surname, and all Joelle Cutter-Crane's old scoops could be found under the the letter *C*, as well as under the first letter of the subject of each scoop. The career of rapidly rising Norbright was stuffed into its envelopes, to be tracked whenever I could find the time. There would probably even be a file on P. Nightingale's Club and its owner. And perhaps starting as early as tomorrow under *G* would begin the clipped and filed documentation of my own rising star.

The librarian for the morgue was the first person in our round of introductions to whom Lou Norbright showed deference. This person sat within her bubble of remoteness, a stack of Sunday *Miami Star*s spread out on a long table perpendicular to her desk. As we entered her glassed-in sanctum, she was in the act of clipping multiple copies of yesterday's front-page lead, WHERE THE DICTATOR STASHED HIS MILLIONS, as its eight-column banner headline read, to go into the various envelopes: "Cutter-Crane," "Jiménez," "Venezuela," "Dictators," "Ex-dictators," plus those of all the minor figures mentioned in the story, and probably even "Cadillacs, custom equipment," from Joelle's very own box idea.

"Moira, this is Emma Gant. We'll be starting her off on the city desk. Emma, meet Moira Parks. I'm sure you know from J-school what an indispensable shop Moira runs." Though Norbright spoke with his usual assurance, he seemed, in Moira's domain, to take up only a normal amount of human space and not flow into hers. Moira Parks ceased applying her massive shears to yesterday's big story and raised her thick, smoke-tinted glasses toward us. It was impossible to guess her age. She wore a shoulder-padded dress in a style from the forties. Her incredible mass of springy gray hair, the bottom clump somewhat restrained by an old-fashioned snood, suggested thousands of quivering electric wires conducting messages to and from her head.

"How do you do?" I said. Her eyes were barely discernible behind the smoky whorls of glass. "You'll probably be seeing a lot of me in here."

"Don't hesitate to ask for help." She spoke in a carefully articulated monotone, as though to a foreigner or simpleton. "That's what I'm here for. The files are organized alphabetically. I ask that you take out only one envelope at a time and replace it before taking another. You'll find tables and chairs behind those shelves. If you need to take an envelope to the newsroom, you sign it out in this book, but it's never to go out of the building."

"I got in big trouble with Moira my first day at the *Star* when she caught me heading out of here with sixteen envelopes," Norbright roguishly confessed.

Moira gave no sign of having heard him. I could picture him gliding out with his hoard of envelopes. It would have been fun to see how she stopped him. Whose trail had he been onto? Which career-promoting story had come out of it?

"Don't hesitate to ask for help," Moira Parks repeated in her remote monotone, and went back to her scissoring.

The city editor, Rod Reynolds, a blond, apple-cheeked man with carelessly pushed-up sleeves, assigned me the desk directly to his left. "That way if you need help I'm in shouting distance. Also, ha, ha, I can keep an eye on you." He was a former Chapel Hill graduate, so we played "Do you know?" for the first few minutes as Norbright, smiling at our repartee, faded from the scene, though leaving behind his gleaming afterimage.

"Old Doc Speers, does he still drop hot ash down the front of his shirt while he's lecturing?"

"He burned two holes during my semester of Feature Writing with him," I was happy to report.

"Lordy, Lordy, the good old J-school days."

He then handed me a list of funeral-home phone numbers to call and showed me the *Star*'s format for standard obituaries. "Anything out of the ordinary, run it past me. I'm not here, look into it yourself, if you think it rates a story."

"Out of the ordinary in what way?"

"Human interest angle, anything bizarre. Switched to an earlier plane and it crashed. Freak accident in the home. Child drowns in half an inch of water. Anything at all to do with a child."

"Will the funeral home tell me these things?"

"Come on, Emma, you know better than that." He ripped a sheet out of his typewriter, slammed it down on the metal spike holding stories ready for the copydesk without looking out for his hand—which made me wince—and retrieved a smouldering cigarette from the ashtray. "Anybody under forty, you ask for the cause of death, even if we don't print it in our routine obits. If it sounds unusual or has pathos, you call the family. And get a picture. Especially if it's a kid, you want to get a picture."

"Like that little boy who drowned at Y camp last week?"

"Good girl. Lou said you'd been studying the paper to see how we do things. It wouldn't go over in Dean Ligon's famous Senior Seminar, but the *Star* is not the good gray *Times* or—what were his other standards of excellence?"

"The Louisville *Courier-Journal* and the *St. Louis Post-Dispatch*?"

"Lordy, yes. Well, our readership isn't the *Courier-Journal*'s or the *Post-Dispatch*'s, either. Miami is not like anywhere else on earth. That's why I love it, it's surreal."

The cutline under the child's photo had read:

Eric's first day at camp . . . and last.

If we seniors in Dean Ligon's Ethics and Responsibilities of the Press Seminar had been discussing that cutline last spring, the dean would have crimped his lips and grumbled, "This isn't as *blatant* as Joe Pulitzer's famous headline, 'How Babies Are Baked,' that ran in the New York *World* after 392 children died in a heat wave, but it has the same yellow tinge. As responsible journalists, you'll want to avoid the yellow tinge as you would want to avoid hepatitis."

SEVERAL HOURS later, I had produced eleven triple-spaced biographies of unmemorable Dade County residents who were on record as having expired in the last twenty-four hours. My first morning's labors had been scribbled over by Rod and slammed down on the spike to await the copyboy's pickup for their trip across to the copydesk and then up to the composing room. I felt distracted and intrigued and excluded by all that was going on around me. What was in the printout that the copyboy tore off the teletype machine and rushed into Feeney's office?

"Did they jail those two witnesses up in Tallahassee yet?" I heard Gabe Truro's bass voice speaking into a telephone somewhere behind me— followed by a burst of remarkably fast typing.

(Since when were *witnesses* jailed?)

Rod Reynolds had introduced me to the *Star's* suave middle-aged crime reporter while I was doing my obits. Being a gent, Truro had paused long enough to welcome me properly before turning aside to Rod to murmur, "Well, the indictment finally came through." *Whose* indictment? Would I have to wait until it was in the newspaper to find out?

I was aware that others around me were taking lunch breaks, and that I was eligible to do the same, but a lassitude seemed to emanate directly out of the fluorescent ceiling lights and keep me rooted to the swivel chair in front of my typewriter pit.

After finishing each obit, I had jotted down the age and gender of its protagonist, thinking I might come up with some clever quip to show Rod Reynolds how I could investigate beyond the ordinary. ("Interestingly enough, Rod, all the deaths under sixty in today's count were women, whereas all those who made it into their eighties were men. That reverses the usual statistics, doesn't it?")

But only a few moments before, Rod had shoved down his shirtsleeves, snatched up his rumpled cotton-cord jacket, and, with neither a word nor a look my way, bolted off in his toed-out Southern-boy swagger.

Although I had known from the movies and from the simulated newsroom set up for us in the basement of the journalism school that my place of work was going to be one big noisy arena jammed with desks at which scores of reporters clattered away, I still must have held out in my imagination for some kind of enclosure affording a sense of privacy between me and my typewriter. To know that I could be observed by others, in all my flattering and unflattering angles, from the front, back, and sides, as I hunched over my machine, pecking away, not to mention spied on from behind management glass by eel-eyed Norbright himself, had produced an unusually concentrated amount of work on my part, but had left me with a tension headache and a sense of unreality.

I sat on in my stupor, adding up the ages of my dead in the new spiral-bound notepad Rod had issued me. Surely there must have been at least one bizarre human-interest story buried in those 909 accumulated years, but if so, I had failed to unearth it.

"You don't get brownie points for skipping lunch around here," said an insolent male voice above me. "Especially when all the brass are into their second martini over at the Yacht Club and can't even see you. I'd be honored if you'd join me for a quick bite at *my* club. It has the best tuna sandwich in town."

I looked up and saw Dave Bisbee with his uncombed hair and crooked red bow tie. What kind of club would let him in? The surprising thing was, he seemed to read my thought and not hold it against me.

"Walgreens," he good-naturedly explained. "It's just down the block. Come on, you need a break. You've worked nonstop since you got here. I'll give you my famous Walgreens Tutorial. Fill you in on who's who and what to watch out for. I gave it to Lou Norbright on his first day, too."

4.

A S WE WALKED DOWN Flagler Street, I assessed my tutor. The
trousers of his summer suit were too short; they made his skinny
ankles in their black socks look comic and vulnerable. As he bounced
along beside me, he kept up a steady banter, gesturing constantly with his
hands—I noted he wore a wedding ring—so that even before we were
settled in our booth at Walgreens he had dispensed much salient information, ranging from how to tell Miami's streets from its avenues to who
had just been fired—the previous occupant of my desk, a reporter named
Kirk. "He was always half crocked, but the real reason was he was trying
to bring in the union. 'Union' is a no-no word in the *Star* newsroom."

By the time our order came, grilled cheese and a Coke for me, tuna
sandwich and black coffee for him, I had Dave Bisbee securely tucked away
into side-by-side pigeonholes of potential buddy and useful stepping-
stone. Though he came across as a bit of a fool, he was an avid observer,
listener, and questioner. He wanted to know why I had chosen to work in
Miami. Did I know anyone here? I smoothly offered up "Aunt Tess" as
my single Miami contact, and modestly went on to confide that, though
I had been pretty much the star of my journalism class *and* had my own
column on the *Daily Tar Heel*, if my dean and Mr. Feeney had not been
Nieman Fellows together, I might not have gotten my Christmas interview at the *Miami Star*.

"Still. It was enterprising of you to come all the way down here for an interview. Not cheap, either, in high season. Even if you could stay with your aunt."

I took an earnest bite of grilled cheese sandwich and chewed thoughtfully, recalling my oceanfront room at the Kenilworth last Christmas, and Paul's rolls of bills passing constantly from his wallet to mine, and Bev calling up on the house phone that afternoon when we were naked under the covers: "Come, child, I want to take you shopping."

After I had washed everything down with a long sip of Coke, I said to Bisbee, "Tell me about Lou Norbright on *his* first day."

"It was like Lucifer in the garden. One morning I looked up from my desk and there he was at the edge of the newsroom. All of a sudden he'd *materialized* there, taking in the lay of the land with that shit-eating grin of his. I was fairly new down here myself, I'd wooed old Feeney for a solid year, sending him my award-winning stories from the *Tampa Tribune*. Soon after that, Feeney brings him over to my desk and says, 'Dave, please take Lou here under your wing and show him the ropes, if you'll forgive my corny mixed metaphors.'

"So Lou and I have lunch his first day, right here in this same booth, and I'm telling him everything I know about how the *Star* operates, who's good and who's not making the grade, who you can trust and who'll stab you in the back—and he's just sitting there smiling, not saying much but drawing it out of me like a suction pump. The first month he was here, we made an effective team. He didn't have a car yet, his wife needed it to get them settled, so I'd call in the stories and he'd write them up and we'd share the byline. He was a speed demon at rewrites; back in North Platte he'd done twenty or thirty stories a day, everything from sports to disasters, whatever came in. What's the big deal, he said. He thought our *Star* reporters were prima donnas, polishing up their one or two precious stories per day.

"By the time he did get his car, he took over the Beach beat while that reporter was on vacation, and within a matter of days he'd uncovered a perfect gem of a swindle, this creep had retirees working a bank of phones, calling people with Italian or Irish names to sell them religious relics, vials of healing water from Lourdes, medals and little figures from the Vatican, blessed by the Pope. There's nothing the *Star* loves more than the human-interest angle, and Lou milked it for all it was worth, all these senior citizens, some of them in pretty desperate shape, willing to fork over their last dollar for these fakes some toy factory in New Jersey was knocking off by the truckload. Lou also interviewed the retirees who had needed the extra income but didn't know they were involved in a federal crime—because the stuff went through the U.S. mails, you know. It didn't hurt, either, that the swindler was photographically loathsome. With his handcuffs on, he looked like a beetle walking upright in a Hawaiian shirt."

"How did Norbright happen to uncover it?"

"Exactly the right question, Emma. If you were assigned the Beach beat to fill in for a colleague, what's the first thing you'd do? Come on, now, remember your News Gathering 101."

"I'd probably check in with the police station, first."

"Which you can be sure Lucifer did. Hi, Sergeant, I'm Lou, filling in for Bernie who's on vacation, what's been happening over here on the Beach? Hmmm, Lou, let's see, a geezer dropped his pipe over the railing and we had to fish him and it out of the bay. Oh, yeah, and this tourist lady reported her wallet stolen, but then she found it in her other purse. Maybe check back later, Lou.

"Where does Lucifer go next? To and fro upon the beach, up and down Collins Avenue on foot, passing the time with nut-brown oldies who have plenty of time to pass. He befriends a group of yentas—you know what a yenta is?"

"An old lady who gossips?" Thank you, Bev.

"Good girl. Yiddish is Miami's second language and Spanish is gonna be its first if these Cubans keep pouring in. How's your Spanish?"

"I had two years in high school and two in college. But except for one conversation course it's the book kind."

"I'd brush up, if I were you. Maybe even find a tutor. It'll get you brownie points at the *Star*. Anyway, here's Lucifer passing the time on the hotel veranda with these old girls playing mah-jongg but not missing a thing going on, and one of them happens to mention her friend's taken this phone soliciting job to supplement her social security check, but is thinking of quitting because something's unsavory about the whole operation—and bingo, Lucifer is off and running."

I slurped the dregs of my Coke through the straw. The jealousy animal had begun to stir inside me. I realized I would not have thought it worth my time to cultivate the yentas on the veranda.

"How about some dessert? I always have the key lime pie. I never knew key lime pie existed till we came to South Florida. My wife tries to make it at least once a week, she knows I'm mad for it, but Walgreens' is better."

"I'll pass on the pie, but I'd love another Coke."

"Coming up. But what made Lucifer a star was his 'Queen of the Underworld' series—the bust-up of this elite house of prostitution run by a mobster over on Palm Island. You ever hear of it? No? The series was picked up all over the country, even abroad. No, that's right, six years ago you would have been just a teenager. The 'queen' herself was still a teenager when she was launched, and twenty-one when she blew the whistle and brought it all down. Look it up in the morgue: Queen of the Underworld trial, also under Ginevra Snow, and the Valentis—they were the Mafia uncle and the nephew. Ginevra was this Georgia fruit-stand beauty who caught the eye of the nephew. He got her to run away with him, promised marriage as soon as he finished law school at the University of Miami. Meanwhile he had his uncle enroll her at Biscayne Academy, that was a posh Miami finishing school for debutantes. Well, she finishes before he does and comes out bearing herself like a queen while the nephew's still goofing off and flunking courses and procrastinating about the wedding. Ginevra moves into the uncle's villa on Palm Island, and one thing leads to another—though at the trial she testified the uncle never laid a hand on her and none of the clients did, either, it was strictly a business arrangement between her and the uncle while her fiancé finished his degree. She kept the books and polished the girls' manners like she'd been taught at the Biscayne Academy, she took them shopping and chose their clothes, and the uncle provided the funds and invited the guests. Well, two more years pass, the nephew's still in law school, she sees him only on the weekends, and sometimes not even then because of studying and tests or he's feeling indisposed. And then one Sunday morning it all blows sky-high when Ginevra wakes up in her Palm Island bedroom and opens the *Star*'s society section to find that her fiancé is engaged to someone else! She picks up the phone and calls the *Star* and asks to speak to a reporter, and guess who just happens to be working overtime on the Sunday morning desk?

"All Lou had to do was make a couple of phone calls and then sit back and wait for Hell-hath-no-fury to drive herself across the MacArthur Causeway to the paper. While she was spilling her story, her unsuspecting pimp was arrested coming out of St. Ignatius Catholic Church with his new fiancée. A raid squad was dispatched to Palm Island to pick up Ginevra's personal belongings, which included an appointment book filled with the names of prominent figures, including a federal judge. Lou took her over to the photo lab and got them to shoot a demure head and shoulders portrait of her just like the *Star*'s standard engagement photos, and then the DA himself arrived and spirited her away to an undisclosed location. The story broke on Monday, circulation started going up and up, prominent heads rolled when the contents of the young lady's appointment book were made known, and during the trial Lou Norbright became as much of a household word as his famous queen."

"Why was she a queen?"

"Lou made her into one. He made her into a modern-day Persephone—you know, the young goddess abducted by Hades, the King of the Underworld. Whereas Ginevra was only abducted from her grandmother's fruit stand by a Mafia brat and transformed by the sophisticated mobster uncle into a highly successful madam while the nephew kept promising to marry her as soon as he finished law school.

"It was what Lou did with Ginevra's testimony and background that hooked readers. He drove up to Waycross and talked to the old crosspatch redneck grandmother, a far cry from Persephone's mother, but it only made readers all the more sorry for Ginevra—the granny had raised her after the child's mother drank herself to death, but demanded her own pound of flesh as soon as the little girl could stand on a box behind the fruit stand and count out change.

"Then he interviewed her high school boyfriend, who confirmed Ginevra had always conducted herself like a queen. She'd never gone all the way with him because they were saving it for their marriage. Oh boy. Circulation kept going up and up, the story had everything, how could Lou top himself after that?

"Next thing, Feeney sends him up to the *Star*'s Washington bureau— ah, my key lime pie. Sure you won't change your mind?"

"No, thanks. But what happened to her—Ginevra—and the uncle and the nephew?"

"The nephew got five years for transporting a minor across the state line, but he jumped bail and vanished, probably abroad, where the uncle had gone to avoid a subpoena for pandering. Ginevra became a local celebrity for a few months, there was talk of her working with disadvantaged girls or collaborating with Hollywood for a movie, but then she married her shrink, a guy named Brown, and dropped out of sight, more or less, on Key Biscayne. She's made a couple of suicide attempts since— I covered them, such as they were—but six years is like a generation in the newspaper business. Now you have to remind readers who the Queen of the Underworld was.

"You know, after Feeney sent Lou up to the Washington bureau, I really missed the guy. Once I conceded his superiority, I got a surge of adrenaline just from watching him operate. When he suddenly returned, none of us could figure it out. His Washington stories had been top-of-the-line; but here he was back *assisting* on city desk, then moving humbly around to sports, business, state, being everybody's friend. He and I had a couple more lunches here at Walgreens and I brought him up to date on everything.

"Well, three months later, Feeney fires the city editor and replaces him with you-know-who. The whole thing had been Lou's idea. Feeney had wanted to bring him back from Washington and install him straight off as city editor, but Lou said no, let him mingle with the staff as their peer first, listen to their gripes, find out who's working and who isn't, get a better fix on the whole operation from inside. In other words be a sneaky, ruthless son of a bitch, which is what people called him afterward, not that he minded, he was the first to admit it himself. He once told me that most people look on a promotion as having arrived but he saw it simply as his next point of departure."

"When I was down here for my Christmas interview," I said, "Feeney was all by himself in there. Yet he seems happy sharing his office with Norbright."

"Feeney's the convivial type; he likes being visible in the community, giving out the awards and scholarships, being keynote speaker at benefits. He never liked the pressure side of the job. Deadlines, crises, resentments and rivalries, all the things Lou thrives on. So now Feeney can be the benevolent overseer while his dark assistant goes to and fro in the newsroom and does the dirty work."

"I wonder what Lou Norbright really wants. I mean, *ultimately*." I loved conversations in which you tried to figure out the motives of sinister or very successful people, who were often a combination of both.

"Lucifer? Power and control, just like his counterpart. Aren't you going to eat your pickle?"

WHEN BISBEE and I returned to the office, I found a half sheet of copy paper stuck under the bar of my Remington.

emma: go see harmon for tests at 3:30

rr

"What's this about?" I showed Bisbee the note.

"Harry Harmon's the personnel director. The *Star* gives personality tests now. Good thing I escaped them, I'd never have got in the door."

"But I thought I was already *in* the door."

"It's a new management thing, probably Lucifer's idea. Don't sweat it. Just don't be too interesting when you go up there is my advice. Harmon's a stuffed shirt."

Having forty-five minutes to kill and no new assignments from "rr," who was nowhere in sight, I picked up my spiral-bound pad and a copy pencil and headed for the morgue. Moira Parks was now cutting up Sunday's inside pages.

"Hi," I said. "Just thought I'd look up a few things, kind of get myself oriented."

"Let me know if I can be of help," she responded without looking up from her scissoring. ALL MY OPPONENTS TRAITORS—CASTRO I read upside down as she severed the two-column story from the adjoining department store ad.

First I looked up Tess, under her husband's name. It was a slimmer envelope than I'd expected. FORMER MISS MIAMI BEACH WEDS PIONEER FAMILY SCION. There was the same three-column wedding picture of the bride that was yellowing in one of Loney's bureau drawers: Tess swathed in acres of tulle and satin, trapped in a circle of train.

I had been old enough then to remember Mother and Loney debating whether Mother should go down for the wedding.

"I'm sure it would mean a lot to Tess," said Loney, "and you certainly have the right clothes."

"Yes, but here I am widowed and working, with a five-year-old child. I'll be damned if I'll set myself up to be pitied by a bunch of Junior Leaguers."

"Well, if you're not going to enjoy it, you oughtn't to go," replied the reasonable Loney, and that was that.

Within a year, infant pictures of the junior scion joined Loney's keepsakes, and the following year came the anguished long-distance call from Miami and Tess's monthlong visit, during which I slept on the sofa while she recuperated in my room from ruining her life.

We knew about the annulment in progress: it was much discussed by my mother and grandmother. "I still don't understand," Loney would say. "How can you annul a marriage when there's already a child?" "Money," my mother would answer, "and you have to be a Roman Catholic."

We also knew that Tess had gone off to live in an apartment, leaving the baby with her estranged husband and his mother. And after Tess came to stay with us, she confided at the table one evening that she had brought down the house by falling in love with her husband's younger brother, a naval officer who had been flown home a wounded hero from the Solomon Islands campaign.

But here in a single-column inside-page story with "May 1, 1944" pencilled above the headline (could that be the younger Moira Parks's fastidious cursive?) was the rest of what had gone unimagined even by us.

PROMINENT WAR HERO
TAKES OWN LIFE

He and Tess had been living together, and it was Tess who found him asphyxiated in the apartment house garage. That she was the former Miss Miami Beach and was estranged from her "scion" husband, brother of the deceased, was in the story, but there was no mention of any child. The family must have used all its clout with some *Star* scion to keep the story so bare and small.

No need to take notes on this one. Hardly longer than the standard obits I had been writing all day, it could be reported from memory to Mother and Loney when I next wrote to them. The deceased hero had been twenty-two and Tess at the time must have been thirty, though her age was not given.

Poor Tess, whom I would be seeing tonight: what a thing to have lived through—and to have it in her newspaper file, where she must expect I would be looking it up. Though maybe her thoughts were elsewhere. She had a boss, who perhaps doubled as a lover, whose praises she sang daily, and she had become fluent in a new language that made her sound like a different version of herself. I replaced the slender file.

More furtively, I moved on to the *N*'s, which were another shelf's distance away from Moira Parks, who was humming a tune under her breath. The *N*'s were at shoulder level, so I wouldn't have to crouch. Even better, they were completely out of sight from the newsroom, in case anybody with an *N* name happened to be passing.

My jealousy animal reared up dangerously on its hind legs when I laid my hands on Norbright's corpus: six stuffed envelopes in as many years. If I was still here in six years, how many would I have? I would be twenty-

eight. Would I have a novel published by then? Would I have won a
Pulitzer for investigative reporting? Oh God, so much to get done.

I checked my watch, a frivolous gold-mesh appurtenance, a graduation
gift from Mother's rich cousin who had wanted to annex us. It was all
wrong for a newspaper reporter: you had to pry open a diamond-studded
cover to see the time. There was a little less than half an hour to go before my date with the stuffed shirt.

I quickly skimmed the first envelope of Lucifer's clippings. The
religious-relic swindler did indeed look like an upright beetle in a Hawaiian shirt. Bisbee certainly had an eye.

Norbright wrote a caustic, cocky prose.

Want to make a easy buck? All you need is a bank of phones, a few
Miami Beach retirees on limited incomes, and a couple of thousand
devout souls in need of a mail-order miracle.

No time today to linger on the early successes. Get to the big one. His
"Queen of the Underworld" series filled an entire envelope. I cursed my
awkward stand-up-and-peek method.

I devoured the series in random gulps, having to unfold and refold
each clipping, casting nervous glances over my shoulder in case someone
came in. Moira's incessant humming spooked me and I was coming to
loathe the foolish wristwatch coyly concealing its one purpose in life beneath the diamond-studded orb.

As I pounced on blocks of type and absorbed image after image of
Palm Island's Ginevra Snow, formerly of Waycross, Georgia—did she
never strike an unbewitching angle?—I felt an increasing attraction to
her. She had the kind of looks I most admired in other women, that
lethal frontage of fine features riding a solid understructure of sex appeal. Her cloud of dark hair, pulled back with a schoolgirlish headband
for the court appearances, still floated like a summer thunderstorm about
to wreak havoc, which she certainly had. Her wide-spaced, slanty eyes
were both hopeful and calculating, and the mouth in the various photos

ranged in expression from affronted innocence to cunning hauteur. I wanted to know her from the inside; I wanted to experience her whole adventure—the motherless childhood with the exploitative grandmother, the abduction by the Mafia nephew, the finishing school for debutantes, the sophisticated mobster uncle, and what it was like to be a madam of nineteen presiding over an elite island whorehouse. In some strange way I felt she offered an alternative version of myself. To follow her story would be to glimpse what I might have done had I been trapped in Waycross in her circumstances.

Perhaps this was why I also felt that Lou Norbright had stolen something rightfully mine, even though I had been a sophomore in high school when this story broke. It was as if he had breached the barriers of chronology and usurped prime material with my name written all over it.

"WHAT STORY does this picture suggest, Emma?"

At first the personnel director had seemed too wet behind the ears to be a stuffed shirt, so I was grateful for Bisbee's warning. By the time we got through the Rorschachs (five black-and-white, five in color), I realized that Harry Harmon did not appreciate whimsy or imagination. Better to have stopped with "butterfly" than to have pushed it with "That's a butterfly looking back at us."

We sat next to each other at a conference table, close enough for me to smell his Listerine mouthwash and ponder his fingernails, shaped like blunt shovels. Not one smile or glimmer of sexual appreciation had I been able to elicit from him. In my category of types, he rapidly rose to the surface as obstacle or adversary, probably both.

"Well," I said, "it's a little boy, about ten, sitting alone in a room with a violin." Sticking to the obvious.

"No, you have to tell me a story."

Mistaking the infinitesimal hint of teasing in his voice as a sign he might appreciate a bit of smart sass, I said, "Well, it can go several ways, can't it? In a minute he'll tuck the violin under his chin and play a nice

first-year tune, or he'll bedazzle us by being a child prodigy, *or*"—I
paused, noting that he was studying me more avidly through his
horn-rims—"he'll put it down and go look out the window and wish he
could go out and play baseball . . . *or*, if he's a bad little boy, he might
smash the violin against the wall."

"What does he do in *your* story?" asked Harry Harmon.

"My story? You mean I have to choose?"

A curt nod.

"Oh, okay. In my story, he's got promise. He's destined to be an artist,
though maybe not on the violin. He is sitting there dreaming of the
greatness that will one day be his."

"How about this one?" said Harmon without comment, turning over
the next picture.

"MISS GANT, some messages for you here."

Alex de Costa, the young manager of the Julia Tuttle, handed over two
pink slips. He looked less preppy today, probably because he was wearing
a guayabera like the Cuban men who seemed to have a game of dominoes
going around the clock. Of course he *was* a Cuban man, I reminded myself, even though he was closer in type to those languid, baby-faced lads
with their feet up on fraternity porch railings back in Chapel Hill. His
book, splayed facedown on the marble counter, was Ortega y Gasset's
Revolt of the Masses.

I stood there, pelvis poked out Bev-style, silently reading my messages
on the pink slips, knowing Alex de Costa was looking me over. Both messages were from Tess, the first, phoned in at 2:15 p.m., said that we would
have to postpone our dinner because she had to make an emergency trip
to the airport for Dr. Rodriguez. The second, phoned in at 4:30, hoped
we could still have it, after all, unless I had made other plans in the meantime.

"Everything all right?" asked Alex de Costa.

"Just my aunt Tess canceling and then uncanceling our dinner
tonight."

"Then that's okay, yes?" He seemed to want me to be pleased that I still had a dinner engagement after all.

"I guess. It's just that I never expected you could get so tired sitting at a desk all day."

"It can be *extremely* tiring sitting at a desk all day." The rolled Spanish *r* reared up like an exotic animal from his American speech.

"I read that last spring," I said, tapping his facedown Ortega with my fingernail. My frosted-rose manicure was set off well by the black cover. "It was the supplemental reading assignment I chose in my Modern European History Seminar."

"Did you like it?"

"My professor gave me a C-plus for liking it too much. It kept me off the dean's list my final semester."

"For liking it too much?"

"The professor—he was really just this Marxist lecturer—told me I was supposed to 'engage with its aristocratic propaganda, not capitulate to it.' I told him I was happy to capitulate to a mind that could put into words a thought I had been groping toward for years."

Actually, I had cried, and when that hadn't worked had begged him to let me write another paper. When the lousy stinker said no, I had stormed out of his windowless basement office. But the person I intended to become would have responded as above.

"What was the thought, do you remember?"

"Of course I remember, it ruined my average."

My combination of attractive surface and interesting mind appeared to be having its effect on Alex de Costa. "Ortega says that a person is a barbarian to the degree that he *can't take others into account*. And so this barbarian, this *mass person*, has a deadly hatred for all that isn't himself. Yet at the same time he's ignorant of how much he doesn't know. That's because he lacks the capacity to go out of himself and imagine life from someone else's point of view. Ortega says the capacity for 'transmigration into another soul' is the highest form of civilized sport."

"Transmigration into another soul," Alex de Costa repeated thoughtfully, as though storing the concept for future use.

"But you're still reading it, so I shouldn't be giving away the plot," I added on a lighter note so he wouldn't think I was just a dull blue-stocking.

"I've read it once before, in Spanish, but I remember very little. I was sixteen and trying to impress my new stepfather when he was consul in Barcelona. Now I'm reading it for clues to what I'm supposed to be doing here."

"You mean on this earth?"

"No, in this ho*tel.*" His voice, rising plaintively, gave the word a Span-ish intonation. "If Ortega, if *anybody at all,* could enlighten me about what is going to happen in Cuba, maybe I wouldn't be quite so in the dark about how to serve my guests."

He glanced up as the female members of the handsome Cuban family clopped through the lobby in beach clogs. The woman and the little girl wore matching dark blue terry-cloth robes over their bathing suits and carried towels over their arms. I still hadn't tried the pool and was won-dering if Paul's black silk dressing gown, which I had brought home last night folded inside my raincoat, would suffice.

"That is Marisa Ocampo and her daughter," Alex said after they went through the swinging doors to the pool. "Last week the Ocampos owned a ten-thousand-acre sugar plantation in Oriente. Now Enrique's not sure what he owns or what his family is going to do next." He shook his head as if he were clearing it, then added savagely, "My mother had a *benefit* for Fidel in Palm Beach when he needed funds to support his revolution. Her Jesuit cousin taught him in school, they were *friends.* Mother raised eight thousand dollars for Fidel. But now he has turned against his friends and the Julia Tuttle is filling up with them and how do I provide the *ambiente,* the environment they need, when nobody has the least idea what he is going to do tomorrow?"

5.

TESS CALLED UP ON the house phone, breathlessly announcing that she had to make that trip to the airport after all. Hector had been expecting some crates of urgent dental equipment that were supposed to have arrived this evening.

"Then we got word they didn't make the flight. Now it turns out the crates arrived in Miami yesterday morning. They've been sitting out there in the terminal collecting dust! If you can put up with my complicated life just a little longer, Emma, we can still have our dinner, it's all prepared, if you don't mind coming to the airport with me first."

"No, I would like to see the airport. Be right down."

AFTER A brief respite of non-rain, the skies had opened again with a fury, and Tess was talking at the same tempo as the windshield wipers. We drove north for a bit and then west for a bit longer. *Avenues in Miami run south to north; streets, terraces, and lanes east to west,* I coached myself from Bisbee's luncheon tutorial, though it was hard to keep track in this rain. Tess again drove Hector's new Cadillac, but she wore off-duty clothes under her yellow slicker: a white scoop-necked blouse with jet beads, silky tan slacks, and thong sandals. She had Bev-perfect feet, though without any nail polish, and their sheer nakedness made me picture them curling as she lay beneath a lover, uttering, as I was sure Tess would, flattering encouragements.

"That horrible man, do you know what he did *today*? But of course you do, you're right there on the newspaper."

At first I thought she meant someone at the *Star.*

"He had the gall to warn *us* not to interfere in his land grab. He steals lands from thousands of farmers and tobacco growers, not to mention *American* landowners, and then has the nerve to call it his 'agrarian reform'! He says we're Goliath and they're David and that we all know the outcome of *that* story. Then he turns around and warns if our 'imperialist agents' so much as set foot on their soil there will be six million Cubans willing to die rather than retreat. Hector says not only is he crazy and power-mad but his warnings aren't even *logical*. Either David slays the giant or the giant slays the six million Davids, Hector says, but he can't have it both ways."

I decided Hector must be her lover. But if the dental equipment was so damned urgent, why couldn't he go pick it up himself and let Tess have her night off?

"You probably know all this from your correspondents," Tess went on. "This is old news to you, but Hector only heard it over the shortwave this afternoon."

"Well, not all of it."

Tess must think "being on the paper," even on one's first day, meant being in on all of tomorrow's big stories. I'd be crouched over my obits of forgettable people on their forgettable streets, terraces, and lanes, and Lou Norbright would suddenly materialize beside my desk with a wire service dispatch in his hand: "Emma, I think you should know that Castro has warned us to keep our imperialist noses out of his revolution."

I would have to wait for a later time to see the airport proper, as Tess's appointment was at a freight terminal. She pulled in beside an oldish-model sedan with its engine running and its lights on, and immediately two men got out and came over. Tess lowered her window and spoke to them in Spanish and they huddled there in the rain in their short-sleeved shirts, getting wet to the bone but seeming not to care. Again it struck me how a person could take on a completely different personality when speaking another language. Her voice was still recognizably that of warm, lovely Tess, but it had an impressive snap of female authority to it. *"Sí, señora Tess,"* they said, nodding rapidly. *"Es lo mismo, señora. De nada, de nada, señora Tess."*

They disappeared into the downpour and returned with an official.

"Here, Officer, let me turn on the light in here so you can see," Tess sang out, handing him some papers. "You know, this is a real shame," she murmured after he had stuck his head through the window and taken in her beauty. "Here Doctor's been waiting desperately for these new drills, and they've been out here gathering dust since yesterday!" His face lingered, close enough to kiss her, as he made a display of checking the papers under the interior light Tess had provided. He then apologized for the inconvenience and suggested she back into the terminal so her assistants could load the dental equipment out of the rain. Tess thanked him profusely and backed us out of the downpour.

"They're such sweet boys," said Tess, watching the men load through the rearview mirror of the Cadillac. "Julio and Genio are Asunción's nephews, they're twins. They'd do anything for Hector."

The Cadillac began to sink as Julio and Genio loaded the crates.

"Heavy stuff," I said.

"Oh, the *drills* are light as feathers," Tess said gaily. "It's the equipment that has to be fixed into the floor to hold them in place that's so heavy. Our patients are going to have so much less pain when Hector gets this new equipment set up."

"What kind of drills are they?"

"Oh, I couldn't tell you the exact *name*, but they're the very latest, Emma. Right from the manufacturer's. Remember those old sledgehammers the dentist used to pump with his foot? No, you're too young for that. But these are like a soft flow of warm, wet air on the tooth. No horrible noises and vibrations. Just a high-pitched little whisper and no pain." This last was almost crooned.

"Boy, Tess, I'm coming straight to you if I have a toothache,"

"Hector would be honored to have you as a patient, Emma."

"No, I meant *you*, *señora* Tess. You'd talk anyone out of their dentist phobias."

"Well"—she laughed—"it's my job, after all."

AT FIRST I had thought we'd be going out to a restaurant, because when would Tess have had time to make dinner for me? But then she'd informed me she had. First we dropped off the Cadillac in the open garage of a modest house, transferred into Tess's seven-year-old Oldsmobile, and were heading down the street again when an approaching car flicked its lights and Tess flicked back.

"Perfect timing!" she cried. "They'll take the equipment on to Hector's office."

"Why couldn't they have taken care of the whole thing?"

"Well, Emma, they could have managed it perfectly well. But at the moment officials in Miami are being very suspicious of Cubans loading and unloading things. I provided the necessary respectability. And now off we go to have our long-delayed dinner. You must be starved."

"Was that Hector's house?"

"Goodness, no. Hector and Asunción have a beautiful home on Alhambra, near the golf course. That was just the little bungalow the boys are renting till they get on their feet. They've only just come over from Cuba."

I had assumed we were now headed for Tess's Majorca Avenue apartment in Coral Gables, to which Mother had been addressing her letters for the past fifteen years, but instead we ended up at a marina on Biscayne Bay. We boarded the ramp of a houseboat. Tess flicked a switch and the deck lit up with a jungle of overgrown plants in big pots and enough nude male statues to be holding a party of their own. As we stepped into the very opposite of what one would expect of a seagoing interior, Tess explained she was house-sitting for an old friend, who directed summer theater in Connecticut, and that this arrangement allowed her to sublet her Coral Gables apartment for the summer.

"It gives me a bit of extra income for all my extravagances. That red door's the bathroom, Emma—or 'the head,' as we nautical types are supposed to call it. Please don't be alarmed by all his mirrors. I usually keep my eyes closed when I'm on the john, but some of the other mirrors can be useful if you need a particular close-up of yourself."

Egads, the mirrors. Virtually every inch of wall was covered with them. Square ones, round ones, heart-shaped, Art Deco, Tiffany, Woolworth's, framed in seashells, the masks of Comedy and Tragedy, you name it. Yet nowhere could you have an extensive view of yourself. While seated, I did not take Tess's advice and partook of snippets of my anatomy, none of which, because of the limited views allowed, was either alarming or flattering. Only when I stood up and turned around to flush did the placement of mirrors over the toilet tank seem more encompassing and take on a pattern. Knock, knock, stupid, I thought. This exhibit was hung for men.

The other exhibit in here was Tess's cosmetics table. Laid out on a cloth of plastic lace was the largest personal collection of expensive potions and lotions I had ever seen. The majority of these bore the Alexandra de Markoff Countess Isserlyn label, and queening it above the assemblage was a twelve-ounce bottle of Joy. These products alone could swallow the entirety of Tess's summer-rental profits.

"See what I mean?" said Tess, handing me a frozen daiquiri when I emerged and disappearing behind the red door herself.

I sipped—"Mmm, peach!"—and took in more of the decor. Could Tess be comfortable surrounded by all these busy fabrics and props? A marble bust of a Roman soldier wore a lavender feather boa draped coyly around his epaulets, and the walls were practically papered with theater posters, including one I lusted for: Sarah Bernhardt dressed as Hamlet. But of course camping out among all these props provided Tess with the extra income for the necessities she called her extravagances.

The waters of the bay sloshed softly against Tess's friend's floating salon. I felt like an actress myself, balanced on the gently rocking stage of my life's adventure. What would the script have in store for me tonight?

Tess returned, glowing ever handsomer, daubed freshly with "the costliest perfume in the world," and took our dinner out of the refrigerator, all on one orange Fiestaware platter. It was an appealing assortment of familiar things I had never seen together: chicken thighs in a spicy sauce, a mound of yellow rice with chunks of pineapple and black olives in it, a creamy relish of avocado and tomato and onion to go over the rice, some nice chewy bread, and, of all things, the frozen green Jell-O salad I had loved as a child.

We ate sitting on bar stools, facing each other across the Formica counter.

"I hope you don't mind," said Tess. "I did consider clearing the dining table over there, but . . ." She waved her hands helplessly at the crowded table hosting the Roman soldier with his boa, a vase of peacock feathers, some Chinese porcelain, a jade Buddha, and about thirty framed snapshots.

"I'm glad you didn't. I love sitting up here on the stools, it's airier. Tess, did you know this is the very same seabreeze salad my grandmother used to make?"

"Of course I did. She made it when I was staying with you all in Mountain City, after everything went to pieces for me in Miami."

I hadn't anticipated her swinging into the subject so easily or so soon, but I had already resolved to say nothing about looking her up in the *Star* file. Let her tell her story her way.

"You were all so good to me. You and Nancy took me for walks to that little park across from your church and you asked if you could hold my hand. I felt so honored."

"You wore a white halter dress that floated as you walked," I said. "You were like some visiting goddess—"

"Oh, no, dearest, I was a mortal in a state of shock. But, Emma, your glass is empty."

To my dismay, she chose this moment to slide off her stool and fetch the daiquiri pitcher from the refrigerator. To hide my eagerness for what she might reveal next, I praised the seabreeze salad again as she was refilling our glasses and derailed the whole thing.

"Yes, I was in the kitchen with your grandmother and she was telling me how you toddled over to her in the garden when you'd barely learned to talk, and said to her, 'You look *loney* all by yourself out here,' and how the name Loney just stuck. And then she got an ice tray of this creamy lime-green stuff out of the freezer and cut little squares of it and laid them out on lettuce, and put a maraschino cherry on each one and a dab of mayonnaise on the side. 'That looks so *festive*,' I said, and your grandmother gave me the kindest smile and said, 'Well, why shouldn't we be festive? *You're* here.' I've never forgotten it. After I went back to Miami, whenever I needed a lift, I would make myself a batch of Loney's seabreeze salad and say to myself, 'Well, why shouldn't we be festive? *You're* here.' "

"That's wonderful," I said. "We need these little reminders."

"I'm so relieved we got Hector's equipment safely home," she said. "I feel almost like a heroine, if that doesn't sound too silly. Everything dovetailing so perfectly, Julio and Genio exactly where they were supposed to be, dead on time, even in all that rain."

"Right out of a spy novel," I agreed. "Only the contraband was painless drills."

"Only painless drills!" She burst out laughing as if I had said something hilarious. It occurred to me she was already tipsy and so was I. But how had it happened so soon?

"Honestly, my *life*. You know, Emma, I'm convinced it all began when I was in the hurricane of 'twenty-six, though please keep that date to yourself. I don't want everyone knowing I was in a hurricane back when they weren't even naming hurricanes yet. I was blown three blocks down Collins Avenue and landed on my feet."

I had heard this story before, both from Tess when she was staying with us, and from my mother later telling friends, "I have this friend who was blown away in a Miami hurricane when she was twelve." Pause for effect. "But she landed on her feet."

Tess's mother had sent her to the hardware store for a rake. They thought the hurricane had passed, but instead they were in the calm eye of it. Tess was suddenly lifted off the sidewalk and *flown* to the hardware store. The hardware store hadn't fared so well, everything was smashed, but the owner told Tess if she could find a rake in the debris it was on the house. Tess found one and made it back home and they raked the dead crabs and seaweed out of the living room for the rest of the week.

"There I was, flying through the air along with coconuts and roof shingles and blowing sand. I looked down and saw this grand piano and some oriental rugs floating down the street on top of the water. Then my feet were on the ground again and I had my arms around this big old royal palm and I held on for dear life till the turbulence was past. Just think of it, Emma. One hundred and thirteen people were drowned or crushed in that hurricane, but *I* landed on my feet. Have you ever heard the sound a hurricane makes?"

"Only in *The Wizard of Oz*."

"Oh, that was just special effects, Judy Garland never even left the ground. The real thing sounds like a freight train heading right at you. You'll hear it in September when hurricane season starts. Ready for some more? We've done this much damage, we might as well finish the pitcher. But here you've let me go on and on about my ancient adventures, when I'm dying to hear about your first day at the *Star*."

"Well, you know, they start everybody off at the bottom." I figured I might as well be truthful and get the obits out of the way. "And then one of the reporters, Dave Bisbee, took me to lunch at Walgreens."

"I've seen his byline. Is he attractive?"

"Not especially, but he told me lots of helpful things."

Tess giggled appreciatively, woman to woman. "Such as?"

"Mostly filling me in on other people. For instance, he warned me not to be too interesting when I went up to have my interview with the personnel director, who's a stuffed shirt."

"But why do you need to be interviewed by the personnel director? You're already hired."

"To have something to measure against my performance later, was the way the stuffed shirt put it. It's a new policy at the *Star*. Bisbee said Lou Norbright probably implemented it."

"That horrible man who destroyed my friend Edith Vine! I thought he was gone. I was hoping something awful had happened to him. You never see his byline anymore."

Edith Vine, Edith Vine, now where had I recently heard or read that name? Damn these sugary alcoholic drinks, the mixture went twice as fast to your brain.

"No, he's assistant managing editor now. He's the one who showed me around today. He's pretty scary, in a fascinating way. Bisbee said the others call him Lucifer. Who is Edith Vine?"

"Poor Edith no longer *is*. She died of heartbreak, though the official diagnosis was heart attack. Her life's work was completely destroyed after the Ginevra Snow scandal. Edith was subpoenaed, she never got over having to testify in a courtroom. People made jokes about her wonderful school, where the daughters of the most prominent Miami families had gone for forty years. The Biscayne Academy of Prostitution, they called it during the trial. Ginevra Snow was this—"

"She was the Queen of the Underworld."

"Honestly, Emma, no grass grows under *your feet*! You already know about that?"

"I skimmed the clips this afternoon. Bisbee told me that's how Norbright got his big break and I was curious. Now I remember. The Mafia uncle sent Ginevra to Edith Vine's charm school."

"Edith would *never* have referred to the Biscayne Academy as a 'charm school,' that was Mr. Norbright's vulgar description. It was more like a finishing school, though Edith always preferred just plain 'academy,' because, as she rightly said, it was a place of training in the special arts of life. Edith herself was classically trained. I took some courses there when I was in the running for Miss Miami Beach, back in, well, never mind what year. You know, Emma, I'm going to suggest you spend the night on board, I'm a bit light-headed, and you're too precious to risk my driving you back through all this rain. I'll lend you one of my nightgowns and I have a shopping bag full of giveaway toothbrushes, compliments of Hector. What time do you have to be at the *Star*?"

"Nine-thirty. But I'd need to go back to the hotel and change first."

"Of course you would. And I have to be at the office by seven-thirty, because Hector and I have to unload our new equipment before the patients come, so I'd have you back at the Julia Tuttle by seven, how's that?"

"Sounds perfect. But you were saying about the special arts she taught you at the academy." Keeping on the scent of the story Norbright had stolen from me six years ago.

"On the first day of every new term, Miss Edith would take the new girls out to the school's enclosed garden. We sat in a circle under her big ficus trees and she told us that Akademeia was the name of Plato's garden in Athens where he taught his students what they needed to know to get on in the world beautifully, and then she'd say, 'and here we are in the middle of Miami in *our* little Akademeia and we're going to learn how to get on in *our* world beautifully.' I helped Miss Edith for a few years after Mother's death. I wanted to have some life on my own before I met someone and got married, and I enjoyed teaching the girls, and learning more myself. There's always more to learn."

"What did you teach them?"

"Well, the very first thing was how to enter a room, and of course the debutantes had to learn how to deep-curtsy and we always had a few clodhoppers every term. And little stickler-things, like you always sit down and get up from a banquet table on the right side."

"I didn't know that." I filed this away for future banquets.

"Most people don't, but it prevents traffic jams."

"And how do you enter a room?"

"Always with an invisible moat of reserve around your person. You keep it in place even when you're being warm and charming. And, let's see, we taught them how to project their voices from their diaphragms and *not* from inside their noses. The ironic thing was—poor Edith confided this to me after the academy closed down—Ginevra was one of the best pupils she'd ever had. 'That little white trash girl had a natural grace and beauty many of my flat-footed debutantes would have sold their souls for,' that's what Edith told me. Ginevra was smart as a whip, she said, and eager to learn everything she could to better herself. Miss Edith gave her private elocution lessons in the evening. Ginevra was boarding there; the Mafia uncle said she was too young to be out on her own in wicked Miami, and Miss Edith accepted his explanation about the nephew and Ginevra being too young to marry yet. Of course, she never dreamed the uncle was a mob person. Ginevra's speech when she came to Biscayne Academy was pure undiluted Georgia cracker, but when Miss Edith got through with her she could read Keats's "La Belle Dame sans Merci" aloud and have everyone in the room under her spell. And all that, Miss Edith said, just to prepare someone for running a whorehouse. As I said, it broke her heart. What do you say to another *half* pitcher of daiquiri, Emma?"

"I wouldn't say no."

Tess had run out of peaches, so it was just daiquiri mix and rum. I felt crammed to the gills with new information about how to get on in this world—from banquet tables to invisible moats. But I was annoyed with Edith Vine for giving up and dying. She should have been proud that she could turn a white trash girl into a queen, even if it was a "queen of the underworld." She could have built on her success with Ginevra to carry on the school with or without the debutantes. What a story I might have done on her!

FORMER DEBUTANTE DOYENNE
RECALLS NOTORIETY

SHARES CHARM SECRETS

Maybe even a series. Who ever got enough of such secrets? As Bisbee said, you had to remind readers now who Ginevra Snow was, but getting ahead beautifully never goes out of style.

WHEN EVENTUALLY we stumbled off to bed, giggling and clinging to each other for balance, it was as if Tess was more my friend than Mother's.

While Tess sat in front of a dressing table and creamed her face and slid metal clips into her marcelled waves, I lay on my side watching two of her performing these motions. The houseboat creaked and swayed as badly as if we were at sea. If I did have to throw up, I would have to crawl all the way to the head.

"Uh-oh, my roots are beginning to show," said Tess to her mirror. "Honestly, my hair seems to grow faster the older *I* grow. I guess I shouldn't complain. Hector's wife, Asunción, says hers is thinning, even though she's—never mind how many years younger than I."

Tess's orange-smelling night cream, mingled with Joy, made it harder for me to concentrate on not being sick. If I closed my eyes, the room spun, or whatever you called this part of the houseboat. As soon as the light was out I would resort to my emergency remedy of putting one foot on the floor to allay my dizziness.

"Well, I'll call Michel on Miracle Mile and ask if he can fit me in this week," Tess prattled on. "He's always so booked, but that's because he's the best in town. *She* goes to him, too, though her name is Brown now. I sometimes see her when I'm having my two-color process. She has a wash and a trim every few weeks. Everyone knows who she is but we respect her privacy. I went through that myself after my marriage blew up and my sad story was in the *Star.* I was so grateful when people smiled or nodded and said hello and treated me like just any woman getting her hair done. Miami is still a provincial town, everybody knows everybody's business. She married her psychiatrist after the trial. He's English or Scottish or something and the rumor is he's kind of a stick-in-the-mud. She's tried to kill herself twice, they can't keep that out of the papers, but everyone at Michel's respects her privacy completely."

Tess finished up her bedtime ritual by slapping her creamed cheeks vigorously and then tying on some kind of bonnet with a chin strap.

"There! That will have to do until I can save up for my face-lift. No, I don't hold *her* responsible, she was practically kidnapped to start with, then set up and betrayed, it could happen to any girl. At least she escaped that Georgia hellhole and learned some graces. It's that vile Norbright and his vulgar, self-promoting 'Queen of the Underworld' series I blame for killing poor Edith."

6.

IMMACULATE IN HER WHITE uniform, with every platinum-blond wave in place, Tess delivered me—with a steaming container of black coffee and a whopping headache—to the Julia Tuttle by seven on Tuesday morning. I wanted to ask her to walk me in, so that if Alex de Costa was behind the desk, he wouldn't assume I had stayed out all night with a man, but I knew she was dying to get to the office and help "Doctor" unload the new dental equipment.

"Thanks a bunch, Tess. It was the first time I ever slept aboard a boat." Every word made my temples throb.

"Not exactly a seagoing boat, but we had fun, didn't we? Only, please, Emma, don't tell your mother I got you sozzled."

"I wouldn't dream of it."

Neither Alex nor gloomy Luís was behind the desk, but a handsome man in a guayabera I knew I had seen before but couldn't place. As I came through the revolving door, he snapped to attention, looking almost painfully eager to be of service. I already had my room key out of my purse and smilingly waved it at him, though it cost my head another twinge. He nodded and sat down on his stool again.

In Room 510 I swallowed two aspirins, set the alarm clock for eight fifteen, and crawled naked into my bed. What would Dean Ligon think if I called in sick my second day of work? What would Lou Norbright think? I slipped into a doze and woke out of it five minutes before the alarm was due to go off.

Somehow I managed to bathe and dress. As I was pinning my hair into its French twist in front of the bathroom mirror, the memory of Tess sticking clips into her marcelled waves last night resuscitated her stories about Edith Vine and the Biscayne Academy, which might otherwise have been lost in the murk of my hangover. Following that, as a piece of forgotten dream will often dredge more of it up into consciousness, came Tess's offhand revelation that she and Ginevra Snow went to the same hairdresser.

ROD REYNOLDS was not at his desk, but there was a torn-off piece of yellow copy paper stuck in my typewriter, to "eg" from "rr," all in abbreviations and lowercase, telling me to call a man in North Miami who was boiling mad about his water bill and see if there was a "huint sty" in it. What on earth was a "huint sty"? After that, my instructions were to "do fun home roundup."

I cracked the "fun home" code first—funeral home—and, after a little more work, realized I was being asked to write a human-interest story.

None of the brass were anywhere to be seen. I would have ambled over to say good morning to Dave Bisbee, but he was hunched over his desk, both hands plunged into his disheveled hair, reading today's *Star* as though it contained the secret to his salvation. Damn it to hell. If I hadn't been de-sozzling myself back at the Julia Tuttle, I could have had a leisurely breakfast at Howard Johnson's with "Florida's Most Complete Newspaper" and been ahead of the game. But alas, Tess, unlike my perfect Paul, did not possess the fine art of controlling the alcohol drip for one's guests.

There was an untouched copy of Tuesday's *Star* on Rod's desk, and I slid it over onto mine and scanned the headlines. H-BOMB BLAST BLINDS ANIMALS 300 MILES OFF was the banner, even though, it turned out, the news was a year old: two multimegaton hydrogen bombs had been fired in the Pacific *last* summer, you learned further down in the story, but yesterday was the first official report by the Atomic Energy Commission.

Dean Ligon would have disapproved of the misleading headline. He also would have raised an eyebrow at the modifier in the cutline under the wirephoto of Earl Long: "Yelling governor is returned to hospital."

The local front-page story, by Joelle Cutter-Crane, with a three-column picture of a weeping mother, was another child's drowning at camp; this time the child was a seven-year-old girl. The cutlines read, "A man's tragic task . . . a mother's unbelieving tears: Mrs. Roberta Grainger sobs as camp director John Travis relays news of daughter's death." "*Star* Staff Photo by Don Kingsley" was the credit line. Dean Ligon would have a holiday of distaste over today's front page. I underwent a surge of revolt myself as I imagined Joelle Cutter-Crane and her pocketbook with the cherries riding alongside the photographer to the Grainger home.

Did the camp director wait for them out on the street so they could all be there *as a team* when the unsuspecting mother opened the door? Was this the actual first photo when the camp director broke the news, or had staff photographer Don Kingsley, popping flashbulbs, said, "Mrs. Grainger, would you please hold it just like that for a few more?"

I felt an overwhelming nostalgia for Dean Ligon's Tuesday afternoons (and today *was* a Tuesday) at home, when his handpicked seniors sat in the book-lined study overlooking the sun-dappled woods, drinking lemonade and nibbling Mrs. Ligon's tea sandwiches, discussing the ethics and responsibilities of the Fourth Estate.

"I think we've pretty much covered today's problem headlines in the *Miami Star*," Dean Ligon would be saying, "but just to keep our ethical sensors on full alert, let's examine the treatment of this grieving mother. The photo *in itself* is acceptable. Human beings have always been drawn to visual representations of grieving mothers, look at Michelangelo's *Pietà*. But would you ever see such melodramatic cutlines in the Louisville *Courier-Journal*? Or the *St. Louis Post-Dispatch*? Or the *New York Times*?"

Of course, Joelle might not be responsible for the cutlines. Though if "the ribbon on our package," as Norbright called her, could dictate the boxes for her stories, she might dictate cutlines for their photos, too. ("I want you to know, Lou, that those cutlines were *my* idea.")

The story that Tess thought was going to be such big news, "Don't Interfere, Cuba Warns U.S.," had been relegated to seven short paragraphs squeezed between sobbing Mrs. Grainger and yelling Governor Long, and ending right above "Today's Chuckle." ("My wife is threatening to leave me." "That's tough. Can't you get her to promise?")

Probably the whole Castro thing was a tempest in a teapot and would be over soon, but people who worked for Cuban exiles or ran hotels catering to them, people like Tess and like Alex de Costa, were bound to take it more to heart.

Now I recalled where I had seen the man behind the desk this morning. He was the father of the Cuban family who'd arrived on Sunday, the man wearing the white suit and ticking off the matching luggage with his silver pencil. The new desk clerk at the Julia Tuttle was the owner of the ten-thousand-acre sugar plantation usurped by Castro.

Before I phoned the North Miami man who was boiling mad over his water bill, I took a respite in the ladies' room to examine last night's damage in the mirror. The overhead fluorescent lights did their worst: I looked green around the gills. I soaked a paper towel with cold water, then locked myself in a stall, sat with my feet up out of sight against the door, and buried my face in the towel. My Emma-ness was at low ebb, and the day had scarcely begun.

Someone else came in and bolted herself into the cubicle next to mine. Platform-soled sandals, thick mud-brown stockings, ladylike tinkle, immediate flush and exit. I held my breath until she would leave the room, since I had compromised myself by hiding out in my stall. But after prolonged hand-washing sounds, I heard, to my dismay, the unzipping of a bag and small items being laid out methodically on the mirror shelf. Whoever it was then embarked on a thorough freshening-up session, complete with the swish and crackle of brushing hair (the person seemed to have a lot of it), the *pock* of a lipstick cylinder being unsheathed and resheathed, followed by brisk, rhythmic rubbing noises and the release of a familiar scent. The person then cleared her throat and burst into a lusty "Habanera," from *Carmen*, in a professional-sounding contralto. It would have been a thrilling moment had I not been afraid I might cough, which of course I proceeded to do. The singer was silenced, and judging from the speed with which she swept everything into her bag and fled, she was as eager as I was to remain anonymous.

It was Moira Parks, I would soon learn. She took regular trips to the ladies' room to wash the newsprint off her hands and massage them with Jergens lotion.

I returned to my desk determined to wrest a notable story from the water-bill protester.

An angry hello answered the first ring.

"May I speak to Mr. Charles P. Rose?"

"Speaking. Who is this?"

"My name is Emma Gant, from the *Miami Star.*"

"What are you, someone's secretary there?"

"No, sir, I'm a staff reporter." The "sir," drilled into Southern children, slipped out on its own and disqualified me further.

"*What* did you say your name was?"

"Emma Gant."

"Now look here, I read the *Star* every day and I never heard of you."

"I just started yesterday. Mr. Rose, could you tell me more about this trouble you're having with your water bill?"

"Now look here, Miss Grant—"

"Gant."

"Okay, *Gant.* I have nothing against you personally, Miss *Gant,* but I haven't been waiting by the phone all morning to be shunted off to some female cub reporter I'll have to explain everything to six times. This is not just 'some trouble' over my water bill. We're talking about manipulation of the populace by a public utility."

"That's a serious charge, Mr. Rose."

"Damn right it is. We were promised a *reduction* in our water rates in North Miami and what we got was an *increase.* It was all a clever wording trick to confuse us."

"And what did the wording trick—?"

"Now look here, Miss Grant—*Gant.* Didn't I just finish telling you I want to talk to someone who can follow me without my having to explain everything six times?"

I felt like hanging up on him. But someone was hovering within earshot behind me, probably Dave Bisbee, though it was too early for lunch, and I had to go on with the audible side of the dialogue and make myself sound confident and professional.

"Mr. Rose, I think it's an excellent idea of yours to go over it six times. That way I can write it down so even the simplest reader can grasp it. You'll be performing that much more of a public service. I've got my pencil and pad ready. Take all the time you need. Pretend I'm just your simplest basic listener who knows nothing at all about water rates."

There was a kind of sputtering at the other end of the line, like a firecracker being doused in water. After a loud sigh, Mr. Charles P. Rose began speaking slowly, exaggeratedly, as if to a dimwit, about the treachery perpetrated on him by the North Miami Beach Water Board. I kept making him qualify and simplify, reading back his answers until I and every cretin subscriber understood base rates backwards and forwards. Once he yelled at me, "Nobody could be *that* stupid!" After we hung up, I called the Water Board and got through to the general manager, who gave me a nice quote—a perfect little dollop of revenge on Mr. Charles P. Rose.

As I was typing up my final draft, Lou Norbright drifted by my desk. "How's it going, Emma?"

"Pretty well, I think."

"That's the impression I get, too," he said, gleaming above me in his white shirt. He regarded me with a certain amusement. Or was there something conspiratorial about it, too? One go-getter recognizing another.

"Keep up the good work," he said cheerfully, and continued on his stealthy glide. It had been the Prince of Ambition himself who'd been lurking behind me as I wrested my first news story out of Charles P. Rose.

My little victory was overshadowed soon after, when the double doors to the boardroom next to Mr. Feeney's office were flung open and out surged all the editors, forming a fawning human horseshoe around Joelle Cutter-Crane and a smallish blond man in his forties with a dark tan. From their complacent expressions and the sudden excitement released into the newsroom you could tell the two were being celebrated for something. My first thought was that they had just gotten married, until an impudent murmur—this time it *was* Dave Bisbee hovering behind—informed me that Joelle and her "favorite visual-aid accompanist," Don Kingsley, were being sent to Cuba to "cover the human-interest aspects of the Revolution."

Joelle was outfitted in smart new safari-type togs and carried a brown leather shoulder-strap purse with lots of buckles and compartments and no cherries. Her visual-aid accompanist walked several paces behind her, like Prince Philip trailing the Queen. He even bore a certain resemblance to Philip, if the Duke of Edinburgh had been shorter and had had all of the expression suntanned out of his features.

Although it was only my second day on the *Star*, my envy of Joelle's assignment actually caused bile to rise in my throat—the hangover no doubt contributing—and once more I sought refuge in the ladies', feet up behind the locked cubicle door, face buried in hands, until someone else came in and I flushed and prepared to return to the bottom rung of the Fourth Estate.

The editor of the Women's Section was brushing her close-cropped silver hair in front of the mirror. She addressed me by name and said she hoped I would join her and a few of the other women for lunch at the Dallas Park one day this week. I politely said I'd love to, and went out thinking, *That's all I need, to get "shunted off,"* as Mr. Charles P. Rose would put it, with the women inside the glass cubicle.

Dave Bisbee invited me to his "club" again, but I declined. I didn't want to be sitting in the basement of Walgreens with an also-ran while Joelle Cutter-Crane and Don Kingsley were flying off to Havana, probably first-class, drinking champagne and planning their assaults on the human-interest aspects of the Cuban Revolution.

("Now, Don, I want you to get a really good close-up shot of a rich landowner just as he's being ousted by the guerrillas, and then I want to pair it with—"

"A really good close-up shot of the happy peasant who inherits the confiscated land."

"You read my mind, Don, but do let's strike the word 'confiscated' from your vocabulary. We're guests of the new government, remember?"

"Your wish is my command, Joelle, but it wasn't me who used the word 'guerrillas.' "

"Touché, but remember, I'm calling the shots. Stewardess, excuse me—Miss? We're ready for another round of champagne over here.")

I rolled a piece of copy paper into my typewriter, cradled the receiver on its rubber cushion between my right shoulder and ear, and dialed the first "fun home" number on my alphabetized mortuary list.

Eventually I took a break and explored the desk drawers I had inherited from the fired Kirk, who drank and tried to bring in the union. The top drawer had copy paper, paper clips, and a half roll of Tums, plus some dirt and crumbs. I threw out the Tums and wiped out the drawer with a Kleenex. In the lower drawer were a pair of men's rubbers, the kind you slip on over your shoes. As I was tossing these in the wastebasket, out fell one unused Trojan in its tinfoil wrapper. Well, I wanted to compete in a man's world, didn't I? I considered dropping in on Bisbee at his desk and making a joke about the pun, but then decided I preferred the moat of my reserve.

TWO MEN, conversing in Spanish, rode up with me in the Julia Tuttle's slow, hiccuppy elevator at the end of the workday.

"*Tengo mi permiso de trabajo,*" said one with a sigh. He must have gotten his work permit.

"*¡Felicitaciones!*" congratulated the other, clapping him on the back.

"*Pero estoy calificado para nada,*" replied the first with a tired laugh. But I'm qualified for nothing. Adding gloomily, "*Mañana, busco un hotel más barato.*" Tomorrow he was going to look for a cheaper hotel. Good going, Emma.

"*¿Quieres que vayamos a tomar algo?*" Would you like to go out and have something?

"*Lo siento, pero estoy muy cansado.*" The man with the new work permit was too tired. I was "*muy cansada*" myself.

"*Bueno, en otro momento,*" replied the other. He had done all he could, and he didn't sound too disappointed.

The gloomy one got off on four. *"Me cago en Fidel,"* he suddenly spat back as he left the elevator.

"Ssst!" the other scolded, shaking his head. As the doors closed us in together, he apologized for his companion's obscenity. *"Perdón, señorita."*

"Oh, *está bien,*" I replied airily, with a dismissive wave of my frosty nails. This obscenity—as well as his standard *"¡Mierda!"*—was quite familiar to me through Pepe Iglesias, my Cuban dance partner from St. Clovis Hall, the male branch of St. Clothilde's. *Me cago en* this and *me cago en* that: Pepe was always "shitting" on someone or other.

The man broke into a gratified smile; he probably assumed that I was fluent. Luckily, my floor was next, so I didn't have to lose face. Like most language students, I could read and write more than I could hear, and I could speak far less than I could overhear. Bisbee had a point, I should find a tutor, which shouldn't be too hard with a hotel full of Cubans.

The galling thing was, I probably had known more Cubans personally than Joelle Cutter-Crane did. At St. Clothilde's, there had been two or three Cuban girls in every grade. Many Cuban businessmen and diplomats posted in Washington and New York sent their daughters there because of its archaic rules and because the nuns absolutely forbade the foreign boarders to converse in their native tongues. In seventh grade, Raquel Cortez had asked me to go home with her for Christmas, which my mother thought would be educational, but I found Raquel off-putting with her melon-size breasts and her painful English, which she sputtered too close to your face, and Loney was able to intervene and convince Mother that I might come down with some awful disease from drinking Cuban water. Now I was sorry I hadn't gone; if this revolution did drag on for a few more months it would have come in handy at the newspaper. ("Yes, I know Havana well, my friend Raquel Cortez lived in the Vedado, I used to go home with her for Christmas.")

After writing a single sentence to sum up my second day at work— "I'm sick of being a goddamned nobody!"—I closed my "Go, Tar Heels!" notebook and sank back on the pillows in Room 510. It was dinnertime and I had skipped lunch. But I was too demoralized to shove my aching feet back into my high heels and clop over to Howard Johnson's or White Castle. What I wanted was someone to bring me a perfectly cooked cheeseburger (slightly pink and juicy in the middle) on a toasted bun with mayo, lettuce, tomato, and a slice of raw onion, with potato chips on the side and a Coke with crushed ice and a wedge of lemon. But the Julia Tuttle didn't have room service; it didn't even have a coffee shop.

I'm sick of . . .

Estoy harta de . . .

being . . .

ser . . .

There was no Spanish word for "goddamned"; I'd have to settle for *una maldita nadie. Estoy harta de ser una maldita nadie.* I'm sick of being a damned nobody.

But wait. *"Ser"* indicated a permanent state of being. I certainly didn't intend being a goddamned nobody permanently.

Estoy harta de estar *una maldita nadie.*

By seven tomorrow morning I could be eating scrambled eggs and bacon at Howard Johnson's. I'd buy Wednesday's *Miami Star,* and there would be, not even an above-the-fold headline, but "shunted off" to one side:

CASTRO'S REVOLUTION FIZZLES

Just an AP wire story, no picture; Joelle and her pet photographer Don Kingsley already would have been recalled to Miami.

At work people would congratulate me on my story about Charles P. Rose. "Nice twist in that last paragraph, Emma" (Lucifer, above my right shoulder); "You're off and running, girl" (Dave Bisbee, at lunch, unless somebody better asked me); "you may think it was just an ordinary story, but his counterpart is found throughout human history, it's the stuff of great literature, the little man trying to hold his own against the giant powers, from David and Goliath and Job right up to Kafka."

7.

ROOM 510 WAS IN PITCH darkness. I had fallen asleep with my clothes on.

What were those snuffling animal noises in the hall? The noises came closer until they were right outside my door. Some small dog trying to find its owner's room? Did the Julia Tuttle allow pets? These Cubans were fleeing with their families, and pets are family. I was sure Alex de Costa would think so, with his desire to provide the right *ambiente* for his guests.

I turned on the lamp. Ten forty-five. My clothes were a wrinkled mess. I decided to investigate, previewing a scene in which I would find a cute little Cuban dog, maybe bring him into my room for a few minutes while I called down to whoever was on the desk and became the agent of re-uniting the little fellow with its exiled owners and having a chance to practice my Spanish.

I undid the safety latch and opened the door, and there, squatting in front of the door opposite mine, was Alex de Costa, a brush in one hand and a woman's high-heeled shoe in the other.

"Oh, Miss Gant," he said, struggling awkwardly to his feet, exposing an ample rear end in the process. He wore a striped bib apron over his shirt and tie.

"I heard these sounds," I said.

"I hope I didn't disturb you."

"I'm glad you did. I fell asleep with my clothes on."

"Luís is indisposed, so I'm doing the shoe detail tonight."

"You mean you're polishing people's *shoes?*"

"It's not an American custom, but yes, our guests expect it. Anytime you want a shine, just leave your shoes outside your door." He looked down at my stockinged feet. "It's not too late for tonight."

"I think I'll pass for tonight," I said, appalled by the notion of handing over my aging high-heeled pumps, stinking of sour feet. "But I'm glad I did wake up, I would have been furious with myself if I'd spent the night in my clothes. That will teach me to work all day and go to bed without eating."

"You haven't eaten?"

"I wasn't hungry at lunchtime, I had this story to write, and then when I came back to the hotel I was too tired to go out again."

"I keep *telling* Abuelito that we need to serve food at the Julia Tuttle, but he's too busy buying up swamps. I have a tin of goose liver pâté and some water biscuits in my room."

"Oh, no, it'll be breakfast time soon. But thanks anyway."

"I didn't mean come to my *room.*" That vehement Spanish *r* bursting out like a drumroll. "I would bring them to you. There are many hours until breakfast."

"Oh, no, really, I—"

"Or we could walk over to La Bodega and have a *medianoche.* That's a popular late-night snack for Cubans, a fried sandwich with fresh pork and cheese. At Bodega's it also comes with fried plantains. I was going myself when I have done with these." He held up the woman's shoe.

A fried sandwich with pork and cheese was a lot harder to resist than goose liver, which sounded disgusting, and water biscuits, whatever they were.

"It'll take me a few minutes—" I looked down at my slept-in skirt and blouse.

"*'Tá bien*—I'll finish the shoes. Shall we meet in the lobby in half an hour?"

———

OUR WALK to La Bodega went in the same direction as my walk to the *Star,* only we turned off at Eighth Avenue. The first thing I accomplished was breaking Alex de Costa of the "Miss Gant" habit. Then he annoyed me in equal measure by drolly inquiring if I was "any relation to Eugene Gant." I had thought leaving North Carolina would rid me forever of that tiresome literary witticism.

"Not any more than I am to the Gant shirtmakers. In England, up in Lincolnshire, they call the crested grebe a gant, and there are lots of Lincolnshire descendants in my part of North Carolina. I doubt if Thomas Wolfe even knew about the crested grebe. He probably just knew somebody in town named Gant and appropriated the name. That was his style. He sometimes put in their addresses and phone numbers as well."

I had spent years perfecting this comeback. Then fatuously I added that I was surprised someone from Harvard had read *Look Homeward, Angel,* only to get shot down when Alex de Costa reminded me Eugene Gant had gone to Harvard.

He had a different walk from the men I was used to; he neither loped or bounced like the big-footed mountain boys, nor swaggered or toed-out in the manner of Southern gents like Rod Reynolds. It was kind of a tight-assed walk, only with his high rump it took on a certain ponderous dignity. Since Bev's tutelage, I had become more conscious of people's walks and what they might reveal about them. The mannikin's walk Bev urged on us was of course the stripping away of telltale idiosyncrasies. When I was trying to look stately and glamorous, I walked in this way, but soon slipped back into my wary sashay, which I supposed expressed my basic mode of encountering life. Paul's walk was a discreet, fastidious stroll. Bisbee's was a nervous dance and Lucifer's was that stealthy glide, as if he moved on invisible wheels.

"How did you know I went to Harvard?" Alex de Costa asked.

Alarm bells jangled aboard my carefully compartmented ship of life. Paul had told me Alex went to Harvard, but that got us into dangerous waters. And I was wary of using Tess, because there was a chance she wouldn't have known and Alex would know she wouldn't have known.

"I heard two men discussing you on the elevator." Opting for the far-fetched lie that couldn't be checked rather than the believable one that could. "They were speaking Spanish, but I heard your name and 'Harvard' and put two and two together."

"Ah." He sounded convinced.

La Bodega was a noisy, pulsating glow in the middle of a dark street of shops with latticework metal grilles pulled down over their fronts. Loud, excited voices, a Spanish crooner on the jukebox, cigar smoke curling upwards into ceiling fans, and sweet, spicy cooking smells embraced us at the threshold. A potbellied man in an embroidered guayabera thumped Alex on the back, addressing him as "Alejito," and made rapid sweeping-away gestures at two men drinking beer at a corner table. They stood up at once and removed themselves to the bar. A waiter quickly put down a cloth on the table, and we were seated with fanfare.

"You must be a favored patron," I said. "He ousted those two men from their table."

"Not really. It's my grandfather's special table; Victor leases this building from him. Abuelito hardly ever comes here at night, so Victor lets others use it with the understanding I may be showing up around midnight. Only I'm ahead of schedule tonight."

"Because of the girl who neglected to eat all day."

"Alejito?" Victor was back. "*¿Qué quieres tomar?*"

"I've been talking up your *medianoches*. Miss Gant has just joined the *Miami Star* as a reporter."

"*¡Felicidades, señorita!* You may do a story on me anytime. *¿Dos medianoches?*"

"Unless you see something else you'd rather have," Alex said to me.

"Oh, no, I've been looking forward to that sandwich ever since you described it."

"What would you like to drink? I'm having a lager."

"Just water for me. My aunt Tess and I overdid on daiquiris last night. I had to stay over at her place." That should take care of my reputation for last night.

"Your aunt makes going to the dentist a treat."

"I'm glad to have her here. And the Nightingales, too. They've been so good to me, Paul and Bev have."

That should take care of his seeing me with Paul on Sunday night.

"How do you happen to know them?" I could tell from the way he asked that he had wondered about Paul coming to the hotel.

"They own a small Jewish family hotel in North Carolina. I worked as a waitress there last summer. They're almost like a second set of parents. Bev's already gone up to North Carolina to open the Inn, but Paul didn't want me to eat alone my first night in Miami."

"I play cards at his club during the season. With my gambling record, it's a good thing he closes down in April. I like to think I'm better off playing bridge with my friends over on the Beach, but lately I wonder if Nightingale's isn't the lesser of two evils."

When the waiter set down Alex's frosted lager, I regretted playing Miss Abstemious. But I couldn't risk another hungover day at the *Star*.

"You look worried," Alex said. I realized he was a face watcher, like me, so I must be superdiscreet. "I hope I didn't give away anything about the card playing over at Nightingale's."

"Oh," I said lightly, "I knew all about that. It's nothing illegal since it's a private club, just like a country club. In fact, he's putting in an upstairs kitchen that will be ready this coming season. So his club members can have late-night snacks."

"If only I could persuade Abuelito to let me open the hotel kitchen! Our guests need to eat, and they're short of cash. Most of them have hot plates in their rooms, which is against the fire code. But we're at cross-purposes. For my grandfather, the hotel is just another piece of North American real estate. He sees the Julia Tuttle as a basic training camp for me. I make all my mistakes here, he declares it a tax loss, and as soon as Fidel's out he'll buy another establishment on the Malecón for me to manage."

"And what do you see it as?"

"Young men with useless degrees and gambling habits need jobs like everyone else. I'm grateful he was willing to set me up, though I never imagined myself a *hotelero*. But when these people started arriving in January, I thought I could be a bridge for them. You know, provide them with a familiar *ambiènte*, help them adjust. It sounds strange, but for the first time in my life, it seemed that this peculiar mixture of me was the perfect fit for something."

"Why are you a peculiar mixture?"

"I'm Cuban on both sides, but raised *norteamericano*. I used to think of myself as a spy, only I was never sure which side I was spying for. I wouldn't make a good spy for *either* side because I have a Spanish accent in English and my Spanish is too *castellano* for my father and half brothers in Camagüey. When I was at boarding school in Palm Beach, I never felt at home with the other Cubans whose backgrounds were similar to mine. Yet with my closest American friends I also held back a part of myself. The same when I'm with my mother and whatever husband she's married to, or when I'm in Cuba on the ranch with my father and my half brothers. Always a part held back."

"Is there one part that you always hold back, or do you hold different parts back depending on whom you're with?"

"You are going to be a formidable reporter, Emma."

"Oh, thank you, I hope so."

It was the first time he had called me by my given name. He broke the syllables delicately between the *E* and the *m*, making it sound both feminine and foreign, less like the name a flat-voiced hillbilly woman might shout across the hollow to her friend. ("Emm-*MA!*")

"To answer your question, it's a combination of both. One part of me is always held back from everybody, the other parts depend on whose company I'm in."

"So right now, with me, what are you holding back?"

"I am trying not to find you too charming."

I kept my moat of reserve intact by folding my paper napkin into small squares. "I suppose you won't tell me about the part you hold back from everyone."

"I hold back the part of me that is *el más mío*—the most mine."

"And what is that?"

"I wish I knew. That's why I'm unable to share it with anyone. But what about you? Have you found your *más mío*?"

"Some days I feel I've been swimming in it all my life, though I don't always remember it's there. It's like this element that can't be separated from me, however wretched I am. My Emma-ness, I guess you could call it." (Thank you, Tess.)

"The last thing you seem to me is wretched," declared Alex with his passionately rolled *r*.

"Appearances can be deceiving. I think I'll change my mind about that lager."

When it came, I clicked my frosted glass against his. "Here," I said, "let's drink to the discovery of your Alex-ness."

I ran past him the names of my old Cuban schoolmates at St. Clothilde's and St. Clovis Hall. He was familiar with St. Clothilde's, some friends' sisters had gone there; he even remembered Raquel Cortez, her brother had invited him to Raquel's *quinceañera*, but for some reason he hadn't gone. He drew a blank on Pepe Iglesias. "But it's a very common surname in Cuba."

He was twenty-seven to my soon-to-be twenty-two, the child of his mother's second marriage to a widowed cattleman in Camagüey with two grown sons. He called his mother by her first name, Lídia. Her first marriage, at sixteen, with a cousin who later became a Jesuit priest, had been annulled by order of her father, Alex's *abuelito*.

"When the romance of ranch life wore thin for her, Lídia brought me to Palm Beach, where Abuelito owned commercial properties. Since the age of four, I was raised by my grandparents. Though Abuelita died when I was twelve."

"What about your mother?"

"Oh, she went off at once to Spain to help lose the Civil War. Lídia loves a cause. Her latest one was Fidel. I believe I told you, she gave a benefit for *la Revolución* last spring. She was in heaven when he took over this past January. She had helped bring down a government at last."

"What is she doing now?"

"She is between causes. At least I think so."

"How many marriages has she had?"

"Five, if you count the one that was annulled. My second cousin once removed, the Jesuit. Then my father, Raul de Costa, the cattleman. Then a Mexican painter, that's the one she went to Spain with. Later was a Spanish diplomat she met in Paris—that was Fredo, my favorite stepfather. I still miss Fredo. Her fifth husband, Dick, her first American, most probably will last."

"Why is that?"

"Because Abuelito made him his partner. Together they're buying up the oceanfront as far north as Cocoa Beach and all the swampland south of Miami. Also, Lídia is getting too old for romance. She's still a beautiful woman, but wealth and power are more important to her now. She ought to have been Cleopatra, or at the very least someone like Eva Perón."

"I'd like to meet her."

"Lídia would approve of you. You're like her in some ways."

Our food arrived just in time to prevent me from saying something flippant, like: I wonder if I will go through five husbands. The *medianoche* was sinfully tasty, a French-toast-like pork sandwich, all bonded together with melted cheese, though impossible to eat neatly without a knife and fork. I also loved the fried green bananas on the side.

Perhaps Alex de Costa would become my symbolic older brother, a male version of my *más mío*, bookish, questing, self-searching, with a less-than-normal family history, who could discuss the intangible things I adored prying into, and whom I could always count on to find me charming. He would help me become fluent in his *castellano* Spanish, and perhaps provide the inspiration for a story I might write along the lines of Thomas Mann's incestuous-sister-and-brother tale, "The Blood of the Walsungs."

All in all, a successful evening, I thought as we walked back through the balmy Miami night, the manager of the Julia Tuttle having slipped his arm through mine in a protective, brotherly way. It occurred to me that

Alex de Costa might even suspect me of virginity, which was a plus. Pepe Iglesias once told me Cuban men expected it of the woman they married. Or, as the incorrigible Pepe had put it, "When I marry I shall tell my bride I have had more experience than I have had, and I shall damn well expect her to tell me she has had less than she has had."

8.

Hot Water Battle

Utility, Customer
Are All Washed Up

By Emma Gant
Star Staff Writer

It may be only a drop in the bucket, but the North Miami Beach Water Board will just have to do without his $2.06, a North Dade homeowner vowed in a torrent of indignation Tuesday.

Charles P. Rose, of 1371 NW 175th St., said he didn't mind paying $15.80 of his $17.86 water-and-sewer bill. But come heck or no water the $2.06 difference was staying right in his pocket.

It started, Rose told the *Star* on Tuesday, when the North Miami Beach Water Board purchased the North Dade Water Co. back in April.

Immediately, the NMB Water Board announced a "reduction" in water rates.

Immediately, Rose's bill went up.

The "reduction," Rose insisted, was nothing more than a "clever wording trick."

True, said Rose, the Board was charging a $1.50 base rate instead of the $2.50 base used by his former supplier. But the $2.50 had been for 6,000 gallons or less. The "reduced" rate was for only 4,000 gallons or less.

Hence, the "reduction" became an increase and Rose became boiling mad.

"A lot of people can be manipulated by words they don't understand," Rose told the *Star*.

He had previously fired off a letter of protest to the Water Board. But the letter, along with Rose's $15.80 check, came back. Attached was a note from North Miami Beach attorney Larry Winthrop, citing chapter and verse on the right of city utility companies to set their own rates.

And saying that Rose still owed the Water Board $17.86.

Rose vowed he would continue his fight.

The Water Board said it wouldn't.

"The next step," said Fred Snead, general manager of the Water Board, "is simply to cut Rose's water off."

My story was on page two of the local section, above the fold, with its equivocal cliché of a headline and a kicker that made it sound as though the battle had been over hot water. Someone had broken up my text and made all these itsy-bitsy paragraphs. Also it had been cut, but as I no longer had the original, I couldn't locate exactly what was missing.

I certainly wouldn't be sending Dean Ligon *this* simpleminded distillation, even if I had promised him my first bylined story. And Charles P. Rose would think even less of me. Any minute my phone would ring. "Nobody's *that* stupid!" he would yell at me from North Miami.

At least there was no Joelle Cutter-Crane human-interest spread from Cuba with heart-wrenching photos by her sidekick Kingsley. The lead story, reported by the AP wire service from Managua, was that rebel forces, said to have been trained in Cuba, had invaded Nicaragua. Not even a picture. The only front-page pictures were of a man skiing in Vermont after a freak summer snowstorm in Stowe, and head shots of

Brigitte Bardot and her new husband, Jacques Charrier, all AP wire-photos. Cuba had slapped an exit permit requirement on Americans yesterday, but this small front-page item was courtesy of the *New York Times* service.

Such were my consolations on this third day at work, the eve of my twenty-second birthday.

Dave Bisbee was sitting at Rod Reynolds's desk. He congratulated me on my story, though without any mention of Job or Kafka or the role of the little man in great literature.

"Rod's been called home, his old man had a heart attack," he went on. "I've been appointed deputy city editor. Lucifer broke the news to me just as he was heading off to Cape Canaveral on some hush-hush mission." Bisbee's usual insolent tone failed to hide his pride and surprise to have been appointed Rod's stand-in, but then he couldn't wait to pull the rug out from under himself by wondering if this was their way of firing him. "It's become a *Star* tactic since Lucifer's been in management. First they blow you up like a balloon and dance you around, get all the mileage out of you they can, then they cut your string."

"Is it also a *Star* tactic to chop people's stories up into moronic one-sentence paragraphs like they did mine?"

"That's copydesk routine, Emma. I wouldn't take it personally."

"How can I not? I don't *personally* write in little jumps and jolts like that."

"They think it's an easy way to jazz up boring copy—not that yours was boring, you made that old curmudgeon come right off the page. But somebody did a survey: people pay better attention. Also, a new paragraph indicates more to come, so readers feel they're getting twice as much news for their nickel."

"Do you honestly believe that?"

"Whether I believe it or not is a moot point. I've trained myself to think in bite-size paragraphs, because that's how they'll end up in the *Star* anyway. If I ever get canned and go off to write my great American novel, maybe I'll go back to my *Tampa Tribune* longueurs. Or maybe I won't. Cheer up, Emma. You're right on schedule, maybe a little ahead of yourself."

"On schedule for *what?*"

"For making it. You will."

"What are you, a fortune-teller or something?"

"No, just an avid people-watcher, not that it earns me many points. What are your plans for the day?"

"Find out who's croaked. Unless you have another assignment for me."

"No, do the stiffs first. Then you could take over my hospital beat: Jackson Memorial, Biscayne, North Shore. I'm going to be pretty busy till Rod gets back. I'll call ahead and set you up with my contacts, if you like."

"Yes, *please.* That way they won't think I'm just somebody's secretary, like Mr. Rose did."

"Who? Oh, your old curmudgeon. Well, you fixed him, didn't you? That coup de grâce last sentence. It *was* yours, wasn't it?"

"Yes, but it was part of a longer paragraph."

THE GRIM Reaper hadn't done much business in Miami the night before. By a quarter to ten, I was clacking out the last obit and planning my next ladies' room freshener when Dave Bisbee hustled over with the tall, gray-haired women's editor, Marge Armstrong.

"Marge has a crisis, Emma, and we could use your help."

Ah, here it came. The bosses hardly out of town and the "deputy city editor," whom I thought I had in my pocket, was already transferring me to the women's department. I lifted my neck and narrowed my eyes at them.

"She'll be perfect," said Marge, smiling down at me. "What are you, Emma, about a size eight or ten?"

"It can go either way." For Christ's sake, they needed my *dress size* before I went into the glass cage with the women?

"We're doing a special feature on raincoats and rain hats, what with all this wet weather," said Marge, "and our model has let us down. I was going to kill the whole thing, then I looked out here and saw you and wondered if—well, if you wouldn't mind coming up to the roof and having your photo taken in a few coats."

"Meanwhile I can call my contacts and get things set up for you," said Bisbee. "Emma's going to take over my hospital beat while I'm deputying for Rod."

"What a good idea!" said Marge. She seemed genuinely pleased for me. As I followed her long tanned legs in their spectator pumps up a flight of stairs to the roof, I decided it was safe to like her.

A striped awning had been set up, flanked by tropical plants in large rectangular containers. It was supposed to look like the entrance to a hotel. There was a coatrack with three raincoats and some wide-brimmed rain hats. The sky glared down on us like a metal reflector, and the photographer started clicking his light meter at me before Marge had even introduced us. He circled me impatiently with a sinister lurching gait, scowling up at my face. His short-sleeved shirt had wet half-moons under the armpits. My own face and neck broke out in a sheen of sweat and I felt my French twist sag in the heavy, sullen air.

". . . bitch . . ." he muttered.

"Excuse me?" I said. What a horrible person!

"This light is a bitch. I'm going to need filters." He plunged his hands into a scuffed leather bag. "I expected her to come more made-up," he growled to Marge as if I weren't there.

"Jake, you weren't listening. The model from the agency didn't *show*. This is Emma Gant, she's a new reporter on the city desk who's agreed to help us out. We need this for the early edition, so we're on a tight deadline."

"Nice of you to fill me in, seeing as I'm just the fashion photographer." He had some kind of Yankee accent.

"Jake Rance won a Pulitzer for his work in Korea," Marge said. "And he's not a fashion photographer, though he could win prizes at that if he chose to. The Photo Department is short-staffed today and this weather is enough to make anyone cross. Do you think we're going to get Beulah, Jake? Unusual so early in the season, but there's a hurricane watch in Panama City."

Marge was apologizing for him and humoring him at the same time.

"A nasty tropical storm more likely." The prospect seemed to improve his mood. "Gulf hurricanes are fickle."

Marge was pinning the back of my raincoat to make it more form-fitting. Gingerly she positioned a wide-brimmed hat on top of my French twist.

"No, she can't wear it like that," said Jake.

"Why not?" asked Marge.

"It makes her face look too fat."

"I don't think so at *all*," protested Marge.

"Let your hair down." Jake Rance's first words to me.

"WHAT A nasty man, that Jake creature," I huffed, back at my desk, my hair pinned up again. "I hope I won't be going out on any assignments with *him*."

"You will be," said Bisbee. "He's just in a snit because he should have gone to Cuba. He's the best man we have. But Joelle likes to travel with Kingsley. He dresses better and she can run him. Nobody runs Rance."

"He has this creepy, lurching walk and he said my face was fat."

"The walk is because one leg is shorter than the other, he had polio as a child. And he's disgusted with the world in general, so don't take it personally. You'll be happy with the photo, wait and see. Here, check this out for me, will you? A young Metro police rescue diver got the bends while trying to locate the body of another diver. See what you can do with it."

The rescue diver was in an iron lung over at Jackson Memorial, waiting to be flown to a decompression chamber aboard a salvage ship in Key West. I scribbled the information from Bisbee's contact at Jackson, a friendly sounding man named Herman Melton.

What were the bends and what was a decompression chamber? There was obviously a whole new vocabulary that went with watery locations, and here I had grown up in the hills. Meanwhile, how to bluff my way through with this liaison who probably assumed I was as informed as Bisbee? What to do? Hang up, run for the big dictionary in Moira Parks's morgue, then call Melton back and say we had been cut off by the switchboard? Sleazy behavior for a heroine-in-progress. Humbly confess I didn't know? Stupidly unprofessional. Indirection was more my style.

"At what *point* did he get the bends?" Ask a slightly offbeat question and hope to squeeze clues from his response.

"That's something only he could answer," said Melton. "He came up too fast, he was down eighty feet. You know what the bends are, don't you?"

"I do in a *visceral* way, of course, but I wish you would tell me, from a medical standpoint, exactly what happens inside the person who's having them. That way I can make it more accessible to our readers." Borrowing from my Charles P. Rose strategy.

"Well, when pressure gets reduced too rapidly, nitrogen bubbles form in the blood. The lungs can't circulate the nitrogen fast enough and there's a lack of blood supply to the brain. The person undergoes disorientation and severe pain, the kind that bends you double—that's where the term 'bends' came from—and then syncope occurs."

"Ah, *syncope.*" I scribbled rapidly. And I had thought I was educated.

"You might want to say 'loss of consciousness,' for the benefit of your readers."

"Thank you, Mr. Melton. Good idea."

"I like your desire to be accessible, Miss Gant. There's too much misinformation floating around about what goes on inside hospitals. And inside the human body. That's why my job was created, to clear away some of the confusion. Now do you know what a decompression chamber does?"

"I believe so, but I'd like to be as clear as possible. And please call me Emma."

"If you'll call me Herman. Come over to Jackson soon, Emma, and I'll show you around. Meanwhile, feel free to call if you need medical translations. I was premed at Emory, but I tripped up on organic chemistry. The terminology stays with you, though."

9.

new words:
moot
coup de grâce
syncope
bends

tomorrow I will be 22

I closed my "Go, Tar Heels!" notebook and slid it back into the bedside drawer on top of the Gideons Bible. An evil sky glowered outside my window. It looked as though Jake Rance was going to get his storm. Nasty man gets nasty storm. The ring of the phone made me jump.

"Hi," said Paul.

"You're here *already?*"

"Nope, I'm calling from your home state. I just fired my chef. His replacement won't be here until tomorrow, if then. I'm not going to make it for your birthday, kid. I can't walk out and leave Bev and Aunt Stella to break in a new guy. You understand, don't you?"

"Why did you have to fire the other one?" I was crushed, but whining wasn't part of Paul's image of me.

"Too slow. Guests were getting restless waiting for their main courses. But he sabotaged himself today when Stella walked into the kitchen and heard him complaining to the sous-chef about having to sacrifice his culinary art to Hymie cuisine. You know how tiny she is, he never even saw her. I went in and told him to pack his bags and drove him to the bus station. He can practice his culinary art at the Mountain City Men's Club, where they drink their dinners and don't allow Hymies. If they'll take him back."

I was bitterly disappointed and tired of being brave. "Ah, I wish I had been at the bus station to go back to the Inn with you."

"There's no going back for people destined for the heights, Emma. I'm hoping to be down the weekend after this one. How's it going at the *Star*?"

"No heights in sight yet. I modeled a raincoat for the fashion page and wrote a story about a police diver who got the bends. It should be in tomorrow."

"We're several days behind here. I just got Sunday's *Star* in this morning's mail. You realize you and I were together Sunday?"

"You think I've forgotten?"

"Just hearing your voice picks me up. I'll be looking for the diver story. And that picture in the raincoat. It's not so long till weekend-after-next."

"It seems very long to me."

"That's one advantage of being old, darling. Time goes faster."

After we hung up, I tried to go on with my rereading of *The Fall*, the one book I had brought with me, like a talisman, to Miami. Just holding it in my hands made me feel closer to the day when I would have a published book of my own. Last spring, I had devoted a *Daily Tar Heel* column to this little masterwork of irony by "the spokesman of his generation," as Camus was described on the dust jacket. That column, titled "We Fornicated and Read the Newspapers," and bearing my mug shot with its flying hair and don't-mess-with-me smirk, was praised and envied by all my literary friends and earned poor Dean Ligon another scolding phone call from the dean of women, saying that I continued to abuse the privilege of my column with provocative language and cynicism.

What kind of thing would I have to write to be called the spokes-woman of my generation? I hugged *The Fall* to my chest. What if I were to be granted a split-second vision of my first published novel, the colors and design of its jacket? *The ———*, by Emma Gant.

Damn it, I was going to be *alone on my birthday*. It was like having a crucial floorboard collapse in my palace of security, sending me plunging right back into the old dungeon of panic and loneliness. I knew it was not the end of the world; if anything, it would only increase Paul's desire for me. But how I hated him for that last remark. By the time I was Paul's present age, he would be sixty-two; when I was sixty-two, he would be eighty-two. I saw us married, Paul on his deathbed, his hair completely white and flowing back from his temples like some ancient rabbi's. He squeezed my hand, and I heard his voice as clearly as a few minutes before: "I've loved you more than anyone, kid, but, darling, I'm old and it's time to move on." Then the pressure of his grasp weakened and dissolved, and I felt the chill of aloneness circulating around my freed hand.

This scenario of my future grief actually brought me off the bed and onto my feet, and I was standing in front of my fifth-floor window, gazing out through a scrim of widow's tears at the weird greenish pallor on the horizon when a rumbling came out of nowhere, like a low-flying plane passing at top speed right outside the Julia Tuttle. Jagged lightning slashed the sky, blue fireworks danced up and down the power lines, glass shattered, awnings collapsed with a *whump*, outdoor metal furniture flipped upside down and shrieked across the concrete. The underwater light in the swimming pool and all the area lamps around the cabanas went out just after a giant royal palm heaved itself partway out of the ground and swayed back and forth over the pool, its tresses dragging the water.

Shouts and Spanish-speaking voices burst forth from all directions. I picked up the phone to ask Luís on the desk what had happened, but the line was dead. The lamp didn't turn on, either, so I slipped on my skirt, grabbed my purse, and headed for the elevator, which wasn't working.

The stairwell was crammed with other guests and their exclamations.

"*¡Dios mío!*"

"*¡Ay, qué susto!*"

"*¿Como salgo de aqui?*"

"*¡Apaga la luz, apaga la luz!*"

"*No puedo, tonto. Hay un fallo eléctrico.*"

"*Un asalto de viento.*"

"*¡Qué ruido!*"

About twenty more had already gathered in the gloom of the lobby, talking nonstop. I was beginning to understand how foreigners feel, but at least these people weren't speaking something impossible, like Russian or Greek. I could recognize about one Spanish word out of ten.

Looking happier than I had ever seen him, Luís scurried about, setting out hurricane lamps and reassuring guests. "*Estamos fuera de peligro . . . Sí, sí, tornado, pero se terminó . . .*" As soon as he saw me he called out, "Is okay, the danger is pass, *señorita*. Was a tornado, but it has moved elsewhere."

The dominoes players had a hurricane lamp on their table and their transistor was tuned to a Miami station. A knot of men clustered around them, translating the news from English to Spanish for those outside the circle. I edged as close as I could and strained at snatches from the bulletins.

Twister heading north, reported to have hit northeast Miami full force . . .

I needed to call the *Star* and offer to come in.

I was on my way to ask Luís where I could find the nearest working telephone when someone touched my arm.

"Mees Gant?" It was the Cuban mother, wearing a turban and lounging pajamas, her frowning little daughter in tow. The girl carried one of the porcelain dolls I had seen her with on the day of my arrival—of all our arrivals—was it only three days ago?

"I am Marisa Ocampo." The name bubbled off her tongue like sparkling water. "Alejito says you are from Mountain City and are also a St. Clothilde's girl, yes?" She was alight with expectancy. Beneath the turban her hair was wet; she must have just washed it. "I was Marisa Velázquez, Class of Fifty-one, my sister Hortensia was Fifty-three."

"I was Fifty-five. Or I would have been if my family hadn't moved away."

"Ah, then in 1951 you were still in the grammar school, you would not remember me."

But I did remember Hortensia Velázquez, in the fragmentary way the handful of Cuban girls had registered themselves upon our cliquish North American concerns. Hortensia's fragment had been her dark moustache, a source of curiosity to us: Why didn't she use a depilatory, or had the nuns confiscated it as a sin against God's will? Naturally, I didn't bring up the moustache, but that I recalled her younger sister was enough for Mrs. Ocampo. She released a flood of news about Hortensia: degree in languages from Columbia, married to an American, both of them working at the UN. "No little ones yet, but they are both so active in their careers. This is my daughter, Luisa. *Luisa, quisiera presentarte a señorita Gant . . .*"

I caught "Mountain City" (*MON-tan CEE-ty*) and "Santa Clothilde" (*Clo-TEEL-day*), of course, but the rest was too fast for me.

Luisa shifted the doll so she could offer me her hand. *"Buenas tardes, señorita."* Her voice was surprisingly unchildlike, solemn, with a gravelly roughness, like a miniature smoker's voice.

"Hello, Luisa. *Me llamo Emma. ¿Como se llama su muñeca?*" I was thrilled to have remembered the word for doll.

"Manuela." She stroked the doll's hair as if soothing her.

"¿Y, donde está su amiga?"

Luisa regarded me with polite incomprehension.

"I mean, let's see . . . Where is your, ah, *OTRA muneca?*"

"Tilda tiene dolor de cabeza," the girl replied in her solemn, gravelly voice.

" *Sí,* our Tilda is upstairs with a headache," said her mother. "Tilda has the headaches and Manuela, she has *las pesadillas,* the bad dreams. The dolls suffer for our whole family, thanks to our wise Luisita here." She stroked her daughter's hair with the same soothing motion that the child had used in stroking the doll's. "Do you know, Emma—may I call you Emma, yes?—I have our yearbook from St. Clothilde's, I brought it with me from Cuba. *Le Flambeau,* from fifty-one, is upstairs in our suite."

"Oh, really?" I needed to get in touch with the city desk. Was Bisbee still on duty?

"Perhaps we can look at it together. If we are still here. We go from day to day, everything depends on that *engañador* Fidel. Do you know, he has taken Enrique's mills in Oriente. And they were at Belén together! That is my husband over there, listening to the radio. Alejito has been so kind, he has given Enrique a temporary job as night clerk so we can pay our bill. We could take out nothing but our clothes from Cuba."

Luís strutted about, relaying the latest tornado bulletins. I strained to hear while attending to Marisa Ocampo, who had attached herself to me like a long-lost best friend.

North Miami hardest hit: up beyond Fifty-ninth Street, houses and stores blasted apart, cars and boats overturned, flying glass everywhere . . .

"Do you know, Emma, I have memorized my class roll from St. Clothilde's . . ."

"Oh, really?"

Dazed and bleeding people wandering the streets . . . ambulances loaded with the injured speeding to the closest hospitals . . .

I needed to get to Jackson Memorial. It was my beat now. My Miami map was in my purse, along with my spiral-bound notepad. I would walk the twenty-something blocks, if necessary.

"Yes, is true! When I have the *insomnio,* I recite the roll: Adelaide Attwater, Caroline Bell, Sue Ann Carruthers, Patty Delaney, Francesca Ford—I remember all the names. And usually I am asleep before Velázquez."

Alex de Costa arrived just as I was heading out the door. He was appalled that I intended to walk all the way to Jackson Memorial.

"There are wires down! Wait five minutes and I will drive you."

He consulted with Luís about damage sustained, spoke individually to guests, announced that he had met a Florida Power & Light crew working nearby and the Julia Tuttle could expect to have power restored any minute. "We got nothing like the devastation in North Miami."

It was the first time I had seen him in his proper role of manager, rather than desk clerk or bootblack, and I was impressed and a mite attracted, watching him take charge, smoothly switching between languages like a diplomat. I was surprised and flattered that he had offered to leave his post to drive me to the hospital. He and Enrique Ocampo consulted seriously about something, from their gestures it appeared to be about the huge royal palm swaying precariously over the pool, and then we were off in his rattly Mercedes sedan.

I was disappointed, as we entered Biscayne Boulevard, to see everything lit up and business going on as usual. Alex told me he had been playing bridge over on the Beach and had just started back across the MacArthur Causeway when he saw the sky explode above the area of our hotel and then had watched the thing snake its way north as transformers went out in flashes of blue light.

"It was all over in a minute. So fast, and so much lost." He sighed morosely. "A fitting parallel to my dissolute evening."

"You've been dissolute this evening?"

"I'm in the hole another three hundred."

We were turning west, onto Northwest Eleventh Street. Must remember directions for when I got my car and could drive myself to assignments.

"But I thought you were playing *bridge.*"

"The people I hang out with would make up a pot if they were playing pin the tail on the donkey."

"Why do you hang out with them, then?"

"I find them charming, I feel at home in their houses. And they like me."

His easy use of the charm phrase devalued his compliment to me from the night before and made me want to be mean. "I guess they do like you, seeing as how you leave behind such generous amounts in their pot."

"I have been known to win on occasion." He sounded hurt.

"How much have you lost in all?"

"Twenty-two hundred." The *t*'s exploded like gunshots.

"Good Lord. Do you pay cash or write a check, or what?"

"They've been very obliging about taking my IOUs, they know my grandfather is good for it. It's not like over on the Beach. Everything's done with chips at that establishment. You pay cash for your chips and when you're out of cash you go home. No IOUs for your friend Mr. Nightingale. It's an all-round business arrangement."

"It sounds to me you'd be safer to stick with Paul and Bev's all-round business arrangement."

Your friend. From now on, it would be "Paul and Bev" out of my mouth every time Nightingale's came up in conversation with Alex de Costa.

As we approached Jackson Memorial, we found ourselves joining a traffic jam consisting mostly of ambulances and police cars. Alex pulled up as near to Emergency as he could get. "Shall I wait for you, Emma?"

Both ambulance bays were full. On either side of us, vehicles were unloading the injured who could walk. A state trooper escorted a dazed woman with a cut cheek and two barefoot little boys in pajamas up the ramp to the entrance.

"No need, thanks. I don't know how long I'll be." My fingers were already fretting at the notepad inside my purse. I could hardly wait to plunge into the urgency.

"Shall I come back in an hour?"

"I'm not sure where I'll be."

"I'll find you. Promise me, Emma, you won't be foolish and try to walk back to the hotel." Assuming the role of my protector.

"Okay." I was already out of the car and chasing up the ramp after an old man with an amateurishly bandaged head.

"Sir? Excuse me. What happened?"

"I seen the thing coming right up the edge of the bay! Streetlights went out, branches and debris flying all around, next thing I know blood's spurting out of my skull. Drove myself here." He seemed elated to be part of the scene, and could hardly contain himself when I started scribbling in the notepad. "You from the press?"

"The *Miami Star.*" I hoped he would not ask to see my press card as I didn't have one yet.

"Name's Henry Sprat, *S-p-r-a-t,* just like in 'Jack Sprat could eat no fat.' Forty-six Forty-four Ingraham Highway, that's in Coconut Grove.

Widower. My dog's name is Lola. Beautiful chocolate Lab. Left her home in case they want to keep me overnight. I built a little runway for her so she can go in and out when she has to do her business. She ought to be in the story, too, on account of we were having our evening walk when we seen it coming."

"Spelled *L-o-l-a*?"

(You see, Mr. Charles P. Rose, some geezers can be downright cooperative with the press.)

"Right you are. Just like in 'Whatever Lola wants, Lola gets.' "

Emergency area a disordered hubbub. Tempers rising. The wounded shouting and snatching at nurses rushing past. Stop. Look around and register what is actually going on in front of you before you begin forming sentences in your head. "Bad journalists arrive at the scene with their lead already written," Dean Ligon had drilled into us in News Gathering Lab.

First thing to register was the confusion and the noise. Screaming children, too many people all demanding attention at once. An overly tanned athletic woman in shorts and sneakers with cuts on her legs and arms snatched at the sleeve of a passing nurse. "Don't you *understand*? A glass *door* fell on me."

"Hon, please be patient. I said I'd get you in as soon as I can."

"I need to be in there with the *injured*," the woman announced to the general public as the nurse escaped through the swinging doors to the emergency room. I was debating whether to interview her—she looked angrier than she looked hurt—or to brazen my way through the swinging doors behind the nurse in pursuit of more dramatic stories when I spotted Dave Bisbee in his crooked red bow tie leaning over someone on a gurney at the other end of the hallway. I hurried over to report for duty, a tad downcast, I must admit. I had anticipated having the field all to myself.

"Emma," said Bisbee, "what are *you* doing here?" The woman on the gurney, hooked up to an IV, seemed to be dozing through all the commotion.

"Isn't it my beat now?"

"Well, yes, in the daytime, when I'm covering for Rod at the desk, but— How did you get here?"

"I caught a ride. I've already interviewed two of the wounded." (Counting my yet-to-be-written-down quote: " 'I need to be in there with the injured,' shouted an angry woman in shorts, grabbing at the arm of a harried nurse.")

"Well, aren't you a trouper." Did I detect a note of resentment? "Anything serious?" Was Bisbee afraid I'd scoop him?

"Just cuts, so far, but—"

"That's just it!" He seemed relieved. "The ER here at Jackson is virtually a sewing room at the moment, people waiting in line to have their cuts stitched up, but nothing major— Listen, step over here, Emma, we need to talk."

Bisbee moved me around the corner from the dozing woman with the IV. "The worst casualties are up at North Shore Hospital where the twister *really* hit. I'm headed up there to meet the photographers."

"Is your contact—Herman Melton—is he around here somewhere?"

"PR people work nine to five, Emma. And Melton lives up in the boondocks of Hallandale. I was on my way out of here a second ago when I happened to glance down at this gurney and thought I recognized the face. I checked the plastic bracelet and sure enough, it's her. Remember, I told you, that trial Norbright covered, the madam who turned key witness—"

"*That's* the Queen of the Underworld?"

"Yep. Another suicide attempt, her third, too bad it got upstaged by the twister. Her husband brought her in, the shrink. Soon as they got her stabilized, he went up to North Shore, where they've put out a call for more doctors. They're parking her out here in the hall till they can find a bed. If you're willing to hang around for a while, you might come up with a nice little human-interest sidebar to the tornado. There are still folks who'll remember her. Phone it in to Vince on the night desk—you haven't met him yet—say I said so."

"What's my deadline?"

Jiggling with impatience to be off, Bisbee checked his watch.

"Half hour at the most. Call in to Vince now so he can be working with the old clips. Tell him to check 'Ginevra Snow' and all the cross-ref files. The other suicides—I mean *attempts*—would be under 'Ginevra Brown' or 'Dr. Brown,' I think it's Edwin. Hey, you may have bopped in here just in time for me to throw you a plum, Emma."

"But what if she hasn't waked up?"

"Come on, Emma, you're a reporter. Give her a little nudge."

A plum or a sop? I wondered as he darted off. Hadn't he told me in Walgreens that the Queen of the Underworld wasn't news anymore? He just didn't want me trailing along with him and divvying up the gorier casualties at North Shore.

Nevertheless, she was my quarry now, this figure who had aroused my imagination from the start, and, after poking my head round the corner to see that she was still in place, I located a pay phone, dialed the *Star*'s number, which I had memorized months ago for just this kind of occasion, and asked to be put through to Vince on the night desk. There was a hold because, as the switchboard operator told me, everybody covering the tornado wanted to be put through to Vince, and then there was a longer wait, after which she asked if it was urgent—if not, Vince said to call back later. I revved myself up into umbrage mode and said I was acting on deputy city editor Dave Bisbee's orders, he'd given me thirty minutes to get a story, and he needed Vince to pull some files this minute.

Vince came on, sounding surly and beset. But when I snapped out the names and background data with telegraphic economy, he changed his tune and I heard him repeating my orders word for word. He said the story of the ex-madam's third attempt sounded interesting, a nice contrast to all the smashed storefronts that were coming in.

"The serious casualties are up at North Shore," I said. "Bisbee's on his way there now to meet the photographers. You ought to be getting something juicier any second now. But save some space for me. And please. Don't put me on hold when I call back in thirty minutes."

Tough and terse. Nice going, Emma. Back to my quarry.

Who was being propped up, none too gently, into a sitting position on the gurney by the same nurse I'd seen escaping the demanding woman in shorts. I approached quietly until I was in hearing range.

"Come on now, Ginevra, hon, can't have you dozing off like that. Not after we pumped that bellyful of chloral hydrate out of you."

The figure, propped up like a life-size floppy doll, was doing its best to slide back into the recumbent state.

"Ginevra, that's a no-no! You want us to have to go back in there with the hose, maybe a bigger one, make sure we got it all?"

"Go away, you sadistic bitch. I remember you from last time. You tried to choke me to death."

Though slurred and barely audible, the contemptuous diction of the contralto voice thrilled me to the bone.

"Well, I remember you, too, hon. Same time last year. Only *this* year there's been a major disaster and nobody's got time to sit with you and keep you from falling asleep."

"I do," I said, stepping forward. "I'll stay with her until Dr. Brown can get back. You've got more than you can handle with this crowd."

The nurse's face was a study in conflict. "You know Dr. Brown?"

"I do," I lied. "I'll be happy to stay here and talk to Mrs. Brown to keep her from falling asleep."

"HOW ARE you feeling?" I asked Ginevra Brown as soon as we were alone.

Though her face was grayish from her recent ordeal, and the hauteur of the slanty, wide-spaced eyes was undermined by puffiness and discoloration, the allure that had been so apparent in the newsprint pictures still emanated from this woman who had just failed for the third time to snuff out her life. My phone call to Vince, and having been put on hold, and then the exchange with the nurse, had eaten a chunk out of my thirty minutes, but at least the patient had been forcibly awakened and was now, I could see from the movements of the smoke blue eyes, making her initial evaluation of me.

"How do you know my husband?"

"Only by reputation."

"His or mine?"

Quick important choice: she was woozy but her sharpness shone through. I opted for truth and surprised myself with a spurt of eloquence. "You've made both of you unforgettable."

"Ha." She closed her eyes and slid down on the gurney.

"Please stay awake," I said.

No response.

For politeness's sake, I allowed her a few moments of peace. Then the hustle of the emergency room going full volume all around us recalled me to my purpose. This wasn't charm school, I was a newspaper reporter.

I stepped forward and touched the shoulder of the Queen of the Underworld. Her hospital gown had slipped down on one side, revealing a widely arched clavicle and a spattering of freckles, which for some reason I found moving.

"Please. Try and stay awake."

The eyelids fluttered open. "What is it to you?"

I removed my hand and risked another flat-out truth. "I'm a reporter on the *Miami Star*. I've promised to call in a story about you and it's almost deadline."

"Promised whom?"

The refined grammar was undoubtedly the result of Edith Vine's coaching after Ginevra's Mafia protector had enrolled her at the Biscayne Academy.

"The city editor."

"I got on with that dark, shiny one who wrote up my trial. He looked like Cornel Wilde."

"Lou Norbright."

"Norbright. Yes. What he's up to now?"

"He's still at the *Star*."

"Haven't seen his name in an age."

"He's risen in power, he's right below the chief." On an impulse I added, "You helped him rise."

"I daresay I did." Now she sounded like a B actress reading lines from a dated script. "Who did you say you were?"

"Emma Gant. I'm a reporter at the *Star.*"

"Emma Gant." Her lips parted on the *E*, kissed the *m*'s, then delivered my patronym with a flash of teeth and tongue. I could see her using this sensuous technique with great effect on men. "And what do you wish to report about me?"

"Why did you do it?"

"Do what?"

"Take the, you know, overdose."

She plucked at the IV line. "Why not?" She closed her eyes.

"Please, try to stay awake, Mrs. Brown."

"Mrs. Brown doesn't wish to stay awake," she murmured.

"How about Ginevra, then?"

The eyes opened. "What do you know about her?"

"I've read all the clips about you from Norbright's series. I felt this immediate affinity with you. I wish the 'Queen of the Underworld' series could have been mine, but I was in high school at the time of your trial. I didn't even know I wanted to be a journalist back then."

"I didn't know what I wanted to do back then, either, except get out of that dump. Then Prince Charming drove up in his Thunderbird and asked me how much for the ripest peach on the place. I started looking him out a good one, but he said, 'No, I mean you.'"

I was disarmed by her unself-conscious switch back into country-girl speech: "looking him out a good one."

"And you said, 'That one's not for sale.' And he said, 'Will you give it to me, then?'"

"Who's telling this story?"

"I'm just quoting from the clips. But readers would be interested in what your life is like now, Mrs.—Ginevra."

"That's a crock, if you'll pardon me. My life now is I'm a married woman who likes to sleep. When I can't sleep, my husband makes up this potion. It's so fast you can feel yourself going out while you're drinking it. Then he worries I'm becoming an addict and hides the ingredients. Edwin's a genius in his field, but not so smart when it comes to hiding things." She gave me a challenging, almost flirtatious look. "End of story."

"Then it *wasn't* a deliberate overdose?"

"How're we doing here, girls?" The nurse was back. "Good news, Ginevra, hon. Your hubby's on the way back from North Shore and the ER doc's agreed to sign you out. You'll be more comfy in your own bed at home, what with this madhouse." To me she said, "If you wouldn't mind staying with her just a teeny bit longer?"

"I'll be glad to."

"Then I'll get back to the *real* emergencies."

"Yes, get your starched ass out of here," Ginevra's contemptuous contralto dispensed with the retreating nurse. "You'd better get going, too . . . Emma. The one thing my husband loathes more than a reporter is a reporter from the *Miami Star*."

"I'd like to stay a little longer. Unless you mind, of course."

"Edwin can be very harsh when he's antagonized," she warned, but I caught a flicker of satisfaction that I wanted to stay.

Even without peeking under the diamond-studded lid of my foolish graduation watch, I knew I had missed my deadline. But I was determined not to let this fortuitous meeting come to nothing. Though I had failed to get a substantial sidebar for tomorrow's edition, I had to do something to impress her before *he* returned, something to make her remember me and be willing to see me again.

Good old Tess came to my aid. "Maybe we'll meet at Michel's on Miracle Mile one of these days," I said. "My aunt Tess says she sees you there sometimes. As soon as I can save up some money, I want to have my hair done properly."

"Which one is your aunt Tess?"

"She's a platinum blonde, up in her forties now." (Sorry, Tess!) "Still beautiful, though she doesn't think so anymore."

"The one still wearing her hair like Jean Harlow. Sometimes wears a nurse's uniform?"

"That's Tess. She's assistant to a dental surgeon in Coral Gables."

"She always gives me a friendly smile." The wistfulness in her voice gave me a further inspiration, which I held out like a carrot.

"Tess has often wanted to speak to you, but like you, she was the subject of some, er, negative publicity a while back. She knows the value of having a place to go where people respect your privacy."

"What kind of negative publicity?"

(Sorry again, Tess, but this is urgent.) "She had a big society divorce here in Miami, and, well, there was another prominent man implicated and he committed suicide. And all of it was in the *Star.*"

Ginevra's eyebrows just perceptibly arched up.

A second carrot came to hand. "Tess went to Edith Vine's academy, too. Before your time, of course. She taught there for a while until she married."

"I still dream about Miss Edith. I'm sorry she passed away before I got a chance to tell her my side of the story."

But you can still tell *me,* I thought. I must start laying the groundwork of trust. "She told my aunt Tess you were one of the best pupils she ever had. She said her debutantes would have sold their souls to have your natural grace and beauty." Of course I left out Edith Vine's "white trash" epithet. "She said you could captivate a whole room when you recited 'La Belle Dame sans Merci.' " I likewise edited out Miss Edith's final summation of her star pupil: "And all that, just to prepare someone for running a whorehouse."

Did I imagine it, or did Ginevra's languor shift a degree toward expectation?

"Next time I see your aunt," she murmured, "maybe I'll say hello."

"Tess would like that," I said.

"Now do yourself a favor. Get lost before my husband comes."

She shut her eyes and slid down on the gurney. I took it I had been dismissed and was steeling myself to make the humiliating phone call to Vince that I had no further story for him beyond the overdose, which she claimed was accidental, and that she was being released from the hospital any minute now in the care of Dr. Brown.

" 'O *what . . .' " she suddenly began.

I was about to reply "I'm still here," but she continued to declaim with closed eyes.

" '. . . can ail thee . . . Knight at arms . . . alone and palely loitering? The sedge has withered from the lake . . . and no birds sing . . .' "

The words rolled forth from her lips. " '. . . O what can ail thee, Knight at arms . . . so haggard, and so woebegone . . . the squirrel's granary is full . . . the harvest done.' "

On she went in her somnolent contralto, like a music box whose top has been lifted.

" ' "I met a lady in the meads, full beautiful . . . a faery's child . . . her hair was long, her foot was light . . . and her eyes were wild . . ." ' "

I hadn't heard a poem being recited since back in eighth grade at St. Clothilde's, when Sister Patrick would entertain us with her sinister rendering of "My Last Duchess." But even she had been reading from a book.

It was utterly spellbinding to be standing in the midst of all the commotion of the emergency room, hearing this beautifully enunciated English poem pour out of the recumbent figure on the gurney with her eyes fast closed. How thankful I was that I'd headed straight for the hospital after the tornado. In a way, I realized, this amazing scene had been my creation.

" ' "I set her on my pacing steed . . . and nothing else saw all day long . . . for sidelong would she bend . . . and sing a faery's song—" ' "

I was so wrapped in my bubble of enthrallment that it took me a moment to realize the bubble had burst. Gone were the enchanted knight and his wild lady, Ginevra's voice had been cut off midsentence and she was warily gazing up at a scowling dark-haired man in a foreign-cut suit looming over me. Beside him stood the nurse.

"How have we met?" he icily inquired of me.

"Well, we haven't, exactly," I said, "but—"

"She said she *knew* you, Doctor," insisted the nurse. "Otherwise I *never* would have—"

He ignored the nurse and continued his interrogation of me. "Perhaps you'll be good enough to explain just what you are doing here." He

was not unattractive, a sort of Orson Welles type, if Welles had been humorless and skinny as a scarecrow and had spoken with a prickly Scottish
burr, but I was glad *I* wasn't going home with him. Had Ginevra actually
fallen in love with him or had she shrewdly chosen someone who would
fiercely protect her from her former notoriety?

Having been warned of his loathing for reporters, especially from the
Star, I said I had been visiting someone in the hospital and on the way out
had recognized Mrs. Brown lying on the gurney outside the ER. "Your
wife and my aunt go to the same hairdresser, and when I heard the nurse
here saying there was nobody to help keep her awake, of course I volun-
teered."

"But you said you *knew* Dr. Brown," the nurse practically shrieked.

"You *asked* me did I know him and I saw you were in such a terrible
hurry to get away that I thought it would be best for Mrs. Brown if I just
said yes."

If looks could kill, I would have been a corpse crumpled at her feet.
My excuse, however, seemed to convince the formidable doctor, who actually went so far as to grudgingly thank me before turning his attention
to his wife.

"Come, love, let's get you home," he said in an entirely different tone.
"I've already signed you out."

"Thanks for your company." I realized she was addressing me. "Please
give my regards to your aunt."

I heard her explaining to her husband as I walked away, "She was making me recite poetry so I wouldn't fall asleep."

"Oh, good, Emma, there you are!"

Alex de Costa was advancing toward me at an alarming speed. I put a
finger to my lips to shush him. I needed to remain incognito to the press-
hating Dr. Brown if I was to follow up on a future meeting. She had left
the door open for it. Though knowing my name, she had referred to me
simply as "she" to her husband.

10.

Diver Gets
Bends in
Rescue Try

By Emma Gant
Star Staff Writer

A 22-year-old Metro police rescue diver was rushed to a decompression chamber in Key West Wednesday afternoon after he passed out in his search for another diver believed to have drowned.

Metro police said Luke Kessell suffered the bends, a temporary paralysis of the nervous system, when he came up too fast from 80 feet of water in a rock pit at SW 80th Ave. and 57th St.

Kessel was searching for the body of Allan Riding, 24, of 505 NE 15th St., a skin diver.

His mother, Mrs. Ruth Riding, of the same address, told police her son had been practicing endurance underwater swimming with a snorkel tube and mask.

The search for Riding was suspended when Kessell became ill. He was taken to Jackson Memorial Hospital in a semiconscious condition and placed in an iron lung before being flown to the special chamber aboard a salvage ship in Key West.

Former Palm Island
Madam Takes Overdose

Mrs. Edwin Brown, of 286 Crandon Dr., Key Biscayne, formerly Ginevra Snow, the madam who turned prosecutor's witness in the 1953 "Queen of the Underworld" prostitution trial in the Dade County Court of Crimes, was treated for an overdose of a sleeping drug at Jackson Memorial Hospital on Wednesday night and later released into the care of her husband, Dr. Edwin Brown.

Buy of the Week:
Swagger Look
On a Budget

Look like Garbo on a budget? That swagger look, characterized by the casually belted trench coat and the nonchalant slouch hat popularized back in the 1930s by movie stars like Garbo and Dietrich, is back in fashion again. And the look is not limited to high-fashion bank accounts. White trench coat worn by our model is $25. Matching rainproof swagger hat is $15. Where to buy: Call FR 9-0000 after 9:30 a.m. today. Or after 24 hours write to the *Miami Star* Shopping Service, enclosing a stamped, self-addressed envelope.

Star Staff Photo by Jake Rance

"*Muy guapa*," pronounced Alex de Costa, running his fingertips along the bottom of my one-column photo in the *Miami Star* spread out on the table of our booth. We had just finished breakfast at Howard Johnson's and he was admiring Jake Rance's image of me in the raincoat and rain hat. "The swagger lady smiles without pity at the world beneath her feet."

It was eight forty-five on the morning of my twenty-second birthday, or, more accurately, the first day of my twenty-third year. It was the morning after the tornado.

TORNADIC WINDS INJURE 100, HOMES, BUSINESSES BLASTED

was the banner, with Dave Bisbee and Vince Gallo sharing the byline for the lead story beneath it:

NORTHEAST SECTOR HARDEST HIT; TERRIFIED, HURT JAM HOSPITALS

"I was smiling with loathing at the crouching photographer at my feet. He made me take my hair down because he said my face looked fat," I told Alex.

"He has captured your *aplomo*, whatever he said."

"*Aplomo* is the last thing I was feeling."

"*No importa*, it is there in the picture. Amazing girl, your first week on the job and you have three appearances in today's *Star*."

I chose not to disillusion him by confiding my darker view. Let Alex de Costa continue to champion my progress. I could use an in-house champion.

Behind my moat of reserve, however, I was festering over what he called my "three appearances" in today's *Star*. Each of them, to me, exemplified a particular kind of failure. The diver story, buried low on an inside page to leave room for all the tornado coverage, showcased my lack of timeliness. The tiny overdose item, called in to Vince by me and printed without a byline, fell mortifyingly short of my original plan. And the "swagger" photo, which, I had to admit, made me look exactly the way I wished to impress others, was hateful because it made me the creation of Jake Rance. Usurpation lurked everywhere, whether in the form of a late-breaking tornado, a contemptuous photographer, or a deadline (plus a husband who hated reporters) arriving too soon.

"How I would love to have a print of that picture," said Alex.

"I'll see if I can get you one." Though I didn't relish asking Jake Rance for a print; he'd smugly assume I wanted it for myself.

"Enrique Ocampo believes the uprooted palm could be saved, but Luís says the machine to lift it back into place would wreck the pool area. It will have to be chopped up in pieces and hauled away. Magnificent old tree, it's like giving orders to chop up a friend. And this afternoon, I must drive to Palm Beach, to ask Abuelito for another loan to pay my bridge debt, which means staying over for dinner at the Bath and Tennis Club so he can lecture me on all the ways I've failed him. I'd much prefer taking you out for your birthday. How late may I call you when I get back, Emma?"

THE *Star* newsroom was electric with postdisaster importance. People rushed about, trailing long streamers of copy. The green-visored copy editors, four of them seated at the horseshoe desk this morning, slashed pages with *aplomo*, as Alex would say.

Adjacent to Bisbee, who was simultaneously scribbling and pulling at his hair, Gabe Truro, the crime reporter, had commandeered my desk and typewriter. My telephone receiver in its little rubber saddle rode between his shoulder and ear as bursts of copy shot from his fingers—he used all ten of them, a properly trained touch typist. I was watching his performance with reluctant awe when Bisbee looked up and saw me.

"Oh, Emma, we're going to move you back to Joelle's desk for the nonce. Gabe is taking down damage feeds from the reporters out in the field and I need him close by."

"Oh." Shunted off to the outskirts, away from the action.

"Thanks again for showing up last night," he added, as a sop.

"Not much came of it. But I plan to follow up on it."

"On what?"

"You know. Mrs. Brown. Ginevra. The Queen of the Underworld."

"What's to follow up on? Here are a few things for you to get started on."

"But you said last night it would make a good human-interest sidebar on the tornado."

"Yes, well, the tornado was last night." He handed me a half page of copy, raggedly torn off from his typewriter bar. "We'll need these for the early edition."

I was stung by being evicted from my desk so someone more proficient could take down the "damage feeds," and even more by Bisbee's implicit reproof about missing my opportunity for a sidebar, but my spirits really hit rock bottom when I read through my assignments.

emma: get update from all three hospitals on tornado victims
& do yr obits

THEN work on these stys for early edition:
—home tips if storm struck you? power out? perishables? boil well
water, etc.—chk w red cross and fp&l & find out frm dademetro
when trash crews resume pick-ups & where
—call ma bell late aft: how many outgoing long dist calls today—
work up coupla hu int grafs on miamians burning up the wires
telling friends and relatives about tornado
—what to do if another comes? 5–6 grafs—get saf-t tips from
weather bureau

djb

The way to the goal is through the chore. I had learned that from my earliest striving days. But however many goals I amassed, the revulsion at the chores never seemed to diminish. This list was so demeaning I didn't dare even take a consolation break in the ladies' room first.

After decoding "djb's" annoying directives (Was I expected to read and write this lingo? If so, why hadn't they coached us in J-school?) and deciding Bisbee's middle initial stood for "Jerk," I launched myself into my chore-attack mode.

Last night Bisbee had offered me the "plum" of a story on Ginevra and today he was withdrawing her again as stale news. If I were a *Star* reader, I would pounce on an interview with a former madam and star witness of the sensational trial that had made headlines in Miami for weeks. And for those readers who had forgotten or hadn't been around at the time, I could provide a juicy recap of the story, using Norbright's series, before heading into my own in-depth conversations with the Queen of the Underworld. What was her life like now, when she wasn't trying to put herself to sleep? What was their marriage like? How had he proposed? Hadn't she been his patient at the time? What were her thoughts and memories from the Palm Island days—and nights? Did she miss the excitement, being with the other girls, getting them ready for the evening, being *their* Edith Vine?

At this point, certain issues discussed in Dean Ligon's Senior Seminar began rearing their unwelcome heads. The challenge would be finding a way to tell Ginevra's story, the intimate, inside story beyond the Norbright series, without violating anybody's right to privacy or incurring libel suits. But first I had to get the story out of her. I couldn't help feeling cross with Edith Vine for dying. If she'd just hung on, I could have set up a reconciliation with the founder of the Biscayne Academy and her star pupil. My God, what a story! Maybe I would write it anyway, start it in my "Go, Tar Heels!" notebook at the Julia Tuttle, as an exercise: a private mood piece to set the tone of the eventual story. I could begin it tonight, while waiting for Alex to get back from his grandfather's scolding at the Bath and Tennis Club in Palm Beach.

I slid out Joelle Cutter-Crane's Miami-Dade phone book from the drawer it shared with her Fire and Ice nail polish, polish remover, cotton squares, and emery boards, and a September horoscope torn from a magazine. "Your success, Virgo, is allied with your capacity to work—and overwork!" had been underscored twice in red. The diarylike snippet sparked my first feeling of kinship with the unfriendly "ribbon" on the

Star's "package." I could see myself in fifteen years, face and nails assiduously maintained, underlining some similar astrological boost. ("See, Gemini, all your efforts are paying off!")

There were two full pages of Browns, but none of them on Crandon Drive, Key Biscayne. Only an office number for Edwin Brown, MD, at the Dupont Plaza.

My contact Herman Melton had Jackson's updated victim list ready when I called.

"That's the trouble with a day job, Emma, you miss all the excitement," he said sadly. "I was all set to drive back from Hallandale when we heard the news about the twister, but my wife was worried about all those wires being down, and since we're expecting a baby, I didn't want to upset her."

"Herman, listen, I talked to this woman in Emergency last night, she was in for an overdose, you may have seen it in today's paper."

"Sure, the former madam married to Dr. Brown. Was that your story, Emma? I didn't know you were at the hospital last night."

"I caught a ride to Jackson. Bisbee was already there but he left to check out the more serious casualties up at North Shore and Biscayne. Do you happen to know how I might get in touch with her again? There's no residential listing for them in the phone book."

"Ah, sorry, Emma, even if I had one, we're forbidden to give out a private number. You could try calling the doctor's office, or there's always the postal service."

"It's just that we were having a pretty interesting conversation I'd like to follow up on. Not for print, just personal."

"Maybe a note to her on personal stationery would be best, then. I understand he's not friendly to the *Star*, though why should he be? It was before I came here, but lots of people still remember the Queen of the Underworld trial."

Of course they do, damnit!

I called Bisbee's contacts at the other two hospitals. The lists were longer; there was one little boy in critical condition at North Shore, but the parents weren't talking to the press.

Next I called my "fun homes." Interestingly enough, the list of the dead was my shortest yet. Maybe there were one or two getting ready to die and then the tornado got them so excited they forgot to.

Then I shut off my emotions, including those of resentment at Bisbee—"home tips" had "women's department" written all over it—and began tackling, item by item, this trivia list of tornado leftovers.

So grim was my momentum that I actually snarled when I sensed someone standing behind me. Not until after I finished banging out my current "graf"

Opening doors and windows on the north and east sides of a house sometimes will reduce damage if a twister hits. Closed-up houses tend to explode due to extremely low air pressure.

did I deign to look around and acknowledge Lou Norbright's gleaming presence.

"What ferocious concentration," he remarked with some amusement.

"Yes, well, the best way to get through chores is just to get through them." Not my brightest comeback. Also it came out surlier than I had intended. Why could I never strike the right note with this man?

He surveyed the pile of typescript stacked to the right of my typewriter. "These all done?"

"Everything's done on the list Dave Bisbee gave me, except the one about how many Miamians called friends and family long-distance with their tornado adventures, but I won't be able to get the figures from the phone company until right before deadline. Now I just need a snappy closing for this one I'm finishing up. What to do if another twister comes."

"Can I have a look?"

"Sure." I handed up my two triple-spaced pages with their six bite-size *Star* "grafs."

Norbright smiled as he read them. Then, leaning forward, he slid a new sheet of copy paper into Joelle's typewriter. Standing beside my chair, he pecked out a few lines with his index fingers. His hands were square and masculine, with well-kept nails and a shiny gold wedding band.

He rolled out the page and passed it over to me. "How's this?"

He had written me my closing.

In any event, keep calm. Even if a tornado warning is issued for your area, the chance that a tornado will actually strike your home is slight.

Just remember this. The odds are in your favor.

"Think it has enough snap?" he asked.

"Oh, yes. And it's upbeat, too."

"The *Star* tries to be upbeat whenever possible."

He opened Joelle's paste pot and brush-stroked my two pages together, then pasted on his contribution. "In the future, Emma, as soon as you finish a story, put it on the spike instead of stockpiling."

"Oh, I didn't think any of them were that urgent."

"It gets them out of the way for when the urgent ones come in. This time I'll be your copyboy and run these over to Dave."

"I met a friend of yours last night," I said. It came out all wrong. Wrong in tone—too coy—and wrong in timing. He had turned to go, but now he swiveled the top half of his body my way and raised an inquiring eyebrow.

"Mrs. Brown," I said, which also sounded coy. "Ginevra Snow, your Queen of the Underworld; she was at Jackson last night, another overdose, though nobody was paying much attention to her because of the tornado."

"Yes, I saw the item in today's *Star*. It was spunky of you, Emma, to report for duty like that. Dave told me. You're showing the makings of a real newspaper gal."

Wasn't he going to ask anything about the woman who'd made his name? "She said you looked like Cornel Wilde."

Norbright flashed me a new kind of smile best described as razor-edged. "Funny, I always thought of myself as more the Spencer Tracy type. Keep up the good work, Emma."

After he had glided away on his invisible wheels, I bowed my head and flipped unseeingly through the pages of my spiral-bound notepad. All around me tomorrow's newspaper went right on being noisily produced by dozens of others, not one of whom, I congratulated myself, had a clue that I was dissolving in my private little puddle of mortification.

When I was able to focus again, the name of Henry Sprat, widower— "just like in 'Jack Sprat could eat no fat' "—bounced up from the page in my last night's scribble and socked me with a wallop of reproach.

I felt Henry Sprat's disappointment in my gut as he opened this morning's *Star*, all prepared to read about his momentous evening walk with the beautiful Lola—spelled *L-o-l-a*, "just like in 'Whatever Lola wants, Lola gets' "—when flying debris from the twister nicked him in the head and he drove himself bleeding to the hospital where this eager young woman reporter chased after him and wrote down his every utterance. Surely it must be in here somewhere, maybe on the inside, though from the interest she showed he'd sort of counted on front page. There were all these *others* being quoted, with stories not half as interesting as his.

His name hadn't been on the updated victim list I'd got from Herman Melton. I hadn't even remembered the old man's existence when I was taking down the names, too preoccupied with my fury at the chore list ahead and my failure to get a phone number for Ginevra Brown. Jackson Memorial must have released Henry Sprat last night. He would be home now, at 4644 Ingraham Highway—"that's in Coconut Grove"—looking in vain for his generously narrated adventure.

"Well, Lola, looks like the young lady let us down. Come over here, give your old dad a wet kiss. I don't mind so much for myself, but I'd told her how beautiful you are and all about your little runway we built for you and everything."

This remorseful transmigration into another soul was mercifully cut short by Dave Bisbee, accompanied by the hateful photographer Jake Rance with two cameras slung over his chest.

"My, you've been assiduous, Emma. How did you get everything done so fast?"

"I haven't got the long-distance figures from the phone company yet."

"How'd you like Jake's photo this morning? Didn't I tell you you'd look terrific?"

"The raincoat came out well," I said, not looking at Jake Rance. "I'm sure there'll be lots of orders for it. What's the latest on the *damage feeds* from your reporters out in the field?"

Bisbee gave no sign of picking up the sarcasm.

"That one little boy is still in critical at North Shore, but the family's nixed any photos. So we'll have to go with damage and destruction in North Miami. Jake got a shot of a woman standing in front of her roof-less house holding her parakeet in its cage, that'll have to do for the human-interest angle. Too bad Joelle's down in Cuba, she of all people could flesh out the pathos of a rescued parakeet."

"If you can see any damn bird flesh at all," said Jake Rance. "I'll get these in the developer and let you know. There's still time to go out and find something else."

"You'd have been better off with a nice big dog," I said to Bisbee, still ignoring Jake Rance. "A large photogenic dog being reunited with an old man hit in the head by flying debris from the tornado—"

"This is not a creative writing assignment, Emma. Reality has supplied us with a parakeet."

"I know where there's a real chocolate Lab and a sweet old widower. They were taking their evening walk when the tornado struck. He took his dog home and drove himself bleeding to Jackson Memorial Hospital. They must have patched him up and sent him home, because he wasn't on Herman Melton's list this morning. Here's his address." I handed over my notepad to Bisbee.

" 'Henry Sprat, Forty-six Forty-four Ingraham Highway, Coconut Grove,' " Bisbee read aloud from my notes. "Where'd you get this, Emma?"

"At Jackson, last night. I met Mr. Sprat going into the ER; he was the first person I interviewed. But then you put me on the Ginevra Brown watch and, to tell the truth, I forgot all about him." I felt it wise, after my sarcasm, to strike a humble note. Bisbee was, after all, my boss for the interim.

"Who is Lola, as in 'Whatever Lola wants'?"

"That's the Lab. Maybe Mr. Rance could shoot a reconciliation scene between man and dog. At least readers will be able to see the dog."

11.

HAVING MADE HENRY SPRAT an extremely happy old man, we roared off again to the *Star* in Jake Rance's low-to-the-ground red Karmann Ghia reeking of pipe tobacco. Rance drove with his chin thrust forward, pipe clenched between his teeth, making an intense to-do about shifting gears, as though he were in a driving contest. The car was loud and we exchanged the minimum of words on the trip out and back. I was trapped in a small, noisy capsule with someone completely uninterested in my proximity. Though, as soon as Bisbee had suggested we go together to Mr. Sprat's house in Coconut Grove, I realized it was in the best interests of my career to be nice to the sullen Pulitzer Prize–winning photographer.

And watching him in action, lunging about on his uneven polio legs, chanting "Beautiful, beautiful . . . oh, that's a knockout, you two!" as he snapped away at the small man with bandaged head and his large dog repeatedly charging into each other's embrace, I did feel an ebbing of hostility. He was so totally absorbed in his work. And when, at the last, he catered to the old widower's timid request for "a portrait of Lola and me" posed in front of a framed photograph of the late Mrs. Sprat, I decided Jake Rance had human qualities after all.

Back at the *Star,* I typed up my specified "four-graf" story, which Bisbee pronounced my "best crowd-pleaser so far," though he immediately went on to spoil it by wondering if Joelle Cutter-Crane's "spirit" had seeped into me since I'd been working at her desk.

When Jake Rance brought the prints out to Bisbee, they were so endearingly packed with man-and-dog love that I found myself gushing, "They're perfect, how did you do it?"

"What is it you always tell them, Rance? Get your frame and then shoot the hell out of it?" Bisbee answered for the photographer.

"Something like that," said Jake Rance, not acknowledging my outburst. "Then shoot a few extra rolls, just in case."

"Well," I said, stung by his ungraciousness, "I'd better get cracking on how many Miamians made long-distance calls about the tornado."

As I stepped into the elevator at the end of my workday, there was Jake Rance, his cameras slung over his chest.

"Hello, again," he said.

"Going out on another assignment?" I kept my tone cordial but indifferent.

"I'm going home. Want a lift?"

Assuming I had misheard him, I didn't answer.

"It's raining," he said.

"Oh no, not *again.*"

"Be glad to run you to wherever you're going."

"Oh, I live . . . my hotel is in walking distance."

"Suit yourself." He looked put out.

"Well, if it's not *too* much out of your way."

"It can't be *too* much out of my way if it's in walking distance." I could swear he was mimicking me. He fished his pipe out of his crumpled fatigue jacket, jammed it between his teeth, and began that infuriating process of putting everything on hold while he lit up. We descended to the underground parking area in silence.

"What's your hotel?" he asked as we rumbled out into the driving rain.

"The Julia Tuttle. You turn right on Miami Avenue and—"

"I know where it is." Deep draw on the pipe. "Why are you staying there?"

"What's wrong with it?"

"Nothing's wrong with it, but it's for Cubans."

"My aunt here knows the manager and he gave me a good monthly rate."

"You speak Spanish?" Glimmer of respect shaded with envy.

"I understand it better than I speak it. There were Cubans at my school in North Carolina. In fact, there's a woman staying at the Julia Tuttle who graduated from my school; her husband just lost his sugar plantation to Castro. She's somewhat older than me."

A sarcastic twitch of his cheek. "And you must be all of what?"

"As of today I'm twenty-two. Today's my birthday."

Why had I played that card?

"Do you drink yet?"

"Pardon me?"

"Partake of alcohol."

"Oh, sure. Wine with dinner. The occasional Beefeater martini."

"Can I buy you a martini on your birthday?"

"Thank you, but I don't think the Julia Tuttle has a cocktail lounge."

"If that's a no, you need to be more specific."

Did this man simply refuse to play the manners game?

I was about to say I was tired of being specific after a day of taking down boring post-tornado data and be rid of Jake Rance then and there, but the mention of a Beefeater had reminded me of Paul and the fact that he was not going to be calling up to my room on the house phone tonight.

"No, it's not a no," I said.

He gave a strange eruption, which I subsequently realized was a laugh. "We'll go over to the Araby on the Venetian Causeway. They're liberal with their cocktail snacks."

THIS MORNING there had been Alex at Howard Johnson's, running his fingers worshipfully along the bottom of my photo in the raincoat, using words like *"guapa"* and *"aplomo"* ("handsome . . . with aplomb") and telling me I was "amazing" to have three "appearances" in today's newspaper.

And now here was Jake Rance at the Araby, spearing a hot sausage with a toothpick and saying he hadn't thought much of me up on the roof when I'd been modeling the raincoat. "When Marge said you were the new reporter, I thought, What are they doing now, recruiting sorority girls? Or does her father know someone on the masthead?"

"It might interest you to know I was too poor to be in a sorority and my father was killed on the way to the hospital on the day of my birth."

"If you'd let me finish, I was going to say I've changed my mind after seeing you in action with old Sprat and then reading your copy."

How to respond? Oh, thank you, kind sir—which could lead into a sarcastic round of fencing and possibly set the tone of all our future exchanges. Or shame him with punctilious cordiality and at the same time "draw him out." As I was beginning to suspect that Jake Rance was just naturally rude the way some dogs are just naturally spotted, I decided I might as well hone my skills as an interviewer.

"What does it feel like to win a Pulitzer?" I asked, helping myself to more crabmeat dip on a cracker.

"You know you've got a meal ticket for the rest of your working life."

"Oh, come on, don't be so cynical. I mean, when you picked up the phone and somebody said—"

"Didn't happen like that. I was in the darkroom and my managing editor yelled it through the door."

"Were you utterly surprised or had you been secretly hoping?"

He winced. "I don't go in for utterlys and secretlys, even in the best of times. And it was a bad time for me. I'd only been back in Detroit for a couple of months and my head was still full of pictures I wanted to forget, including the ones that won the prize. As I recall, I went out to a bar that night and tied one on."

"What were the pictures of?"

"You can look them up in the morgue. The *Star* did a spread when I joined the staff here."

I contemplated the winking sign over the bar. A fat little neon sheik riding cross-legged on his magic carpet:

THE ARABY—FOR A "POTENT-DATE"!

Sheik = potentate. It took me a minute to work out the pun. The silence felt good, as my cordiality reserves were depleted. This was anything but a potent date. I helped myself to a sausage. Might as well fill up on snacks. Maybe Alex would get back in time to take me out for another of those *medianoches*.

"Two million lives lost in three years," Jake Rance was muttering between pipe puffs as he drove me to the Julia Tuttle. "And the thirty-eighth parallel didn't move a goddamned inch. Any day now, we should be invading Cuba. If we went around the world to fight Communists in Korea, what's stopping us from going ninety miles south?"

"*Señorita* Gant, you hab mail!" handsome Mr. Ocampo announced happily, pushing two packages, some cards, and two pink message slips across the desk. "*Espera,* is more!"

He ducked around a corner and returned bearing a long florist's box. Meanwhile I had read the messages, both from Alex, a 3:10 p.m. one saying "Delayed until tomorrow" and a 5:30 p.m. one saying "Return with mother tonight. Will call if not too late."

"*Perdón, señorita,* but you need *un florero* for the flowers!" Mr. Ocampo's hands made sweeping undulations, pantomiming the thing he lacked the word for. "If not, we search you one."

"You mean a vase?"

"*Sí,* base! Thank you."

"No, I don't have a vase."

"*Pronto,* I have send to your room."

"Well, if it's not too much trouble."

"No trouble, *señorita.* Our pleasure."

On my upward elevator journey, I transmigrated briefly into Mr. Ocampo's soul. A very short time ago he had been riding around on his sugar plantation giving orders and greetings in his native language. I pictured him symbolically on horseback, though with ten thousand acres to cover, it was more likely he would bop around in his own little airplane, dropping down to consult with his overseers and bestowing señorial encouragement in his upper-class Spanish on the tired but smiling peons leaning against their machetes. And now here he was making Spanglish hash, a part-time desk clerk in a foreign hotel. If, overnight, I were to be deprived of the fluency I took for granted, the rug would be pulled out from under whatever *aplomo* others thought I possessed. My familiar consonants would mutate into God knew what mush, and even my posture would suffer from all that obsequious bobbing and flailing to make myself understood.

I opened the flower box first. A dozen roses in many colors, each stem immersed in its little ampule of water.

Happy Birthday, darling.

It was the precious illegible scrawl, but the message was uncompromising enough to have been penned by anyone. It was the first time he had written the word "darling" and the first time he had left off the "Paul." This card could be on exhibition to anyone who came into the room. Whom did he imagine coming to my room? I felt a double wrench of love for my secret man. He had made arrangements for these flowers before he left Miami so he could write the card himself. And what he had written not only conveyed his love but made room for me to have a life without him.

Mother's package included my Spanish-English dictionary—this was Mother at her best, anticipating my needs—and the white silk head scarf I had hinted that I wanted. As always, she had made her card, this time a watercolor of a Chinese mother and daughter jointly flying a striped kite, and inside, only "Love, Mother." Enclosed in the same envelope, to save postage, was a tiny second painting, not as well executed, of three Chinese children waving from a hilltop, with the signatures, such as they were, of the little ones.

Loney had sent me some lavender bubble bath and the present I knew I was getting: a white Ship 'n Shore drip-dry blouse with my initials embroidered on the breast pocket. I had picked out the cursive script I wanted from a book of designs, made a stencil of the *EG*, and chosen the colors (carmine letters edged in royal blue, ornamented with arabesques and foliations in jonquil yellow and verdant green), and Loney's exquisite needlework had done the rest. My escutcheon, at last.

Loney's love could transform a store-bought card (this had a simple spray of violets on the front) into a message for you alone. Often I had watched her perform this magic in the drugstore, picking up one card after another, sniffing at the pictures as she always sniffed at milk, rejecting one verse after another until suddenly a connection would be made with a particular card, which she would proclaim to be "just right" for the receiver. The invisible-ink message inside this card assured me not only that I was the dearest person in Loney's world, but that I was altogether pretty exceptional.

A knock at the door: Enrique Ocampo himself delivering a chipped cabbage-colored plaster vase that had never been a beauty.

"*No es hermoso*, this base, *señorita*, but is the only one we meet." His gaze danced approvingly on the display of roses tumbling out of their florist box on my bed. "But soon you will disappear it with your . . ." He mimed someone arranging flowers. "Your . . . *composición! ¡Felicidades, señorita!*"

The door swung shut on his retreating figure before I could thank him properly. Shouldn't I have tipped him?

Then it occurred to me that this might be the very awkwardness he was fleeing from.

There was one more card to get out of the way before I turned to the sacred task of "composing" Paul's flowers. (Some of Mr. Ocampo's hit-or-miss translations were downright inspiring; I loved the idea of meeting a vase.)

Any missive from my stepfather, even a commercial birthday card, could be counted on to pack a wallop of encroachment and insinuation. How did he do it? In his own way, Earl was as effective as Loney when it came to sending his spirit through the mail.

This one came with *layers* of intrusion. Somehow Earl had managed to locate (it looked a little shopworn) a birthday card of a Vargas Girl, with hair exactly my color, looking provocatively over her shoulder at the viewer. She sported a fishing rod and wading boots and a man's denim jacket, which, along with her let-down hair, barely covered her naked butt. Now, to be fair, I liked Vargas Girls—even though Earl had introduced them to me. He had allowed me to cut them out of his old GI calendar to paste in my scrapbooks, along with my Jon Whitcomb magazine girls with their tip-tilted profiles and off-the-shoulder gowns. But, right off, here was Earl shoving his way in with a shared memory. The greeting alone ("To a very special Miss on her birthday") could have been for a girl turning twelve, were it not for the bosomy Miss on the front. Likewise, the message inside ("To tell you on this special day that you're specially nice to know") was harmless in itself, but not with the pinup. This card was probably designed for a *Playboy* subscriber to send to his paramour.

To up the ante, Earl had appended two postscripts in his pert block-print handwriting. Following his favorite quote to annoy me with, "I count only the sunny hours" (Hazlitt's "On a Sun-Dial," from *A Treasury of English and American Verse*), came one of his typical out-of-left-field rebukes: "Pick up the phone occasionally and make your mother and grandmother happy."

AFTER DISPATCHING Earl's card to the bathroom wastebasket, I took a few deep breaths before embarking on the arrangement of my flowers. Paul was not here, but his roses were. Not tonight, but next weekend we would be sipping our Beefeaters and eating our New York strip steaks and snuggling together afterwards in the "ambassador's" quarters over at P. Nightingale's, where poor Alex lost less money gambling in the winter season because no IOUs were accepted there. (Why was Alex bringing his *mother* back from Palm Beach?)

Meanwhile Paul loved me, I was his darling, he might well be thinking of me right now, almost 6:30 p.m., which he knew was the time of my birth. It was also when the doors opened for dinner at the Nightingale Inn and Paul put the march from *The Bridge on the River Kwai* on the stereo and stood by the door in one of his elegant suits, greeting the guests as they filed in.

Here's the first rose, a red one, for you, Mr. Nightingale, gent extraordinaire. You gave me the courage to come to this city, you restored my faith in men.

And, well, maybe a red rose for my father. Without Preston Gant's biological contribution, Paul would have no Emma to send flowers to. Thank you, Father, for charming my mother, at least long enough to get me under way.

What *right* had Jake Rance to be so rude? Driving me back to the Julia Tuttle, he had lashed out savagely when I asked, mainly to seem interested in Korea and his Pulitzer, about the significance of the thirty-eighth parallel: "How uninformed women are! You never know any *facts*. You were how old in 1953, sixteen? Where *were* you? What were you thinking of? Didn't you ever pick up a newspaper or hear people talk?"

Now a yellow rose for Paul. The first time I saw him he was wearing a yellow polo shirt. Last June, I had answered an ad for a waitress at a "small family resort" on Lake Henderson, thirty miles outside Mountain City, and he had come to the house—Earl and Mother's—to interview me. The waitress job at the plush resort in Blowing Rock had fallen through at the last minute, and I was willing to take anything with room and board to get me out of the range of Earl's temper and his nightly prowls.

I was in the front yard, reading a library copy of *The Confessions of Felix Krull, Confidence Man (The Early Years)* and watching my little half sister and half brother splash in their plastic wading pool while Mother, seven months pregnant with a third child, took a nap indoors.

A dark green Buick station wagon with wood panels drew up in front of the house and a middle-aged man with tawny skin and cropped crinkly gray hair rolled down his window. "Is this the Gant house?" he inquired in a soft nasal drawl.

"It's the Brady house, actually," I said, rising from the deck chair, "but you're in the right place. I'm Emma Gant."

He stepped out of the wagon, a trim Levantine figure in pleated silvery trousers, yellow Lacoste shirt tucked neatly inside his alligator belt, and black-and-white spectator shoes.

"I'm Paul Nightingale."

We shook hands. The sophisticated scent emanating from him was a universe away from the college-boy brands I was familiar with.

"So you worked for the peerless McCord last summer at Blowing Rock. I've seen him in action over at the Deauville during the winter season. I have a modest establishment on the Beach myself."

"He wrote me in May that Blowing Rock had been sold and the new owners weren't hiring college kids anymore," I said. "He's gone back to Europe because of the terrible winter in Miami; nobody made any money."

"It was the worst winter in tourist history."

"Did you have a bad winter at your place?"

"No, we had a fair season, but thank you for asking. My place on the Beach is a supper club, mostly locals who know one another and want a good steak and some light entertainment. When it hit forty degrees, we turned on the heat and opened the cloakroom. The ladies were tickled to have a genuine excuse to get out their minks. Too bad about McCord. The spectacle of him setting his long legs in motion and sailing across a dining room with his tasseled menus was something to see. You must know your stuff if he trained you. Our Nightingale Inn will be small potatoes for you."

"We had to make these tiny diagrams on our order pads," I said. "If Mr. McCord ever overheard a waitress asking her table 'Who gets the chicken and who gets the fish?' she was down the mountain in a flash."

Paul Nightingale laughed. He had small, even teeth with no fillings.

"Out of the twenty of us who started with him," I went on, hell-bent on landing this job, however small-potatoes it was, and getting out of Earl's clutches, "eleven of us survived the training week. Only eight of us lasted out the whole summer."

Mr. Nightingale was looking more and more delighted with me.

"Wouldn't you like to bring your visitor in?" Mother, finished with her nap, had called from the porch.

THERE WERE four red roses, two yellow, two coral, two pink, one white, and one mauve. The florist's random selection from the day's offerings? ("He said a mixed bunch, might as well get rid of some of these stragglers.") Or had Paul specified how many of each color? I wouldn't put it past him, the man who knew to the ounce how much gin you needed before your shrimp cocktail came. I fantasized that I was tapping into his private code. What, for instance, if not my bruised face, could this single mauve rose represent in our shared history?

My heart still sank when I remembered Paul Nightingale's recoil at the sight of me when I stepped off the Trailways bus from Mountain City the morning after our interview.

"Christ, kid, how did you get that shiner?"

"Oh, saying goodbye to my stepfather." I tried to keep it light, but I could see he was shocked by the sight of me. This was not what he had come to pick up from the Lake Henderson bus station and take back to his "family hotel" to wait on his guests.

"Let me understand this," Earl had begun the night before, his throat already engorged with the tension that heralded a conflict. "You prefer to wait tables at a kike 'family' hotel, when you could stay in your own home in comfort and lighten your mother's load and get paid a substantial weekly allowance by me. Those Miami Jews will run you ragged and then stiff you and you'll come bellyaching to me at the end of the summer that you didn't make any tips and can't go back to school."

"Please, Earl"—my mother, resorting to her peacekeeping role— "we're not even sure it *is* a Jewish hotel. And Mr. Nightingale seemed a gentleman in every respect."

"Hell, if his name is Nightingale, mine is goddamn Woody Woodpecker. And everybody knows Lake Henderson has been ruined by the Jews."

"Well, I'm going all the same," I said. I folded a sweater and laid it carefully in my suitcase. "I don't care whether his name is really Nickelbaum or Noodleberger."

Stop now, while you're ahead, a well-known inner voice urged—in vain. "Whatever his name is, he's more of a gentleman than you'll ever be."

WHAP.

RED, RED, yellow, and now the mauve. As Enrique Ocampo had predicted, my flower *composición* was "disappearing" the dowdy vase. The dusky purple added a lugubrious note to the festive hues of its companions, reminding me that my shiner from Earl, as unpropitious as it had seemed that day, had set up the ideal circumstances for Paul's and my affair.

"Kid, I can't take you to the Inn looking like this," my new boss had said, driving us past the entrance to the Nightingale Inn. "But I don't relish the idea of sending you back to Mountain City on the next bus."

"I don't want to go back."

He was driving slowly around a lake choked with water lilies. "Here's what I'm going to propose, then." He turned off the main road. "All this property used to be a girls' camp," he explained as we bumped along a rutted dirt road winding between clusters of abandoned cabins. We passed through a tunnel of towering rhododendron until the road ended in front of a solitary cabin with new porch furniture and venetian blinds.

"My aunt Stella fixed this up for me," he said, idling the motor. "It's supposed to be my hideaway, where I can come to collect myself and make payroll. I'm going to suggest you stay here until that shiner fades. Then you can join the rest of my staff up at the Inn. As I told your mother, the young people have a wing all to themselves. The cabin's amenities are pretty basic, but it's peaceful and you look like you could use a little peace. I'll send Stella down, she's a wizard with skin, she worked for Guerlain in Paris before the Occupation. Now she creates custom scents for her Miami clients. We'll just say when I picked you up at the bus station you had a bad cold, so we quarantined you here. If that's agreeable to you."

"It's very generous of you. And don't worry, I heal pretty quickly from this kind of thing."

He gave me a sharp glance and seemed on the verge of asking me something, but didn't.

"I'm going to do a good job for you as soon as I'm presentable," I said.

"I haven't the least doubt of it." He switched off the ignition. "I'll go in with you and remove my things. My wife Bev was in such pain just before we flew her down to Miami for the hysterectomy that she wanted our room to herself up at the Inn."

Thanks to the resilience of my young skin, and to Aunt Stella's comfrey poultices and cosmetic arts, I was on the job within the week. Yet, also thanks to her, I never did move up to the employees' wing at the Inn. I forged an immediate bond with this independent little wrinkled fashion plate, with her French scarves and scents, and her curious amalgam of Gallic and Yiddish witticisms. While she ministered to my face, we exchanged pivotal chapters from our past struggles. My black eye naturally led into the saga of my decadelong campaign to escape Earl-dom. Which elicited Stella's tale of how she had escaped bourgeois life with her department-store-owning father in Leipzig after her younger sister Lily ran away to America with one of the salesclerks. ("Poor Ernst was not at all comme il faut, and he was a *schmendrick* in the bargain, but he rescued Lily from Leipzig; they even produced darling Paul between them before Ernie perished from a burst appendix. But who was going to rescue *me* from the family store? I had to think fast or surrender my fate to my father's will. You see, Poppa had decided that I was to take over the business.")

IT WAS Stella's judgment, at the end of her ministrations to me, that I was too mature to be herded into dormitory quarters with the "boychiks and girlchiks" up at the Inn. "She's going to be a writer," she told Paul, "and she needs her privacy."

Whenever I indulged myself in connecting the dots of my fate as it was unfurling, I had to wonder how much my remaining in the cabin had contributed to Paul's and my love affair. It would have happened sooner or later, I was sure, because there was a mutual attraction from the beginning. But, just as Earl's whack had necessitated my temporary asylum in the cabin, Stella's suggestion that I stay on there certainly expedited things.

The story got around that I had begun a novel and that Stella and Mr. Nightingale had turned over the cabin to me so I could write during my off-hours. This gave me a certain mystique among the other college help, who were eager to go out and party as soon as serving hours were over. When Bev returned from Miami after recuperating from her hysterectomy, she added her respectful enthusiasm to my literary ambitions, meanwhile teaching me how to walk and to pin up my hair in a French twist like hers.

One of the two remaining red roses would commemorate the inauguration of my idyll with Paul. Still hiding out with my black eye, I had asked him to bring me the second volume of *Felix Krull* from the library when he drove into Mountain City for supplies. He had returned looking as crestfallen as a father who has failed his child.

"Kid, I couldn't get it for you because there *isn't* a volume two. Mann died before he got a chance to write it, the librarian said. She sent this, though; I hope you haven't read it." It was a much-tattered copy of *Death in Venice and Seven Other Stories.* I said I hadn't, and went on to thank him profusely. A new look flickered across his face. He tripped over the doorsill as he backed out of the cabin.

That was as far as it went. But a few days later, after it had gone a lot further, he told me that's when it had begun for him. "I saw your disappointment and how you decided to lie about the other book so I wouldn't feel bad. Also I was touched that you didn't know he hadn't finished it, a smart kid like you. Like with the shiner, I wanted to protect you. But now I also knew I wanted to make you happy. If it had been in my power, I would have produced that second volume out of thin air so I could bring you the rest of your story."

I WAS about to unplug the third red rose from its capsule when my phone rang.

"I was just putting in a red rose to commemorate the first time you kissed me in the cabin," I would say. Though it was unlikely he could get away to call me when the guests were still filing in to dinner.

But it was only Tess, full of excitement, wanting to know how I'd weathered the tornado.

"Well, a big royal palm fell into the pool, and our power was out for a while, but I went right over to—"

However, Tess plunged into her own adventures before I could embark on mine. "Julio and Genio's bungalow had extensive water damage, so we've been busy all day transferring some important equipment they were storing for us to dry locations."

Julio and Genio? Oh, right, the twin nephews who'd just come over from Cuba, who had loaded the dental equipment into Hector's Cadillac—good Lord, was it only three nights ago? I'd been meeting more new people than I could digest the names of.

"Was it those drills we picked up at the airport?"

"What drills? Oh, of course, the *drills!* What a good memory you have, Emma. No, *that* equipment is in place, this is . . . some more equipment. But enough about me—are you okay?"

Just as well Tess either didn't know or hadn't remembered it was my birthday, since I had something more important I was dying to tell her. "Listen, Tess, guess who I met last night at the hospital?"

"The hospital! What were you doing in the hospital? Here I've been going on about our silly equipment—were you hurt?"

"No, the hospital's part of my beat now. I'm taking it over for Bisbee while he's deputy city editor. As soon as the tornado hit last night I went right over to Jackson."

"You amazing child. *You'll* be an editor next—"

"No, listen, Tess. I met *her* last night. The Queen of the Underworld. She was lying right out in the hall, on a gurney."

"The queen of *what*? You met *who*? Oh, my God! You mean Ginevra Snow? You met Ginevra Snow? Was she in the tornado?"

"No, she'd taken another overdose but they'd pumped her out and couldn't pay much attention to her because of all the people coming in with injuries. There was a small item in today's *Star*—I guess you missed it."

"Emma, I haven't even had a chance to sit down, much less look at today's paper. You say you *met* her?"

"We talked."

"She was able to talk? What did you talk about?"

"Well, for one thing, she said she still dreamed about Miss Edith. She said, 'I'm sorry Miss Edith passed away before I got a chance to tell her my side of the story.' "

"She actually *said* that? Oh, Emma, this makes me want to cry! But why were you talking about Miss Edith?"

"Well, because of you. I'd said you'd seen her at Michel's on Miracle Mile and I described you and she said oh yes, you always smiled at her and you look like Jean Harlow."

"Did she really say that?"

"Yes, and I told her you would have spoken, but you valued your own privacy and wanted to respect hers."

"Well said, Emma. That's very true."

"But I did tell her you had both gone to Edith Vine's Biscayne Academy and that you had taught there before you married. That's when she talked about wishing she could have explained herself to Miss Edith. I hope it was all right I told her you went there, too."

"Perfectly all right. Emma, all this is giving me goose bumps. I certainly *will* speak the next time I see her at Michel's. But is all this in your story?"

"No, see, that's the problem. Her husband, that Dr. Brown, showed up and put a stop to it. What's in the paper is just a teeny item telling about the overdose and reminding readers of who she was. It doesn't even have my byline. But here's where you come in, Tess. I know she wants to talk to me again, but we have to do it without him knowing. If you could find

out when her next hairdresser's appointment is, I could maybe arrange to
be there."

"Well, I don't know, Emma. I don't think I can ask Michel. He's fierce
about protecting his clients' privacy."

"Couldn't you just look through his book?"

"If Michel caught me looking at his book, Emma, I'd be looking for
another hairdresser."

"Sorry, bad idea. Forget it, I'll think of something else. That's part of
the challenge of being a reporter."

"No, wait, Emma, let me give this some thought. We need to get together again soon for dinner anyway. I want to hear all about it, but right
now, I'm still at Hector's office, rescheduling appointments in *our* book.
I just wanted to see if you were okay."

"I'm fine, Tess. And I really appreciate your concern."

"When you next write to your mother, be sure and send her my love."

"I certainly will. And will you please forget my stupid idea?"

"No, Emma, just let me give it some thought. I'd like to help you if I
can. Why, I'd like to get to know her myself! Let me see what I can
arrange."

ANOTHER THUNDERSHOWER was in progress outside my window.
I'd been in Miami five days now without seeing the sun. Huge severed
chunks of the poor royal palm lay ready to be carted away. I was certain
Alex had closed his eyes when the chain saw took its first bite. It had been
"like giving orders to chop up a friend," he'd said. If I'd known about him
bringing his mother back, I would have stuffed myself with more hot
sausages and crabmeat dip at the Araby. Best thing to do probably would
be swallow two aspirins and hope they'd make me fall asleep before I got
hungry again.

Tess had broken the spell of my color-coded-rose ritual, but I made
myself complete it anyway. Mother surely deserved the last of the reds
for having me. Then I'd switch to the coral, which were also beautiful, to
commemorate another high point with Paul: when he had driven me back

to college at the end of last summer. We had stopped overnight at a famous "restricted" golf resort in Pinehurst, where Paul signed us in as Mr.
and Mrs. Tom Mann. Next morning he played nine holes on foot with
me tagging along. The autumnal air was poignant with our imminent
parting. We were plotting our keeping-in-touch tactics for the long separation, when Paul sank a putt with the ease of someone in a dream and
announced: "Got it."

"You sure did," I replied, thinking he meant the hole in one.

"No, I've got it figured out," he said. "At Christmas we'll get you to
Miami, and then next June you'll start work on the *Miami Star.*"

When I asked how all this was going to come about, he said, "Easy.
I'll take care of the Christmas part and you're gonna do the rest."

Loney wouldn't care what colors she got, as long as they were from me,
so I gave her the remaining yellow and both pink, since Mother couldn't
stand pink. That left the other coral, which I dedicated to my first raise
on the *Star.* That left the single white rose, which I decided should por-
tend my satisfied death, knowing I had fulfilled my destiny—unlike the
stay-at-home old maid who had died while hearing my train pass.

Later, as I was soaking in Loney's lavender bubble bath, I recalled these
serials in her beloved magazines. *"To be continued,"* or *"To be concluded,"* it
would say at the end of each installment. And then at the top of next
month's continuation, there would be a little box in italics: *"The story so
far . . ."*

The story so far: Emma has arrived in Miami, and . . .

I got into my pajamas—the drip-dry blue ones with white sailboats
that Loney and I had bought in the boys' department at Belk's before I
went off to college. I also had a yellow pair with navy stripes from the
same shopping trip. After seven years of having been forced to wear the
shortie nightgowns Earl brought home from the chain store where he was
training unsuccessfully to become management material, I had wanted
classic sleepwear with legs and arms and some privacy.

I swallowed three aspirins—surely nobody died from just *one* extra—

and settled back on the pillows to await sleep. If Paul called, it would be a pleasure to wake up, and if Alex called later for *medianoches*, I could always dress again.

I played with "Emma's story so far" awhile longer and then, rather than counting sheep, began making a mental list of all the people I had met since boarding the train last Saturday.

First Major Marjac ("Weaponry is opening up to women in an unprecedented way!"), and then Luís at the hotel desk, and the exiled Ocampos surrounded by their stockade of luggage, and Clarence the bellman, and Alex, and the potbellied proprietor in the pink guayabera at La Bodega. Then the whole *Miami Star* crew: Rod Reynolds; Bisbee; Joelle Cutter-Crane; Pat and Ed on the copydesk; Gabe Truro, the touch-typing crime reporter; Bert, the books and religion editor; Moira Parks of the morgue with her massive shears; Marge, the friendly Women's Section editor, whose glass cage I was determined to avoid; humorless personnel inquisitor Harry Harmon; Mr. Feeney and his capable secretary, Liz; and of course Norbright, "Lucifer," though he seemed to require a class of encounter all his own. And Jake Rance the Rude. And Julio and Genio, the Cuban twins, who had slipped my mind; and Mr. Sprat with his Lola; and Ginevra and Dr. Brown and the nurse Ginevra had called a "sadistic bitch."

But then, what about the borderline cases, like the photographer Don Kingsley, who had gone to Cuba with Joelle; or Charles P. Rose, who had yelled at me over the phone, but whom I hadn't seen in the flesh—and, likewise, Herman Melton, my hospital contact?

I made a second column for these "once-removed" people I had merely brushed against but hadn't actually met. They kept popping up in no particular order: the two men who were ousted from Alex's grandfather's table at La Bodega, the men playing dominoes in the lobby of the Julia Tuttle, the airport official who had stuck his head into the Cadillac and been dazzled by Tess's beauty, the waiter at the Americana who hadn't been quick enough to light Paul's cigarette. ("But we'll give him three out of ten," Paul had said, "because he recognized his mistake and because I'm happy tonight.") And the two men riding up with me in the hotel elevator, the gloomy one with the new work permit, who "shat" on Fidel, and his friend, who had apologized to me afterwards for the obscenity. Oh, yes, and the three middle-aged people in their bathing suits and rain hats on the passing yacht that first rainy afternoon.

And what about the "twice-removed" people I had heard about through the stories of the first-column people? Did they need another column? Tess's boss Hector and Hector's wife, Asunción; and Tess's hairdresser, Michel, and her late friend Edith Vine; and the fired reporter, Kirk, who had "tried to bring in the union," and had left his condoms and his rubbers in my bottom drawer. And Alex's mother, Lídia, with her quintet of husbands and her causes, who was en route with her son this very evening into my first column.

"She is between causes," Alex had said. "At least I think so." And then had added: "Lídia would approve of you. You're like her in some ways."

Part Two

Each one of us is in danger
of not being the unique
and untransferable self
that he is.

—JOSÉ ORTEGA Y GASSET,
The Revolt of the Masses

12.

I WAS WALKING DOWN a road, watching myself walking down a
road, and someone was walking toward me.

"What you need to do to protect yourself," coached my watcher self,
"is say this person's name loud and clear." But the sun was in my eyes and
all I saw was the figure approaching. I couldn't even tell whether it was a
man or a woman.

I awakened sweaty in a cradle of buttery morning light for the first
time since I'd taken up residence at the Julia Tuttle.

Still under the omen of the dream, I snapped up the window blinds to
confront an almost aggressive tropical blue sky. To the right was the roof
of the *Star* building, where I had posed for Jake Rance on the eve of the
tornado. Down the Miami River puttered a motorboat towing a barge.
The barge had an outlandish little house sitting on it—did someone actually live in it? The whole affair was too low for the drawbridge to need
to ring its bells and go up, and recalled to me against my will a joke told
by a boy at a fraternity party back in Chapel Hill.

"Hey, girls, wanna know the height of male vanity? This gnat is floating down the river on his back, and he calls out, 'Raise the drawbridge!' "

Followed by the pause it took for the girls to "get it," and turn the
obligatory shade of pink; followed by the prurient haw-hawing of the
joke teller, who happened to be my date.

The chopped-up giant palm down by the pool looked sadder than ever in this cruel sunshine. When would Alex have the pieces removed? I wondered. As if conjured by my question, a whiplash of a little woman in a white dress and Panama hat shot into view, trailing two brown-chested men in Levi's jeans and work boots. She jabbed her finger toward the dismembered tree, then with other staccato hand gestures appeared to be describing more things she wanted done. The hulking men nodded. Her hat and wraparound sunglasses hid her face, but even from five floors up I could tell she was used to having her orders carried out promptly.

Alex, in a baby blue polo shirt, ambled into view, hands thrust deep into his pants pockets, pulling the material of the chinos tight across his rump. He slouched apart from the action with a sort of languid resignation while the woman, followed by her bare-chested retainers, continued to dart about, jabbing and pointing and making her designs in the air.

Damn, damn, damn. Though I was ravenous to get to Howard Johnson's to have my breakfast and check out my stories in today's *Star*, I took extra time dressing and making up my face in case I had to run Lídia's gauntlet—for who else could it be down there but Alex's mother?

They were in the lobby when I came down, Alex chatting in Spanish with the men at their dominoes table in the corner, their little transistor turned faithfully to Radio Reloj for the minute-by-minute news update from Cuba. The woman had removed her Panama hat and was frowning down at the Mediterranean tiles. (Was she thinking of replacing them?) Her dark glasses now perched tiara-like on top of her head, the way I could never get mine to do. As soon as I stepped off the elevator, Alex called out, "Oh, there you are, Emma. I want you to meet my mother."

I lowered my eyes as we converged, but could feel her going over me from French twist to stockinged ankles.

"Lídia, this is Emma Gant. Emma, this is my mother, Lídia Prieto Maldonado y—"

"Please, Alejandro, enough," the little woman cut him short in a voice more masculine than his. She stuck out a manicured hand with a gigantic pink pearl ring on the middle finger and gripped mine. "I have had too many names. Please call me Lídia. So you are the young *periodista* on the *Miami Star.* He talked about you all the way from Palm Beach, and when we arrived, I wanted to telephone you and take you out for a birthday toast, but *he* insisted it was too late." Though she spoke with a much heavier Spanish accent than her son, she raced pell-mell through her sentences, never pausing for a word and never messing up the grammar.

"We got back at half-past ten," said Alex. "I was afraid you'd be asleep, Emma."

"Nonsense," Lídia said. "When I was her age, I never went to bed before three in the morning."

"I hope you didn't go to bed hungry again," said Alex.

"As a matter of fact, I did. But now I'm headed out for a huge breakfast at Howard Johnson's."

"May we *take* you to breakfast there?" Alex's mother was the most formidably groomed female I had so far encountered. The sleeveless white sundress showed off her exquisitely sculpted arms and neck; every hair of her cunningly tinted coiffure (subtle stripes of rich reds and golds against a base of caramel) was in shining place. The earrings in her pierced ears were smaller versions of the pink pearl on her middle finger. (Why middle? To show she had grown tired of advertising her husbands?) Her narrow feet were shod in high-heeled pumps of woven straw that matched her Panama hat, and her stockings were of the palest beige. Even Bev Nightingale, my arbiter of style, suddenly seemed a piecemeal effort next to the effect of this Lídia. Alex had said his mother was "still beautiful," but "still," in her case, seemed beside the point. You could imagine her looking exactly the glossy same at sixteen or sixty, given regular tucks and tints and frequent assaults on expensive boutiques. Tess, though "still" more naturally beautiful, would sag in comparison with this highly carved, coutured creature.

"But, Mami, Emma likes to read the *Star* with her breakfast and check her stories."

"Oh, no, I—"

"Of course she must!" cried Lídia, giving me a sly wink. "We shall be very quiet at breakfast and allow Emma to check her stories."

Girl-to-girl, she linked her arm through mine as the three of us walked to Howard Johnson's. "Alejandro says you admire my great friend Pepe Ortega." Then, seeing me draw a blank, she added, "Y Gasset."

"You *knew* José Ortega y Gasset?"

"We became close friends when Alejandro's favorite stepfather was cultural attaché in Madrid in 1948. Ortega had recently come back from exile. He was extremely *galante* with all women, but he especially enjoyed my company. 'A little Spanish gentleman with the face of an old *torero*,' that's how Pepe described himself. Franco, *de mala gana*—with not very good grace—had allowed him to return to Spain, but Ortega never got over his exile, he felt he had lost his best years. He loved when we would argue politics and philosophy. 'Lídia,' he would say, 'you argue like a man.' " She gave a throaty chuckle. "However, it was at a bullfight that I won his heart for *not* being a man—Alejandro, *por favor*, walk on ahead of us—my son hates when I tell this story. I had talked Pepe into coming with me to the *corrida*. Though he was fascinated by the sport, the history and theory of it, and so on, he had no stomach at all for the actual thing—"

"You're going to spoil your story if you're not careful," Alex warned his mother.

"*Gracias, hijo*, you are right." She gave me another wink. "So there we were at the *corrida*"—Lídia's rolled *r*'s were a splendid percussive instrument all her own—"and the picadors had sunk their lances, and thank God not one of the horses had been gored; that would have done in poor Pepe, although I didn't know it at the time. And then the *banderilleros* came running out and the first of them plants his *banderillo* into the neck of the bull and Pepe closes his eyes, and exactly (*ess-ACK-ly*) at that moment I feel a gush of blood you know where—walk on ahead, Alejandro, and order our coffees—and I said: 'Listen, Pepe, I hate to tell you, but something very embarrassing has just happened and after the *corrida* you are going to have to help me.' I was wearing a white dress, as I am now, only now I am past the time to worry about such accidents anymore. 'After the bullfight,' I said to Pepe, 'I will not be able to rise from my seat until I have something to cover me from behind.'

"Well! Dear Pepe was overjoyed! He jumps up immediately. '¡Voy en *seguida!* I'll go at once, *querida,* there is a lap robe in the boot of my car.' 'But we parked far away,' I said. 'If you go now you'll miss the *faena*'—that's the final third of the *corrida,* when the matador does his work with the *muleta* and then kills the bull. I begged him to stay but he wouldn't hear of it, and that is exactly what happened, he missed the *faena.* By the time he returned with the lap robe, they had already cut off the tail and presented it to the matador. I proposed that we stay for the next fight, now that I was 'covered,' but Pepe wouldn't hear of it. I tied the lap robe around my waist, like a sweater, and off we went for our cocktails. Pepe treated me like a delicate flower the rest of the afternoon and was in an extremely cavalier mood. Only later did I learn from a friend that my 'accident' had saved him from revealing he was squeamish about the sport he found so fascinating in theory. Despite his liking to call himself an old *torero,* Pepe lacked the stomach for watching an actual bullfight."

I was itching to suggest that this was perfectly in keeping with Ortega's transmigration theory; he was imagining himself inside the soul of the bull. But this was obviously one of Lídia's pet stories, and at this early stage it seemed imprudent to try to impress her with my grasp of Ortega's philosophy.

"Poor Pepe, it's hard to believe he has been dead four years," concluded Lídia, sailing ahead into Howard Johnson's while I held the door for her.

Alex had ordered our coffees and bought the *Miami Star,* which was placed reverently in front of the space where I had sat across from him yesterday morning. It was even the same booth.

8-Inch Rainfall Slows
Mop-up After Tornado

Gabe Truro, the reporter who had commandeered my desk, and two other "field" reporters shared the byline for the banner story.

$5 Million
Loss Seen
In Miami

I skimmed the table of tornado-related stories at the bottom of page one, ticking off my contributions: "These Are Still in Hospital," "How to Handle the Home Problems," "Miamians Burn Up Long-Distance Wires," and "What to Do if Another Comes," with Lou Norbright's snappy ending. Oh, good, here it was: "Man and Best Friend Reunited after Twister," A7. Heart already contracting at the possibility someone had left off my byline, I rattled through to the page. Whew, no, there it was. Plus the story was *above the fold*, taking up three columns, with Jake Rance's great photo. Wouldn't Mr. Sprat be pleased! He'd probably gone out at daybreak to buy copies, one for himself and one for Lola. Now to relax and order my breakfast. I could check on my other stories later and look less avid about it.

"How many appearances do you have today, Emma?" Alex asked.

"Five, not counting the obituaries. But only one biggish one."

"May I see the biggish one?" asked Lídia, who had seated herself next to me.

I folded the paper and slid it over to her.

"What will you have, Emma? Same as always?" Alex made it sound as if we'd been having breakfast together for years.

"No, I think I'll have the blueberry pancakes today with bacon and a large orange juice. And some grits on the side, with melted butter."

"Lídia?"

"Just a small baguette," Lídia said, without glancing at the menu. "With two pats of butter, *not* melted, on the side."

"My mother means a hard roll," Alex explained to the waitress.

"Sorry, sir, but all our rolls are baked fresh every morning; we wouldn't have any hard ones."

"Well, then a *fresh* one will have to do," said Lídia, sending her son a superior smirk. "With two pats of cold butter on the side."

"Yes, ma'am. May I freshen up your coffee?"

"Please." Lídia seemed on the verge of adding something else, then resolutely pressed her lips together.

"And you, sir?"

"I'll have the fruit plate with cottage cheese again," said Alex. Something was different about him today. Cross? Disturbed? Less in charge? I would have to think about it at work.

Lídia uttered another guttural chuckle as she read my story. "This is *muy simpática*, Emma, very dear—and so clever. You are totally inside the personality of this old man."

"That's his late wife in the picture frame," I said. "He asked that we include her in the photo."

"Yes, but anyone can see that now he is married to his dog," said Lídia.

Our breakfasts came. I tucked into mine. Lídia pinched off a tiny piece of her Howard Johnson dinner roll, scrutinized it, buttered it slowly, and popped it in her mouth. She made a few perfunctory chewing motions and swallowed. "Well, it is certainly *soft*," she said. "Almost like whipped cream. *Escucha*, Alejandro, we must do something about breakfast at the Julia Tuttle. *En seguida*, right away. Our Cuban guests must have their *desayuno*."

"Yes, Mami, but we need a permit to serve meals, and Abuelito insists Fidel will be out and all our guests gone back to Cuba before we can even schedule an inspection and fill out the forms."

"Your *abuelito* is too busy buying up real estate in the swamps north of Pompano to keep up with the important gossip. When I saw Dolores López at our planning meeting of the Society of Four Arts, she told me the Wald brothers are in Havana this very moment, negotiating the official 'life of Castro' film. They've set up preproduction headquarters in a mansion in the Country Club district and turned the lawn into a helicopter pad—that seems to be the preferred mode of transportation for this regime. They are hoping to cast Marlon Brando as Castro if his price is not too high—Brando's, not Fidel's: Fidel is delighted. Even Fidel's army is excited about being in the film. Now, I ask you, does it sound like the Revolution will be over tomorrow when Marlon Brando is on his way to Cuba to grow a beard and be fitted for fatigues?" (Lídia pronounced it 'COO-bah.') "So I think we must purchase one of those rolling *cocinas* like the street vendors have, that run on gas, and offer a *petit déjeuner* to our guests. We could start tomorrow."

"What sort of *desayuno*, Mami? And who is going to prepare it?"

"Who do you think? Didn't I organize breakfast and canteen food for the *periodistas,* including Hemingway and Martha Gellhorn, during the Spanish Civil War? When supplies were not only scarce but one had to dodge the bullets to get them. Leave it to me, *hijo.* You have more important things to do today. As does our clever young journalist, Emma. It will be nothing fancy, baguettes from a bakery, *jugo de naranja, huevos*—hard-boiled—perhaps some *jamón.*" She swallowed a sip of her coffee and grimaced. "The important item is the *cafecito,* good strong Cuban coffee, not this *agua sucia,* like dirty water."

AT LEAST, I congratulated myself as I walked through the dense heat to the *Star* building, I had stopped short of blurting out, "You knew *Hemingway?*" As for the Spanish Civil War, I would look up who was on which side and what they were fighting for in the morgue's encyclopedia. No more displays of historical ignorance like my thirty-eighth-parallel gaffe. Though Lídia, of course, would not lash out at me as Jake Rance had. That devastating little smirk of hers would simply fly through the air to her son, as it had when the waitress had mistaken the meaning of "hard roll," and Alex would think I was slightly less amazing. The odd thing was, I wasn't sure I even liked Alex's mother, but I was determined that she should like me. And, though her presence did in some way diminish Alex, I knew that life would never be boring when she was around.

ROD REYNOLDS was back at his desk in his role of city editor. "Emma, they tell me you've been going great guns around here."

"I guess I've been keeping busy." Who were "they"? Norbright? Or just Bisbee—who was nowhere in sight. "How is your father doing?"

"He's stable, thanks. Had one heart attack at home in the bathroom and then a second in the ambulance. All his cronies have been sneaking him cigarettes in the hospital. I told him I myself was not proud of my nicotine habit but I definitely was not willing to die for it. He just laughed and said, 'I'd rather be a dead tiger than a live chicken, son.' And that's when I decided the father-son cord was fraying and it was time to get back here. Just in time to miss all the tornado excitement. Your friend Herman Melton over at Jackson Memorial wants you to call him. He has something for you. What a beguiling little piece you wrote about that Sprat fellow."

"Thank you."

"Just the kind of thing *Star* readers lap up. Not what Eisenhower is doing—the Queen's trip to Canada, eh, maybe, and Castro's daily antics, if you're a Cuban refugee waiting it out in Miami until he lays an egg—but an old man reunited with his dog? They can never get enough of that. I stuck an interview possibility in your typewriter bar—about this woman meteorologist over at the Weather Bureau. But get your funeral homes done first."

"Naturally."

I settled into my rightful slot that the tornado rewrite man had pre-empted yesterday, and dialed Ken at my first "fun home." Since Monday, I'd established "once-removed" relationships on the phone with the various undertakers, and so far I liked Ken at Pedersen's best, with his exotic Minnesota accent and his sympathetic attention to detail.

"Good morning, Emma. Nice to see the sunshine for a change, isn't it? I have two for you this morning. Ready?"

One woman and one man: a ninety-year-old widow of a druggist and a seventy-two-year-old switchman for the Seaboard Railway. Nothing newsworthy about either, until Ken pointed out I'd want to be sure to mention that the widow had been active in "the following local charities" (a list of ten) and also said to remind readers that her late husband had been proprietor of the first drugstore in Miami, which still bore his name. The switchman had been grand master of his Masonic lodge.

"Those details make all the difference," I said, scribbling in my pad. "They catch the eye of more readers. All the people who know the drugstore, all the Masons."

"You're too young to believe this, Emma, but most older people—and there are lots of us out there—read the obituaries before they read any-

thing else. Well, but these folks got to live out their full lives. Our establishment up in Lauderdale got such a tragic call this morning. A three-
month-old baby was smothered by the new curtains blowing across her
crib. The young parents had gotten alarmed by all the recent stories of
plastic-bag fatalities and thought it would be safer to replace the plastic
curtains with gauze ones. Talk about the ironies of fate."

Rod Reynolds, slashing up someone's copy at his adjacent desk,
perked up when I exclaimed, "God, how awful!"

"Get on the phone and call Lauderdale," said Rod, when I relayed the
incident after hanging up with Ken.

"You mean call the Pedersen funeral home in Lauderdale?" I was already fiddling with the words for my lead. ("An infant girl suffocated in
the new gauze curtains that her parents, alarmed over recent plastic-bag
fatalities . . .")

"No, our bureau in Lauderdale. One of our Broward reporters will
call Pedersen's and get in touch with the parents and write the story."
Seeing my disappointment, he added, "That's what bureaus are *for*,
Emma."

I'D BEEN hoping while typing up my obits that Herman Melton had
decided to sneak me Ginevra Brown's home phone number after all. But
no, when I returned his call, he only wanted to proffer a tip for what he
described as "a nice little feature for you." A registered nurse at Jackson
Memorial was also a professional hula dancer, currently starring in a
Hawaiian production over at the Roney Plaza. Herman said he could set
it up so she would pose both in white uniform and in sarong. I supposed
this was his way of making it up to me for withholding Ginevra's phone
number.

I then set up an interview for three o'clock with the lady meteorologist at the Weather Bureau, reported my appointment to Rod so he could
assign a photographer to drive me, and set off with my spiral-bound pad
for the morgue.

Moira Parks, in smoke-tinted glasses and snood-restrained hair, was busy with her massive shears. Multiple copies of

First Lady
Of Stage
Dies at 79

lay awaiting their separate envelopes on the long table perpendicular to her desk.

"Good morning, Moira. I'm just going to research something in here." I could never look at her without remembering that burst of operatic splendor when she thought she was alone in the ladies' room.

"Don't hesitate to ask for help."

"What would be the best source for a concise summary of the Spanish Civil War?"

"*The Columbia Encyclopedia*, I would think," she replied in her monotone. "That would be the best place to start."

I had already planned on starting with the *Columbia*, but it seemed the cordial thing to take Moira up on her inveterate offer of help. I lugged the tome from its shelf, established myself at one of the library tables, and experienced a pang of nostalgia for college days and looking things up. I had particularly relished the research on the young Elizabeth for my Tudor History course. That's when I had become smitten with the concept of usurpation and all the ways a person could be usurped.

A virginal copy of this morning's *Miami Star* had been placed at the end of each table. In my earlier self-oriented perusal of the paper at Howard Johnson's, I had missed Ethel Barrymore's front-page obituary, wedged as it was under a bigger story

Senate Rejects Strauss
As Commerce Secretary;
Ike "Good 'n Sore"

Also, the one-column photo of the dowager-ish woman in her black dress was very overlookable. The "First Lady of the American Theater" had died at age seventy-nine, on my birthday. "She was in good spirits right up to the end," reported her nurse.

And who was to contradict the nurse? What was to stop people from telling whatever stories they liked about their deceased friends, especially if the friends had been famous—like Lídia telling about Ortega at the bullfight.

As I scanned the lengthy entry under "Spanish Civil War," I fought down the familiar agitation of *losing ground*. For a college graduate and news reporter, I knew such a little about such a lot. Jake Rance had certainly made his point. Where had I *been* all those years? Surely some adults must have discussed the Korean War during my young life, and most likely they had discussed this war in Spain that had begun shortly after my birth. What had I been thinking of? During the Korean War, I had been tethered to Earl and Mother's gypsy caravan, moving from high school to high school, in every one of which the only war we ever seemed to study was the American Civil War. I had made A's in these history courses, and could still recite by heart, and in order, all the battles of the four-year conflict our Southern teachers enjoined us to call "The War Between the States," because "civil war" meant a divided nation and made the Confederate states seem more at fault.

How would I ever catch up and fill in the gaps of my ignorance?

"You've been scribbling so assiduously I'm loath to interrupt you," said a familiar insolent voice over my left shoulder.

"Bisbee! I've been wondering where you'd got to."

"Can you join me for a quick bite at my club? I've got news."

"About *what?*"

"About myself."

I couldn't read his face. "Is it . . . good news?" I remembered his prediction of a few days back that the *Star* sometimes elevated you like a balloon, then cut your string.

"*Commensurately* so. I'll tell you everything when we get to Walgreens and you be the judge."

———

"SO, TELL me, how has your first week gone?" Bisbee had started right in, after ordering my grilled cheese sandwich and Coke and his tuna sandwich and black coffee.

"Well, you've been my boss for a good part of it," I said. "How do you think it went?"

"Oh, I know how *I* think it went. You get five stars from me."

"Out of a total of how many?"

He laughed. "That's such an Emma question. Out of five, of course."

Had I detected a twinge of ruefulness in the laugh? Bisbee seemed altogether *tamped down* today. And I found it ominous that his hair was for once smoothly combed, his bow tie perfectly straight. "But that's not what I asked you," he went on. "I want *your* assessment of your first week at the *Star.*"

"Won't you please tell me your news first? I'm dying of curiosity."

"A reporter should always be dying of curiosity; it should be his or her chronic ailment, to be exacerbated at every opportunity. Nope, I want your assessment first. Consider it your final assignment for my Walgreens Tutorial."

He leaned forward, training his full gaze on me. I noticed with surprise that his eyes were a serious pale gray, not the nervous brown I'd just assumed were under the wild brown eyebrows.

"Well, sticking with your five-star system," I said, "I'd give myself five for overall effort. And for endurance. Definitely for endurance. And for not sassing back. Though, no, I did come close to the line when you wouldn't let me follow up on my Queen of the Underworld story yesterday. But I don't think you caught my little sarcasm."

"Oh, I caught it, all right. In some things I'm your equal, Emma. But in the perspicacity department, I'm leagues ahead of you. I've had more opportunities to fine-tune my instrument. I have more to say about your Queen of the Underworld, but for now continue with your assessment."

"I'd have to give myself a low mark, say a one, for not following through on that Ginevra opportunity at the hospital. I really bungled my chance. It wasn't completely my fault, I ran out of time, and her husband showed up, but the ideal me would have done more with our time together. Actually, I won't even give myself a one, because not one thing came out of it. Just a stupid paragraph I called in and someone else wrote."

"I see," said Bisbee. "Zero stars for Ginevra. Go on."

"I'm going to give myself another five for Henry Sprat and Lola; even though they weren't as thrilling a story as Ginevra would have been had I made the most of it, I squeezed the most out of Mr. Sprat. Of course, Jake's photo contributed. Which brings me to something else that's figured largely in my week. Keeping my temper under control. Jake Rance isn't exactly a picnic to go on assignment with. And on my first day there was this old man, Charles P. Rose, who kept yelling at me over the phone, 'Nobody could be *that* stupid!' And I just went on being sweetly patient and saying let's go over this again so that every reader, no matter how simple, can get it—"

"The curmudgeon and his water bill," recalled Bisbee. "But you nailed him with that last sentence. Though you weren't happy about the way the copy editors chopped up your paragraphs. How many stars for that story?"

"Two, I think."

"Only two?"

"Yes, because, let's face it, it was a scrap flung at a cub reporter. But there's another aspect of it that I'd give myself five for."

"And what aspect is that?" Bisbee was looking amused.

"Norbright was standing behind me, eavesdropping. I could tell he'd been impressed, because afterwards he complimented me, only I can't remember what he said. I never can seem to remember my compliments."

"That doesn't surprise me," said Bisbee. "Given your punishing standards for yourself."

"Well, but I award myself five stars for earning his respect on that one occasion."

"He's impressed with you altogether."

"What makes you think so?"

"He told me so a few minutes ago, when I was in there with him and Feeney."

"Why don't *you* stop punishing me now and tell me what your news is."

"You don't want to hear your compliment from Lucifer first?"

"I'm dying to. I'm just trying to exacerbate my chronic ailment."

"Lucifer said, and I quote verbatim, 'Emma has a great facility with words and applies herself ferociously. If she keeps it up, we'll make a real newspaper gal out of her.' "

"Thank you. *Now* will you tell me your news?" Something about Norbright's compliment was less than pleasing, but I would figure it out later.

"They're sending me to open a new bureau in Pompano Beach. Ever hear of it?"

"Sure." I would look it up later.

"There's only a weekly up there now, but the place is growing. The *Star* bought the weekly and the building and I'm going to be bureau chief."

"Oh, Bisbee. Congratulations."

"You think it's good news, then?"

"Don't you?"

"As I said, commensurately so. Kicked upstairs to the boondocks. My reward for being a good soldier. Like getting promoted to sergeant when you're not officer material."

"But couldn't a bureau chief be considered an officer?"

"Not in this case, the timing's wrong. I've been in Miami too long for this move to be a compliment."

"I don't understand."

"The normal drill is they start you off in the main office and see where you fit. If you're officer material, you stay here and move up. Or you go to the Washington bureau and come back, like Lucifer did. If there are gaps in your training, you get sent to one of the smaller state bureaus after a few months and learn your trade there. Some grow and make it back to the main Mecca, and some don't."

"What happens to the ones who don't?"

"They rot in the bureaus till they retire or get the sack. If you want to know the truth, Emma, when Feeney and Norbright called me into their sanctum this morning, I was positive I was getting the sack."

"Having your balloon string cut after being deputy city editor."

"You got it. I'm going to have the key lime pie one last time. Will you join me?"

"No, thanks."

"Another Coke, then?"

"Yes, please. How soon will you be leaving for Pompano Beach?"

"I'm driving up this afternoon. I'm booked into a motel until I find out what my wife wants to do."

"What do you mean?"

"She likes Miami. She's fixed up the house exactly the way she wants it. She might choose to stay on. In that case, I'd get myself an apartment on the beach in Pompano and come home for weekends. Might spiff up our marriage, having some time apart. Not that we hate each other, but things aren't what they once were. And who knows? Having all that time to myself at night might force me to make a start on my Great American Novel."

"Do you . . . have an idea for it yet?"

Bisbee's "last piece" of key lime pie arrived along with more steaming black coffee and my Coke.

"I've had the entire novel written in my head for the last fifteen years. With most of the periods and commas in place."

"But how—?" I was not only nonplussed but envious. "I can't *imagine* carrying around a completed novel in your head without writing it down!"

Nodding in agreement, Bisbee attacked his pie.

"I mean, it would be like being notified you'd won a prize and refusing to go pick it up, or something," I went on.

"That's a pretty good analogy. But what if you weren't sure you'd like the prize once you saw it?"

"But if you have it all pictured in your head, you ought to *know* whether you'd like it. You really do have the whole thing completed in your head?"

"It's not long, only about forty thousand words. It all takes place in a single summer evening. From the point of view of a nine-year-old boy whose mother dies while he's outside catching fireflies in a jar."

"Did—are parts of it autobiographical?"

"Everything from the fireflies to the dance music on the radio next door. It's very lyrical. In fact, it's perfect. The only trouble is, James Agee got his written down first. And it was his father, not his mother, who died."

"Well, if I were you"—I decided to ignore this latest attempt to pull the rug out from under himself—"I would check into that Pompano motel and start writing mine down this very afternoon."

"And if I were you, I might do that very thing," replied Bisbee, smiling broadly.

"Does it have a title?"

"It's called *August,*" he said quietly, rounding up the last vestiges of pie with the underside of his fork. Having chewed and swallowed the final morsels, he pushed the plate aside. "Now, tell me, Emma, how this 'ideal you' would have 'done more' with your meeting with Ginevra Brown."

"Well, I mean, there's so much more to be done, isn't there? Ever since we were at Walgreens last time and you told me about Lucifer's 'Queen of the Underworld' series, I haven't been able to get her out of my imagination. Doesn't that make her still a good story? You yourself said at the hospital that I might get a human-interest sidebar to the tornado out of it, don't you remember? You said, 'There are still folks who'll remember her.' You even said you were throwing me a plum."

Bisbee sipped his coffee. "Let's see if I can account for what kind of plum I had in mind. Okay, you're hard on yourself, so I'm going to be hard on you, too. Here's the 'plum,' the ideal sidebar, the most you could have done with it: a five-inch, one-column sidebar whose main gist would have been that the notorious young madam who six years ago queened it over the local headlines, and was now married to a doctor, was in Jackson

Memorial Hospital for her third overdose in as many years. The tornado upstaged her, but that wouldn't need to be put into words. The fact that it was a sidebar would be enough for readers to see the irony. Readers who remembered, that is. *Sic transit notitia* and so on."

"But that's more or less what was in the paper," I said. "Only I didn't write it, I just called it in, and that Vince on the desk slapped something together. He expected more, too. The thing that gets me is there *was* so much more. It was a real interview, I kept waking her up, like you said to. We talked about Norbright—she said he looked like Cornel Wilde— and about that Biscayne Academy. I told her my aunt Tess had gone there, too, and she and Tess share the same hairdresser. And we talked about Miss Edith, the woman who had groomed her, not knowing what she was grooming her for, and she even recited some poetry with her eyes closed. 'La Belle Dame sans Merci.'"

"Keats."

"Yes, and then Dr. Brown showed up and there wasn't time to shape it into anything."

"Look, Emma, let's say you'd had another hour to shape it into something. Based on what you've told me, how much of that something could the *Star* have printed? Think about it. Could there be an angle you've overlooked here?"

"You mean about lawsuits and all?"

"For a start."

"I considered that. The challenge would be finding a way to tell the intimate story beyond the Norbright series, without violating anybody's rights. If I were a *Star* reader—I mean one who remembered the series— I would *adore* a follow-up. What's her life like now, when she's not taking the overdoses? Does she miss the Palm Island years, all the excitement of being with the other girls, the men arriving in their evening clothes, or sometimes docking their own yachts behind the mansion? And that whole transformation story of how a girl from Waycross trained with the debutantes at Edith Vine's academy and outshone them all."

"How do you know she outshone them all?"

"Tess told me. Miss Edith confided to Tess that Ginevra had more grace and beauty than all those clumsy debutantes put together. Miss Edith was crushed by all the publicity of the trial and the series. Tess said it killed her. It's a shame, because I really would have liked to interview Miss Edith as well."

"Make it up, then."

"You mean, like fiction?"

"You should see your face. As if I'd suggested you rob a bank. Why not? Pursue your fascination while it's hot. Just don't expect to have it run in the *Star*."

"At the hospital Ginevra told me she wished she'd had a chance to tell her side of the story to Miss Edith. How I would have loved to eavesdrop on that conversation!"

"Eavesdrop to your heart's content. Satisfy your curiosity. It won't be a waste of your time. The simple act of getting it down on paper will develop your writing skills."

Look who's preaching getting it down on paper, I thought.

Bisbee, who of course had read my face, looked guilty, then had the grace to laugh. "I'm going to miss our talks, Emma. Both of us enjoy going into things."

"I'm going to miss them, too," I said, really meaning it.

13.

A S I LIMPED HOMEWARD on the pavement that was rapidly eroding my only pair of heels, I resolved to take my first plunge into the Julia Tuttle's pool, even though the sky had clouded over again. But was I up to offering Lídia the chance to scrutinize my figure in the faded St. Clothilde's racing suit? I decided I was. Going down on the elevator I could wear Paul's black silk dressing gown, then I could slip it off at the edge of the pool. But what about footwear? I had no sandals; my Bass Weejun loafers would have to suffice. I was not going to let Alex's rabidly groomed mother keep me from the pool.

Bisbee's lunchtime revelation about his entire novel languishing up there in his head was scary. I must never let such a thing happen to me. And his abrupt departure had left me a bit disoriented. After lunch, I had ridden with an elderly photographer to do the profile of the weather lady amid all her meteorology gear and afterwards cranked out eight inches of copy with a lead that made Rod Reynolds smile.

When it rains, Martha Seawell looks out the window and says stoically, "Hmmm . . . low-pressure area."

Late in the afternoon some news had come clacking over the wire from our Washington bureau that made me dash for my notepad. There was a proposal that Congress levy a special tax on Cuban sugar exports and set this money aside in a fund to reimburse owners who didn't get fair value for their sugar plantations. But while copying down the story, I realized that the fund would be for American landowners only. Shit. How I would have loved being the bearer of good tidings, hot from the *Star*'s teletype machine, to the usurped Ocampos.

Alex was behind the front desk, frowning over a book. The smile that transformed his earnest, square-chinned countenance when he looked up and saw it was me was like a scented bath of approval just waiting for me to step into. I do not need to do one single thing more today to earn points, I told myself.

"Pool's closed?" I asked, seeing the sign at the entrance.

"Until seven. My mother has been very busy. Come back at seven and you will find tapas out by the pool, also illegal drink until we get our license, and a Cuban band that Lídia hired off the street. Also, it seems she has invited every Cuban she met today."

"What's the book?" As I tapped the spotty old tome I realized my nails needed redoing. Especially with Lídia on the scene.

"A Galician cookbook belonging to Marisa Ocampo's grandmother. I'm making a list of tapas. Lídia wants to have a rotating selection each evening; they're like canapés." He passed across the pink telephone-message pad on which he had been writing. "Here is tonight's menu."

" 'Huevos rellenos,' " I read aloud in my best accent. " 'Almendras fritas, ensalada de pimiento y pepino, jamón serrano con quesos . . .' It all sounds lovely, but unfortunately my Spanish isn't good enough to connect me with any pictures of food."

"I shall translate," said Alex indulgently, proceeding to roll out the Spanish in his haughty Castilian, followed by the descriptions in English: "Deviled eggs, spiced fried almonds, roasted red peppers and chopped cucumbers in garlic and oil, cured Serrano ham with cheeses, and peasant bread. On Monday they will deliver the gas *estufa* on wheels and then there will be hot tapas cooked out by the pool—shrimp fritters and spiced meatballs and so on."

"But who is making all these tapas?"

"Lídia and the Ocampos and any of the guests Lídia can enslave. Enrique opened the cans, young Luisa peeled the eggs and helped Marisa roast the peppers in the kitchen range, and Lídia oversaw the chopping and told her stories about dodging bullets and making sandwiches for the Loyalists during the Spanish War. If you're not careful, you'll find yourself in her assembly line."

"Oh, I don't mind a little chopping for a good cause."

"What kind of day did you have, Emma?"

"Nothing spectacular. I did a story on a lady meteorologist and went to lunch with a colleague who's being sent to Pompano."

"I'm glad to hear you had lunch. You mustn't skip meals."

"I'll miss old Bisbee. But it's a promotion, even if he does have to leave Miami. Pompano is growing so fast that the *Star's* opening a bureau there and he'll be the chief."

"That's the sort of news that will please my grandfather, since he has been buying up all the land around Pompano."

WHEN I got to 510, I went immediately to the window to see what was going on down by the pool.

Where the poor royal palm's stump had been this morning was a brand-new garden, a raised triangular bank of closely planted red and white flowers, the white ones forming a star in the middle of the red, to coordinate with the Cuban flag now flying above. Enrique Ocampo and Luís, the other desk clerk, were setting up trestle tables and Marisa and Louisa were covering them with white cloths. Lídia was nowhere in sight.

My stomach growled angrily and it was still an hour until seven. Much of my existence thus far at the Julia Tuttle, I realized, had been spent thinking of food or finding ways to fill in the time until I could eat. I was looking forward to the deviled eggs. Thank goodness Lídia was such a monster of action. There might even be some kind of on-site breakfast tomorrow morning.

Paul's birthday roses in the homely "base" brought by Enrique had altered since yesterday, some having unfurled to fuller beauty, others gone past their prime.

As I shook Loney's lavender flakes into my running bath, I wondered what was transpiring up in the mountains at the Nightingale Inn. Going to bed early last night to forestall hunger pangs, I had assumed Paul would be phoning later to wish me a happy birthday, and, if so, it would be a pleasant thing to wake up for. But then, today, the meeting and breakfast with the formidable Lídia, followed by Rod Reynolds's return and Bisbee's news, had derailed my habitual reflections. This neglect, for the first time ever, to keep Paul always somewhere within the range of consciousness felt ominous, as though my not thinking of him for a whole day could make him stop existing.

Soaking in the fragrant hot water while removing the chipped polish from my nails, I reminded myself that Paul had a separate life to lead and people to take care of and a hotel to run. In the next room were his roses, and a week from tomorrow we would be plugged into each other again.

While my fresh polish dried, I lay in bed naked under the sheet with the air-conditioning on full blast and looked up some things in my Spanish-English dictionary, after which I committed a few jottings to my "Go, Tar Heels!" notebook.

commensurate

sic transit notitia

curiosity = a reporter's chronic ailment, to be exacerbated at every opportunity

Sp. Civil War, 1936–39

"Loyalists" or "Republicans" = Lídia's side. Middle-class liberals or socialists who were part of the 2nd Spanish Republic gov't (1931). They began attacking privileged structure of Sp. society. Large estates were broken up and redistributed. They murdered priests and bishops and burned down churches. Also called "La Causa" and "International Brigade," when foreigners (like Hemingway and journalists) started volunteering, and later "Communists," when USSR sent supplies and got politically involved.

> *"Nationalists" or "Rebels"* = *Franco, the military elite,*
> *the Church, and the upper class, later called "the Fascists" or "the*
> *Falange." Hitler and Mussolini sent supplies to Franco and*
> *the Nationalists committed their own atrocities, bombed hospitals*
> *and the working-class section of Madrid. German Condor Legion*
> *units used their latest modern weapons to carpet-bomb Guernica.*
> *One-third of the population killed or wounded. Sheep and cattle ran*
> *burning through the streets until they disintegrated.*

Frankly, I would have been more comfortable around Lídia knowing less about La Causa. Neither her and Hemingway's side nor Franco's with his carpet bombers seemed worth risking your life to make sandwiches for. And none of it was good news about the evolution of the human race.

I gingerly tapped one thumbnail against the other; the polish was still tacky, which meant at least ten more minutes before risking contact with elastic and zippers. Why not use these extra drying minutes to "eavesdrop" on Ginevra and Miss Edith, when Ginevra returns to tell her side of the story?

Set the scene in the same room where Miss Edith taught Ginevra to enunciate "La Belle Dame sans Merci." Evening. Maybe a fire in the fireplace—nope, not in Miami. Also, they needed fictional names: Miss—what was old-fashioned and had a classy simplicity? Edna, perhaps. And what to call the girl from the Waycross fruit stand? A slightly pretentious name that could take on a romantic aura after she achieved notoriety. Or *notitia*, as Bisbee would say.

Miss Edna is standing by the mantelpiece, maybe some magnolia leaves arranged in the grate, a Southern custom during the hot months. She's looking at a piece of priceless porcelain, a gift from one of her satisfied debutantes in the days before the debacle. The doorbell rings. She is expecting nobody. She can't have a fire but it could be dark and raining; I certainly knew how to describe rain in Miami. Miss Edna descends the stairs with her usual stately posture, though haltingly. Ever since the trial her heart has been acting funny. She opens the door and there is a woman in a raincoat and a white silk head scarf. At first Miss Edna assumes it is a stranger come to the wrong door.

"You have every right to slam the door in my face," says the woman in the silk scarf, and her old teacher recognizes at once the thrilling voice whose diction and modulations she herself had created. She presses her hand against her heart; it is beating so erratically she can't speak at first.

But when she regains her breath, she hears herself, ever the lady, kindly addressing the star pupil who dragged her name and her life's work through the mud.

"Won't you come in out of the rain, Delfine?"

This completely satisfying opening seemed to have flowed out of its own need to exist. The trouble was, my nails were hard-dry but I hadn't written down a single word.

I looked out the window. Not yet seven, but people were gathering down by the pool, being received by Lídia, gaily turned out in a red flamenco dress. Some paused to admire the new red-and-white flower garden and point at the matching flag, while a few purposeful souls headed straight for the tables with food and drink.

I dressed hurriedly. Deviled eggs always went first.

14.

S TILL AT THE FRONT DESK, Alex was checking in an unusual couple. A beautiful young mulatto woman, arrayed in swirls of green taffeta reaching to her ankles and a matching picture hat, was filling out the register while a rotund old man in rumpled white suit and dark glasses leaned on his cane, puffing his cigar and holding forth in a booming sepulchral voice.

"*Oye,*" he addressed both Alex and the lobby at large, "*lo único que necesitamos aquí es una habitación sin barbudos.*"

The dominoes players exploded with laughter. Damn it, I recognized every word but the last one, which was obviously where the joke was. The only thing we require here is a room without—what? It probably took years before you could pick up jokes in another language. The old man spoke in the heavily lisped upper-class Spanish, to which Alex, putting forward his *castellano* self, was responding in kind.

"See you later, Emma," he said as I passed by. "Enrique and I will take turns on the desk so no one misses Lídia's party." I could actually hear the woman's voluminous skirt rustling as she wrote in the register. What an outlandish outfit to travel in! Were they fleeing Cuba, too?

Lídia took possession of me as soon as I stepped outside. "*Bienvenida,* Emma! What exquisite needlework on your blouse! Did you do it?"

"No, my grandmother did. But I designed it."

"Ah, I have committed acres of embroidery in my time, all girls were taught in the schools. While I was married to Alejandro's father, I embroidered everything in sight to keep from dying of boredom on our cattle ranch in Camagüey."

As she clamped her fingers onto my forearm, I noted that she, too, had refurbished her social talons—this time to match the flamenco red of her party outfit. Awesome woman, to squeeze a nail job into the rest of her day's accomplishments.

"Marisa Ocampo has been telling me you also were at St. Clothilde's," she went on. "Do you know, I came dangerously close to going to St. Clothilde's myself? Papi said he couldn't control me anymore, he had even paid the nonrefundable tuition to the nuns. However, I managed to elope instead. Come, let me present you to some friends. *¡Ay!* Here is Dr. Rodriguez, our fantastic dental surgeon—or you have met already through your aunt?"

"No, I—"

"Oh, good, it will be my pleasure. *¡Hector, ven acá!* Here is our young *periodista*, Emma Gant. The niece of your amazing *señora* Tess."

The dental surgeon in his pleated guayabera kept my hand firmly in his while permitting his gaze to take a cursory roam over my entire person. "I have heard many wonderful things about you, *señorita* Gant." He was small and debonair, with close-cropped reddish-gray curly hair receding at the temples and snapping dark eyes behind wire-rimmed glasses.

"Tess isn't actually my aunt, but she's the nearest thing I have to one." I felt I'd better say it, since he must know it anyway.

"I understand completely. We all admire her so much, it is natural to want to claim her however we can." His accented English was fluent and soothing. I could imagine his warm, elegant hand lingering in that of a nervous patient. ("I understand *com-PLIT-ly*. Is *NOT-ur-all*, your pain. But we are going to make you feel better soon.")

So this was Tess's "Doctor Magnánimo." Selected images passed through my mind.

"A pity Asunción couldn't come," said Lídia, a shade accusingly. "Your maid said she was out for all day and evening. Off on another of her rescue missions, I suppose. Organizing housing and schools for more of our *pobres exiliados*?

"Asunción sends you her regrets. She would not have missed this for the world, but she has her book club tonight and has been working extremely hard on her presentation."

"Oh, *I* once organized a book club in Havana," said Lídia. "*Por lo menos*, we called it a book club. We were fomenting with sedition and used it as a cover. This was after that thug General Machado closed down our colleges."

"What is your wife's presentation on?" I asked Hector Rodriguez.

"*Doctor Zhivago*. You have read it?"

"It's wonderful." I meant to read it as soon as I had time, but had browsed through reviews enough to discuss it intelligently, had Lídia not preempted this feat.

"Ah, here is our little *orquesta* come to play! Do you know, I found them performing in the street? *Por favor*, Hector, Emma," waving us toward the table. "You must excuse me while I show the musicians where they are to set up. Please! go and help yourselves to food and drink."

"*¡Señorita Gant! ¿Qué quieres tomar?*" Handsome Enrique Ocampo, the ousted sugar heir, was cheerfully tending bar in a striped bib apron. "There is sangria, *ron*, Coca-Cola, ginger ale *y* soda."

"What are you having?" I deferred to Hector, to whom, as my accompanying male, Enrique's eye contact had addressed our choices.

"No, please, you first, *señorita*."

"Well, then, maybe a Coca-Cola."

"I will join you, as I have work to do tonight. *Dos* Coca-Colas."

"Another patient in pain?"

"Ah, no, *por suerte*. Just some office work."

It was clear from Hector's offhand tone in ordering our drinks that he took Enrique at face value: a bartender. Should I perhaps try to introduce them? But what to say? This is *señor* Ocampo, who last week owned a ten-thousand-acre sugar plantation but now is serving us so he can pay his family's hotel bill? What with Enrique's meager English and my not knowing the Spanish for "dental surgeon," I decided not to attempt it.

I did, however, take advantage of the sudden bustle of the dominoes players moving their table outside to sidle quickly over to the tapas and dispatch a deviled egg while Hector waited for our drinks. As soon as I had swallowed, I restationed myself by his side.

"What do you think is going to happen in Cuba, Dr. Rodriguez?"

"Ay, it is a mess!" He warmed to the subject with alacrity. "It is much more serious than we originally think." He gestured toward the gathering with his Coca-Cola glass. "All around you are people who completely opened their hearts and their pockets to Fidel. Lídia was one of the first to take up his cause to free Cuba. And now, what does the great liberator do? Overnight he turns into a little dictator himself. Yes, *señorita*, you are in the midst of some very disillusioned people at this little *improvisado* gathering of Lídia's. Here are many, many *desengañados*, everywhere you look. And many more arriving even as we speak."

"That man over there serving drinks?" I felt now was an opportune time to inform Hector.

"*¿Sí?* What about him?"

"Well, that is Enrique Ocampo. Fidel has taken over his sugar plantation. And he and Castro went to school together! They couldn't take any money out, so Enrique is working at the Julia Tuttle to pay his family's hotel bill."

"I am hardly surprised," replied Hector, after studying Enrique in this new light. "*¡Caramba!* I am hardly surprised by anything these days. This new '*ley agraria*' of Fidel's, his 'land reform,' is nothing but an excuse to take what he wants. But do you know what keeps me hopeful, *señorita*? My respect for history. Yes, I am a great fan of *la historia*, especially the history of my country, and what gives me the hope are two things. One"—he held up a finger—"no Cuban ruler has ever held power for as much as ten consecutive years. And two"—up went the second finger—"is for certain the Americans will *never* allow a Communist regime to come so close to their shores."

"That sounds pretty astute to me," I said. "I mean, if we went completely around the world to fight the Communists in Korea, what's to stop us from going a mere ninety miles south?" (Thank you, Rancid Rance.)

"You are an informed young lady. However, there is an old Spanish proverb: *'El que espera desespera.'* He who waits will despair. Now I think we must do more than just waiting. Lídia understands this and I support her completely. We must have some plans of our own, all of us working together every single moment, not just waiting for the American government to act. *¿De acuerdo?"*

"*De acuerdo.* Doctor, what is the Spanish for 'dental surgeon'?"

"Ah, *odontólogo."*

I repeated it, trying to do the tongue thing with the *"tó"* syllable.

"*Muy bien, señorita.* It is a family profession. Both my father and grandfather practiced *odontología* in Havana. My great-uncle Hector in Madrid, whom I am named after, was dentist to King Alfonso *Trece."*

At this moment, the Miami sunset plunged behind the cabanas and Lídia's little street *orquesta* struck up with "Cherry Pink in Apple Blossom Time." There was no singer, only two guitars, an accordion, bongo drums, and maracas, but the tune was instantly recognized and a cheer of approval went up from Lídia's guests. Dancing began at once, and when Hector saw me swaying to the music he gallantly opened his arms and we slid right into the *cha-cha-cha.* Bev Nightingale had taught me to do it and some other Latin dances last summer; she insisted that I join the dancing in the evenings. Under her encouraging eye I would cha-cha or rumba or samba with the guests and also with Paul.

Paul was a smooth dancer—Bev had been his teacher, too—but Hector Rodriguez made more complicated moves with his torso. Did he and Tess ever dance?

As though he had read my mind, he began to talk of her. "Your adopted aunt, she is a pillar of strength, as you say in English. If she had been Spanish, the name Pilar would have suited her well. Our Tess is *bien segura,* she has an adventurous spirit. I am giving her flying lessons in my Cessna; she has perhaps mentioned it?"

I did my best to cover my surprise: not of Tess flying—I could perfectly picture her serenely guiding the aircraft above tropical clouds, her lovely profile intent on the controls in front of her—but that she had *not* mentioned it to me made me wonder whether I was less important to her than I had supposed.

"She didn't tell you? *¡Ay!* I have spoken out of turn."

"No, maybe she *did* mention something," I hastily reassured him. Could she possibly have said something that night on the houseboat after I was too daiquiri-sozzled to take it in? "But maybe I confused it with that time she flew through the air in the hurricane. Did you know that story?"

"Oh, yes, with the piano and the carpets floating below." He forced a laugh, but still looked worried. "Perhaps she is waiting to surprise you with her pilot's license. Please, *señorita,* don't mention my indiscretion."

"Of course I won't."

And here came Marisa Ocampo, accompanied by her little daughter, bursting with news. "Hortensia *remembers* you, Emma, she remembers you from St. Clothilde's! She telephones us daily from New York and she was so excited when I told her you were here in our hotel. 'Of course, Emma Gant, she was one of the leaders in the younger grades,' that's exactly what my sister said!"

I introduced Dr. Hector Rodriguez to Marisa and Luisa Ocampo, keeping straight who got presented to whom and doing a pretty agile job of pronouncing "*odontólogo.*" I saw Hector register at once that these were the usurped sugar heirs, and as he gently began evoking from Marisa a blow-by-blow account of the Ocampos' reversal of fortune, both of them still speaking in English out of courtesy to me, I transferred my attention to sedate young Luisa.

"Well, Luisa, where are the dolls tonight? Your *muñecas?*"

"*Las muñecas estan arriba,*" Luisa replied in her disconcerting gravelly little voice.

"Ah, they're upstairs. Does— Now is it Tilda who has the headaches? *¿Tiene Tilda otro dolor de cabeza?*"

"No, *señorita.*" Luisa gave me her polite stare. If I had hoped to score a point about Tilda's headaches, I was out of luck.

"Oh, *sí*, well, that's good. I mean I'm glad—*estoy muy alegra* . . . no, *me alegra de que* . . . *de que Tilda NO tiene un dolor de cabeza.*" Oh Lord, this was torture.

Tilda y Manuela desprecian las fiestas," Luisa explained simply before I mangled her language any more.

"Oh, I see. Tilda and Manuela don't *like* parties." I flailed my hand around at the chattering crowd and scrunched up my face to mime disgust.

At last I won an affirmative nod. "*Sí. Manuela, ella tiene miedo del ruido, y Tilda es muy crítica de la gente.*"

"Yes, our wise Luisita's amazing dolls," interjected Marisa, who must have been listening to our exchange. "Manuela is afraid of noisy crowds and Tilda is so critical of people, and both of them hate parties." She stroked her daughter's shiny dark hair, parted in the middle like her own. Their look-alike dresses of lilac dotted swiss had the odd effect of bringing out the budding womanhood of the girl and revealing the girlhood still lingering in the mother. "We are so fortunate to have Tilda and Manuela! They wear our deficiencies for us so that we can make a brave appearance."

I caught Luisa gazing longingly toward the food.

"I don't know about you, Luisa," I said, "but I'm famished. *Tengo mucho hambre.*" Even though she was still a child, I hesitated to use the familiar *tú*. "*¿Usted, también?*"

"*Sí, señorita.*"

"*Escucha, querida . . .*" Marisa Ocampo instructed Luisa in Spanish, then switched back for me. "Please, Emma, go with Luisita and sample the tapas we made together before all of them disappear."

Luisa and I left Marisa confiding to Hector that her sister Hortensia's husband at the United Nations said diplomats in high places thought it was only a matter of weeks until America kicked Fidel out. "But the delay is still a disaster, my husband says—that handsome *camarero* serving drinks is my husband—because those *esbirros* who confiscated our mills won't know what to do with the harvest . . ."

Language barriers crumbled as Luisa and I got into a little game of filling each other's plates.

"This looks good, Luisa. May I put some on your plate?"

"*Sí, señorita Gant.*"

"*Me llamo Emma.*"

"*Gracias . . . Emma.*"

"What do you say we rescue those last two eggs from their loneliness? One deviled egg for you . . ."

"*Gracias, Emma.*" Then Luisa took the serving spoon and slid the second and last onto my plate. "Devil egg," she said, glancing up at me with the tiniest twitch of humor.

"Thank you, Luisa. Oh, this all looks so good. Will you permit me to help you to some of these red peppers and cucumbers? What are they called in *Español?*"

"*Estos son pimientos, y estos son pepinos.*" She pointed to each in turn.

"*Pimientos . . . y . . . pepinos.*" I echoed her pronunciation. "And *you*"—I pointed to her and then made slicing gestures—"you prepared them? *Sí?*"

"*Con mi madre, sí.*"

"*Claro. Con su madre.*"

After each of us had heaped the other's plate, Luisa got a Coca-Cola from her father and I decided the time had come to switch to rum and Coke, which Enrique presented to me with a ceremonial flourish: "One Cuba libre for *señorita* Gant!"

Then off we went with our hoard to the far end of the pool, where we stood companionably stuffing ourselves like two schoolgirls excused from the social restraints of the adult scene.

The street *orquesta* launched into something faster, with an African beat, lots of drum and maracas. Many couples were dancing now. Hector Rodriguez and Marisa had joined Enrique behind the bar and the two men were speaking with intensity, both sets of hands flying, while Marisa in her girlish lilac dress smiled on them with approval.

"Do you like to swim, Luisa? *Quiere nadar?*"

"Me gusta cuando hace calor."

"Yo también. I hate chilly water. *Desprecio agua fría."*

"En Oriente, la temperatura de nuestra piscina está ideal."

Of course. She missed their pool at home, always the right temperature. Before I knew it, I had transmigrated into Luisa Ocampo's usurped young soul. When Mother and Earl had dragged me out of St. Clothilde's and away from Mountain City, at least I still had my native language to make new contacts. What would it have been like to start all over, as poor Luisa now had to do?

"¿Cuentos años tiene, Luisa?"

"Tengo nueve años."

Nine years old. Thirteen years' difference between us. *"Y, yo"*—I soldiered on, pointing to myself—*"yo tengo veinte y dos años."*

"Viente y dos," Luisa repeated respectfully, picking at one last roasted almond on her paper plate. I must seem ancient to her.

"Desde ayer," I added. "Since yesterday. *Ayer* was *el dia de mi nacimiento,* my birthday."

"Felicidades . . . Emma."

"Gracias, Luisa. Y qué es el día de su nacimiento?"

"El segundo de Julio." Adding with a little sigh, *"Espero que estemos de vuelta en Cuba por mis cumpleanos."*

And if Hortensia's UN husband's hunch was right, the Ocampos would be back in Cuba in a matter of weeks and Luisa would be entertaining other children in her pool on her birthday, perhaps sparing a fleeting thought for that American *periodista* with her lousy Spanish who had befriended her beside that chilly North American pool. Or, worse, remembering me as a minor character in a bad dream that was now over.

"Y yo espero tambíen, Luisa." Nevertheless, I wished her home in time for her birthday.

A sudden tropical breeze animated the colored lights strung around the pool and sent the red-and-white Cuban flag into a patriotic flutter above the flower beds. Spanish and English phrases tumbled together in the dark tropical air and wafted across the pool to us, amplified by the water:

"Oye, chico . . ."

"Claro, but . . ."

"Ay, in COO-bah, we . . ."

" 'La ley agraria.' ¡Cuantas mentiras!"

"¡Ay, te lo dije!"

"Excuse me, can you tell me where is the best . . . ?"

"Es un cotilleo."

"No, querida, es cierto. Llegó la hora . . ."

By this time, my Cuba libre had kicked in. I had ceased straining over translations and just let the words wash over me, making perfect sense in a larger way.

Darting busily about was Lídia in her red flamenco dress, pouncing on her guests, arranging and rearranging them in designs of her own making, like a creative artist whose material just happened to be other people.

Alex appeared and spoke to his mother, who immediately pointed to Luisa and me at the far end of the pool. So she had known exactly where we were in her pageant the whole time.

Alex made directly for us in his dignified, high-slung walk. My first thought was that he was coming to ask me to dance.

"There's a long-distance phone call for you, Emma. It's Mrs. Nightingale. You can take it on the house phone in the lobby."

15.

Y OU MEAN *MR.* NIGHTINGALE, don't you? I had to bite my
tongue to keep from saying it. If Alex had said "Mrs." he must
have *meant* "Mrs."

As he accompanied me back to the hotel, Lídia shot forth from a cluster of guests and grabbed his arm.

"*Hijo,* why are all the lights on in the penthouse suite?" She pointed at
the string of lit windows on the top floor of the Julia Tuttle.

"I guess because Don Waldo Navarro wanted them on."

Why on earth was Bev Nightingale calling me?

"*¡Dios mío, Alejandro!* You mean to say Don Waldo has arrived and you
didn't even tell me? I wanted to be there to greet him."

"You were busy greeting your guests, Mami. Not even you can be two
places at once. Come, Emma, I'll show you where the house phone is."

"Wait!" cried Lídia. "Did he bring his old housekeeper? Altagracia?"

"The name of the lady who signed the register was Altagracia
Navarro. But she's not old and he introduced her as his wife."

"No, Alex, you are mistaken. Altagracia is his old housekeeper—"

"Excuse me, Mami, while I go and put Emma's long-distance call
through."

"Ah, long-distance," said Lídia, sending me a significant look. "A tardy
birthday call from someone special, perhaps."

Alex pointed the way to the house phone, then went back to the switchboard to connect us, while I edged into the booth in a swirl of possibilities:

"Emma, it's Bev Nightingale here. Paul has been so busy he hasn't had a moment to himself. He asked me to phone you and wish you a tardy happy birthday from us both."

"Emma, this is Bev, your former friend and admirer, whose husband you've been having an affair with for the past year. I just found out today and I'm disgusted with you both. I'm filing for divorce and you can have him all to yourself."

"Oh, Emma. Be strong. I've suspected all along about you and Paul, but now it falls to me to tell you that he's been seriously injured and is asking for you."

"Oh, Emma, be strong. Paul was in a bad accident and we have both lost him. Now all we have is each other."

Would Paul want to marry me? Did I want to be Paul's wife? Would I continue my job, changing my byline to "Emma Nightingale"? Would I live in the same house he had shared with Bev? I hang my clothes in her spacious walk-in closet?

How seriously was he injured? Would I still want him if he was maimed or blind? Would Alex offer to drive me to the airport to catch a night flight to Carolina?

If he was already dead, wouldn't it show goodwill to fly to Carolina anyway to comfort Bev and Aunt Stella? Could I get away without letting Mother and Earl know I had been thirty miles away?

As Bev began speaking to me on the phone, I was so caught up in my forebodings that when she said "We've had an unexpected loss, Emma," I was already en route to the airport in Alex's car, struggling to hide my grief until I was alone on the plane. But then I heard her say that Stella had suffered a massive stroke on Thursday and died an hour ago. "It's just as well. She would have been helpless, she would have hated it."

Paul would be accompanying his aunt's body back to Miami on the noon plane.

"Jews are supposed to go into the ground quickly, that's the tradition, even though by law everybody has to be embalmed now. We were wondering, Emma, if you could get something in tomorrow's *Star,* so Stella's friends and clients will know about the funeral. It's at noon on Monday at Fisher's, with burial immediately after at North Shore, next to Paul's mother. I've never seen him so torn up. He was much closer to Stella than to his mother. He stayed all last night at the hospital and earlier today was making arrangements for bringing Stella back to the Inn and hiring round-the-clock nurses. Which she would have detested, she was such an independent little *berrieh.*"

"Little what?" So that's why Paul didn't call on the night of my birthday.

"A woman who can do everything better than everyone else, including taking care of herself."

If Stella had been locally prominent—or locally notorious, like Ginevra Brown—there would still be time to squeeze something in by deadline, but the standard obits had been locked into their trays for hours. Yet I heard myself promising I'd go over to the newspaper right away and see what could be done.

"In the worst case, Bev, it will have to be in Sunday's *Star.* But people spend more time browsing through their Sunday paper, so more of her friends would be likely to see it on Sunday."

"That's a point. I'll tell Paul you said that."

"Still, I'll see what I can do tonight. I'm heading over to the *Star* as soon as we hang up. At least I can write it and have it ready to go."

"Paul was hoping you'd write it. Keep an eye on him, will you, Emma? He admires you so, and you seem to appreciate him. Someone has to stay here and run the Inn, with our new chef starting. Paul's determined to start clearing out her house. She left it to him, along with all her Old World furniture and her thousands of *tchotchkes* that will have to be disposed of—he knows better than to bring them home. And then there are all those little bottles and essences and funnels she used for her perfume business. I hate to think of him facing all that *stuff* alone. I would consider it a real *mitzvah,* Emma, if you could spare him some time this weekend."

"I was about to offer. Stella was very good to me when I first came to work at the Inn."

"Oh, yes, the week of the black eye. That's when I was having my surgery in Miami. Paul told me all about it, the way you looked when you got off the bus and the lie to everyone about the bad cold and all Stella's packs and potions. He said he didn't have the heart to send you back, you were such a nice kid. And he was right."

"I'll keep the weekend free. Tell him to call me as soon as he gets in."

"Bless you, child."

ALEX'S MOTHER was leaning over the front desk, lecturing him about something in rapid Spanish.

"Everything all right, Emma?" he called rather plaintively as I emerged from the booth.

I gave him a breezy flip of my fingernails and ducked into the open elevator.

In 510, I hung up my new blouse to keep it fresh for Paul, slipped back into my workday shirt, and grabbed my purse and notepad. In the hallway, I waited impatiently for the slow elevator to return. It seemed stalled on the top floor. I headed for the staircase, remembering the panicky Spanish-speaking exodus during the tornado. All that was left was to get through the lobby without Lídia pouncing, or Alex insisting on walking me to the *Star* because it was after dark. How had this happened? In less than a week I found myself kicking against brand-new familial demands and constraints from people who weren't even my family.

I was in luck. Lídia was gone and Alex was engaged at the switchboard. I slunk out successfully, the clackety-clack of my heels beating a solitary tattoo along the after-dark Miami sidewalks. My shoe soles felt closer to the pavement than ever, but I couldn't have the shoes resoled until I had a second pair, and payday wasn't till next Friday.

An evening crew of reporters, many of whom I hadn't seen before, populated the newsroom, and one of them was ensconced at my desk.

The only familiar face was that of Marge Armstrong, bent over some layout pages inside the women's glass cage. She gave me such a friendly wave that I stopped in the doorway to say hi.

"Emma, what are you doing here on a Friday night?" She wore jeans and a tee shirt and a terry-cloth turban from which some damp gray curls escaped.

"A friend just died. I promised the family I'd try to get something in the paper so people would know the funeral was on Monday here in Miami. But my desk has been usurped."

"Plenty of room in here. Come keep me company. Dear me, was this friend someone your age?"

"Oh, no, she's the aunt of some people I worked for last summer. They run a summer hotel in North Carolina, and in the winter they have a nightclub in Bal Harbour. The aunt came over from France during World War Two and started a perfume business on the Beach. She made individual scents for people."

"You don't mean Stella Rossignol."

"You know her?"

"I'm a faithful customer. How strange. During my swim this evening, I was thinking, It's time I phone Stella and get a refill of my lotion. Then I remembered she goes away in the summer."

"She was up in North Carolina, helping out at the Inn. She had a stroke last night and hung on until today. Her nephew is bringing the body to Miami on the morning plane."

"I'm so very sorry. Did you know her well, Emma?"

"She was sort of a fairy godmother and confidante to me when I worked at their Inn last summer. I guess there's not much chance of getting something about the funeral in tomorrow's paper."

"If she had been the mayor, or even an alderman, yes."

"That's what I told the family. But at least I can write up the obit now and check it with Fisher's and it'll be ready to go for the Sunday paper."

"More folks will see it on Sunday anyway."

"That's what I told the family."

"You'll find a substantial file on her in the morgue. I did a piece on her myself in the late forties when I was filling in temporarily over here and trying to dream up features to make the *Star* hire me. A friend smelled wonderful and I said, 'What *is* that?' and she said, 'There's this darling little European woman has a shop over on the Beach—you go in, it's like going to a fortune-teller. She asks you questions and while you're talking she plucks out vials and asks you to sniff them and describe your associations, and a week later you pick up a bottle of your very own scent. She sold perfume for Guerlain in Paris and during the Occupation she was in a French concentration camp with one of the Rothschild women. She's like a chic little witch. You ought to interview her.'

"So I hightailed it over to the Beach and mentioned my friend's name and asked Stella to let me interview her. She said, 'Why not let me interview you first, *chérie*? Let me create a scent for you. Then, if you like, you may describe what I do.' She said the scent would be on the house, but I explained that the *Star* was rigorous against anything that could be construed as payola. I paid for my scent and it certainly wasn't cheap. She made me an 'unguent,' as she called it, because if you're a sun worshipper like me the carbon in a perfume's alcohol can damage the skin. I haven't used anything else since, but I guess now I'll have to. You know, there *was* a witchy something about Stella that made you assume she'd just go on and on, like her fragrances, until she evaporated into the Great Atmospheric Scent.

"Anyway, the women's editor was impressed with the feature and hired me full-time, and if I do say so myself it was an entertaining piece. Stella was one of the first custom perfumers in this country, it turns out. After I became women's editor, we ran a full-page spread on her, with mug shots of her prominent clients. She had a waiting list by then."

I went to the morgue and pulled Stella's file from the *R*'s, then, in a jolt of remorse, back-stepped to the *N*'s and, for the first time, extracted Paul's envelope. It was surprisingly thin. Almost as if my weeklong negligence had diminished it. How could I have waited so long to look him up? Too obsessed with fatter envelopes in the *N* drawer: the burgeoning documentation of Norbright's enviable rise. Even Tess's modest archive of social ups and downs was thicker than Paul's.

I took both aunt and nephew to a library table and, in an act of contrition, read every word of Paul's clippings before I went to work on Stella. It was soon done. All were from "Nightlife with Marty Lang" columns, which ran in the *Star* every day except Sunday. A subhead, "Old Friends to Shmooze at New Bal Harbour Club," announced the opening of P. Nightingale's "just in time for the 1951 Season. Hosts **Paul Nightingale,** a local boy, and his glamorous wife, Beverly, want a congenial meeting place where old friends can get together for a good steak, dancing, and entertainment from comedians of the **Lenny Bruce** ilk."

This was the longest entry, the only one with its own subhead. The other clippings, five in all, were announcements of Borscht Belt "headliners" at P. Nightingale's, their unrecognizable names hurriedly wedged between unrelated items like "**Herb Shriner,** currently at the **Fontainebleau,** has leased an apartment at the new Southgate Apartments on Miami Beach" and "**Jackie Heller, Eden Roc** show host, was a classmate of **Martha Raye's** in one of **Benny Davis's** learn-while-you-work travel units."

I felt the spirit of Moira Parks training her thick smoked lenses on the world of newsprint, as watchful of every name, from the gaudily famous to the most obscure, as God of each sparrow, tenaciously keeping track of us all with her scissors.

She might have been looking over my shoulder as I replaced Paul's meager mentions in chronological order and returned his envelope to the *N* drawer before turning my full attentions to Aunt Stella.

Miami Beach Perfumer
Creates Custom Scents

By Marge Armstrong
Star Writer

"You don't choose your perfume on an impulse, like a pastry in the bakery," says Stella Rossignol, the chic, petite perfumer on South Miami Beach who creates a unique fragrance for each of her clients.

"And never, *never* assume that the bewitching scent worn by the woman across the room will smell the same on you. If you do, *chérie*, you are courting disaster, because each person's body chemistry is completely different."

The jealousy animal began to stir as I read the interview that had earned Marge her full-time job just as Norbright's exposé of the religious-relic hoax had launched his investigative career.

Compared to Lucifer's cocky, egocentric voice, Marge's style was practically transparent: you saw and heard Stella without Marge's personality coming between you. Here, in this lead feature in the *Star*'s Home Section, as it was called back in 1948, was Paul's beloved aunt, a person with whom I had spent hours and hours, who had applied her magic poultices to my black eye, intermittently coaxing confidences from me and sharing highlights of her colorful history. It was her voice, her gestures, her Yiddish and Gallic witticisms. Yet I was reading things about her I hadn't known, or else had listened to with half an ear and hadn't had the curiosity to draw out of her. In Marge's piece, she came across as a more significant person, and consequently I seemed less significant because, despite all the time I had spent with Stella, I couldn't have written it.

For instance, Stella's imprisonment in the French internment camp for Jews had turned her preoccupation with personal smell into an obsession, which she later passed on to her nephew Paul. I knew this, as I knew she had made friends in the camp with the woman "who was a Rothschild." But the game Stella and her friend had dreamed up to distract themselves from the nauseating stench of the camp, a game that served as a crucible for Stella's olfactory skills, well, it killed me to admit that she had alluded to this game a number of times. And each time I had passed up the opportunity to probe for the salient details that had given Marge's portrait of Stella both its shape and its vividness.

Both women had previous experience of scent combinations, Stella having worked for Guerlain both as floor saleswoman and as a copywriter, and her friend having studied organic chemistry in Paris before joining the family's wine business. Both were aware that the most lasting and costly ingredients of perfumery were derived from the excretions of animals: civet from the civet cat, ambergris from the sperm whale, musk from the deer, and castoreum from the beaver. The scents of these excretions were foul by themselves, but contributed crucial base notes to the most enchanting perfumes.

"One morning, as we were setting out for the latrines, I said to my friend, who was already retching: '*Écoute, amie,* what if we dilute *un petit soupçon* of today's Essence of Latrine in fifteen milliliters of alcohol, and then we add equal parts of jasmine and tuberose?'

"At first she thinks I'm talking *mishegoss* but then she catches on. She laughs and actually takes a sniff.

" '*Non,*' she says, 'too sickly sweet. We need a musky touch of *ambrette*. And, *peut-être*, something spicy?'

" 'How about a *shtikl* of nutmeg?' I suggest.

"We named our first fragrance 'Latrine Oh Là Là.'

"Our next creation was 'Pour la Femme Négligée,' which means 'For the Woman Who Neglects Herself.' To the stifling base note of seventy unwashed female bodies we added the fresh citrusy scent of oil of neroli combined with infusions of cypress and eucalyptus.

"All this in fantasy, of course, but it amused us and took our minds away from our nausea."

The Stella of the 1948 photo was less wrinkled than the Aunt Stella I knew. The Colette bangs were darker, the Chanel suit a bit spiffier, but the *sportif* neck scarf and the sibylline little side-grin, which had so appealed to me from the start, were exactly the same. She was posed beside her portable perfume organ, a leather carrying case that unfolded into a triptych of shelves with holes for several hundred tiny vials.

Next came clips from the nineteen-fifties, when the Home Section had become For and About Women.

In a feature on gifts for Valentine's Day by Darcy Feinstein, staff writer:

. . . Perfumer Stella Rossignol, who creates individual scents for her Miami Beach clients, offers the following tips to would-be perfume givers.

"If you know her preferred scent, you can't go wrong in presenting her with an ounce of the *parfum*, which is the extract in its most concentrated and lasting form."

But Rossignol, who once wrote ad copy for Guerlain in Paris, warns against choosing a perfume for your beloved on the basis of fancy packaging or exclusive brand name.

"I know a girl who broke her engagement after her fiancé gave her a twelve-ounce bottle of . . . let us just say a French perfume that advertises itself as costly.

"Poor *shlemiel*, can't you see him striding up to the perfume counter. 'I want the biggest size you've got of that perfume that costs so much.' But when his fiancée opens the package, his goose is cooked. 'I realized he didn't know the first thing about me,' she says. 'I wouldn't be caught dead stinking of that hothouse *dreck*.' "

Next came an un-bylined clip:

Perfume for Men
In Fashion Again

It was Napoleon Bonaparte who put the lid on men's perfumes.

Though he went through several bottles a day of Farina eau de cologne, which you can still purchase today from Roget & Gallet, he forbade all "floral, musk, and amber scents," maintaining that they incited lust and indolence in his troops.

But now, 150 years later, the winds of masculine fashion are shifting again.

"Perfume for men is hardly a new idea. Men have been anointing themselves with precious oils and spices since the beginning of civilization," says Miami Beach's popular custom perfumer Stella Rossignol.

"King David saturated his clothes with aloe and cinnamon. Who knows, it was maybe the king's 'custom scent' that snared Bathsheba!

"The Roman emperor Nero bathed in attar of roses.

"And according to the memoirs of the Duke of Saint-Simon, the court of Louis the fourteenth positively *reeked* of civet," Rossignol adds with a chuckle.

However, Napoleon's moratorium on sensuous scents succeeded in cramping the style of perfumers until the last years of the nineteenth century.

It wasn't until 1889 that the famous House of Guerlain broke the taboo, says Rossignol, who once worked for Guerlain in Paris.

"That year Aimé Guerlain, the head of the house and a famous 'nose,' as perfumers are called in our trade, created a sensational perfume that became an instant must-have for *La Belle Époque*'s aesthetes.

"He named it after his favorite nephew, Jacques ('Jicky') Guerlain. Some people were scandalized by Jicky's audacious civet base note and its indefinable appeal—what the French call *je ne sais quoi*," explains the diminutive Miami Beach "nose."

"But the dandies adored it. And soon it became a favorite with the type of woman who is not afraid to be original."

Stella was obviously the pet source when it came to scent lore, though, two-thirds through the piece, the writer of the men's feature had dutifully squeezed in quotes from perfume buyers for Burdines and Jordan Marsh. Both said that men were definitely buying more colognes and scented soaps, leaning toward Caron's Pour un Homme and Rochas's Moustache, the classic favorites, though Dior's Eau Sauvage was the current rage among young men-about-town. But the standby, they agreed, was still Shulton's Old Spice.

Then back to Stella for a snappy windup. Yes, she had created custom scents for many men since coming to Miami Beach; she couldn't divulge names, of course, but they included entertainers, athletes, attorneys, hotel directors, law enforcement officers, sales representatives, "and the kind of man who has grown bored with the same old de rigueur *shnook*-splash after his morning shave.

"This type of man wishes to go deeper into himself, to experiment with the subtleties of scent, to stir up new moods in himself and others."

Rossignol cites the case of a young man who, just before opening a new business establishment on the Beach, decided to Anglicize his surname.

"He wanted a scent to affirm his new identity. For him I made a fantastic cologne with a dry note of blond tobacco, the clean mossy scent of vetiver, and a base of costus root."

Rossignol laughs. "By itself costus smells of wet dog, but if it is used sparingly in combination with other ingredients, it creates a potent and provocative mix.

"As a matter of fact," the perfumer roguishly confides, "costus is a time-honored aphrodisiac."

I scanned all the intervening minor clips on Stella, snipped and archived in chronological order by the ever-vigilant Moira: a reference to Stella's "Scent Booth" in a trade show; her "Sidewalk Saturday" schedule on Lincoln Road during high season; her advice about making potpourri for the home ("White flowers do not dry well, they turn brown . . . Choose glass or porcelain containers, which don't react with the essential oils of a plant."); her suggested ingredients for "Your Personal Bath Blend": pine needles, sweet orange, lemon, juniper berries, or rosemary for an invigorating uplift; chamomile, clary sage, sandalwood, or ylang-ylang—which Rossignol called "your budget jasmine"—for a calming, soothing bath.

Last in the envelope came the page-one spread in For and About Women, after Marge Armstrong had become the *Star*'s women's editor and Stella Rossignol had her waiting list of clients.

Perfumer Designs "Character Scents" for Miami Notables

By Alma Olsen
Star Staff Writer

The feature had run on the first Sunday in October of 1956. Or, as Paul, always generous about establishing my whereabouts during his own important moments, would have said, "when you were starting your sophomore year in college."

Compared to the other profiles of Stella, this one was drab and uninspired. It was just as well for the reader that the arrangement of the head shots around a new photo of a more-wrinkled Stella with her portable perfume organ took up more space on the page than the writing, which concentrated on the prominent clients displayed in the head shots: Arthur Godfrey; Xavier Cugat and his wife, Abbe Lane; Tommy Dorsey's widow, Jane Dorsey; and Fontainebleau architect Morris Lapidus.

For the Stella parts, the writer had simply lifted chunks from the earlier stories, especially the one Marge wrote when she was a temporary. There was the scent game the two women had played in the French internment camp, though Alma Olsen had managed to drain it of all quickness, humor, and dialogue. There was the "beware" quote about coveting another woman's fragrance, but with the *"chérie"* omitted. As in the previous stories, Stella remained the "chic" or "diminutive" perfumer "who had worked for Guerlain in Paris."

The most interesting observation in the whole piece was the Morris Lapidus quote, which the copydesk had incorporated into its headline: "Just as I imagine myself as a movie set designer when creating a hotel for my client, I see Stella Rossignol as a character designer who employs scent to help define her clients to themselves."

AS THE reporter was still occupying my daytime desk in the city room, I had no choice but to return to the women's cage, where Marge was now seated at her typewriter, pecking out copy. She had shed her terry-cloth turban, and her close-cropped gray curls, dry again after her swim, sprang up around her pleasant tanned face.

"Well, Emma, you must have had a productive hour."

"Was it an hour? This stupid watch, I forget to look at it. It's designed to pass itself off as a bracelet. The minute I get my paycheck I'm going to go to Woolworth's and buy a straightforward timepiece."

"Did you find anything useful in the clips?"

"Well, first of all, I wasn't aware Stella was so well known. And then that game you wrote about? The one they played when they were prisoners in that camp? She sometimes spoke of it, but never in all that great detail. Your interview made me realize I need to pay more attention. I need to get better at drawing people's stories out of them. You really caught her personality, the way she talked."

"Thank you, I worked hard on that piece. I can assure you it didn't look like that the first few times it came out of the typewriter."

She tapped a cigarette out of the open pack on her desk, and glanced down at what she had been writing. "I used to think it would get easier, but it doesn't. I'm still Tillie the Toiler when it comes to prose. Why don't you use that desk, the neat one. It's Darcy's, she's away on her honeymoon."

"She wrote the Valentine piece about Stella."

"You're right, she did indeed. Was it helpful?"

"Next to yours, it was the most help."

"Darcy's my star. I hope we can keep her. What did you think of the other pieces?"

"The one on men's perfumes was interesting, I don't recall the byline."

"It didn't have one. It was assigned to someone we'd just hired, but she dropped the ball. I had to phone Stella and do a makeover."

"The 'de rigueur *shnook*-splash' and the aphrodisiac that smells like wet dog, that was yours?"

"It was vintage Stella. All I did was write it down. If you ask me, Emma, you pay pretty close attention."

"I'm trying to train myself. My stepfather was always telling me I never listened. This person who dropped the ball, was it Alma Olsen?"

"No, the poor ball-dropper didn't last the summer. What made you think of Alma Olsen?"

"Well, because her piece on Stella wasn't very original, just quotes from other people's pieces—she drained the oomph out of those. The only good part was that Morris Lapidus quote about Stella."

Marge made a not-very-serious attempt to suppress a smile. "Originality was never Alma's leading quality. But she has organizational skills, so they tell me. She's Broward women's editor up in Lauderdale now."

As I set up shop at Darcy's desk, I made a mental note to read the complete works of Marge's "star" on a future trip to the morgue.

I flipped open my notepad—all the "fun homes" numbers and contacts were penciled inside the front cover—and dialed Fisher's. The mortician on duty—alas, not my usual contact—said he was still compiling the information on the deceased. Could the *Star* call back tomorrow morning at the usual time?

"Actually, we're trying to put together something a little special about her for the Sunday edition. Miss Rossignol was an interesting figure locally, she created custom scents for many famous clients like Arthur Godfrey and Morris Lapidus—there's lots of material about her in our files for me to work with. All I'll trouble you for tonight, if you could spare me a minute, is her date of birth, and the place—I think it was Leipzig, Germany, but I need to be sure. And could you just confirm that the funeral service is at noon at Fisher's on Monday, with burial immediately following at North Shore?"

It would have been humiliating to have Marge overhear me fail, but he stayed on the phone and warmed to his task the longer we talked. At last I thanked him profusely, hung up, and set to work, stuffing as much color and detail into the limited inches of the *Star*'s standard obit as I thought could make it past the copydesk slashers.

Meanwhile the women's editor pecked and paused and x'd out lines, drawing ruminatively on her cigarette. As she typed, her long-waisted torso rose and sank like that of someone posting on a horse. The aroma of her tobacco I found nostalgically pleasing. Mother had smoked the same brand in her newspaper days, using an atomizer to douse herself with Tweed cologne and chewing clove Life Savers at the end of the day so Loney would believe it was the smoke of *others* that had seeped into her clothes in the newsroom. All the smooth girls at college had smoked, choreographing the act into a rite of seduction. In the early days, before I had cut a dash with my *Daily Tar Heel* column "Carolina Carousel," I always carried a pack of Camels in my purse as a kind of emergency social accessory, though I never learned to inhale.

Marge Armstrong and Major Marjac were both handsome, affable women with careers. They had an aura about them that deterred you from categorizing them as old maids. What if I ended up without a husband at their age? What would I need to have accomplished by then to deter people from pitying me for being single?

My obit was an inch and a half over the limit, but, reading it over, I thought it was substantial enough to make it past the copy editors. I delivered it to the copydesk in person.

"I know it's too late for tomorrow," I told the old slasher on duty, someone I hadn't seen before, "but I want to be sure it'll be in Sunday's paper because the funeral's at noon on Monday."

"Take it to the night city editor," he replied gruffly. "That's the chain of command here."

The night city editor was Vince, from the tornado night. Well, at least he knew who I was.

"I know this is probably too long." I handed him my two pages of copy. "But there was so much interesting stuff about her in our files I decided to risk it."

"Working late again, are you?" He took my obit without so much as glancing at it. "I'll get to it, but not now. It won't run till Sunday, anyway."

"I know. Just so her friends and clients know about the funeral on Monday."

I returned to the women's cage, planning to thank Marge for her hospitality and beat a thin-soled retreat to the Julia Tuttle.

"In the hopper?" She smiled up at me from her copy, which had lots of lines x'd out.

"It's wending its way down the chain of command. Vince says it'll run Sunday."

"Were you happy with it?"

"Such as it was, though he'll probably kill a third of it. At least I can assure the family she's in for Sunday. Which is why I came back to the office."

I tucked my notepad inside my purse and heaved the purse over my shoulder with a sigh.

"It's been a long day for you, hasn't it Emma? Are you tired?"

"No. More like *thwarted*."

"Really? How?"

"I could have gone on much longer. She had an interesting life. From all she told me and then what I read in the clips tonight, I could have done a good piece if I'd had more space to work with."

"Say, twelve inches under a three-column picture?"

"Well, *yes*, but they only allow a one-column head shot. Even for a lead obit."

"I had in mind more of a feature on her life. Liggett's has just pulled a half-page ad on hair care scheduled to run Monday because a shipment of conditioner didn't arrive. That's why I'm working late, to remake Monday's pages. If you felt up to tackling a piece on Stella tonight, I could make it my lead story on Monday. Her friends would be sure to see it then, and still have time to make it to the funeral."

"Twelve inches is . . . ?"

"Four pages of triple-spaced copy. I'd run the photo across the top, under our logo, and have three columns of four inches underneath."

"How much time do I have?"

"Oh, why not just start writing? I'll go upstairs to the photo lab and see what pics are available."

"There's that one where she's posed with her portable organ—"

"I was thinking of that one, too."

ALONE IN the women's cage, I rolled a sheet of copy paper into Darcy's typewriter.

Just start writing.

I'd had no problem tossing off that lead for my woman weather fore-caster—Lord, was that also today?—that made Rod Reynolds happy: "When it rains, Martha Seawell looks out the window and says stoically: 'Hmmm . . . low-pressure area.' "

Now, just do the same for Stella.

Stella Rossignol, who . . .

"Under our logo" meant top right-hand front page, the spot that first attracts the eye of the browser, as we learned in Layout Lab.

The popular Miami Beach perfumer, Stella Rossignol, who . . .

Paul would be surprised and pleased. "Hey, kid, you've got clout."

Glad Stella didn't die on my birthday, or he'd always connect the two events. "I've never seen him so torn up," Bev had said.

Stella Rossignol, Miami Beach's popular creator of signature scents for her clients, many of them household names . . .

Don't panic, Emma. What needs to be accomplished here? "More of a feature on her life," Marge said.

Stella's life. Germany, France, the United States. Leipzig, Paris, Miami Beach. Three countries, three languages—four, counting Yiddish.

Sixty-five. Loney was seventy-three, but much less wrinkled.

Stella Rossignol, the custom perfumer about whom one of her famous clients said . . .

Stella Rossignol, the Miami Beach scent sorceress described by Morris Lapidus as "a character designer who uses scent to define her clients to themselves" . . .

Calm *down.* Stop x-ing out. Write something, anything, whatever comes to mind, and *leave* it, even if you paste it somewhere else in the copy later on.

discovered her perfect pitch for scent while in an internment camp for Jews in Nazi-occupied France . . .

Marge came back with our photo.

"How's it going, Emma?"

"Oh, I haven't hit my stride yet, but I'm getting there."

"Good girl. Big excitement on the front desk. Joelle's just delivered her firstborn from the new Cuba, so we're not the only ones remaking a front page tonight, only theirs is for tomorrow. I ran into Vince up in the photo lab looking for a halftone of a plow to go inside the box head."

"What's it about?"

"The reaction from different levels of society to Castro's land reform. I grazed the wire copy while we waited up in photo. I had my order in first, but of course Vince took precedence because his deadline is in twenty minutes."

"So, what did you think of it?"

Marge gave me the same equivocal smile as when I had asked about Alma Olsen. "It's the quintessential Cutter-Crane recipe for success. First paragraph describes the wealthy, arrogant landowner playing roulette at the Hilton casino and cursing Castro's landgrab; second paragraph describes the dirt-poor couple who've been tilling other people's land for centuries; next paragraph quotes their joy and humility at the prospect of having sixty-six acres of their own. 'Now we will be rich'—followed by alternating pro and con quotes from an unnamed Cuban businessman friendly to America's interests, an unnamed official in Washington who sees gradual land reform as preferable to chaos and Communism, and a final quote from an unnamed spokesman for an American sugar corporation hinting at a possible right-wing counterrevolution being plotted right now. Plus some historical filler about mankind's attempts at redistributing wealth since the French Revolution."

"But why did he need a halftone? She took a photographer with her."

"Oh, there's a nice Don Kingsley shot of the smiling dirt-poor couple. The halftone of the plow will go inside the box head as a logo for the series, 'Cuba's Great Experiment.' "

The positive thing about my envy of others was that it could be depended upon to rev up my incentive motor. I sat up straighter at Darcy's Remington, pounded its keys harder, and mentally steamrollered over my picky inner critic holding out for the perfect lead. The day would come when, like Joelle, I could effortlessly knock out a story—an Emma Gant story—and everyone would run around remaking the front page.

16.

AT 10:26 P.M., HAVING finished the piece on Stella to my satisfaction and Marge's, I stood in the humid dark outside the *Star* building, waiting for the presses to roll.

Five nights ago, Paul's car was pulling up directly across the street. Five nights ago, Aunt Stella was up in Carolina, flitting about the Inn, helping out. She had three days to go before overhearing the chef complain about "Hymie cuisine," and two more days on this earth after that.

The folder spews the first complete paper onto the belt, the foreman does his quick page-through, then signals for the presses to accelerate to full speed. Faster and faster chop the folder knives until the beat merges with the roar of the presses into a screaming blur of sound. The pavement vibrates beneath my thin soles and last Sunday's Paul cups my knee with his hand.

"Seventy thousand newspapers an hour. Just think, kid, your byline hitting the streets seventy thousand times."

My rapturous flight took an abrupt plunge as someone touched my elbow.

"Yikes! *Alex.*"

"Oh, Emma, you were watching the presses?"

"I *was.*"

"Sorry if I startled you."

"How did you know I was here?"

"I phoned your room. Then I phoned the paper. They said you'd just left."

"Who's they?"

"First a man, then he transferred me to a woman. She said you'd just left."

"What's up? Is Lídia's party still going on?"

"The food and the drink are finished, but they are still dancing and talking. Everyone is very excited. Don Waldo Navarro and his new bride came down to the pool and now the women are busy taking apart Altagracia's traveling dress and liberating the note cards that will be Don Waldo's new book. Listen, Emma, I'm starved. The tapas were long gone when it was Enrique's turn at the desk. Will you join me for a *medianoche* at La Bodega?"

"ALEJITO, *señorita* Gant! As you see, my *clientela* has abandon me for a party at your hotel. *¿Qué pasa, Alex?* Your lovely mother—she has just telephone for us to send over six dozen empanadas and two cases of beer. What is the occasion of this party?"

"Probably she is organizing a new *movimiento*. We'll take that booth by the window, Victor."

"Not your *abuelo*'s usual table?"

"I think not. Tonight I am slightly overdosed on *la familia*."

"Ah, *sí* . . . ha, ha . . . *entiendo*. And how is the newspaper business, *señorita*?"

"WHY WERE you working so late at the paper, Emma?"

Though I was dying to hear more about the interesting old man who had smuggled out his book inside the dress of his bride, I explained about Aunt Stella and the feature I'd written that would run on Monday.

"Ah, so that was your phone call from Mrs. Nightingale. To tell you her aunt had died."

"*His* aunt. Stella was his mother's sister. He's bringing the body back to Miami on the morning plane. Bev asked me as a personal favor if I could help him go through Stella's things and sort of bolster him up over the weekend. Bev says he's really cut up about it, Stella was closer to him than his mother." Two "Bevs," three "Stellas," and a smattering of mere pronouns for him. Way to go, Emma.

"A little woman with dyed hair and an old-fashioned suit?"

"That's her. The suits were Chanels. She worked for Guerlain in Paris." I was offended by his description of one of the first female perfumers in the country.

"Yes, I've seen her over at Nightingale's, running up and down stairs, making herself useful."

"That was in her spare time. She was a very renowned perfumer on the Beach; she created custom scents for famous people like Arthur Godfrey and Morris Lapidus."

"I met Morris Lapidus once, at Joe's Stone Crab. I was with Abuelito, he introduced us."

As he fitted together the missing pieces of my itinerary and found connections to his, Alex's mood was improving noticeably, even before Victor brought our lagers.

"It's a good thing you don't drink the Mexican *cerveza*, Alejito, because I just send over my last cases to your mother's party. Your *medianoches* are on the grill. *Es mi ronda, amigo.*"

"*No, no, Victor, gracias, pero—*"

"*De nada, de nada. La próxima la pagas.*"

"Well, thank you, Victor."

"My pleasure. Enjoy, *señorita.*"

"What was that all about?" I asked.

"Victor insisted on buying our lagers. *Salud*, Emma."

We clicked our glasses and sipped.

"It has been an extremely turbulent day," declared Alex with his vehement rolled *r*'s. "It is a relief, having you across from me, Emma. Being around my mother gave me asthma as a boy; now she gives me vertigo. You remember our *más mío* conversation from last time?"

"Yes, of course."

"Well, Lídia, when she is at full force, makes me *menos mío*."

"I also have people who make me *menos mío*."

"Do you really, Emma?"

"Sure, though I didn't think of it in those terms until you said it just now. My first close-range *menos mío* person was my stepfather, Earl. He could make me feel really stupid. He could even cause me to make the mistakes he predicted I was going to make. And now at the *Star*, there's Lou Norbright, the assistant managing editor, who really runs everything. He is a master confidence-leacher. He has a way of *gleaming* at you so you see yourself in his mirror and you can read his reservations about you in a sort of subliminal text. Is that anything like what Lídia does to *you*?"

"It is difficult to describe. When I am in my mother's presence, I stop thinking of myself as the main person in my own life. It is *Lídia* who is the author *and* the central character. I am there to carry out her wishes, to facilitate the things she has decided must happen next."

"Somebody needs to invent a kind of spray-on *menos mío* diffuser. Maybe an aftershave for you and a cologne for me. I'd call mine 'Get Thee behind Me, Satan.' They actually do call him 'Lucifer' in the newsroom. What would you call yours?"

"You're so agile with words, Emma. I must think. '*Déjeme*,' perhaps? Leave Me Alone. Or '*Mejor que no*'. I'd Rather Not. Wait! What was the phrase Bartleby the Scrivener used in the Melville story?"

" 'I would prefer not to.' "

"Yes! Until I come up with something better, dear Emma, I shall think of my spray simply as 'I Would Prefer Not To.' "

"Or just 'Bartleby.' And, on second thought, 'Satan' is a giveaway, so I'll call mine, let's see, 'Deviled Egg.' 'Bartleby' and 'Deviled Egg.' Code names to cover our tracks if we need to warn each other in the proximity of the enemy."

Seeing Alex de Costa laugh gave you a glimpse of the boy he may have been before he got all entangled in separate selves. It was the laugh of a boy who was part of an insider gang and could let himself erupt naturally. It attracted me, just as I had been attracted when he was being so managerial on the night of the tornado, switching languages and taking charge of the fallen palm tree and the well-being of his guests.

"Speaking of words," I said, "what does *'barbudos'* mean? I missed out on a joke by that Don Waldo when he was checking in because it was the single word I didn't know."

"Yes, I remember. He said all he required was that their accommodations be free of *barbudos*. *'Barbudos'* means bearded. *'Los barbudos'* has become the epithet, not always flattering, for Fidel's revolutionaries. Though Fidel's *barba* is rather *flaca*. Che Guevara has the most photogenic beard."

" What is *'flaca'*?"

"Oh, thin, wispy. Not curly like Che's. I'm sure Fidel envies Che's beard and hates when they are photographed together. Fidel is much taller, however."

"It's a wonder anybody ever becomes bilingual," I said morosely. How had I managed to drink three-fourths of my lager?

"Don't worry, Emma. All those years you spent at St. Clothilde's and now surrounded by so many of us at the Julia Tuttle, you're ahead of the game."

Where else had I heard that phrase recently? Ah, yes, Major Erna Marjac, assessing the bright and shining product in front of her, minus all the Earl shadows.

"*¡Aquí están! Dos medianoches. Buen provecho, señorita, Alejito!*" With great flourish Victor presented our sinful sandwiches, still crackling from the grill and oozing bubbly cheese, and flanked by those sweet-smelling Cuban banana halves. "Careful, *señorita* Gant, that plate is very hot! Alejito? *¿Otra de lo mismo?*"

"*Sí, Victor*," said Alex, after checking the state of our glasses. His was half empty. "It seems we are thirsty tonight."

"Now tell me," I said to Alex, "who is Don Waldo and what is this book he smuggled over in his wife's dress? I *thought* that billowy dress was an odd choice for traveling, it rustled like it had crinolines sewn into the skirt."

"It was Altagracia's wedding dress, which was permitted to be rustly and billowy, and the 'crinolines' were his long-awaited *memorias*, written in tiny script on both sides of note cards. Who is Don Waldo? Where to begin? He is listed in professional biographies as a Cuban essayist, critic, and educator, born in Madrid in 1882. I have a few of his *obras* in translation, which you are welcome to borrow. Who is Don Waldo to our family is more complex. He is my second cousin twice removed and became Lídia's father-in-law briefly. Later he was her favorite professor at the University of Havana until the dictator General Machado closed it, and he has been her cherished mentor and correspondent for years, though she writes to him more often than he writes to her. I took Don Waldo's Poets and Rebels Seminar during his visiting semester at Harvard and made an A-plus. Lídia, of course, took the credit when she found out about it later, but I wrote the best term paper of my life."

"How could she take the credit?"

"Because Don Waldo belonged to her first, and because she knew Lorca and Jiménez—my term paper was about the influence of New York City on Martí, Lorca, and Jiménez. Martí alone escaped her clutches by dying before she was born. Otherwise it would have been, 'My son Alejito is writing his paper on three of my good friends: José our great liberator, dear naughty Federico, and poor Juan Ramón.' At Harvard, Don Waldo assumed I was simply Alex de Costa from Palm Beach, he didn't connect me with the de Costas from Camagüey Province, not that Don Waldo would have reason to know any cattlemen. He had known my mother as Lídia Prieto Maldonado, and I wasn't about to reveal myself as Lídia's son, until the course was over. How is your *medianoche*, Emma?"

"Even better than last time. I've been trying to figure out why. It's crisper and butter-ier on the outside, and the filling is nice and runny, yet the pork and cheese maintain their separate textures."

"That's the mark of Victor. He made them himself."

"Good Lord, is the *cook* at Lídia's party, too?"

"I wouldn't be surprised. Look around you. Only a few *turistas* who wouldn't know a good *medianoche* from a perfect one."

"Do you really think your mother is starting a new *movimiento*?"

"Lídia adores having a new cause. She has the time and most decidedly she has the energy. And she rides into town with my grandfather's and stepfather's blessings and on their bank accounts. Fidel can't bite the dust soon enough for Abuelito and Dick. His messy revolution is delaying their plans for that new hotel on the Malecón."

"The one you're going to manage?"

"*¿Quién sabe?* Today my crystal ball is *ess-TRRREME-ly* vague." Alex's savagely rolled *r* gave emphasis to his suddenly clouded-over face. He was feeling edged out by Lídia, displaced from his role as person in charge at the Julia Tuttle and manager-in-training for his grandfather's future hotel in Havana. If I had been a better person, I would have rerouted the conversation back to his successful term paper, New York's influence on Martí, Lorca, and Jiménez—Why was Lorca "naughty"? Why was Jiménez, who had won the Nobel Prize in Literature only three years before, "poor"?—but my curiosity had its own system of priorities.

"How did Don Waldo happen to be Lídia's father-in-law?"

"She eloped with his son, Jorge, when she was sixteen. Abuelito got it annulled and Jorge entered the Jesuits."

"Now wait, was this the same Jesuit who taught Castro and became his friend and supporter?"

"You remember everything, Emma. Yes, that is Jorge, but Don Waldo was telling us tonight that Fidel is now beginning to turn a cold eye on all priests and nuns, even those who were his dear friends. Poor Don Waldo is going blind. His wife had to sign the register."

THE POOLSIDE party I walked away from three hours earlier had undergone changes of tempo, set, casting, and even lighting. The little orchestra Lídia had hired off the street was playing a slow, romantic dance tune. A singer had been found from somewhere and he was crooning a song many of the guests sang or nodded along with. I picked out the words *"dos gardenias," "te quiero," "te adoro," "mi vida," "corazón," "calor,"* and *"beso"*—all of which suddenly recalled to me that my own *corazón,* Paul of the Roses, would be with me as soon as tomorrow. A few couples danced; the other guests chattered in Spanish around the wrought-iron tables that

Wednesday's tornado had sent shrieking across the concrete. Waiters (from where? La Bodega?) served drinks on trays.

But all this was background, the guests (who appeared to be a fresh batch) relegated to the role of extras hired to provide ambience for the center-stage pageant.

NEAR THE entrance to the pool, two floor lamps with fringed shades had been brought outside and hooked up to extension cords to illuminate the wondrous-strange proceedings. Within the twin circles of golden lamplight were gathered what first appeared to be three seamstresses bent over their work: Marisa Ocampo, her daughter Luisa, and the tall young mulatto woman who was Don Waldo Navarro's bride. Flanking them and facing each other in matching wing chairs dragged out from the lobby were portly Don Waldo, cheerfully puffing a cigar, and Lídia, arranged like a compliant schoolgirl, ankles crossed demurely below the flounces of her red flamenco skirt, head modestly lowered, reading aloud the topmost note card from the stack in her lap.

"Cuando no puede vestirse de piel de león, vístase en la de vulpeja." When you cannot dress yourself in the something-or-other of the lion, dress in that of . . . Damn it, what was a *vulpeja?*

Appreciative nods and murmurs. A sweet little twitch of Luisa Ocampo's mouth.

"Saber ceder al tiempo es exceder . . ." To know blank of the time is to . . . what? *¡Mierda!* Poor show, Emma.

The voluminous taffeta traveling dress was spread across the laps of the three who were intently picking out its seams, squeezing out one after another the contraband note cards of Don Waldo's memoirs, and handing them over to Lídia, who all of a sudden became aware of Alex and me observing their tableau from the sidelines.

"Niños, come and join us! Don Waldo, this is our young *periodista* I was telling you about, Emma Gant, who writes for the *Miami Star.* Emma, *querida,* may I present my dear cousin and mentor, Don Waldo Navarro, one of our great men of letters."

Gripping the arms of the wing chair, Don Waldo with a rolling motion of his rotund belly was making ready to rise.

"Oh, please don't get up," I said.

But already he had nimbly sprung himself to full towering height. "Why not?" demanded the jovial sepulchral voice. "I am still a vertical animal."

He laughed and grasped my hand in both of his, as Hector Rodriguez had done earlier. A Cuban masculine thing?

"Encantado, señorita Gant."

Though Alex had said Don Waldo was almost blind, the old man appeared to be taking me in with the full advantage of twenty-twenty vision in its prime.

"They tell me you have been working late at the paper, *señorita*."

"Yes, a good friend just died. I wrote her obituary."

"Ah, I doubt I shall have such good fortune."

"Sir?"

"I mean that a good friend will write my *necrología*. It is especially unlikely in Cuba now. Certainly not in *Granma*."

Delighted laughter from his adoring circle, except for his wife Altagracia, who simply kept on picking out stitches from her amazing traveling dress. Perhaps she knew little or no English.

"The official newspaper of the Revolution," Don Waldo explained to me. "*Granma* was the name of Castro's sailing vessel in his botched attempt to bring down Batista in 1956."

"Alejandro!" Lídia called sharply just as Alex was edging away. *"Una silla* for Emma, *por favor."*

Alex turned on his heel. *"En seguida, Doña Lídia,"* he replied dryly, executing a curt bow.

"And—and bring a chair for yourself, too, of course," Lídia called after him, a mollifier he gave no sign of having heard.

"Tell me, *señorita* Gant, how do you find living among this hotbed of exiles?"

"It has given me a taste of being an exile myself."

"*¿De verdad?* I am curious to hear more."

"Language, for a start. I guess it's mostly about language."

"Please continue!"

"Well, here I am among people who speak a language I have studied in school and still I can understand only about one word in every five, if that. But the situation could be much worse. What if the Julia Tuttle were a hotel filling up with Polish exiles or . . . or *Swahili* exiles?"

"Then both of us would be in trouble," remarked Don Waldo, with his basso profundo laugh. "But please, go on!"

"And then, looking at it from the other side," I continued, aware that I had captured his interest, "these people . . . I don't mean like yourself or . . . or Marisa Ocampo, who went to an American school . . . but many of the people here find themselves having to start all over with little or no English. And it's demeaning. You lose your *graces*. Being bereft of your native language even affects your posture." (I was thinking of the gesturings that accompanied the Spanglish hash of handsome Enrique Ocampo, whom Alex and I had just glimpsed hunched at the switchboard, waving his hands wildly in an attempt to make himself understood to the party on the other end of the line.)

"A very perceptive observation, *señorita* Gant."

"I wish you would call me Emma, Don Waldo."

"With pleasure . . . Emma. One of my favorite heroines. We are on our way to Princeton, where I will deliver a lecture titled 'The Journey from Delusion to Reality in the Novels of Jane Austen.' With particular emphasis on *Emma*, and, to a lesser degree, *Pride and Prejudice*."

Don Waldo's fluent British English was lavishly colored with Spanish intonations, and his Spanish *s*'s and *z*'s thick with the *castellano* lisp. "Providential for Altagracia and me, the Princeton engagement was confirmed eighteen months ago. It afforded us the perfect opportunity to vamoose.

" 'You are traveling light, *compañeros*,' they said while pawing through our things at José Martí Airport today.

" '*Ah, sí, compañeros*, only these lecture notes on Regency literature you have examined from my briefcase, a change of shirts, an extra pair of eyeglasses, a change of outfit for my wife—*pasamos la luna de miel*, we are making a short honeymoon out of my lecture obligation before we return home.'

" '*Ah, felicidades, compañeros. Buen viaje. ¡Hasta pronto! ¡Viva la Revolución!*'

" '*¡Viva la Revolución, compañeros—hasta pronto!*' " Don Waldo lowered his voice to a throaty whisper. " '*¡Pero no aguantes la respiración, compañeros!* Or as we say in English, don't hold your breath! Then, very calmly, with deliberation, I replaced the lecture notes into their little hammock where they ride in my *portafolio*, I closed it with a smart click-*click*, and then, very calmly and with majesty, Altagracia took my arm and she and her whispering skirts swept us through the last barrier into the departure lounge, which we call *la pecera*, the fishbowl, because it is enclosed by glass."

"And nobody suspected the whispering skirts?"

"*Por Dios*, nobody. Again providential that <u>susurrating</u> skirts are in fashion."

I was racking my brain for a half-remembered line of poetry, *the susurration of the pines*, something like that—Poe? Whitman? Milton?—to keep up my end in response to Don Waldo's agile parlance, when Enrique Ocampo brought out "my" chair. He was placing it according to Lídia's instructions—next to her, not to the great man of letters—when the musicians struck up a jaunty little number that elicited a roar of joy from Don Waldo.

"Ay, 'Bonito y Sabroso'! Who can resist? Emma, may an old man have the honor of this dance?"

Having acquired the rudiments of Latin dancing under Bev Nightingale's tutelage, I accompanied Don Waldo more or less confidently to the dance floor. The music was fast, but hadn't I cha-cha'd successfully with Tess's precise and sinuous Hector Rodriguez earlier this evening?

However, I was no <u>terpsichorean</u> match for Don Waldo. At first I tried to follow, always a half beat or more out of time with his confident, high-bellied prancings. We were doing, as it turned out, the mambo, a much faster and more syncopated cousin to the rumba and the cha-cha. Every time I tripped over one of his sudden dips or pivots I apologized profusely, but he gamboled blithely on, singing the words to "Bonito y

Sabroso" along with the vocalist, smiling as though he had Isadora Duncan in his arms. He was astonishingly dainty for a man of his height and girth. When I finally went limp and let him take over, it worked better. Several times he literally swept me off my feet.

Once the ordeal was over, I expected to be led back to my appointed chair next to Lídia, after which he would select a more competent partner—his lovely young wife, for instance, or Marisa Ocampo, or Lídia herself, who had shot several disapproving looks my way.

But the next song was "El Manisero," which Pepe Iglesias and I had danced to at St. Clothilde's. Pepe had brought his very own 45 single of "El Manisero" to a tea dance and Mother Patton had allowed it on the turntable—"A simple Cuban folk melody about a peanut vendor," she had announced. (She also endorsed the rumba, with its arm's-length requirement for good form.) With no part of our torsos touching, Pepe took gloating pleasure in coaching me in the song's double entendre lyrics. "Here, listen: in this passage, the *manisero*, the peanut vendor, is advising the housewives and young girls not to go to sleep without first tasting some of his hot nuts!"

With a rumba one could combine conversation. For half a second I was on the verge of sharing my Pepe and "El Manisero" story with Don Waldo, but I realized in time that the possible loss of respect from that gent was not worth the joke. I opted instead for safe Old World courtesy and congratulated him on his marriage.

"*Muchas gracias*, Emma. Altagracia has no need for an old rooster like me, but it is my good fortune that she desires to serve. I don't mean like *una criada*, a servant, but like a *religiosa*. She has the soul of a nun. She offered to leave me and enter a convent, but I said, Wait! Enter my convent and see the world. She was raised in my house, her mother abandoned her to her grandmother, Altagracia, who was my *ama de llaves*, my housekeeper. When Altagracia died, the girl asked permission to take her grandmother's name. Rosita, the name the girl was given by her unfortunate mother, did not match with her soul, she said. She was perfectly willing to leave Cuba with me as my *ama de llaves*, but I explained why she must go as my wife. In Cuba, you see, we are all shades of the rainbow. Batista himself was a mulatto, though he'd have you executed if you reminded him after he became dictator. *Mulato lindo*, that's what they called him when he worked as a water boy on Enrique Ocampo's father's plantation, 'the pretty mulatto.'

" 'We are going to the United States of America,' I told Altagracia, 'where people of color use separate *baños* and must sit in the rear of the *guagua*, the autobus. You must be Doña Altagracia Navarro in order to receive the respect to which you are entitled.' "

"What is the difference between calling someone *señora* and calling her *doña*, Don Waldo?"

" *'Don'* and *'doña'* are marks of respect to a superior person—or else to a very old monument like myself. The use is dying out, however."

Alex must really be vexed with his mother to have addressed her coldly as "Doña Lídia." And she, who now regarded me none-too-warmly from the sidelines, had picked up on it, too.

The peanut vendor was urging the housewives and maidens to partake of his hot wares before they went to sleep, and I thought it prudent to cast my eyes down while knowing laughter rippled from the surrounding tables of Cubans.

"How long will this revolution of Castro's last, do you think?" I asked Don Waldo, when we were back on safe ground.

"It is not easy to predict, Emma. Fidel insists that his revolution is as green as the palm trees. But there are those of us who have lived through previous revolutions who are saying this one begins to look more like a watermelon, green on the outside and red on the inside. If Mother Russia does decide to play godmother, we may live to see some very strange fruits growing from Cuban soil."

17.

"COME, EMMA," BOOMS Don Waldo's sepulchral voice.

"Where are we going, Don Waldo?"

"You are embarking on your journey. Tell me when you are ready."

"Is it far?"

"Geographically, no. We need only cross the lobby of the Julia Tuttle."

"The Mother of Miami. My aunt Tess's grandmother sewed Julia's dresses before her untimely death. Julia's death, I mean, not Tess's grandma's. Julia worked too hard at her dream and now nobody knows who she was."

"*Granma* in COO-bah is the official newspaper of the Revolution."

"The Watermelon Revolution."

"Very perceptive. May I offer you my arm? We will cross the lobby together."

Our passage is sluggish, as though we are dragging through ankle-deep water. But there are the dry Mediterranean tiles below us, though for the first time I notice that each tile bears the face of a different primitive god. All of the faces are spiteful or malevolent.

Don Waldo stops to converse in Spanish with the dominoes players. I can follow the gist, though they rattle along at breakneck speed. Don Waldo is explaining that the American *señorita* understands more than she lets on. He tells them I am going on a journey.

"We will miss her," says one.

I feel ashamed of not perceiving them as individuals. When will I learn to pay more attention?

Now we're standing outside the Julia Tuttle, where the cars pull up.

"Any minute now," says Don Waldo. "Ah, here they come."

A sleek black Cadillac materializes out of the darkness and glides to a stop under the canopy. The chauffeur, in full livery, is Tess. In the backseat, head modestly bowed, is a woman whose face is obscured by a dense bridal veil. Next to her, looking heartbreakingly desirable, is Paul Nightingale in wedding clothes.

"It is a great match," Don Waldo intones. "Beneficial to everyone! They are embarking on their honeymoon."

"*La luna de miel*," I translate, trying to hide my pain.

"You will be bilingual in no time, Emma. Aren't you going to offer them your *felicitaciónes?*"

"They aren't even looking at me, Don Waldo. I seem invisible to them, or are they under a spell?"

"The spell of *el corazón, sí.* But you are a young woman who started ahead of the game and will want to do the correct thing. Think of Jane Austen. Ay, *niña*, don't let them see you cry!"

"I can't—" I am dissolving.

"Then simply raise your hand in farewell, *señorita.* They are your *compañeros primeros*, the ones closest to you when you fall asleep."

I make a supreme effort and lift my arm and flutter the fingers in a limp, childish way. Tess in her natty chauffeur's cap continues to face front serenely, but Paul has seen my gesture. He gives me a cool, curious look—Who is that woman going to pieces outside the car?—then returns his attention to his bride. He lifts her veil and raptly contemplates his prize: Ginevra, Queen of the Underworld.

"They were made for each other," booms Don Waldo. The front door of the Cadillac swings open and Don Waldo moves forward and without a glance at me folds his great bulk into the front seat, beside Tess. The black door swings shut and the four of them glide soundlessly off into the night.

Oh God, how did I not recognize it, when the signs were all over the place? Tess putting me off about getting together with Ginevra, Paul pretending to be up at the Inn in North Carolina, Bev offering the decoy of Aunt Stella's death, Don Waldo keeping me dancing and chattering inanely to "El Manisero." This was too much to bear, it must be a dream, any moment now I would wake up.

But it's not a dream, a voice-over says, *because didn't you see the Cadillac sink when Don Waldo transferred his weight inside? That is a detail from reality. And here is Lídia in her red dress of the evening: more reality.*

"Oh, there you are, Emma. I have been looking everywhere for you. We are going to need your help in the kitchen."

"But Don Waldo said I'm going on a journey."

"What journey? Nobody told me about a journey. Your journey is here with us. Look what I have done, to save you time."

She unfolds an apron with something embroidered on it. "You like it, *querida?*"

She has cut my initials, Loney's beautifully embroidered handwork, out of my new blouse and carelessly tacked them onto the apron, which she now attempts to tie around my waist.

"Hold still, Emma, there is much we must do. *Dios mío,* what is the matter now?"

YOU . . . YOU . . . HAD NO RIGHT . . .

Though my wail of outrage was enough to awaken me mid-cry, the malign residue of the experience hung thick in the room.

What was the purpose of these melodramas authored by the nether side of my own mind while I slept? Or *was* there any purpose? Assuming there was, then you either looked for omens—Joseph interpreting Pharaoh's dreams—or you looked for a pattern in the story that pointed to something in your waking life that you needed to pay attention to.

I lay very still and set about detoxifying myself. This was Room 510 at the Julia Tuttle and it was Saturday. For the second day in a row there was sun on the other side of the blinds. The television was on in the next room. The electric clock on my bedside table said half-past nine. The first week at work was over. I had comported myself honorably throughout and shone on one or two occasions. Lídia was miffed that I had danced

and jabbered with Don Waldo and then added insult to injury by pleading journalistic exhaustion and leaving the party without ever sitting
down in the chair she had ordered placed next to her. Tess was learning
to fly an airplane and had neglected to tell me, but that did not mean she
was plotting perfidies behind my back. Ginevra was not on her honeymoon but most likely lying in bed over on Key Biscayne right now, post-
poning beginning another day as Mrs. Brown. Did her dreams assemble
collages torn from the colorful old days and nights on Palm Island when
she supervised wardrobes, ordered food and drink and flowers, penned
Federal Judge So-and-so's name neatly into the incendiary little black
book, summoned the girls when their escorts arrived by Cadillac or
yacht? How frequently did *her* unconscious construct melodramas from
which she woke herself wailing? Or did the chloral hydrate Dr. Brown
doled out to her smother all dreams?

Bev had said Paul would be arriving in Miami on the noon plane. Even
if the plane was dead on time, it would be close to one before he could
get to the Julia Tuttle. I had three, maybe four hours to put to use.

First, as always, came sustenance, but how was I going to negotiate the
distance between me and breakfast without passing through Lídia's orbit?
She was sure to be whipping about, radiating her *menos mío* toxins, and a
quick flip-up of my window blinds revealed this to be so.

There she was below on the pool terrace, darting from table to table
in a pert white blouse with sailor collar, navy pedal pushers, and matching espadrilles, pouring coffee from a silver pot. You could see from five
floors up that she was playing herself as the *"doña,"* who had instigated *desayuno* for her guests in less than twenty-four hours and was now graciously serving them.

Though I had met her only yesterday, I felt capable of providing her
lines as she addressed the captive audience under each umbrella. To the
dependable beat of "I" and "my," every topic from revolutions to embroidery would be orchestrated to provide a gloss on the life and times of
Lídia Prieto Maldonado (plus wherever the surnames of her five husbands wedged a place for themselves).

I could sneak out to Howard Johnson's, but what if Paul got delayed or something and tried to reach me and whoever was on the desk said "Five-ten doesn't answer." What would he think then? Ah, the kid couldn't be faithful to me for one week.

I picked up the phone and dialed the desk. Please let Alex, or at least Luís, be on. I wasn't up to communicating with Enrique Ocampo without benefit of gestures.

"Emma! Good morning, how are you?"

"How did you know it was me?"

"Your room lit up on the switchboard."

"Listen, Alex—"

"You don't sound so good, Emma."

"As a matter of fact"—he had given me the perfect alibi—"I'm definitely under the weather, but I've got to feel better because I've promised to help Bev's husband clear out his aunt's house this afternoon."

"You need some nourishment, Emma. Mami and her minions have assembled the promised *desayuno*, such as it is, down here, but I rather think you'd be better off with American coffee and your usual eggs or pancakes. Shall I send Luís over to Howard Johnson's?"

"Oh, Alex, would you?"

"Our pleasure. I'll send up a paper, too. You have a nice big appearance today on the front page of the Metro Section—about the lady who forecasts the weather."

"Oh, is it in already?" With all the events of yesterday, I had completely forgotten about Martha Seawell and her low-pressure area.

"It's on the upper half, or whatever you call it—"

"Above the fold."

"Above the fold, with her picture, and a nice big byline that says 'By Emma Gant, *Star* Staff Writer.' Now, would you like Luís to order you eggs or pancakes—or perhaps both?"

"Just maybe some soft scrambled eggs and toast." Pancakes on the side, while tempting, might seem excessive for someone claiming to be under the weather.

"With melted butter, right?"

"Please."

"And don't you want your *grits*?"

"Well, maybe yes."

"Melted butter on them, too, right?"

"Right."

"And a large orange juice?"

"Uh—"

"For the energy, and vitamin C."

"Oh, true. Alex, thank you so much."

"*El gusto es mío. Señor* Bartleby must take care of his Deviled Egg."

WHILE WAITING for my breakfast, I slipped Paul's dressing gown over my pajamas, plucked out several wilted roses from my birthday bunch— two of the reds, the mauve, and a coral—forcibly restraining myself from looking for meanings in their order of decay, and then sat down at the desk and dashed off a letter to Loney on Julia Tuttle stationery.

Loney was the easiest, because I didn't have to marshal my thoughts as I did with Mother. Mother expected some semblance of narrative form in a letter, with little asides of philosophy interspersed to show I was paying attention to my life's voyage. Whereas Loney relished simple details of weather, clothes, food, and gossip. Whatever ones I served up on the page, in whatever order or no order at all, would provide savory fare for Loney's rereadings.

I started with the tornado and said I was fine, even though I had been out in the thick of it, doing stories about the injured at the hospital. Then I went right on to the seabreeze salad Tess had served me and what Tess had said about Loney making her feel special all those years ago in Mountain City after she had just ruined her life. I said I had looked up the hitherto-left-out details of the ruin in the *Star*'s files and that the young war-hero brother-in-law Tess had gone to live with had asphyxiated himself in their garage. I thanked Loney for the lavender bath salts and nylons and said I hoped I didn't wear holes in the stockings before I got some money to buy another pair of heels, as the soles of my college ones had become thin as sandpaper after just one week of walking to work. I told her I had inaugurated "our" embroidered blouse at last night's poolside party given by our hotel manager's elegant Palm Beach mother, who had effusively praised Loney's embroidery. I wrote that there had been almost solid rain here until yesterday, but now that the sun had at last acknowledged my arrival I planned to take my maiden swim in the beautiful Olympic-size pool today, though I did not have a proper beach robe or shoes. My raincoat and Bass Weejuns would have to suffice. My faded old one-piece racer from St. Clothilde's swim team was ludicrously unfashionable in a place like Miami, but it had the advantage of modesty while at the same time emphasizing my long waist and narrow hips. Before sealing the letter, I included clippings of my tornado story on Mr. Sprat and Lola, and Jake Rance's fashion photo of me modeling the raincoat and hat.

I HAD made it halfway through a letter to Mother by the time Marisa Ocampo brought my breakfast tray. "*Lo siento,* Emma, sorry for the delay. Oh, what beautiful roses! You see, the food was not hot when Luís returned from the Howard Johnson's, so we warmed it for you in the oven. And here is your newspaper. *¡Y mira!* I am bringing you my yearbook from Santa Clothilde's, *Le Flambeau* from 1951. Of course, you were still in the lower grades, but you will recognize some of the girls and all of the nuns. Please, keep it as long as you like. *¿Está bien?* And now Luisa and I shall walk with Altagracia over to Gesu Catholic Church. It is a good thing it is so close, as Don Waldo says his wife is extremely *devota*. Altagracia is beautiful, don't you think?"

Cuba's Great Experiment

**Castro's Land
Swap Triggers
Hate and Joy**

*Staff Writer Joelle Cutter-Crane is touring neighboring Cuba to report
firsthand on Fidel Castro's new policy of taking land from the rich
and giving it to the poor. This is the first in a series of articles.*

So there it was, taking pride of place in a two-column boxed presentation, top front page left.

Marge's summary last night of Joelle's "firstborn from the new Cuba" had been right on the money. The "quintessential Cutter-Crane recipe for success" was a perfect little crowd-pleaser of a fable. The arrogant Cuban landowner losing money at the Hilton casino's roulette table and snarling at Castro; the humble peasants elated over their very own acres. And there was the Don Kingsley portrait of the smiling peasants, the wife bent and toothless, the husband leaning against his hoe. Followed by a mixed chorus of "unnamed" denigrators, well-wishers, and fence-sitters.

"Prices Highest Ever (AP)—$1.24 Today is $1 of 1947–49" and "Work Crews Return City to Normal after Tornado" shared the rest of the above-the-fold space with Joelle, while below were "Prosecutor of Tokyo Rose Takes Life in Seattle" and "Grizzly Bear Mauls Man in Glacier Park," both from AP, plus "Today's Chuckle." (Is your wife economical?" "Sometimes. She used only 30 candles on her 40th birthday cake.")

Then on to the Metro Section.

She Charts Steady Course

Martha's Career Is Stormy

By Emma Gant
Star Staff Writer

When it rains, Martha Seawell looks out the window and says stoically, "Hmmm . . . low-pressure area."

Then, if it's a working day, she puts on her slicker and goes down to the Weather Bureau. If you are one of the people who call that day to ask whether downtown Miami is flooded or whether you should plan that barbecue, you'll probably talk to Martha.

Miami's only lady meteorologist, she's accustomed to answering the phone and having a voice say, "Please connect me with someone who knows something."

"Lately, it's gotten better," Martha says wryly. "Now they call and say, "Let me talk to someone.""

The city's lone weatherwoman has been measuring cloud heights and mapping low pressure areas here for 16 years. When she came to Miami after finishing a weather-observer course in Atlanta, she told friends: "It'll be easy predicting the weather down there. It's always sunny."

"That was before I met a hurricane," she says today.

During Hazel, in 1954, which kept the Weather Bureau on a 24-hour vigil, Martha issued scores of bulletins heard on radio and TV. When her time came to go home and snatch a few winks on the Friday night Hazel struck, where did she go?

Martha drove over to Haulover Beach to watch the waves. "I'd never seen hurricane swells before," she said. "I'd been so busy predicting them or drawing them on charts. This was my chance to come face-to-face with the real thing."

On her days off, Martha and her husband, Alan Seawell, drive to Tampa Bay to collect minerals and gems (they belong to the Lapidary Guild and the Miami Mineral and Gem Society). If it rains, they stay at home in North Miami and mull over their extensive collection.

"That is, until the phone rings," laughs Martha. "Usually it's one of my friends calling me instead of the Bureau to ask when I think the weather is going to clear up."

On Martha's behalf, I deplored the tiny one-column profile head shot. She could have been any female with cast-down eyes, lipsticked mouth, and the glint of an earring. The cropping excised all traces of her wit or professional status. I had liked her on sight and felt a surge of comradery when she confided her "Let me talk to someone" experience. I wasn't the only professional woman who had her Charles P. Rose cross to bear.

I glanced over my "fun home" obits, adding up to eight this morning in their tiny, tedious format.

Mrs. Rebecca Brule

Services for Rebecca Page Brule, 82, of 500 N. 17th Ave., who died Thursday at Jackson Memorial Hospital, will be at 2 p.m. Saturday at Fairchild Funeral Home. Interment will follow at Evergreen Cemetery. Mrs. Brule, who moved here 35 years ago, is survived by a sister, Mrs. Elizabeth Kuntz, and a brother, Robert Page.

Elmer F. McConnahey

Services for Elmer F. McConnahey, 77, of 42 Sidonia Ave., Coral Gables, will be at 7 tonight at the Washburn Funeral Home. Mr. McConnahey, who came here seven years ago from Baltimore, was a retired auto dealer and a member of the Coral Gables Country Club. He is survived by his wife, Becky. Burial will be in Baltimore.

Everybody who croaked—as Bisbee so elegantly termed it—got one of these 8-point notices. From their boilerplate group appearance under "Dade Deaths," it was hard to believe each one had been individually composed about an untransferable self by another untransferable self.

Even if you were the mayor, you got the 8-point in addition to your front-page story. In Sunday's paper Stella would have her boilerplate, which I had labored to expand and individualize as far as the space limits allowed. And on Monday Paul would open up his paper and there would be her front-page profile in For and About Women. I would tell him today, of course, so he would know it was coming.

Very soon it would be time for my bath—late enough to maintain the clean scent, but early enough to avoid being in the tub when Paul might phone from the airport.

In the interim I took up Marisa Ocampo née Velázquez's handsome 1951 *Le Flambeau*. Each graduating class got to choose the color and style of its leather cover, as long as the icon of the lit torch was somewhere in sight. Marisa's year had distinguished itself with smooth, plump cream leather bisected top to bottom by a fiery red torch. My own Class of '55, of which I was no longer a member when it came time to graduate, had chosen a flattish crimped leather in powder blue with a door-key-size torch in the lower right-hand corner.

I recalled a vexing afternoon in Chapel Hill when a former classmate from St. Clothilde's discovered me in the student lounge and insisted on dragging me across the street to the Chi O house to show me "our" year's *Flambeau*, assuming I was dying to see it.

"There's Julie Orbach looking sultry, you'll remember even back in ninth grade what a terrible flirt she was. She dropped out her first semester in college to get married—they say she had to."

It was an ordeal to sit hip to hip with this girl I had never much cared for on her Bates bedspread in the overheated room choked with ruffles and be led page by page through memories in which I figured as a ghost. There was the row where I would have appeared among the seniors, alphabetically flanked by Melanie Jane Frazier and Stephanie Goode, each of us in a dark, round-necked sweater set off by a single strand of pearls. There were my absent pale thighs in the swim team lineup, my editorial influence missing from the yearbook staff. ("Listen, we can do better than this wrinkly powder blue—and that insignificant torch wouldn't attract a moth.")

"Of course, *you* would have been one of the Outstanding Seniors, if you hadn't moved away," the yearbook owner assured me, with a little butt-wriggle of complacency, as she herself had made the list of eight, her specialty having been "best personality."

Yes, there I *wasn't*, a missing full-page portrait of myself at eighteen in V-necked velvet evening dress with sleeves, the St. Clothilde Honor Cross on its gold chain resting in my modest décolletage—and below, my stash of ghostly accolades: "With scholarship offers so far (as this book goes to press) to Radcliffe, Bryn Mawr, and Salem College, Emma Gant (Please! No relation to Eugene!) is headed for success whichever alma mater she picks, etc., etc.

At last I had escaped the Chi O hothouse—a yearbook with a graduating class of twenty-one girls contained only so many pages, after all—and trudged back to my dorm in a blue funk. It was impossible to locate the cause of my disquiet. After all, hadn't I made it anyway? Here I was, a junior in college, even without the tailwind of strenuous St. Clothilde's; I loved being on a university campus where there were ten males to every female; and I had my own column bearing my mug shot twice weekly in the *Daily Tar Heel*. ("Why, you're already famous on campus!" cried Best Personality of '55 as she pounced on me in the student lounge.)

What's going on here? I asked, kicking savagely at the fallen leaves in my path. Whence came this sudden wind-rush of miasma? Surely I can't be mad because someone else wrote the class poem when I could have done a better job. Who on this earth has ever managed to live two lives at once?

That I couldn't track the miasma to its source made it all the more oppressive.

When I got to my dorm room, I found my roommate, a devout Christian Scientist, crumpled on the floor "working on" an injury. Someone had kicked her in the stomach at basketball practice.

"Can I do anything?" I asked.

She said no, but it was comforting just having me there in the room. So I propped up pillows on my bed, intending to sketch out my next *Tar Heel* column in a notebook. But what came instead, like ointment being squeezed urgently from a tube, was the class poem I didn't get to write.

On a fair hill stately set,
Saint Clothilde, you claim us yet.

We who came of age
Within your cloistered walls
Still haunt your winter-lit schoolrooms,
While nuns chant psalms in chapel gloom,
Hearken to your raven's call,
Tilt on wings in his deep air,

Ride his mountains range on range,
Peaks inflamed with autumn change.

Time was prime.
The soul unfurled
Midst sullen winds and rain
And crisp blue space again,
Scudding drifts of colored leaves,
Hoary frost on Hallows Eve,
Nativity beneath the throbbing stars.

Spring's wild green hour!
A girl's song floats from topmost tower:
"Saint Clothilde in thee we glory,
All thy daughters love thee well,
We hail your name in song and story,
Would that we knew more to tell."

A god-struck Queen,
Pet raven on your arm
Converts your king
And lures us hence from harm;
Your dream of lilies in a field
Replaced the frogs on France's shield.

Name Saint of our beloved school
On fair hill stately set
Mysterious Queen, though you entice me yet,
I fain would fare thee well.

—Emma Gant, '55

Even as my pen rushed across the page, doubled back to cross out, tried a different scan, a better rhyme, I could hear Mother Patton, principal of the high school, revising over my shoulder:

"I can assure you, Emma, we don't think of our chapel as *gloomy* . . .

"You will need to capitalize 'His' if you mean God's deep air. You don't? Then whose? Are you implying the *bird* owns the air?

"That raven she's holding, by the way: I know of no hagiography that mentions Saint Clothilde having a pet raven. Falconry is more of a king's hobby.

"And the frogs definitely have to go. They set the wrong tone. We know Saint Clothilde had a vision of lilies and that's how King Clovis's banner came to have fleurs-de-lis instead of toads—in ancient France the toad symbolized protection against armed attacks. Yes, I agree, 'toad' is an ugly word in a poem, but 'frog' has other unfortunate implications, it's a slur word for the French people. You'll need to rework those lines, Emma."

But I didn't have to change a damn thing, because the poem belonged to me. That was one advantage of nonpublication. By then, the troubling afternoon had darkened into supper hour, my roommate had prayed herself out of her stomachache, and both of us in better moods walked uptown in the Halloween weather for hamburgers and coffee at Harry's Grill.

THOUGH I had no school memories of the eighteen-year-old Marisa Velázquez strolling through the grounds of St. Clothilde's, her every appearance leapt boldly out at me as I leafed through the yearbook she had brought back with her from Cuba. Someone—not hard to guess who— had *colored* all the Maria Teresa Velázquezes throughout the black-and-white pages of *Le Flambeau 1951*: the senior portrait with pearls, the secretary of the Pan American Club, the member of the Glee Club and the Children of Mary Sodality, the subcaptain of the Tennis Team. It was a child's job, but that of a careful child, who kept within the lines and had a flair for realism in skin tone and clothing, considering her limited palette of crayons.

18.

"YOU'RE DIFFERENT," PAUL SAID.

"But you were with me last Sunday and today's only Saturday. How could I be different in less than a complete week?"

"That's what I was asking myself."

"In what way am I different?"

"You're not a college girl anymore. That's as far as I've got."

I kept quiet. I knew he'd share his insight as soon as he found words for it.

He was by no means the wreck Bev had prepared me for. He looked tired and older, but not red-eyed or bereft. He was more like someone who's had a serious setback and in a thoughtful manner is assessing the damage.

We were in a booth at Wolfie's on the Beach. Paul had hot tea in a glass fitted into one of those metal holders, but so far he hadn't touched it, whereas I had sipped my iced tea down to the ice level. He expected me to eat, it made him happy, and though not enough time had elapsed for me to be truly hungry again, I chose the hefty-sounding Reuben, which was still only just a sandwich, which I could cut into pieces and consume slowly. After a cursory glance at the menu Paul settled for a lox and farmer cheese omelet ("Tell the chef to make it dry, please") and some rye toast on the side.

He had driven his rental car straight from the airport to his house to take a shower before coming to get me. So typically Paul. His clothes were fresh Paul-clothes, the dark gray Lacoste today, with his silky silvery jacket. His signature scent, created by Stella, emanated from those little sunken notches above his collarbone where I liked to bury my face. Had he choked up when splashing it on? The salt-and-pepper hair was slightly ragged at the nape of the neck, but he had just informed me that his next stop was the barber. ("Meanwhile you can case the shops on Lincoln Road.")

I had been all prepared to comfort him, whereas here he was sitting across the table puzzling out in what way I was different since last Sunday.

Things had gotten off to an unpropitious start when he picked me up at the Julia Tuttle. As I stepped off the elevator, Lídia was just sinking her claws into Paul, who was waiting near it.

"Ah, Mr. Nightingale, our dear Emma here has told us your sad news—we heard it from her last night when she returned to the party—after she wrote your aunt's *noticia* for the newspaper. My son Alejandro, the manager, has gone out on an errand, otherwise he would join me in offering our condolences. Do you know, I myself once visited Stella Rossignol in her little shop over on the Beach! I went with someone who was having a personal formula made up for her and she urged me to choose one for myself. Your delightful aunt was extremely (*ess-TREME-ly*) patient with me. We tried many combinations from that adorable little cabinet of hers until she finally said to me, '*Je ne suis pas une sorcière, Madame, mais je vous parie quand même*'—we were speaking in French—'I am not a sorceress, but I can tell you all the same: you are an original. Your only *parfum* is a certain soap.' And she named the soap, a Spanish one which I order from abroad. I was extremely impressed! 'You may not be *une sorcière*,' I told her, '*mais vous avez une nez formidable!*—you have a formidable nose!'"

If Lídia had been getting her revenge on me for leaving her party early, she couldn't have done a better job. She made it sound as though (a) I belonged to *them* now, and (b) that I couldn't wait to get back to the party after fulfilling my chore of writing Stella's obit. This before I'd even had the chance to tell him about the feature.

Paul continued to study me, but not in a critical way. I didn't think my "difference" had anything to do with Lídia's preemptive assault. In fact, he'd said as soon as we were in the car, "The lady comes on strong, doesn't she?"

As we drove to the Beach ("You hungry?"), I'd told him about my feature on Stella, which would be running on Monday—"That's in addition to the obit"—and he'd covered my hand with his. "You never cease to amaze me," he said.

Last Sunday, after having been apart for half a year, he had covered my hand exactly like that as we drove to the Beach. "How is it you are always better than I remember?" he had asked.

"And how is it you are always more important to me than I remember?" I was about to respond, but didn't. It might sound as though I devalued him in his absence, when what I meant was that each time we got back together I was reminded, with a shock of surprise, how deeply I could feel for someone.

Now he was shaking his head and smiling faintly.

"What?" I asked.

"The fights those two used to get into."

"Who?"

"My mother and Stella. After Stella got out of occupied France and came to live with us in Miami Beach."

"What did they fight about?"

"Oh, they stuck to a pretty standard menu, but they never lost their appetite for it. Family matters, for the most part. Which sister had been the more favored. My mother was the beauty and Stella was the brains, so this fight had several outcomes, depending on which parent was being accused of favoring beauty or brains. Then there was the bigger bone of contention: who was to blame for their mother's running away. This also had a variety of outcomes, depending on the emphasis."

"She really ran away?"

"When Stella was twelve and my mother ten. Left a note saying not to try and find her, she wasn't worth it."

"What did the father do?"

"Depended on the fight my mother and aunt were having. He hired detectives, was convinced of foul play, never stopped looking for her. Or he wrote her name in the Book of the Dead and destroyed her letters to the girls. Or he himself sent her away and paid her to stay away."

"Was she a bad mother? A bad wife?"

"Ah, that's material for another fight." At last Paul sipped his tea. "Phew. I've let this go cold. She was fifteen years younger and her parents were Silesian garment workers. She ran away to the big city of Leipzig and got a job in a department store and married the owner. Then, thirteen years later, she ran away again. And that led to the next item on the menu: which sister got off easier putting up with the father afterwards. As my mother eloped to the States when she was nineteen, Stella usually won that fight because she stayed in Leipzig and helped run the store until she was in her thirties and took off for Paris.

"Of course the prize fight was always over which sister had suffered the most for being Jewish." For the first time he laughed, showing those small, level teeth with no fillings, recalling to me that first day when he came to Earl's house to interview me and I entertained him with my story of the tough maître d' who'd fire a waitress if she asked her table "Who gets the fish and who gets the chicken?"

"But surely, Stella— I mean, Stella was in a *camp*—"

"That was always my mother's opening shot. 'You think, Stella, just because you were the one who was in *the camp*—'

"And then Stella'd jump in with *her* lines: 'I know, I know, Trude-*lein*— only seven months in that *bubkes* camp, who am I to complain? A few shit smells, a little dose of daily fear, a nice mattress of straw, so what? Mere *bubkes*! While you in this free country, *pauvre petite soeur*, are still being tortured by those disrespectful signs in the windows of *goyisher* hotels.'

"When the hair really started to fly they'd switch to German and up the ante until Stella would draw herself up and assert her dignity as the elder sister and say in English, 'Listen, Trude, it's time I stop being a *bor-derkeh*, I'm crowding you and Paul in your nice apartment.'

"And she'd put on her French suit and one of her scarves and go off to look for a place of her own. And as soon as she was out the door my mother would start to cry. 'Run after her, Paul,' she'd say, 'she's my sister, she's the only family I have left in the world.' "

"And you were how old?"

"Twenty-four. Night manager at the Miramar and still living with my mother. I wasn't in uniform yet. Pearl Harbor was still to come. You were, let's see, four years old."

"So, you ran after her?"

"I didn't have to run very far. She'd be waiting for me at the deli around the corner. 'You want tea or root beer, *chéri*? I advise the tea. Hot tea on a hot day cools the body.' Of course, I'd have the root beer, hot tea was for older ladies. Stella was all of forty-eight at the time. Now I'm almost there myself, and you know what?" Paul raised his tea glass in a sort of toast and now I could see the sorrow in his face. "She's right. Only I've let this tea get cold." He signaled a passing busboy. "Would you please ask our waiter to bring us refills on our drinks?"

"And would she then go look for a place?"

"After we'd had our *petit déjeuner*, as she called it, Stella'd have the prune Danish with her tea and I'd have the almond Danish with my root beer. We pounded a lot of pavement before she found her little hacienda on Espanola Way."

"The place she's been in ever since." Both of us, I noticed, were still using the present tense for Stella.

"She knew it was for her the minute she saw it, though by then Espanola had turned into the opposite from what old Roney, the big developer back then, had envisioned. Somewhat the same story as my club in Bal Harbour—the developer has a vision, but reality turns it into something else. Some vacationing friends from New York had told Roney that what Miami Beach needed was an artistic quarter with a foreign atmosphere, like Greenwich Village, or Montmartre in Paris. So Roney hires an architect to make Espanola Way look like an old Spanish village. He builds a couple of hotels, some apartment buildings and shops, all small-scale, with stucco façades and wrought-iron balconies and red-tiled roofs, gaslights, the whole works. He even hires Spanish-looking girls to drift about with shawls and fans. My mother and her cronies had a good laugh because most of these dark-eyed beauties were local Jewish girls. But he'd got half of the street built and the businessmen still weren't biting, so he dropped the project and transferred his energies to creating his masterpiece, the Roney Plaza.

"Espanola Way went to seed fast. During Prohibition, it was mostly bootleg operations posing as news shops and shoeshine parlors. Stella's little corner building had been designed to be either a fancy shop with an upstairs apartment or a Spanish bistro with a walled patio, but when we saw the Realtor's For Sale or Rent sign in 1941, the windows were broken and the floors were full of trash and worse. It was demoralizing just to stand outside.

"But Stella, she looked through the broken windows at the ripped-out staircase and the dog turds and said, 'I can have my flat upstairs and my shop down here.' It was the first I'd heard mention of a shop. We'd assumed, as soon as she had her naturalization papers, Stella'd get a job maybe as a buyer in a store like Jordan Marsh, with her fashion sense and French airs. I asked what kind of shop, she tells me she hasn't decided. Antiques or cosmetics, maybe a combination of both. 'Anything's possible,' she said. 'After you've been as good as dead, Paul, you stop making difficulties for yourself in your imagination and just get on with what you'd like to do next.' I date the change in my life to when she said that. She made it sound so sensible and easy. My mother, you see, was always imagining the worst and then being, well, almost let down when it failed to happen. So why not just cut the dire imaginings out of the deal and take the chance and bet on something you'd like to do next?

"Even the Realtor tried to discourage Stella. The last tenants of the building had run a rumba studio fronting for a bookie joint, and when they did their midnight flit they took all the moldings and fixtures with them. The place would need major work, and he'd hate to see a lady like herself go to a lot of expense and then have the owner, who was pretty disgusted with Espanola Way, sell it out from under her to the first *shlemiel* buyer who made a reasonable offer. He said he'd show her better rental properties on better streets, some with ocean views, places she could move right into. How much was she willing to spend? 'No, you don't understand,' she tells him, '*I* am your *shlemiel* buyer—if your disgusted owner is willing to accept my reasonable offer in cash.'"

"But where did she get the cash?"

"She kept it in a false-bottomed scent case she had had made for her, right after Paris fell—the one your manager's mother called her 'adorable little cabinet.' When Hitler passed the law forbidding Jews to own property, her father sold the family store in Leipzig. He divided the proceeds, wired half to us in Miami and half to Stella in Paris, then shot himself."

"Stella never told me that part. She said he expected her to take over the store when she'd had her fill of Paris."

"That's Stella for you, always emphasizing the positive and leaving out the negative. After the nonownership law was passed, some Jews would let a Gentile buy the business on paper and they'd wait it out till things got better. My grandfather obviously didn't think things were going to get better. My mother bought a house with her share; we took the top floor and rented out the downstairs. Stella lived on hers in Paris and rescued what was left from the bank as soon as France fell. She left the case with a friend when she had to go to the internment camp. Here comes our food. It's about time. Lucky for her, the case was still intact when we sent the affidavit that freed her to come here. Waiter, we need refills on our tea. I guess the busboy didn't deliver my message."

"So you get your beverages *and* refills on us. Be right back, sir, with the drinks. You and the lady enjoy your food."

"What score do we give him?" asked Paul.

"Five out of ten?"

"If he hadn't thrown in the free beverages. Refills are always free. Plus he's been hustling a loaded station, five full tables and our booth."

"So, what do you think?" I was impressed that all during the time he'd been reminiscing about Aunt Stella, Paul's managerial eye had never stopped keeping watch.

"How about six out of ten and a decent tip?"

As we strolled down Collins, Paul to his barber and me to case the fancy shops on Lincoln Road, he said, "Walk on ahead of me."

"Why?"

"Go on. Just for a minute."

I obeyed, swinging into my conscious Bev-walk.

"Okay, that'll do."

"What was that about?"

"Bev made me promise to check out your shoes. She said, 'If they're her same ones she had at Christmas, they'll be getting run-down at the heels.' " He pulled out his wallet. "This is from her. Go into Saks and get yourself a new pair."

"That's way too much."

"It's what she specified. And if anybody should know what shoes cost, it's Bev. There's the Raleigh, it's supposed to have the most beautifully designed swimming pool in the country. We'll go for a drink some evening. And that's the Delano, interesting story there. Just after the war, the city council passed an ordinance prohibiting construction work from November to April within fifty feet of any existing hotel. To protect the seasonal guests, you know. All we had was the winter season back then. Well, as soon as the Delano broke ground, the hotel next door set up a howl and the police swept in and arrested all the Delano construction workers. So the Delano developer sues not only the city but the individual council members. The council calls an emergency session and amends the ordinance to read fifty *yards* instead of feet. But that wasn't good enough for the developer, he didn't withdraw the suits. A month later the council decided to lift all bans on construction, whatever the season, and the postwar boom was on with a vengeance."

"The hotel next door must have been furious."

"It was demolished soon after. True to Miami Beach jungle law. Some always going up, others always coming down. Speaking of jungles, here's Lincoln Road, a mangrove jungle less than fifty years ago. According to

Bev, Saks has the widest choice of shoes. I'll come looking for you after I get shorn. Forty-five minutes give you enough time?"

Warily entering the perfumed chill of Saks, I paused beside a counter heaped with delectable silk scarves and made sure my moat of reserve against fashion intimidation was intact before continuing on. I'd been in Saks with Bev at Christmastime, when she had sprung her shopping trip on me, almost catching Paul and me in bed at the Kenilworth, but on that day she had marched me in and out of stores with a specific purchase in mind, the black dress we subsequently found at Lily Rubin's for which she had insisted on paying half. Now, however, there was no well-disposed guide to shield me from the competition.

You'll be fine, if you'll just remember you can't be everyone at once. Loney's advice.

Okay: not that rich spoiled teenage goddess trying on belts over her sexy tennis dress; not those two glamorous matrons spritzing themselves with cologne testers and then solemnly sniffing each other's wrists; not the regal old girl in black picture hat and elbow-length gloves being shown the inside of an alligator handbag by a reverent saleslady.

Just Emma, with her lover's wife's cash gift in her purse, headed for Shoes.

Ginevra from her Palm Island days dropped down and strode along beside me, the Mafia uncle's roll of bills zipped into her purse. ("Here, get what you need in Saks for the party tonight. And better pick up some stockings and costume jewelry for the girls. Forty-five minutes enough?")

Two salesladies were tracking me; they were probably on commission here. Lídia would simply whirl around and fasten her talons on the nearest one.

"Yes, can you help me? What I am looking for is a good-quality dress pump. Three-inch heel, in black leather. And it must of course be satisfactory for walking."

"Certainly. What size does madam take?"

"Well, you see, my heels are an eight *narrow* but my toes sometimes require an eight *medium.* I also have an *ess-TREME-ly* high instep. So I may want an eight *and a half,* depending on the brand of the shoe." Bombarding her with my idiosyncratic requirements from the start so she can come staggering out with a double load of narrows and mediums in two different sizes.

Impersonating Lídia—or a toned-down version of her—turned out to be a practical move. It streamlined the transaction and left me with time to spare. I stopped off at Costume Jewelry, my Saks bag dangling like a prize from my arm, and browsed the offerings under glass. Returning to my fantasy of Ginevra in Saks, I now pretended to be the young madam choosing baubles for my Palm Island girls. Maybe the pearl drop earrings for Dolores, whose lobes were pierced; the rhinestone hair clip for Mona's thick dark locks; the dinner ring for Celeste's tapered fingers. Was that the sort of thing Uncle had in mind? Or would his taste be too gaudy for someone trained to Biscayne Academy standards? Avoid ostentation, Miss Edith—like Loney—would surely have preached. Make classic simplicity your Royal Road; though, with costume jewelry, you can allow leeway for wit and humor.

"See something you like?" asked Paul, who had stolen up beside me.

"Oh! You look—"

"Is it too short? We got to talking about one thing and another. And he knew Stella."

"No, it's—" It's beautiful, you are beautiful to me, was what I was actually thinking. "It brings out the noble shape of your head," I said. It did, he looked like the immaculately groomed prince of some small kingdom tucked away in another hemisphere.

"As long as you like it, I'm satisfied."

We stood there in a sort of rapt contemplation of each other until he broke the spell by nodding toward the shopping bag on my arm. "I take it you had success?"

"I'm afraid so. I spent all Bev's money."

"I told you she knew what shoes cost."

BACK IN Collins Avenue sidewalk traffic, we threaded our way between beach-attired bodies ranging from the reproachfully perfect to the obscenely gross.

"Your Carolina mountains have declimatized me," Paul said. "I never used to notice the Florida heat in summer. I'm going to propose a change in plans. Instead of rushing down to Espanola Way to deal with Stella's stuff, let's get the car and drive up to Bal Harbour and see if the ambassador is upstairs in his bedroom at the club. What would you say to that?"

"I'd say it's a five-star plan."

We switched directions and crossed to the shadier side of the avenue. "Here, let me carry that," said Paul, relieving me of the bag inside which the costly shoes snuggled head to toe in the tissue of their I. Miller box.

A feisty little beige dog with a pink bow in its topknot lurched toward us on its taut leash, dragging a beefy, perspiring man. The man saw Paul and stopped in his tracks, all but garroting the little dog, who let out an aggrieved yelp.

"Paulie the Stern!"

Paul squinted hard at the man. "Irving Katz," he said neutrally. "You've filled out some since we last met."

"All that starchy Cuban food. And the sugar in the drinks—disgusting! I'm a lot trimmer now than I was back in January. Been on a strict steak and J&B regime since Manny brought us back home to the Beach. You've stayed your same old stern skinny self, Paulie. You look swanky as a peacock. Or I guess I better say nightingale now, ha, ha."

"Emma, this is Irving Katz. We went to high school together."

"Yeah, I taught him everything he knows, ha, ha. A pleasure, Emma. You a local girl?"

"Emma is a reporter for the *Miami Star*," said Paul, whose demeanor was growing frostier by the second. He had neither presented me to Irving Katz nor supplied my surname.

"Oy! I better mind my p's and q's, hadn't I? Don't want to get off on the wrong foot with the *Star*. You should write about his club, Emma, or maybe you are. Everyone's talking about Nightingale's up in Bal Harbour. I hear the artwork upstairs is exceptional, the paintings and decor and so on. Putting in another kitchen, too, Paulie? For late-night schmoozing? But listen, enough. None of us wants to fry on the sidewalk. Plus I got to get Trixie back to the hotel. Manny's a strict observer of the Sabbath, so it falls to an infidel like me to open and close his refrigerator and turn on his lights and walk his pup. He's gonna be tickled pink when I tell him I ran into you, Paulie. You know, we need to talk sometime very soon. Because I'm thinking we could provide some additional services for your expanding operation."

"I'm not looking for additional services, Irving. I plan to stay small."

"Ah, still the same old Paulie the Stern. The bird moniker hasn't lightened you up, has it? Well, don't rule it out, Paulie; I just seriously would not rule it out if I were you. Manny was saying just this morning that with all these refugees from Castro pouring in, the sons of Abraham are gonna need to close ranks against the Cuban Mafia. You know the funny part about all the spics flooding in, I said. Now it's gonna be someone else's turn to 'ruin the beach.' We get to be the old settlers for a change, ha, ha. We can put up our own signs: 'Restricted to Members Only. If your grandparents didn't come over on the Yiddish *Mayflower* before Prohibition, don't bother to apply!'"

19.

"IT'S NOT YOU," SAID PAUL, wrapping himself around me under the sheet. "It's nothing to do with you."

"It's not important."

"It is important. We're two fine-tuned individuals who can't shut off our minds from our bodies. It's always been more than just the act for us."

"What I meant was, it's not important to me as long as I know I haven't turned you off in some way."

"I repeat, it's nothing to do with you. I'm just sorry I had to introduce you to that bum."

"But you didn't introduce me. You never said my last name. You just told him where I worked."

"I was of two minds about that. But people in his racket cultivate a healthy fear of the press. And I didn't want him making any impertinent assumptions about you."

She is his mistress and they've been shopping at Saks.

"What *is* his racket?"

"Does the name Manny Lanning mean anything to you?"

"He's some kind of gangster, isn't he?"

"A charter member of our Miami Beach Shady Hall of Fame. When Kefauver killed local gambling, Manny packed his roulette wheels and took off for Cuba. Batista welcomed him to the table—he skimmed off his own juicy cut, naturally. They shared a profitable coexistence until Castro took over and they both fled Cuba on New Year's Eve. Now he's relocated back here on the Beach. Gambling's always been Manny's first love. He thinks he owns the sport."

"But what do they want from you?"

"It's called protection. They want to guarantee protection for my 'expanding operation.' "

"Oh, God, even I know about that from the movies. But he called you 'Paulie.' Was that your high school name?"

"My *friends* called me Paulie. Every time I heard it out of Irving's smarty mouth, I wanted to mash his face in. He was an insufferable tagalong, a would-be punk. He was always trying to do something showy and dangerous to impress us. He stuck to me like chewing gum on a shoe because I was halfway decent to him. My mother told me I had to be, because his mother cleaned hotel rooms, but it wasn't easy. When he turned sixteen and started running betting slips and money for the S&G syndicate, he became truly insufferable."

"The S&G syndicate?" Foreseeing more homework for myself in the *Star*'s morgue.

"A cartel of local bookmakers. Highly organized and controlled by Manny and his cronies." Paul tugged up the lightweight blanket and rearranged us under it so that he lay on his back and I fit into the crook of his arm. It felt cozy and privileged to be tucked up close with him against the air-conditioned chill when people outside were sweltering in the streets. Paul's old-fashioned desk lamp with its green glass shade bathed us in its underwatery glow. As always, the blackout shades were drawn, cloaking us in an aura of fantasy and—had our encounter with Irving Katz not tainted the word with irony—protection.

What had happened, or not happened, between us in bed was a first for me. It was fraught with complexities that called for a new kind of response. Before Paul, the omnipresent—omni*pressing*—urge of the male member had demanded simple responses from me, depending on the person attached to it: outright blockade ("Nope, that's as far as *you* go"),

postponement ("I'm not sure how I feel about you yet"), or erotic dé-
tente ("Okay, you definitely arouse me, but please take precautions").
The few times I had awarded my body as a sort of merit badge for someone's persistence had left me feeling queasy and untrue to myself. With
Paul, I had been the one yearning for his body while he was still in the
stage of wanting to protect me. In a way, I had seduced him by falling in
love with him. And now, this afternoon, when I was more in love with
him than ever, the requirements had suddenly changed. He was my first
older man. What were the courtesies older people showed each other
when their bodies sprang surprises? It had always been more than just the
act for us, he'd just said, and whatever this unpredictable afternoon turned
out to require of me, I wanted to honor that notion.

"Supposedly 'S&G' stood for Stop and Go. Meaning sometimes the
heat was on and the syndicate had to lie low and other times there was no
heat at all, everybody had been paid off, you could flourish openly in the
bright sunshine. As I said, Manny was the kingpin and it was a highly organized affair. S&G would negotiate the concessions for its bookies,
paying a top hotel like the Roney up to fifty thousand dollars for a
winter-season rental. The syndicate took care of all the business details:
accounting, payoffs to law enforcement, you name it. It was so prosper-
ous and smoothly run that it achieved a sort of respectability. The S&G
boys dressed well, gave money to charity, and were not harassed by the
police, who went after the sleazier bookies. S&G bookmakers had their
own cabanas at the big resort hotels, and guests who wanted to play the
horses could lounge by the pool and summon a boy like Irving Katz to
run their bets to the cabana while they ordered another Tom Collins and
waited out the race. Meanwhile back at headquarters, the syndicate was
taking care of all the organizational details and deducting a king-size
chunk from each bookmaker's profits."

"Is this what they're after with you? They want to take part of your
profits and in turn they'll keep the police away?"

I burrowed deeper into the cave of his armpit, picking up for the first
time, beneath Stella's custom scent, a personal odor. It was not a sweat

smell or an unwashed smell—an unwashed Paul being a contradiction in terms—but it had a distinctive acrid pungency, like a glandular release of the afflictions playing out inside him.

"It's not the police I'm worried about. My members pay dues and if they want they can go upstairs and have a game of cards or dice. Cabbies don't drop off tourists at my place and get a fifty-dollar thank-you note from the doorman."

"Then—I don't understand—what would this Manny be protecting you *from?*"

"Oh, small mishaps, to start with: a small electric fire in the kitchen when no one's there. A faulty stair riser so someone falls and breaks a leg. Then, if the owner is being stubborn, something foul finds its way into the water lines and the club has to close down till it's fixed. If the owner is still holding out, next is maybe a major break-in by hoodlums who completely wreck the place—"

"But . . . those are *threats.* Like the mob or something."

"Darling, this *is* the mob. Miami Beach is mobbed up, that's what my barber just got finished telling me. The old gang's back in town, he said; Manny Lanning has a suite at the Sherry Frontenac, and everyone's wanting a piece of the action."

"If only we hadn't crossed to the other side of the street! You wouldn't have run into that Irving creature."

"He would have come looking for me. It was only a matter of days. I was already on their list. Not a big fish, but at this stage they're testing the waters. You heard him going on about my upstairs kitchen, the 'paintings and decor.' He's already been inside. He knows what's behind the big fox-hunting painting. Probably one of the construction crew let him in, someone on the payroll. Construction people make ideal snoops. No, at this stage they want to find out who's for sale and who isn't and blow the isn'ts out of the water early in a style that will make other isn'ts reconsider. A small fish like me could be a timely warning to others."

"But what are you going to do?"

"I want no part of it. He's peddling his gefilte fish in the wrong market."

"But then, won't they start engineering their 'mishaps'?"

Paul freed his arm and rearranged me so that my head rested against his chest. "That's what I'm lying here thinking about. I'm happy you're here with me, so we can think about it together. Say I phone the Sherry Frontenac tomorrow and say, Manny, I'm willing to talk—"

"But you just said you didn't want any part of it!"

"Shhh, hear me out, kid."

He began stroking my hair back from my face in a soothing rhythm that seemed to blend with the beat of his heart. "We're just going through the options. Think of it like someone's writing a story. Maybe your good friend Thomas Mann. So far he's got this guy who's built a nice little business for himself, a private club on the Beach, open during the winter months, where members, many of them prominent lawyers and business types who have known one another since childhood, can go and feel welcome and have a good dinner and some entertainment or wander upstairs and join a bridge or poker game or open up the door behind the painting and play the wheel. The last few years he's even realized a profit, which he decides to reinvest in an upstairs kitchen for late-night short orders, just like the country clubs and the old-time 'gentlemen's casinos,' like the old Royal Palm over on Biscayne Bay. So. Everything's going great until there's an upheaval in a little entertainment capital to the south and the gambling mob has to leave that little country in a hurry and restart its business in the old neighborhood. It takes them a few months to set up headquarters, hunt up old contacts and make new ones: find out who's doing what, and who's doing *well*. And on the list of those doing well is a small, discreet club, a sole-owner operation, that's investing in improvements. A lackey checks out the site himself, recognizes it belongs to an old buddy, or would-be buddy, from high school, and soon afterwards has the luck to bump into him in broad daylight.

"We'll skip the next scene, with the Sabbath dog-walker and who said what on Collins Avenue. Your friend Thomas Mann's already got that part written and we've just read it. Now we have to move on to where the story can branch out in a number of different ways. You still with me?"

"Yes."

"Let's start with the surrender option. I call Irving and say, Okay, let's talk. I'm invited over to the Sherry Frontenac suite and they roll in the hospitality wagon and there are little kosher delicacies and sealed bottles of Black Label and Cuban cigars. Irving calls me 'Paulie' a few thousand more times while Manny treats me like the prodigal son and makes optimistic talk about partners in an expanding business. I walk out a protected man but not my own man anymore. Or ever again. And once a week during season some bagman, maybe an Irving Katz in training, pays me a visit, probably to this very room, and I open that right-hand desk drawer and hand over an envelope full of bills. That goes on for a while. Until they up the ante to the next denomination of bills."

"But what if you aren't making enough money to cover all these pay-offs?"

"Ah, that branches out into a subbranch. We have a talk, he buys me out, sets me up somewhere else as an employee. Or maybe I stay put at my club, everybody thinks I still own it, but I'm a dummy front, I'm in *their* club now, and once you're in their club you can never get out other than feetfirst. There are some grislier outcomes to this subbranch, but we'll skip them since I have no intention of becoming a dues-paying member to those *gonifs.*"

"But what can you *do?*" I sat bolt upright. My heart was pounding with indignation.

"Easy." He reached for me and pulled me back to his chest. "I need you right here. We're working it out like a story. Try to keep a distance."

"I don't see how *you* can. It's your whole life, everything you've worked for, and it's not a story. Some real-life crook comes up to you in broad daylight and says, 'You've done well, Paulie, now fork over our king-size cut'—"

"Yeah, I've worked hard for it. But it's by no means my whole life." He was stroking my head again, a steady fatherly stroke.

"How can you be so philosophical about it?"

"That's a good question. Maybe because"—his chest heaved and I felt him swallowing hard—"I've just lost something that puts it in a less world-shaking perspective."

"You mean Stella?"

"I told you, she changed my life when she said, Why not dream big? After you've been as good as dead—"

"You stop imagining difficulties for yourself . . . and just get on with what you'd like to do next," I finished chapter and verse for him.

"So I went ahead and seized an opportunity and made an elegant club for people like myself. It was the first of its kind, you know, and I'm proud of that. I'd say we've had a pretty good run. And I've gone year by year without imagining the worst until today it came waddling toward me behind a little dog. What a fatso Irving's become."

"But is it really the worst? Aren't there still options?"

"For me, oh yes. I'm still my own man. There are plenty of things I could see myself doing next. But for P. Nightingale's, I'm afraid the options have run out. It's fitting, in a way, that it should be happening now. Stella was the club's godmother. She lent us the down payment. It's even named after her—"Rossignol" is the French for nightingale, and that's the name she chose for herself in Paris after my grandfather killed himself in Germany. His name was Rosenthal. After my mother died, I decided to make a new start myself, change our name to match the club's. Bev gave me some flak, you know her special brand of humor she wields like a weapon. Oh, great, she says, for the first twenty years of my life I'm stuck with a Polish name nobody can spell or pronounce; then I get one that suits me, that has some gravity to it, and now you go renaming us after a frivolous foreign bird. But she went along, she even said it had a cozy element to it that would be good for business: Mom and Pop Nightingale welcoming their friends to P. Nightingale's in Bal Harbour. Well, Monday Stella goes in the ground and Nightingale's goes on the market. I'm going to offer the exclusive listing to an old friend, Martin Feldman."

"But then . . ."

"What?"

Wait a minute, I was silently protesting. We barely got going on our Thomas Mann options and you're *selling* the club while we're still lying in it?

Not only that, what was the meaning of all these sudden first-person plurals? She lent *us* the down payment . . . I decided to change *our* name to match the club's—and the "cozy" image of Mom and Pop Nightingale welcoming their friends! Where was I in this new plot development where he was "still his own man," still very much married to Bev, but putting P. Nightingale's in the ground along with Aunt Stella?

"What?" he repeated.

"Oh, just thinking . . ."

"About what, my darling?"

Was it possible he would leave me behind in Miami, settle year-round in North Carolina, which, as far as I knew, wasn't "mobbed up" yet? Would it have been better for my love life if I had gone to the *Charlotte Observer*? Oh, damn, blast, hell.

"In one of the clippings about Stella I was reading last night, she told the interviewer about a young man who had just opened a new business on the Beach and wanted a new scent to affirm his new identity. Was that you?"

"It was. In the write-up about more men starting to use cologne?"

"Yes. She said he had also anglicized his surname. So you made Rossignol into Nightingale. But you never told me what your name was before that."

"I never told you that? I guess not. It never came up. It was Stern. My father's name was Stern. You heard Irving call me Paulie the Stern."

Earl's response to first hearing Paul's name rang jeeringly in memory: "Hell, if his name is Nightingale, mine is Woody Woodpecker." And I had replied, "I don't care whether his name is Nickelbaum or Noodleberger. Whatever his name is, he's more of a gentleman than you'll ever be," and earned a black eye.

"She made you a cologne with—she listed the ingredients. Vetiver, some kind of tobacco, and some root that smells like wet dog—"

"Costus root," supplied Paul, laughing softly.

"Which, if used in the right combination with the other ingredients, creates a . . . well . . . a time-honored aphrodisiac."

As I quoted Stella's words, I felt the terrain of Paul's body changing.

Lose a few, win a few, I thought, tucking myself under him.

"We're plugged in again," Paul presently exulted.

To keep myself from wriggling and cutting short our "refueling," I pondered the question of surnames. The name Emma Stern as a byline was certainly more formidable than Emma Nightingale. Bev was right, it had gravity.

Though, to borrow Dave Bisbee's term, it was probably a moot exercise on my part.

Part Three

Al andar se hace el camino
y al volver la vista atrás
se ve la senda que nunca
se ha de volver a pisar.

As you go you make the road
And if you turn to look behind
you'll see the path your feet
will never tread again.

—ANTONIO MACHADO,
Proverbias y Cantares, 34

20.

new words:
cartel
bagman
gonif
STERN

I have been in Miami exactly one week today.
I feel a thousand years older and a million times more ignorant.

I closed my "Go, Tar Heels!" notebook and dropped it into the bedside drawer, on top of the Gideons Bible. Then, pricked by some atavistic need for divine judgment, I slid out the Bible, opened it at random, and stabbed at a page with my finger.

"For the good that I would, I do not; but the evil which I would not, that I do." Romans 7:19.

Well, that would certainly do in lieu of church, where everyone seemed to have gone except Don Waldo, who, last time I looked out the window, was breaststroking up and down the turquoise pool, his leonine head erect, his undulations making sun-dappled wavelets on either side of him. There was something noble and touching about the international man of letters in his billowing maroon trunks sedately propelling his blimp shape through the water.

Presently I would dress and head out for an American breakfast at Howard Johnson's with the fat Sunday issue of the *Star*. But now, while my brain was still uncluttered after sleep, I sank back on the pillows to ruminate further on yesterday.

I was almost glad Paul had pleaded urgent business errands today and would not be picking me up until early evening. I needed time to assess the damages.

Yesterday afternoon in bed at the club, we had found our way through a menacing impasse back into our realm of matchless rapport. Only to end up having our first falling-out in Stella's apartment on Espanola Way.

Though how could you call it a falling-out when he hadn't even reproached me? I remembered last summer when I'd been complacently folding napkins for the next meal and "letting the garbage pile up" at the Cohens' table. It was the first time I had disappointed him, and he was sharp with me. *Stern*. But last night had been much worse: I could gauge from his carefully chosen words, spoken almost apologetically, how far I had fallen from grace.

How presumptuous of me to think I could pep-talk him out of his pessimism about Manny Lanning and his gang! I had been so triumphant after our sublime lovemaking, giving myself full credit for "honoring" the earlier bout of impotence with mature tact and composure, yet also feeling flush with my youthful aphrodisiac powers. I suppose I had assumed it would be a cinch to recharge his fighting spirit as well.

If only I had stopped short of making that stupid comparison with his grandfather shutting up shop in Leipzig and killing himself "without fighting back."

("How could anyone be *that* stupid!" Charles P. Rose accused in his single-note refrain while Jake Rance raged contrapuntally up and down the scale: "How uninformed women are! You never know any *facts*! Where *were* you? What were you thinking of? Didn't you ever pick up a newspaper or hear people talk?")

Up until then Paul and I had moved about Stella's apartment in harmony, making plans for the dispersal of her worldly goods. In the final third of her life, her American years, she had kept faith with cherished parts of her past while leaving plenty of space for new interests and acquisitions: her "perfume corner" with its vials and beakers, the beautiful rugs and antique furnishings bought at Miami Beach auctions. The rooms testified to a personality that had kept growing branches right to the end.

"I'll bring boxes tomorrow," said Paul. "The books I'll keep. One of these days maybe I'll find time to read the ones in English. And the others have sentimental value."

He pulled down a volume from the shelf, Goethe's *Faust* in German. The frontispiece was Delacroix's painting of Faust being tempted by a robust Mephistopheles. At the top of the facing title page, *Stella Rosenthal* had been penned in a girlish formal hand. "You've read it. A college kid like you."

"No, I haven't, but I need to. Thomas Mann wrote his own version of it in his novel *Doctor Faustus.* And when he was working on *Felix Krull* he said he felt he was living in Goethe's sphere."

"Maybe we'll read it together someday. My mother could quote long passages. I know some of them by heart without fully understanding which word means what."

As he recited the German lines, his voice took on a harsher character. I heard a different Paul. Just as I heard a different Tess when she spoke in Spanish.

" '*Verklungen, ach, der erste Widerklang. Mein lied ertönt der unbekannten Menge.*' Which more or less means that the friendly crowds of old are gone and my song of grief now falls on indifferent ears. That was the passage she quoted the most. It summed up my mother's philosophy of life."

I had been thinking many things at once—too many, the ideas bouncing off one another. How would my character change if I were to speak in a different language? Would I gain more authority, like Tess, or sound foolish, like Enrique Ocampo? What image of our future was Paul glimpsing when he said maybe we'd read it together someday? And I thought of all my new friends at the Julia Tuttle, from the young Luisa to the old Don Waldo, all of them suddenly uprooted from the home they took for granted; and of Thomas Mann himself having to begin life all over again in this country when he was sixty-three. And now the same old enemy was threatening Paul. Usurpation was knocking on his door in the form of Manny and his mob.

"You know what?" I blurted, full of zeal. "I think you ought to fight them. The law is on your side. This isn't Nazi Germany. You don't have to be like your grandfather in Leipzig."

Paul frowned. The four slashes of wrinkles that resembled the beginning of a tic-tac-toe game deepened in the center of his brow.

I thought he was considering my advice and plunged recklessly on. "And, I mean, who knows? Maybe he shut up shop too soon. Instead of killing himself, what if he had stuck it out and fought back?"

Paul replaced *Faust* on the shelf. He gazed obliquely down at the richly patterned oriental carpet on which we stood. "Hindsight and history tell us he wouldn't have lasted very long," he said quietly after a pause. "Someone else would have put the bullet through his head, or packed him off in a boxcar."

Still focused on the carpet, he went on, more gently than ever, as though trying to shield me from the disgrace of my own ignorance. "You've got to remember we're a very ancient race, Emma. We've learned to read the writing on the wall. It's construed as cowardice by some, but it can also be a form of wisdom."

Iowa Mother of 4
Is Mrs. America

By Marge Armstrong
Women's Section Editor

was the local lead story on page one—not in the Women's Section, either. Last night, Mrs. Margaret Priebe, the "slender 36-year-old graying wife and mother" (in the two-column photo you could see the gray) had been crowned Mrs. America of 1959 in Fort Lauderdale's War Memorial Auditorium about the same time Paul was driving me back to the Julia Tuttle.

I read through Marge's Mrs. America story, increasingly appalled. It was enough to put you off the whole prospect of becoming a Mrs.

"I didn't do my best," the new Mrs. America, wearing a pale green floor-length strapless gown, had gasped after being crowned. "Everyone else was better than I was."

Her husband, a purchasing agent, declared himself stunned and of course proud. "Who's the boss? I am—at least sometimes," he said.

The runners-up were listed.

Mrs. Alaska had been voted "Mrs. Congeniality" by her fifty sister contestants.

Hundreds had jammed the hot, sticky lobby of the auditorium, each clutching $4.50 to buy admission to the show.

But because the event was staged mainly for a telecast, the un-air-conditioned auditorium was crammed with TV equipment and many in the audience had to make do with watching the ceremony on TV monitors spotted throughout the orchestra.

TV technicians wore shorts and sport shirts while the fifteen Mrs. America finalists sweltered in their formals.

Primarily a test of homemaking skills, the Mrs. America contest awarded $13,000 in prizes to the winner. The winner's awards would include a completely equipped new kitchen, an in-ground swimming pool, a South American vacation for two, and a $1,000 savings bond.

To win the coveted crown, Mrs. America had "cooked, cleaned, and scrubbed her way through the three days of competition."

The homemaking judges narrowed down the fifty-one contestants to fifteen. Next they got together with the poise-personality judges to choose six finalists. Then the poise-personality judges selected the winner.

Though hacked into the *Star*'s typical bite-size "grafs," Marge's keen but unobtrusive reportage carried you right into the event.

You saw and heard the Iowa housewife, admired her efforts to remain slim after giving birth four times, were disarmed by her modest self-put-down after the gasp of surprise at being chosen, and by the strands of gray she hadn't chosen to dye.

You pressed against the other spectators in the sticky heat and were indignant at having forked over your $4.50 only to get shunted off to monitors so the usurper medium of television could lord it over reality.

You sweated under the hot lights in your strapless formal with your sister contestants who for three days had scrubbed floors and baked cookies with poise and personality to make this event possible, while the TV technicians strutted about in their shorts, making themselves the indispensable feature of the show.

Marge must have been bouncing up and down in her typing chair right down to the wire before deadline last night, x-ing out whole paragraphs ("I'll always be Tillie the Toiler when it comes to prose") to turn out this keenly observed slice of American life with its subversive subtext. For the subtext was there, I could swear it.

Castro and his doings were nowhere to be seen, neither on the front page nor in any part of the A section. Promising harbinger!

Joelle Cutter-Crane and her well-dressed photographer that she could "run" could be on a plane back to Miami this very moment.

("Well, Don, at least we got our first story in. I was the one, by the way, who suggested the headline, Castro's Land Swap Triggers Hate and Joy.'"

"What do you think will happen to that couple, Joelle?"

"What couple?"

"The smiling dirt-poor couple I shot those moving photos of. Do you think the next dictator will take away their sixty-six acres and give them back to the rich?"

"Well, Don, if so, we'll go back as guests of the new government and do another human-interest series: 'Volatile Cuba: Setbacks for Poor, Reprieve for Rich.'"

"The new government might not take kindly to being called 'volatile,' Joelle."

"Touché, Don. Oh, dear, I think you have spilled food on your tie again.")

And Lídia's *movimiento* plans for a backyard revolution would be nipped in the bud. She'd take her checkbook and organizing skills back to Palm Beach and leave Alex in peace to run his hotel until his *abuelo* had time to build the big one for him to manage in Havana. And Luisa Ocampo would be able to have her tenth birthday party with friends in her own warm pool back in Oriente. And Don Waldo, after delivering his lecture, "The Journey from Delusion to Reality in the Novels of Jane Austen," at Princeton, could return home with his young bride and invite his son the Jesuit over to dinner. Afterwards, over cigars and brandy, they would talk of Lídia, the former wife and daughter-in-law.

("She has not changed, *hijo*. If you want to take orders, it is far more enjoyable to be taking them from Ignatius of Loyola.")

THE INTERNATIONAL headline story, side by side with Mrs. America, was about the Dalai Lama, who had escaped to India from Tibet. (One-column picture of a dark-haired, very young man with horn-rimmed glasses; cutline: "I must tell the world.")

1,000 Monasteries Sacked

65,000 Slain, Says Dalai

MUSSOORIE, India (UPI) — The refugee Dalai Lama Saturday accused the Chinese Communists of killing 65,000 Tibetans and destroying 1,000 monasteries in a "reign of terror" designed to smash the ancient Tibetan culture. He challenged the Reds to an on-the-spot investigation by an international commission.

At his first mass press conference since he fled his capital of Lhasa March 17 and took asylum in India, the Tibetan god-king charged the Reds had submitted members of his family to indignities and had even removed the lock on his mother's bedroom door.

The twenty-three-year-old Dalai Lama made no attempt to conceal his concern over the plight of his people.

He said he would welcome a meeting of Indian Prime Minister
Jawaharlal Nehru and Premier Chou En-lai of Red China to work
out a "peaceful and amicable solution of the present tragic problem." But he stressed that he will not return home unless the Communists promise to restore the full powers he exercised before the
Red Armies invaded the Himalayan country in 1950.

The Dalai Lama ruled out any direct negotiation with the Reds
because, he said, he feared they would go back on their promises. He
said mediation was possible only through a third power.

The crew-cut Dalai Lama said that almost daily reports of the
"suffering and inhuman treatment" of Tibetans by the Reds com-
pelled him to level the series of indictments against the Peking
regime.

"The time has manifestly arrived when, in the interests of my
people and religion, and to save them from the danger of near anni-
hilation, I must not keep silent any longer but must frankly and
plainly tell the world the

Continued on Page A2

I'd get to the jump page later. God, twenty-three was five years younger
than Alex, and only a year more than myself. There seemed to be an epi-
demic of usurpations spreading around the globe.

Having checked as soon as I sat down in Howard Johnson's to make
sure Stella was in today's *Star,* I now turned to B9 to read through her obit
word for word, as Paul would do.

Stella Rossignol, Perfumer
Services for Stella Rossignol, 66, of 15 Espanola Way, Miami Beach, will
be at noon on Monday at Fisher's Funeral Home. Interment will follow
immediately after at North Shore Cemetery. Miss Rossignol came here in
1942 from Paris, France, where she worked for Guerlain up until the German Occupation. By 1948, she had become a much-in-demand perfumer

who would create custom scents for such notables as Arthur Godfrey, Xavier Cougat and his wife Abbe Lane, and Morris Lapidus. She is survived by a nephew, Paul Nightingale, of Miami Beach.

Though severely cut—as I had feared—by the copydesk, Stella's was the lead obit, with a half-column head shot of her. I hoped this would redeem me a few notches in Paul's estimation.

In other news, Miami's rainfall had already topped the all-time record for June; Secretary of State Christian A. Herter held a lunch in Geneva for Soviet Foreign Minister Andrei Gromyko "at which neither man backed down an inch" on the Berlin crisis; in Chicago, a five-year-old boy playing hide-and-seek was found suffocated in a discarded icebox; Italy's oldest retired admiral had committed suicide at ninety-eight by jumping out a window in Turin; and Elvis Presley, an Army jeep driver on furlough in Paris, confided to a UPI interviewer that the thought of returning to television in eight months gave him "the shakes."

"Aw, Dry Up!" was the rubric for today's weather: temperature in the eighties, partly sunny with intermittent showers.

BY THE time I got back to the Julia Tuttle, the sun had disappeared behind a solid cloud cover, but there was not a soul in the pool area and I decided the time was ripe for my inaugural swim. The longer I put it off, the more self-conscious I was going to be about crossing the lobby in my unorthodox beach costume. Before I could talk myself out of it, I hurried into my faded St. Clothilde's suit and Bass Weejuns, wrapped myself in Paul's black silk dressing gown, stuffed my bathing cap and comb in the pocket, draped a towel casually across my shoulders, and headed for the elevator.

I was happy to find the lobby at an all-time-low intimidation level: Luís was occupied at the switchboard and the dominoes players were either at church or out to lunch.

Where was Alex? When Tess had delivered me to the Julia Tuttle a week ago today, Luís had told her Sunday was Alex's bridge day. Had he managed to elude his mother and assert his Bartleby-ness by slipping across the bay to lose more money to his charming friends?

Had I been sure of total privacy, I would have taken my own sweet time lowering myself down the ladder at the pool's deep end, acclimating my anatomy in gingerly stages to the 15- to 20-degree drop in temperature. But on the off chance someone happened to be watching from the hotel, I executed a shallow-entry racing dive into the chilly waters, did a fast-bobbing breaststroke until I stopped shuddering, then lapsed into my languid long-distance crawl. Back and forth, back and forth, with an open turn at each end: approach, rotate, push off; approach, rotate, push off. Not counting laps. This was a Sunday swim, not a competition.

I was proud of my swimming, it was the only sport I could do. Mother had taught me to how to float and dog-paddle in the shallow end of the municipal pool. A Girl Scout counselor later talked me out of my terror of depths and cheered me as I thrashed and flailed across a narrow branch of a freezing mountain river. For the rest of the camp season she coached me in a proper crawl.

In seventh grade, the new gym teacher at St. Clothilde's, ambitious to get us into intramural sports, made us choose between tennis and swimming "to excel in." Somehow she had convinced the nuns to refill the indoor pool left over from the school's days as a hotel. My choice was instant. I hated to sweat, I informed my circle of friends; moreover, propelling myself gracefully back and forth in the water while lying prone and thinking my own thoughts was infinitely more appealing than dashing about on a hard court at the mercy of someone else's backhand. They were used to my sassy mouth, and I doubt even the subtlest of them guessed there was a third reason: that I knew I could never catch up with all their childhood hours on country-club tennis courts.

Approach, rotate, push off.

After we made intramural, the gym teacher was eagerly training us in the freestyle flip turn until Mother Patton, dropping by to watch a practice, put a stop to it. That half second when our somersaulting butts mooned above the waterline was "not in the St. Clothilde tradition."

Lulled by my partial submersion in the watery element, and by the discipline of rhythmic breathing, my mind began to unclench and let go of its habitual frets. My thoughts lapsed into a freestyle of their own. Associations spooled out and made new contacts. Tough subjects and their interconnections pulsed with interest.

Paul was a mature and honorable man—his own man. What he already was would shape the rest of what he would be. Whatever transpired for each of us in the future, we would have affected the other's design.

The same went for all the others involved in the writhing organism of my present life: Lídia, Alex, the Ocampos, my *Miami Star* colleagues bright and dark; Tess and her "Doctor Magnánimo," Ginevra and her Dr. Brown. Our designs-in-progress collided, intermingled, left behind imprints, created more options, each with its set of branches and subbranches.

I really should swim more. From now on I would get up an hour earlier and do laps before I went to work. Think of what I could accomplish at the *Star* with this agile, freestyle mind!

As I approached the shallow end, I saw a pair of little-girl legs beneath a frilly bathing skirt hopping up and down in my underwater view.

"Luisa! *¿Cómo está?*"

"*¡Ay, frío, frío, frío! Emma, la piscina está helada!*" Wet up to the hips, she shivered extravagantly to mask her delight in finding me here. I had been a little girl myself once.

"You'll never get in *that* way, Luisa. You need to have a game . . . *es necesario hacer un juego . . .* a goal . . . *un gol.*"

"*Enséñame, entonces. Enséñame el juego . . . Emma.*" She wanted me to teach her this game.

"Well, *primero*, you have to think"—I pointed at my head—"you have to make a picture of the thing you want most . . . *hace una imagen de la cosa lo te quiere el más.*"

"*La cosa que quiero el más,*" she repeated solemnly.

"*¡Sí! ¿Tienes una imagen?*"

"*Sí, la tengo.*"

"And now, *ahora*, I imagine *la cosa que quiero más,* and BY THE TIME I

COUNT TO THREE . . . *a las tres* . . . I must be COMPLETELY IN
THE WATER." I mimed imagining this thing I wanted more than anything, squinching my eyes shut with concentration. *"Uno, dos . . ."*

At the count of three, I pinched my nose and sat down on the pool
floor, sending up a noisy array of bubbles. Above the water, Luisa
laughed.

"Okay, now it's your turn. *Uno, dos . . ."*

With a shriek she sank to the bottom of the pool. I had been using
this method on myself for years. It always worked if you found something to want fiercely enough. I would bet anything that what drove her
under even before the count of three was the image of going home.

I floated on my back at the shallow end, sculling myself around so I
could watch Luisa rock from side to side in a primitive crawl, her head
arched adamantly away from the water. At least she had her arm motions.
I saw myself coaching her in the late afternoons after work. I'd pull her
along on her tummy and teach her to dip her head in and out of the
water and coordinate her flutter kick with her breathing. If Castro blew
a fuse in the next week or so, she'd have new skills to show off at her
birthday party back in Oriente.

DON WALDO in floppy sun hat and dark glasses issued forth from the
hotel, followed by Altagracia carrying a wicker tray. His faded terry-cloth
shirt, which once upon a time must have been blue, surmounted the
globe of his belly and then billowed loosely outside his khaki shorts. Vestiges of the dandy were still apparent in his shapely legs and small, elegant feet in their canvas espadrilles.

Altagracia set him up at a corner table near Lídia's new red-and-white
garden and directly behind the flagpole, where he could preside over the
scene without being too accessible. After adjusting the umbrella and laying out his things, which included a giant magnifying glass, a thermos, a
legal pad, and writing instruments, she touched her forehead briefly to
his and murmured something that made him laugh. Walking away in her

narrow-waisted white dress, her hair in a thick plait trailing down her back, she could have been a girl of sixteen. Imagining bedroom scenes was impossible to resist. Should the seventy-seven-year-old bridegroom be arrested by a bout of impotence, I was sure he would meet the challenge with gaiety and aplomb. (*"Un momento, mi amor,* he is doing his utmost to become vertical. How *simpática* you are to be so patient with your old rooster who loves you.")

AS WHEN Luisa and I had been filling each other's plates at Lídia's party, comprehension became less of a chore as soon as we let ourselves go in a mutual activity. Luisa managed to penetrate my spotty comprehension and I learned that someone had indeed been watching me from a window and that as soon as Marisa Ocampo had seen me dive and swim she permitted Luisa to come out to the pool by herself if she promised not to be *"una molestia"* to me.

After our swim, Luisa led us to the table where she had propped Tilda and Manuela side by side to guard her things. As we passed Don Waldo's table, we circumspectly averted our faces to indicate we had no intention of becoming *molestias* to him.

"¡Ven, ven acá!" he thundered after us. "Come and join me!"

"Won't we interfere with your work?" I asked.

"No, I am only gloating over these precious note cards redeemed from my wife's skirt. It pleases Altagracia to think I am out here with something to do, because she is hoping to be majordomo to Lídia's exciting schemes. They attended Mass this morning at Gesu Catholic Church and Lídia conscripted a small platoon of new exiles from Cuba. She is mobilizing them in the kitchen, Altagracia tells me."

"I wondered where everybody was," I said. "Even the dominoes players have deserted their station."

"Perhaps they have heard the news and are also seeking assignments from the benefactress in the kitchen," said Don Waldo. " 'From each according to his ability, to each a free room at the Julia Tuttle' is, I understand, Lídia's new order of the day. And there is other news. Alex has gone to pick up one of his brothers from an airfield in Fort Lauderdale. It wasn't clear which brother, but he flew himself over from Cuba.

"*Eh, chica . . .*" He turned to Luisa, who had fetched her dolls and was arranging them side by side in a chair. "*¿Como se llaman tus amigas?*"

"*Está es Tilda, y está es Manuela.*"

"*Majestuosas,* are they not? Rather *feróz.* They remind me of my great-aunt from Bilbao. Tía Guillerma. As a child I was awestruck. They say she died without ever once touching her back to a chair."

The great educator's consecutive translations into Spanish on Luisa's behalf bore no trace of pedagogy. Don Waldo made it seem merely as though he suddenly chose to complete the rest of his discourse in another tongue.

And as Luisa explained to Don Waldo the different temperaments of her dolls, I suddenly realized I was following every Spanish phrase. While Tilda suffered the headaches and was very critical of people, Manuela had the bad dreams and was terrified of noise.

"*. . . y las dos desprecian las fiestas,*" Luisa concluded in her gruff voice.

"Yes, they both hate parties," I happily glossed.

"*Yo tambíen,* I also deplore *fiestas,*" said Don Waldo. "Not because I am *tímido,* no one has ever accused me of being a shrinking violet, but parties, generally speaking, are not hospitable to the sort of talk I enjoy most (*no soy una violeta retirada . . . el tipo de conversación que me gusta más*)."

"What sort is that?" I asked.

"It has substance but one also feels refreshed afterwards (*. . . sustancia . . . refrescante . . .*)."

"*¡Hay las tarjetas!*" Luisa had spotted the note cards, stacked in several piles on the wicker tray.

"*Sí,* my memoirs. Which you ladies so graciously helped Altagracia unpick from her skirt, *muchas gracias.* And so now, *entonces* (the *en-TONTH-es* heavily lisped), *mi memorias* are preserved from the *barbudos* and I am allowing myself this tranquil Sunday to rejoice in their safety and fondle them a little. Won't you each take some?"

To Luisa's and my mutual enchantment, Don Waldo plucked a handful from the top of a pile and began dealing them out like playing cards.

"*¡Qué pequeñitas, estas palabras!*" said Luisa, squinting at the tiny writing on her cards.

"*Sí, muy pequeñitas,*" rumbled Don Waldo. "That is my own tiny handwriting, which I can no longer read without my *lupa.*" He patted the large magnifying glass. "*Este juego,* this game we are about to play is called *Destinos y Desatinos* because that is the title of the work. It is a work, *sí,* a memoir, in the '*cahiers*' style, with chapters on many different subjects, some aphorisms, and, as I say in the preface, things too simple or unpopular to have been said by me before. But for now, since I have the pleasure of your company, instead of my reading it to myself under the umbrella, we shall play it aloud, like a game. *Vamos a ver,* let's see. Five cards for each of us, Luisa, Emma, and Waldito el Tremendo—that is my son Jorge's nickname for me, *mi apodo.*

"Now, we each have our five cards, but before I create the rules for this game"—Don Waldo's translations were so seamless that I no longer kept track of which language I was hearing—"before I continue with the rules, I had better explain to Emma that in English the wonderful play on words in my title is completely lost.

"*Destinos,* in English, are 'destinies,' and *desatinos,* in English, are 'mistakes.' In Spanish, that little devil of an *a* turns a destiny into a blunder. That's why I love it for a work of *autobiografía.* Because often in life it is difficult to tell one from the other when you are in the midst of it. Of course, later, *más tarde,* it is easy to look back and say, Ah, yes, *this* was part of my destiny, and *that* was my foolishness: *ah, qué desatino!* What rubbish was I thinking?

"Now for the rules. I shall be what you call 'it' in English games. I shall play the one on the defensive. Just as at university, a student must defend his *tema,* his thesis.

"So: Luisa, you will begin. Look quickly at your *tarjetas* and read aloud the first word or phrase that jumps out at you."

Should it be serious or funny (*serio o divertido*), Luisa wanted to know.

"*Cualquiera, niña,* whichever you choose."

As Luisa frowned at her cards, I tried not to look at mine and get ahead of the game. Even with the teeny writing, several candidates leapt up at me: the names of Ortega and Camus . . . that "skin of a lion" passage Lídia had read aloud during the communal unpicking of Altagracia's skirt . . . and, God! There was "my" word, *usurpado,* in a chapter heading: "Exiliados, Usurpados, y Gusanos."

But for all I knew, Don Waldo would make up different rules for me.

"*¡Ay!*" screamed Luisa, bouncing up and down in her chair, "*¡Platero! Aquí está Platero!*"

"I see you have picked my chapter on empathy, *la empatía.* 'Platero the Donkey: Jiménez's Emblem of Empathy.' Now, here are your rules. I must explain to you the *esencial,* the meat, of this Platero chapter in one minute. Not a second more. *¿Comprendéis?*"

He unstrapped his watch, which had a second hand, and laid it between Luisa and me on the table.

"One of you stop me when the *segundero* has gone once around. *Vamos,* let's begin!"

But the second hand swept past five . . . ten . . . and Don Waldo had yet to say a word. Already he had thrown away a quarter of his allotted "defense."

Then he said, "*Ay, niñas,* we shall have to continue our *juego* at a later time."

Excited Spanish-speaking voices grew louder. Facing the hotel, Don Waldo had been the first to see we were no longer alone.

Lídia, in a pink linen suit and matching straw hat, had the air of one bringing home her trophies from battle and parading them out to the pool to show off to Don Waldo. Trailing in her wake came the Ocampos and an assortment of men and women in churchgoing attire.

Clamped into Lídia's grasp so securely he might have been handcuffed to her was the only un-well-dressed member of the party, a short, solidly built man in jeans, sweaty fatigue shirt, and dusty cowboy boots.

What followed for me was as thwarting as having the English subtitles snatched away from a foreign movie just when it becomes urgently important to know who is saying what.

The stranger, handsome in a sexy, brutish way, was Alex's half brother Nestor, who had just flown himself from the Camagüey ranch to Florida in the family's plane. This much I caught, even though the rat-a-tat of everyone's Spanish, Lídia's included, was going a mile a minute. If Alex had gone to fetch this brother, what was he doing now? In my frustration, it even occurred to me that Lídia was deliberately speaking fast to exclude me; she had not once looked my way. Probably she was still punishing me for asserting my independence on the night of her party. She also had dispensed with her refined diction and adopted her stepson's lazy manner of slurring words together. I was bombarded by a completely different Spanish from Don Waldo's courtly back-and-forthness with Luisa and me.

Whatever Nestor was relating in his indolent, slurry mumble was eliciting wave after wave of mounting indignation in his listeners.

"*¡Bárbaros! ¡Gamberros!*"

"*¡No me lo digas!*"

"*¡Ay! ¡Qué injusticia!*"

"*¡ . . . y qué idiotez!*"

"*¿Han estropeado todo ya, los Fidelistas?*"

"*¡Es verdad: Lo ha estropeado todo . . . desde hace seis meses . . . tantas mentiras!*"

"*Qué verguenza . . .*"

"*¡GENTUZA!*"

"*¡CANALLA!*"

"*¡No puedo creer que esto me está pasando!*"

Back to square one, Emma. Just as on the night of the tornado, I was the foreigner in their midst. Recognizable words flew by—there went one! there went another!—but, given my kindergarten-level skill in assembling them, they added up to a great big nothing. I resolved to enroll in a night course in Spanish conversation at the University of Miami as soon as I had my first paycheck. Even if I hadn't got the new shoes from Bev I would now have given the Spanish lessons priority.

"Papi, él no quiso hacerlo," Nestor continued to regale them in his lazy, mumbled Spanish, *"y . . . lo hicieron, los brutos . . . lo hicieron lenta y mal—"*

"¡Horroroso! Tremendamenta mal . . . !"

"Es puro barbarismo . . ."

"¡Pobre animalucho!"

"Brutalidad . . . criminal . . ."

Marisa Ocampo, seeing her daughter's teeth begin to chatter, hustled Luisa into a nearby cabana to strip her out of her wet bathing suit. They returned, arm in arm, a well-combed Luisa bundled snugly in her terry-cloth beach robe her mother had a matching copy of upstairs.

I was recalled to the state of my own appearance. My "beach robe" was clearly a man's silk dressing gown, and was wet all down the back. My hair, I knew, had dried into a weedy, shoulder-length fright. No wonder nobody had so much as glanced my way. And there was no longer a mother close by to shepherd me off to a cabana and lick me back into shape. Where was Alex? If only I could *just arrive* in my room without having to shuffle in my Weejuns, with my wet backside, past this church-clad crowd.

Don Waldo unscrewed his thermos, poured out a steaming cup, and offered it to Nestor. *"Cafecito, hijo,"* he softly lisped. And then in a Spanish I could completely understand: We are very sorry about what has happened. You must be exhausted (*agotado*) after your terrible experience."

June 21

. . . It's Sunday afternoon and here's the rest of the letter to you I started yesterday. I mailed Loney's letter yesterday, you'll be glad to know, with news of weather and what I found out in the Star*'s morgue about Tess. I included a clipping of my "most crowd-pleasing story" so far (according to one of the editors) and a Garbo-ish photo of me in raincoat and hat because the model from the agency failed to show up.*

The Miami Star *is not exactly the* New York Times, *but I am holding my own and the assistant managing editor (whom everyone calls Lucifer because of his ambition and quick rise to power) has already indicated I'm making the grade. I just have to work very hard and come up with more crowd-pleasing ideas so they won't shunt me off to one of their boondock bureaus.*

Your presents were perfect. Nothing is more mysterious and seductive than a white silk scarf crossed under the chin and tied at the back of the neck and wraparound sunglasses, which I need to get. The Spanish dictionary is a godsend. Thank you for anticipating my needs. I have been making lists of words ever since I came back from a FLUMMOXING experience downstairs at the pool. As you know, the Julia Tuttle caters mainly to Cubans—that's why Tess, with her Cuban connections, was able to get me the special rate. So far I have managed to get by because most people speak some English, like Marisa Ocampo, who was at St. Clothilde's a few years before me, and Alex de Costa, the Cuban-American manager, who is twenty-eight and has a degree in Comparative Lit. from Harvard. (He has a little crush on me, but he's more like a fellow voyager, if you know what I mean.) His mother is another story, which makes me realize how fortunate I am to have been born to you. But more on that later.

Also staying here is an internationally famous writer and critic, Don Waldo Navarro, who's seventy-seven—he arrived Friday with his young mulatto bride. He smuggled his politically seditious memoirs out of Cuba on note cards sewed into her long skirt, and he and I and Marisa's little daughter (whom I am teaching to swim) were playing a game out by the pool late this morning with the note cards, all of us getting along fabulously in this effortless mixture of English and Spanish, when out comes Alex's mother with a whole parade of Cuban refugees she picked up at church and is offering free rooms to in exchange for work. She also had in tow Alex's half brother from her second marriage—she's had five husbands, but would really rather be organizing a revolution, but more on that later—and it was clear the half brother had been through something awful. He'd just escaped from Cuba in the family plane and everybody was talking fast in a non-Castilian Spanish, saying how horrible and what barbarians (I could follow that much), but it wasn't until after Alex's mother led everyone off again for a buffet lunch that Don Waldo was able to fill me in.

The revolutionaries (called "barbudos" because of their beards) had just confiscated the de Costa ranch in Cuba as part of Castro's new "land reform," and they wanted to have a barbecue to celebrate. They ordered Nestor's father—at gunpoint—to slaughter his $20,000 breeding bull! He and the other son refused and were locked in a military truck to be taken off to prison. The sons' wives were put under house arrest in the servants' quarters and Nestor was allowed to help them move their things. Then, while the "barbudos" were inexpertly slaughtering the bull, and the animal was screaming bloody murder, Nestor managed to flee in the family plane. Now he is on his way to the Dominican Republic to join some exile brigade being trained there. He is distraught but says he can do more to fight Castro this way than sitting in prison with his father and brother.

Never a dull moment at the Julia Tuttle. Or elsewhere in Miami, for that matter. While interviewing the wounded at the hospital after the tornado, I spent half an hour talking to a famous ex-madam of a Mafia "house" on Palm Island who had just tried to kill herself for the third time. She's married to a psychiatrist now, is "respectable," and goes to Tess's hairdresser. I think there's a novel here if I can succeed in imagining it all from her side. Tess is going to try to arrange another meeting between us. Of course, I'd have to do a lot of research, but already yesterday I met an actual gangster walking his boss's dog on Miami Beach.

There is still so much to get done, but boy am I ever thankful I had you as my mother. It has certainly put me ahead of the game . . .

21.

FISHER'S FUNERAL HOME WAS a Spanish-hacienda-style establishment with verandas and hanging plants, sloping red-tile roofs, and a meticulously barbered turf lawn. A winding drive flanked by royal palms meandered discreetly around to the rear of the house and a parking lot bordered by tasteful utilitarian outbuildings, also roofed in red tile. This rear view, including the hearse waiting to carry Stella's body to the nearby cemetery, was rendered invisible from the street on either side by high flowering hedges.

I was going to have to bone up on tropical flora.

I had assumed that Stella would be buried in some lovely cemetery over on the Beach, where she had lived the last third of her life. But as Marge Armstrong drove us to the funeral on Monday in her sporty little MG she explained that there *were* no cemeteries on Miami Beach. "The Chamber of Commerce considers them bad for tourism," she said. "People aren't supposed to die in Paradise."

We entered the floral-scented chill of Fisher's reception hall, where a man in a dark suit stood by to greet us with just the right professional touch of lugubriousness and asked us to sign our names in Stella's visitors' book beside a spray of orange flowers. It wasn't yet noon and already there were several pages of signatures ahead of us.

As I was recording my presence in my best St. Clothilde's penmanship (for I knew Paul would cherish this book for the rest of his life) and wishing for a finer instrument than the blue ballpoint provided by Fisher's, my covetous eye jumped to a wide-nibbed bold script a few lines above. Damn it, *someone* had come armed with his own personal fountain pen flowing with jet-black ink.

Emmanuel Lanning

"Oh, *no!*"

"Anything the matter?" asked Marge.

"Oh, no, no. Just having a little trouble with this pen."

The greeter in the dark suit of course heard me and was instantly proffering apologies and a fresh ballpoint.

"We didn't expect so many mourners. There was a very prominent write-up about the deceased in this morning's *Star.* We've had to switch to one of our larger parlors."

This larger parlor was all but filled. I slid into a chair in back next to Marge, folded my hands on the lap of my dark green shirtwaist, and tried to anesthetize my too-many feelings.

Paul and I had said our goodbyes last night; he would be driving the rental car straight from the cemetery to the airport. ("I can just make the one forty-five to Raleigh and catch the feeder to Mountain City and be at the Inn for dinner. Bev's up there all by herself with the staff, and we've got forty-two guests.")

Stella's plain pine box on its gurney looked stark against all the floral arrangements. "She would have fit easily inside a child's coffin," Paul had said last night.

Paul stood beside the lectern in murmured consultation with a fresh-faced, skinny rabbi who looked, and was, young enough to be his son. ("I lucked out. One of my club members has a son a year older than you, just out of a Reform rabbinical school. Reform Jews have more tolerance for us nonpracticing types. Stella never liked synagogues because she felt they didn't give proper privileges to women, but she told me she hoped I'd say Kaddish for her and said that if I went first she intended to say it for me.")

Paul and the rabbi and the other male mourners wore black skullcaps that I now knew the name of. Before I came to Miami, I couldn't have told you the difference between a yarmulke and a guayabera, so I was making some progress toward the international.

The women in this room greatly outnumbered the men. Covertly I canvassed the heads in front of me. Which of the skullcaps perched on the head of the notorious Manny Lanning? What was he doing here? Had he spoken to Paul yet?

The sartorial aspect of Paul had always had the power to render me weak-kneed, and today set a new record. The dark suit, more somber than anything I had ever seen him wear, coupled with the yarmulke, put a new kind of distance between us. Today he was a mourner and he was a Jew. How could I compete with such profundity?

I hardly dared look at him, not only because I was loath to risk another gaffe that would send him off with bad memories without my having a chance to undo the damage, but also because I feared the intensity of my feelings might become obvious to Marge, who didn't miss much.

I had only limited preconceptions regarding funerals, since my experiences of them so far added up to the grand total of two.

In one of the five high schools I attended while tethered to the gypsy caravan of Earl's early "career," a boy playing chicken with a friend had smashed his car into a stone abutment, and I went with some classmates to an open-casket service at a mortuary. I was appalled not so much by the heavily made up mannikin of the boy I had barely known laid out in a dress suit and bow tie but by the number of people, including the boy's parents, who'd commented on "how good they'd made him look."

And several years ago I had accompanied Loney to the funeral of her best friend Cora's paying boarder, Sam. Sam drove Cora everywhere in her car, smoked a perennial cigar, and behaved with Cora's friends like a tolerated old spouse. Loney herself often speculated that there was "more than just boarding going on over there." Sam's casket was also open, with a mirror tilted so you could see his face from the entrance to the parlor. When Cora implored Loney to "come up closer and see how peaceful he looks," Loney had begged off, saying she'd rather remember

Sam as he was. Midway through the service, the minister invited any among the mourners who felt so moved "to say a few words about the departed," and one of Sam's brothers went on too long with an ill-timed reminiscence about a "damsel" whose "favors" he and Sam had vigorously competed for back in the Roaring Twenties.

AFTER SOME opening remarks of welcome, the rabbi, who had a sonorous voice for one so skinny and was remarkably in command for one so young, recalled Stella Rossignol as he had observed her on several occasions while dining with his parents at P. Nightingale's in Bal Harbour.

"While I can't claim to have known her in any personal sense, some people have the gift of conveying themselves simply by brushing past you, and what she conveyed to me *in essence* was this tiny blur of unstoppable energy. Once I even saw her bussing a tray, though you could hardly see her underneath it as it went past our table."

Appreciative laughter.

"Stella Rossignol also created essences for others—one per customer, no two alike, as the lovely big write-up in today's *Miami Star* phrased it. She saw each of us as one of a kind, and the great architect Morris Lapidus, who was one of her clients, said, and I quote from today's *Star*"—he was actually reading from the clipping of my story—"Lapidus said of her: 'Just as I imagine myself as a movie set designer when creating a hotel for my client, I see Stella Rossignol as a character designer who employs scents to help her clients define themselves.'

"Now, to help someone define himself, or herself, is no small *mitzvah*. Because the more we can define ourselves, the clearer it becomes to us where our essential powers lie and how we can best put them to use during the short span allotted us on this earth.

"Stella Rossignol went through her own 'definition' ordeal in her forty-eighth year, when she was interned for seven months in a French camp during the Nazi Occupation. Up until then, she had worked for a famous perfume house in Paris, as a saleswoman and copywriter. Now she found herself surrounded by the stench of latrines and unwashed bodies. But instead of despairing, she and another lady by the name of Rothschild dreamed up a game to distract them from their nausea. Both ladies had some knowledge of scent combinations and knew that the most valuable ingredients of perfumery were derived from animal excretions.

"One morning as they headed to the latrines and her friend was already retching, Stella said, and I quote again from today's *Miami Star* write-up, 'Listen, *amie*, what if we dilute a dash of today's "Essence of Latrine" in fifteen milliliters of alcohol, and then we add equal parts of jasmine and tuberose?'

"And the friend laughed and made herself sniff the putrid air, and said, 'No, that's too sweet. We need a musky touch of ambrette'; and then Stella suggested a *shtikl* of nutmeg, and they named their first 'fragrance' 'Latrine Oh Là Là.' "

The rabbi waited for the ripple of laughter to subside.

"After that, the ladies continued to invent scents to take their minds off their surroundings, but this 'game,' conceived to defy despair, revealed to Stella her own perfect pitch regarding scent. After she got her exit visa and came to this country to join her sister Trude and her nephew Paul, she would fully develop this happy talent discovered in an internment camp. Her last eighteen years in Miami Beach were spent giving others the pleasure of knowing themselves better, which in many cases led to transformations in their lives. As a matter of fact, the headline given to Stella's story in today's *Star* is 'Popular Perfumer Transformed Lives.'

"May we all be so honored in our epitaphs."

Here he unfolded a beautiful shawl with fringe and draped it around his shoulders.

"The language of the Kaddish is not Hebrew but Aramaic, the vernacular spoken by Jews in their Babylonian exile and during the days of the Second Temple, or Commonwealth. Although it is known as the Mourner's Prayer, it contains not one reference to death. It is a prayer of praise. In reciting the Kaddish we affirm our awareness of holiness in our world. Much of our experience of divine goodness, grace, and love has come to us through those whose lives have brushed ours. We stand joined together in a great web of being. Let us praise, let us love the life we are lent, passing through us in the body of humanity and our own bodies. Please stand.

"*Yitgadal v'yitkadash sh'may raba . . .*"

As the rabbi prayed in the plangent syllables of this strange "everyday" tongue that went back to the Babylonian exile, and the mourners answered in shorter bursts of it—the man in front of me was being particularly vociferous in his responses—I bowed my head and focused humbly on my beautiful black I. Miller pumps and suffered afresh Paul's gentle admonishment of Saturday night: "You've got to remember we're a very ancient race, Emma. We've learned to read the writing on the wall . . ."

After the last "Amen" had been said, I dared to look at Paul to see how he was faring. His eyes were red, but he was looking fondly at me.

"WHAT A wonderful tribute to Stella," said Marge, angling her MG into the cortege forming in the parking lot. "You must be feeling pleased with your contribution."

"I only built on what was already there in the file, your piece especially. And after all, you were the one who suggested I do the story." Feeling generous, I added, "Even the Alma Olsen piece contributed to the overall effect because it contained that Lapidus quote."

"Alma phoned me from Lauderdale this morning. She's taking an indefinite leave of absence—her mother in Wisconsin has cancer—and she wanted to know if I could spare someone from my team to fill in for her at the Broward bureau. I told her my 'team' was scarcely a team just now, with my star player off on her honeymoon, the society columnist on vacation, and the homemaking editor going in for knee surgery on Wednesday. Poor Alma, I had to disappoint her."

Shit, here it came. Blindsided by my benefactor. By Wednesday I might find myself in Marge's glass cage, calling up housewives to get their key lime pie recipes, typing up housekeeping tips:

Here's How to Keep Mildew
From Usurping Your Closet

I gave what I hoped sounded like a sympathetic sigh, praying that the next thing out of her mouth would not be an invitation to take up the slack on her depleted team.

My prayer seemed to be answered. Marge dropped the subject of Alma Olsen cold and in a livelier tone returned to our present journey together.

"I was impressed with that young rabbi, weren't you? I liked the way he added his own midrash-like interpretation to your words about essences and definitions. I'm no stranger to Jewish funerals, but I learned a few things today. Great turnout, too. Did you happen to notice the man in front of us praying so loudly? That was the infamous Manny Lanning, the gambling-syndicate king. I'd heard he'd come back from Cuba. I wonder if Stella created a scent for *him*. I'll bet she enjoyed herself if she did."

"You recognized him?"

"He's an old familiar face in the columns of the *Star*. And I saw him in person once. He had some business at the courthouse and my father pointed him out. Father was a circuit court judge."

WE WERE a smaller group at the cemetery. The same greeter in the dark suit passed out laminated cardboard fans, compliments of the funeral home, as we took our places on folding chairs under the awning. Most of the fans were already in motion against the stifling midday heat. They pictured an evocative ocean sunset with a cluster of palm trees in the foreground. If your loved one couldn't be buried on the Beach itself, your keepsake fan might gradually blur that fact in your memory. Under the picture was the motto "Fisher's Funeral Home, Inc., Serving Dade Families of all Faiths since 1910." On the back was the Jewish Mourner's Prayer, each verse printed in phonetically spelled Aramaic, followed by an English translation. For Christian burials there undoubtedly would be another set of fans with the Lord's Prayer or the Twenty-third Psalm.

And perhaps there would be a third set for the religiously disinclined, with verses from Kahlil Gibran or Edna St. Vincent Millay.

Once again we sat directly behind the loudly praying man, whom I could now study—and even sniff—at close range, knowing it was Manny Lanning. There was nothing sleazy about him. He dressed like the kind of person who would insist on signing his name in black ink with his own expensive fountain pen. He was smallish and trim in body, with a fleshy face. His thick black hair under the yarmulke had recently been barbered, and, given that he was at least fifteen years Paul's senior, most likely dyed. His well-cut lightweight charcoal suit belonged in the same club as those worn by Mr. Feeney and the other brass when they headed out to lunch. The only item of questionable taste was the pinky ring with a large diamond on his left hand, with which he fanned himself.

The back of his neck gave off a musky scent. If it had been Stella's custom creation for him, what a pity she couldn't be here to tell us about the "interview" preceding it.

("Now, *Monsieur*, please tell me a little bit about yourself."

"Well, ma'am, I'm in the sporting business. I founded a cartel here on the Beach, built it up from scratch, to make things run smoothly for people who like to, you know, place bets, throw a few dice, pin their hopes on a little ball running around a wheel."

"A man who feels at home with risk, *n'est-ce pas?*"

"Oh, yes, plenty of risk involved in my business. My job, you might say, is to bring organizational clout to these games, streamline the business angle."

"*S'il vous plaît*, take a sniff of this little vial."

"Mmm. Nice. What's it called?"

"Perhaps first you will tell me what associations it brings to your mind."

"Oh, something dark and classy . . . mysterious . . . maybe a yacht gliding into port with its lights off and its engines cut."

"You are a poet, *Monsieur. Voilà*, I think I've got it!"

"Got what?"

"Your base note. The most lasting part of the fragrance; we call it also the dry-out note. A very important beginning: we build your middle and top notes on it. Now, *Monsieur*, what does *this* little infusion bring to mind?"

WHEN ALL the mourners were seated, the rabbi signaled for the lowering of the coffin, which had been poised on its trestles above the grave. Draping himself in the shawl, with no prefatory remarks this time, he began to chant once more in the plangent tongue. His singing voice was at least an octave higher than his speaking voice and brought prickles to my face.

I suddenly teared up as Aunt Stella's coffin began its hydraulic descent into the freshly dug trench, beside which Paul had stationed himself. This was *final*. This was the end of Stella's story, as experienced by herself. From now on her life would exist only in memories: the resourceful twice-exiled little woman who had rubbed unguents into my cheek and covered my black eye with compresses; the beloved aunt whose name Paul took, who had inspired him to start his club and had lent him the money.

Then I thought of Loney. How long would it be until I stood at her open grave? How could I bear it? And this image, along with some from last night in the upstairs bed at P. Nightingale's, evoked full-fledged sobs.

"There'll be other hideaways," Paul had said, his voice so close to my ear I couldn't see his face. "This wasn't our first one and it won't be our last. I feel I've always known you and always will. There's something timeless about this thing we have. I sometimes feel I *am* you. Does that make any sense or does it sound crazy?"

"No, I feel the same."

"I'll be there for you, whenever you need me, and I think you'll be there for me. I knew where you were today and you knew where I was. You were with me all day long and it made the day easier. You're a sort of extra intelligence I carry around with me. When the men were dismantling the roulette table and lugging it piecemeal down to the van, I was hearing myself telling you the details, like a bedtime story. Then, of course, I had to install a safe, to make a reason for all that empty space behind the foxhunting painting. The place is already on the market, by the way. I called my friend Marty at home this morning. He says with the new upstairs kitchen we ought to get double what we paid for it. He was sad, though. A lot of friends are going to miss the hospitality at P. Nightingale's."

STELLA WAS in the earth beside her sister, and Paul was receiving condolences. One of the first to reach him was Manny Lanning, who shoved his hand into Paul's and began to speak in a low voice. I realized from the look of surprise on Paul's face and then his bodily recoil that he had not expected this meeting and perhaps hadn't even recognized the racketeer among his aunt's mourners. Then Paul must have said something cutting, because the older man looked taken aback, though he quickly recovered his composure and even managed a hearty slap on Paul's arm as he made his exit.

I introduced Paul to Marge and vice versa, getting the priorities right. My face was still teary, but after all, this had been Stella's funeral. Marge told Paul she had been a faithful customer of Stella's, and Paul thanked me for the feature on Stella and thanked us both for coming. "We'll be in touch," he said to me, keeping custody of the eyes, and I couldn't resist saying, "And please thank Bev for her thoughtfulness."

"A VERY personable man, Mr. Nightingale," Marge remarked as she drove us back downtown.

"And his wife is just as wonderful a person as well," I immediately chimed in.

"Yes, they usually are," said Marge pleasantly, facing ahead with her equivocal smile.

22.

Days, she dons a white uniform and plays Florence Nightingale.

When the sun sets, she slithers into a bright sarong and does the hula-hula.

Lovely Luz (which means "light") Aquino leads a double life.

A Filipina by birth, she serves as a dandy Hawaiian

At Jackson Memorial Hospital she is known as Miss Aquino, RN. A very gifted nurse, say doctors.

In the entertainment world she is Luz, just as gifted as a hula dancer.

She was adjusting her Hawaiian costume for rehearsal at the Roney Plaza's lush new Polynesian Gardens, where she is starring in the South Seas "Show of Shows."

Luz came to Miami two years ago from New York, where she undulated hips and hands at the Hotel Lexington's Hawaiian Room. She learned both nursing and dancing in the Philippines.

"I always wanted two careers," she explained. "I love to help make people well. I also love to dance."

One column inch of space to go. Now I needed a snappy punch line. But what? The quote I'd just typed was pretty much the full extent of Luz's contribution to the interview. My hospital contact Herman Melton, who'd proposed the story to me, had delivered Luz from Jackson Memorial to the Roney Plaza so our photographer could save time by snapping her in both nurse's uniform and hula costume at the same place. Once there, the four of us were accosted by the hotel's high-powered publicity director, "Ken," who pressed on me as well as on the diffident Herman a sheaf of colorful press releases telling everything we wanted to know, and more, about the lush new Polynesian Gardens and the "Show of Shows" ("Outdoor Extravaganza! Hawaiian Luau! Flashing Swords! Tahitian Volcano! Hulas and Native Love Dances!").

Miss Aquino in her pristine white uniform and cap was so demure and self-effacing I couldn't imagine her drawing blood from a patient's vein, much less swiveling her hips in native costume.

It didn't facilitate matters that the assigned photographer was Jake Rance—being his usual corrosive self. Pipe clenched between his teeth, he bitched all the way to the Beach, murderously wielding the shift stick on his noisy Kharmann Ghia. ("They call this a *story?*") Over Ken's protests and Herman Melton's apologies to Ken, Jake refused to snap the nurse pictures anywhere but in the dullest corridor, which took some finding in the plush hotel. ("It's phoney enough that this *isn't* Jackson Memorial, but I see no reason to advertise the amenities of the Roney Plaza *twice.*") If I had been cowed by his unflattering comments during our rooftop trench coat session, no wonder the shy Filipino nurse looked ready to flee. I was surprised when she returned barefoot—and smiling for the first time. Either Ken had fortified her with a pep talk, or she knew how appealing she looked in her sarong. Jake positioned her in the grass, in front of a totem pole stacked with grimacing Polynesian-god masks, and ordered her to dance. That's when she came to life, enchanting us all. Jake went into action, lunging about on his polio leg, chanting, "Beautiful, beautiful . . . oh, that's a knockout!"

"Watch my hands," she told him, swaying and smiling. "They are telling a story."

Luz began the sinuous Hawaiian dance, swaying with a liquid grace and intricate arm movements.

"Watch my hands," she said, swaying lightly on the balls of her feet. "They tell a story."

But who was watching the hands?

Not my proudest feature, and queasy-making on a couple of counts. "A very gifted nurse, the doctors say," had come from Herman Melton's mouth alone. And the ending was worthy of "Today's Chuckle"—or Earl.

As I was pasting up my three sheets of triple-spaced copy to drop in Rod Reynolds's metal basket, the double mahogany doors to the board-room next to Mr. Feeney's office swung open and released the editors from their afternoon meeting, minus Mr. Feeney, who was on vacation in Maine with his family. Lou Norbright was in command until mid-July.

I had been waiting to spring two new feature ideas, both timely and both concerning Cuba, on Rod as soon as he emerged from boardroom, but seeing that Lucifer was gliding alongside him back to our city desk, I postponed my trip to the ladies' room and briskly rolled a blank sheet of paper into my typewriter, though I had nothing further to write.

"Well, Emma," Rod greeted me, "I hear from Marge that your feature on that little perfume lady packed the house at Fisher's Funeral Home this morning."

Norbright, sinisterly tailored all in gray, white, and black today, flashed his gold-edged canine at nobody in particular. He seemed to float in the ether of his yet-to-be-revealed intentions toward the newsroom over which he now held sway.

"I just finished that hula-dancer nurse," I told Rod. "I was about to put it in your basket."

"That it?" He snatched up the streamer of copy, still smelling of glue. "Immm, ha! Ha, ha. Good girl. This kind of thing comes easy to you, huh?"

"*Moderately* so. It wasn't all that big a challenge. I'm hoping Jake Rance's pictures will bump it up a notch or two in pizzazz. She was such a com-pletely different creature in her two outfits."

"Good old pizzazz, eh?" Rod laughed, flinging off his seersucker jacket, de rigueur for the boardroom, and shoving up his shirtsleeves. "Though I'm not sure our Dean Ligon would approve of pizzazz."

To Norbright he explained, "He was our ultratraditional J-school dean at Carolina."

"Different strokes for different folks," mused Norbright cheerfully.

His bright eyes behind their silver-rimmed glasses were trained on the sheet of paper in my typewriter as if something not to my advantage had suddenly appeared on its blank surface.

"I told Marge at our editorial meeting," Rod informed me, "I said, 'That was a beguiling story Emma wrote for you about the little perfumer on the Beach, Marge, but don't go trying to kidnap her from the city desk.' Didn't I, Lou?"

"Oh, we're keeping a close eye on Emma," Norbright smilingly replied before gliding on his way.

"LISTEN, ROD, have you got a minute?"

"Sure, what's up?"

"Well, I have some ideas for features about the Cuban refugees staying at my hotel. They're pouring in every day, and one's a world-famous teacher and critic who just smuggled his dangerous memoirs out of Cuba in his new wife's skirt, and the other escaped just yesterday in his family's plane when their cattle ranch in Camagüey was confiscated by Castro. The soldiers slaughtered a twenty-thousand-dollar breeding bull for a *barbecue* and arrested—"

"Hey, slow down, Emma, let me get my book."

He rummaged in a drawer and snatched out a dog-eared ledger of blue cloth with red leather corners and spine, bulging from things pasted into it.

"Oh, what's that?"

"My futures book. Don't tell me they left that out of your training."

He was riffling through the dated pages at the hectic rate he did everything.

"Where you record the daily news calendar and store reminders for upcoming stuff," I said.

Dean Ligon had done his job there, too; it was just that I had never met a futures book in person. I loved its archival appearance and determined to get one for myself as soon as I received my paycheck. What a perfect repository for my "appearances," as Alex called them, plus jottings for future *Star* projects to further my own star. It would be my business record, to be kept separate from my "Go, Tar Heels!" plaints, pep talks, and fantasies.

"Okay," said Rod, shoving up the loose cuff of his rolled-up right sleeve as he scribbled, "roasted a twenty-thousand-dollar breeding bull— and then what?"

After I had filled him in on both stories, he suggested I start on Don Waldo, since there were some sensitive issues about the Camagüey takeover.

"For a start, Joelle and Don are still running around loose in the countryside, representing the *Star* under the protection of the new regime, and we don't want to embarrass them or put them in any jeopardy. The other thing is, John, our editorial page editor, is writing an editorial to run on Saturday, the day after Joelle and Don get back, in which he'll state the *Star*'s position on the landgrabs—"

"What *is* the *Star*'s position?"

I could see from the city editor's flung-up eyebrows that I had overstepped my humble-cub-reporter bounds, but he sportingly rallied.

"John's still working on that. It's not all that cut-and-dried, Emma. There are so many ramifications. Even Ike is being cautious in his pronouncements about Castro's Cuba."

I finished off the afternoon tracking down Don Waldo in the morgue—what there was of him. Moira Parks, having finished scissoring and storing Sunday's bulky edition, was working on today's, humming under her breath. Not in sight on her clipping table, but somewhere in the pile, if not already filed, was "Popular Perfumer Transformed Lives," tucked into separate envelopes for Gant, Emma; Rossignol, Stella;

Lapidus, Morris; Godfrey, Arthur; and Nightingale, Paul—I was glad to have added some more bulk to his file.

He should be on the feeder flight now, somewhere between Raleigh and Mountain City. For once, *he'd* had more time to think about *me* than the other way round. During the first leg of his journey, I had returned to the paper with Marge. (What an odd remark of hers, "They always are." Was she intimating that she knew I was Paul's lover? Had she herself had similar experiences?)

Then back over to the Beach again with crosspatch Rance, my interview with Luz at the Roney Plaza, back once more to the *Star*, with Jake growling about Ken and something called "space graft," which I misunderstood as "space *graf*," provoking another tirade: "No, graft, GRAFT, with a *t*, as in bribery and corruption. The sole aim of his despicable breed is jimmying free advertising into newspapers."

I had composed my flimsy piece with its cheap punch line, been elevated sky-high by Rod's warning Marge off trying to "kidnap" me from the city desk, only to be shot down again by Norbright's oblique response.

Don Waldo's *Star* file contained only two items. A non-bylined 1957 announcement, with a one-column head shot, of his upcoming lecture on *Don Quixote*, sponsored by the Department of Hispanic Studies at the University of Miami, free to the public; and a 1958 AP wire story containing Don Waldo's "when reached by phone in Havana" reminiscences of his contemporary and friend Juan Ramón Jiménez, who had just died in exile in Puerto Rico. "When Juan Ramón was informed he had won the Nobel Prize in Poetry in 1956, his wife, Zenobia, was on her deathbed and he told reporters to go away, that his wife should have had the prize and he would not go to Stockholm. After Zenobia's death he wrote no more poems."

Twentieth Century Authors and *The Columbia Encyclopedia* added a bit to Alex's résumé of Don Waldo from the other night in La Bodega: Fernando Waldo Navarro y Cabrera, born in Madrid in 1882; studied at the University of Salamanca; professor of literature at the University of Madrid; married Maria Teresa Bombal, one son, Jorge; exiled from Spain with family in 1924 for criticizing the dictator Primo de Rivera; professor of rhetoric and literature at the University of Havana; fled Cuba with family when General Machado closed the colleges in 1931; taught at Fordham and Columbia; death of wife in New York; returned in 1933 to Cuba after the installation of President Grau. Followed by a list of works in Spanish and a much shorter list in English translation.

After I had laboriously copied it all out, including the complete list of works, I peeked under the diamond-studded dome of my foolish graduation watch and discovered it was past my quitting time.

THE NEW man behind the front desk was superfluent in English and slicked out like a professional ballroom dancer. He greeted me by name and, introducing himself as Salvador Barca, kept up a sociable stream of patter as I quickly sorted through the mail he handed over. Besides letters from Loney—hers and mine must have crossed—and my former roommate at Chapel Hill, there were two pink slips with phone messages, one from Tess ("Can you manage an early supper with us on board tomorrow? Call me at the office, I'm working late tonight!") and the other from Alex, asking me to phone his room as soon as I got in.

I was so eager to be in my room, I considered running up the four flights of stairs. But one had to keep up appearances for the desk clerks of the world, as well as for two tables of dominoes players, who were being served coffee by a waiter. Assuring Mr. Barca I had everything I needed (room service was now available, he'd informed me, if I would like refreshments sent up), I wished him *buenas tardes,* Bev-walked to the elevator in my new I. Miller pumps, and stood coolly enduring its maddeningly slow descent.

"Us" *had* to mean Tess and Ginevra—what else could it mean? Tomorrow! So she had done it, old Tess, as she said she would. I absolved her for learning to fly without telling me, I even forgave her for chauffeuring the newlyweds Paul and Ginevra in my recent nightmare.

———

"TESS?"

"Emma, love! You got my message? You're free, I hope? Tomorrow's good for her because he has some shrink seminar over at the Americana."

"Oh, Tess, how did you do it?"

"Emma, sweet, I'll tell you all about it tomorrow when I pick you up at the Julia Tuttle. Is six okay? I'm afraid I can't talk now. Doctor and I are up to our ears in work, we've overscheduled ourselves. So much going on! So many people with emergencies!"

"ALEX?"

"Oh, Emma, oh, good, you're back. I mean, you *are* back, aren't you?" He sounded flustered and excited.

"I'm in my room. Which has been done up royally, I must say. Even the end of the toilet paper roll has been folded like a table napkin."

"Yes, we have four new maids and a housekeeper. All overqualified for their jobs, but happy to have somewhere to wait it out. The housekeeper was head of millinery at El Encanto, the great department store, and the outgoing man on the desk, *señor* Barca, was maître d' at the Havana Hilton."

"Good Lord. Is this all from your mother's churchgoing roundup yesterday?"

"Yes. She has been very busy. Lídia is truly in her element." His voice had that same edge as when he'd addressed her as "Doña Lídia" on Friday night.

How could so much have happened in so short a time? It just now struck me that I hadn't seen Alex since he brought back his half brother from the Fort Lauderdale airfield.

"How is your brother Nestor?"

"Nestor is resting. We also have been busy. Emma, I must talk to you. Would you mind coming down to my room?"

"You mean right now?"

"*Por favor.* Second floor. Room two twenty-seven. And listen, Emma, would you mind very much taking the stairs? I'll explain when I see you."

HE HAD the door on the latch and must have been waiting right behind it for the sound of my steps.

He whisked me in and bolted the door.

"Ah, Emma, was anyone—did anyone see you?"

"Not a creature was stirring, not even a maid."

I don't know what I expected. I hadn't really spent much time imagining Alex's room beyond the books I knew it must contain and the goose liver pâté and water biscuits he'd offered me that night I caught him polishing shoes.

It was a much larger and longer room than mine, with a view of the bay and ocean, and what struck me first was how comfortable he had made it, with bookshelves, lots of them, containing real books, many of them leather-bound, not just tattered student paperbacks left over from college. There were upholstered club chairs, a sofa, a coffee table with magazines and more books on it, a writing desk with a leather top, a hi-fi system with speakers placed high on the walls, and even a knee-high wood-paneled refrigerator, where the pâté must live. Had I visited this room earlier, I would have been in an agony of envy. It was exactly the room I would have liked for myself at this point in my life.

Now, however, there were boxes all over the place, a tray piled with dirty dishes and coffee cups on the elegant writing desk, and a jumble of male clothing strewn across the bed and the sofa. A pair of lace-up work boots that looked brand-new stood guard rather incongruously beside a stack of *Saturday Reviews* on the coffee table.

"What's *up*, Alex?"

"Shhh, we have to keep our voices low. Nestor's asleep in the next room." He indicated a closed door. "This was meant to be a suite and will be again shortly. Listen, Emma, I need your help tonight. There is no one else I can trust. This is all very, very secret. If Lídia finds out, she'll ruin everything. But first I must ask, can you drive a car?"

"Well, of course." To give credit where credit was due, Earl had taught me. With plenty of cursing and faultfinding, of course.

"My old Mercedes has a stick shift."

"It was a while ago, but that's what I learned on."

"Fantastic!" He strode about the room, in a kind of high-tension reso-luteness that suited him. "Now, listen very carefully, and if you have second thoughts about any of this, you must refuse."

"But you said you have no one else you can trust."

"That is true. We'd have to do it on our own, then, which would be somewhat riskier and much more inconvenient for my mother. But we could still manage it, and we will do so, if you have the least hesitation."

I concentrated so intensely as he outlined the plan that I missed crucial chunks and had to ask him to repeat. I thought I heard Nestor snoring in the next room.

"What should I wear?" I asked, after Alex had gone through everything again.

ZERO HOUR was set for nine and now it was just past six. There were letters to open and read, thoughts to think, good old bathing and grooming to get through, and, of course, my next meal to be eaten.

Under ordinary circumstances, marking time until a date or an appointment would have been a simple matter of organization. But now there was this added element of secrecy to be observed.

I was not exactly a novice at subterfuge—hadn't I kept Paul a secret from everyone I knew for an entire year? But putting something over on a predator like Lídia Prieto Maldonado de Costa, etc., etc., etc., was a far riskier exercise than keeping something they would rather not know anyway from my family and from Paul's wife.

"When I am in my mother's presence," Alex had said at La Bodega, "I stop thinking of myself as the main person in my own life. It is Lídia who is the author *and* the central character. I am there to carry out her wishes, to facilitate the things she has decided must happen next."

When someone has that power over you and you need to keep a secret from them, the smart thing to do would be to stay *out* of their presence.

That, however, Alex could not do. To make tonight's plan go forward, he had to take part in Lídia's evening fanfare, which she and her newly recruited minions were setting up right now beside the pool. "Her" stepson Nestor was to be given a hero's send-off by the exile community before Alex drove him to the Fort Lauderdale airfield, from whence he would pilot himself into counterrevolutionary territory.

I, however, pleading more work to do, was to make a brief and gracious early appearance, wish Lídia *buena suerte* on behalf of her stepson— since Nestor and Alex wouldn't be down yet—and head back to the *Star*.

While still in Alex's room, I had concocted the perfect alibi for myself simply by moving up a day the homemaking editor's knee surgery Marge said was scheduled for Wednesday. ("Of course I have my city desk duties during the daytime," I would tell the partygoers, "but the women's editor is so shorthanded I offered to write a few features for her this evening.")

This was all very well until I realized, once back in my room, that I had been caught up in the fantasy I had fashioned for Alex's purposes. Marge did not expect me tonight, as I had *not* offered to take up the slack on her team; she might not even come back to the office herself. And it was not in my best interest, while Lucifer as deputy managing editor might still be gliding to and fro in the newsroom, to be seen taking up space with no clear purpose.

So here's what I would do: present myself early at Lídia's party, maybe set up an interview time with Don Waldo for my feature on him, then make my excuses and head off as though walking to work, detour over to Howard Johnson's for a frankfurter with baked beans and cole slaw on the side, and vanish into one of the movie theaters on Flagler Street until just before nine, when I would station myself at the *Star* entrance and wait for Alex and Nestor to pick me up.

I checked the *Star's* movie listing, "Let's See a Movie Tonight!" with its separate categories for "Theaters," "Drive-ins," and "Negro Theaters."

My Flagler Street choices were *Say One for Me*, with Bing Crosby and Debbie Reynolds, and *El Dolor de las Hijas* and *El Enmascarado de la Muerte*, running as a double feature; both Spanish-language movies sounded

promising in their different ways and would improve my Spanish comprehension, regardless of their quality.

Bell, Book, and Candle, with Kim Novak, playing at the Negro theater,
would have been my definite first choice, but I didn't have the courage for
that. What if they refused me admission at the box office? In Mountain
City, theaters simply reserved their balconies for Negro moviegoers and
everybody watched the same show the same week.

"*Bienvenida,* Emma! Don't you look adorable in those capri pants
and flats! So casual and *désinvolte.* May I pin a *clavel* on your blouse? Everyone is receiving a white carnation tonight. A sort of party favor."

Up close Lídia smelled of what must be the scent Aunt Stella had
identified, the very special soap imported from Spain because Lídia was
such an "original" she eschewed *parfums,* even custom ones. She was wearing the red flamenco outfit with a burst of white carnations pinned to the
waist.

"But you are very early, *chica.* The hot tapas are not out yet. Hardly anyone has arrived, except Hector, who has to leave promptly at seven and
return to his office."

"I'm afraid I have to leave before that. I promised the women's editor
at the *Star* I'd write some features for her tonight. She's very short-staffed
with one of her editors going in for knee surgery tomorrow and her star
writer away on her honeymoon."

"Such enterprise, Emma. You are turning into a real *carrerista.* But you
must at least stay and shake hands with Nestor, who was always my favorite stepson. Here he is flying off into danger and you haven't even met."

"But I saw him yesterday, when you brought him out to the pool to
meet Don Waldo. I hope Don Waldo will come out soon, I need to ask
him something important."

"That will be difficult, *hija.* Don Waldo and his wife left for Princeton
this morning." Lídia divulged this, I thought, with a certain amount of
sweet revenge. "He is to deliver his Jane Austen lecture, you remember."

"When do you expect them back?"

"Oh, it is a *little* up in the air. There is some research he needs for his *memorias*, and, as you know, this is also their honeymoon. But Altagracia told me confidentially she hopes they will return by the end of the month; she is so eager to help with all our projects. By the way, congratulations on your adorable story about the little *parfumeur* on the Beach. Your friend Mr. Nightingale must have been extremely pleased with you."

"Oh, I think both he and his wife, Bev, were very—"

"Here is Hector, whom you've met. Have you seen your lovely aunt recently?"

"We're going to have dinner tomorrow, she—"

"Hector! Come and say hello to our ambitious *periodista* who, like you, says she must leave early, such a shame. I was just telling Emma that Nestor was always my favorite stepson, so much more *confiable* than his brother Carlo. God knows I don't wish anyone in prison, but if one family member was to escape it is lucky for the de Costas that it was the dependable son."

"So how is the newspaper business, *señorita* Gant?"

"A bit hectic. That's why I have to go back to work. Tess tells me you have been pretty hectic yourself. Lots of emergencies."

"Emergencies, yes," repeated the debonair dental surgeon rather dreamily, cradling my hand in both of his and giving me the male-female once-over. The white carnation was pinned high on the chest of his guayabera. "There is much going on at the moment, yes." He seemed bemused by the activity of all Lídia's minions rushing around. "All these new Cubans," he said.

"She recruited them after Mass at the Catholic church yesterday. They get room and board in return for whatever work they do at the Julia Tuttle. Alex says the new housekeeper was the head of the millinery department at El Encanto, and the man on the front desk was the maître d' at the Havana Hilton."

"I don't see the owner of the sugar mill. Perhaps it is his night off.

Well, *señorita,* may I accompany you to the beverage table? What will you have?"

"Just a Coke, thanks. I've got to keep my mind clear, especially tonight."

The dental surgeon laughed. "I also must stay clear. *Entonces: dos Coca-Colas por la claridad.*"

"How do you think things are going in Cuba, Dr. Rodriguez?"

"*Calamitoso.* Pure and simple. What a deceiver! He has betrayed everyone, including himself." He absently stroked the white carnation. "There is that old Spanish proverb, I think I told you. *'El que espera desespera.'* He who waits will despair. We must be organizing plans of our own now, not just sitting around waiting for the American government to act for us."

I TOOK an aisle seat in the air-conditioned dark of the Tivoli, wishing I'd brought a wrap and already regretting the hot fudge sundae after my Howard Johnson frankfurter and beans. ("There are no subtitles," the girl at the box office had warned me in accented English, to which I had coolly replied, *"Gracias, señorita, pero no importa."*)

A desert chase on horseback was in progress, shots rang out, the rider in the black mask bit the dust, pulling his horse down on top of him. (I hated when they did that. How many movie horses had to be put out of their misery without ever knowing their riders were only stuntmen and the chase that broke their legs hadn't even been necessary?)

Then a close-up of the victor trotting off in the opposite direction. Against a background of swelling guitar music a dark-haired beauty on a balcony anxiously squinted into the distance until it became clear that her man had won.

End of *El Enmascarado de la Muerte.* The dim lights came on. About half the audience, mostly under fifteen, got up to go, noisily racing each other up the aisles. A few rows ahead of me, a good-looking man in a row all by himself stood up, raised his arms in a luxurious masculine stretch, exchanged comments in Spanish with a couple of teenage boys who stood aside to let him pass, laughed indulgently at something they said, and then swaggered out of the theater, head held high, as though he owned

the world. Only after he had passed my seat did I realize it had been Enrique Ocampo, the ousted sugar heir. He had not seen me.

El Dolor de las Hijas opened with a close-up of the father, a dour corpse
with melancholy profile, in his casket. Unless there were flashbacks to
come, that was the end of his role in the movie. The tensions between the
mother and her three daughters blossomed at once, prompting me with
hopes for emotional understanding without the aid of subtitles. The
mother was a black-eyed termagant with a mean mouth and forbidding
posture. (I was reminded of Don Waldo's *"feróz"* great-aunt from Bilbao
who died without ever touching her back to a chair.)

Power was clearly the mother's forte, with a dose of sadism thrown in
for good sport. She missed nothing, and everything in the drab, boring
village referred back to her. She was definitely a *menos mío* type, like Lídia.
The daughters were no match for her, the eldest being *una solterona*, the
old maid and family slave; the middle one an ineffectual, dreamy beauty;
and the youngest a religious sadist in training. In the cortege from the funeral to the house was a young male cousin, just back from some war. He
had eyes only for the ineffectual, dreamy beauty, and she only for him,
but tradition dictated that the eldest sister must be married first, so he allowed himself to become engaged to the old maid. You definitely got the
impression the mother knew exactly what was brewing. And when the
married couple took the middle sister to help them set up their house in
a neighboring village, you felt she had instigated this, too. Now there
were the two women left, mother and daughter sadists, sitting upright in
their chairs and mean-mouthing each other.

Where could this story go next? Unless this was a very short movie,
this couldn't possibly be the end.

It wasn't. Another war breaks out and the young husband departs
promptly with his fighting gear. His wife and her live-in younger sister,
the ineffectual beauty, are left alone together, both seemingly happy with
their shared life. Each glows privately as she goes about her chores, smiling to herself a lot, until the termagant mother comes for a visit, the termagant daughter having entered a convent. The sharp-eyed mother ferrets
out at once what no one else, including us moviegoers, has noticed: the

wife is in the early stages of pregnancy. When the mother announces this, the married daughter admits it is true and the ineffectual beauty goes off and hangs herself.

At the funeral (closed coffin this time), the mother, speaking in close-up to the camera, proclaims herself a *mater dolorosa*.

"But life cannot be all sadness," she fiercely concludes, adjusting her black mourning veil and rising to new heights of posture. "I had three daughters. (*Tenía tres hijas.*) One lives as the happy bride of Christ, one will soon give birth to my grandchild, and one died a beautiful virgin. I refuse to deplore my destiny. (*Yo me niego a deplorar mi destino.*)"

The aftereffects of *El Dolor de las Hijas* accompanied me as I left the chill of the Tivoli and set out down hot and humid Flagler Street, now lit up for nighttime pleasures. I kept my stride purposeful, my eyes cast down. It was almost seven minutes before pickup time in front of the *Star*, a few minutes more than I needed, but if I slowed to a pedestrian stroll, I might be inviting another kind of pickup.

Now I wished I had stayed for the credits instead of making for the ladies' room—there would have been time for both. Had a man or a woman written that screenplay? Was it adapted from a story or taken from someone's experience? If the latter, who had suffered, and who had artistically avenged himself or herself? Despite the mother's speech at the end, it *was* titled *The Pain of the Daughters*.

Or was it just a cold-blooded bit of cinematic whoredom: a bunch of cynical scriptwriters sitting around with their cigarettes and whiskies, catering to the lowest emotional denominator? Yet something about the story dogged me, and encouraged me to play with it. Perhaps my emotions were not as elevated as I liked to think.

Which daughter, in such a family, would I most likely have been? Probably the termagant in training, but allowing myself some verve and wit. I had read enough about Saint Teresa of Ávila to know you could join a convent and still get away with being yourself if there was enough of a self to start with.

————

ENGINE RATTLING, the Mercedes was already waiting across the street from the *Star* in the same spot where Paul and I had parked to watch the press run my first night in Miami.

Alex stepped out of the driver's side as I approached; he must have been watching for me.

"Perfect timing, Emma. But why are you walking in this direction? I expected you to come out of the *Star*."

"Change of plans. Marge couldn't make it, so I went to the movies."

Keep the lies short and simple: complications were compounding by the minute. Still under the miasmic spell of the mother in *El Dolor de las Hijas*, I was having serious qualms about deceiving Lídia. It would be no picnic returning to the domain of such a woman after having put one over on her—and didn't I still have to live at the Julia Tuttle?

"Will you drive, Emma? That way you'll be familiar with the car when you return."

Nestor slid out of the front seat and transferred to the back. After helping me adjust the driver's seat forward, Alex went around to the passenger side.

When we were all inside, Alex introduced me to his half brother, calling him simply *mi hermano*.

"*Mucho gusto, señorita*." Nestor gave no sign of connecting me with yesterday's frowsy Emma in the man's wet silk dressing gown when Lídia had paraded him around the pool. "*Usted es muy amable de ayudarnos este tarde*." (You are very kind to help us tonight.)

"*El gusto es mío, Nestor. Y me llamo Emma, por favor. Yo siento mucho lo ocurrido en Camagüey*." (The pleasure is mine, Nestor. And please call me Emma. I am very sorry about what happened in Camagüey.)

"*Usted es muy amable . . . Emma*."

"Emma, your Spanish gets better and better," Alex proudly noted.

"I've just come out of a Spanish-language movie, that may have something to do with it. Oops, *sorry*." I had let out the clutch with a violently amateurish jerk.

"*¡Él respinga!*" said Nestor, with a good-natured machismo laugh. (He bucks!)

"This will take a little getting used to. Last time I drove a straight shift, I was sixteen."

"Take all the time you need, Emma. I want you to get used to it. I'll be your navigator. Go straight down to the end of Flagler and take a left onto Second Avenue. There won't be so much tourist traffic as Biscayne."

I committed a few more clutch clinkers, and as I was making the turn onto Second Avenue, I heard Earl say, as distinctly as if he had traded places with Alex, "Now, don't let up or she'll cut out on you again," and of course that's just what happened. The Mercedes cut off and we stopped traffic in both directions.

"You're going to be fine, Emma," Alex said as I lurched us forward again.

"*Bueno . . . ha domesticado el caballo,*" said Nestor from the backseat when at last I found my rhythm with the pedals.

"*Sí,* Emma, you have tamed the bronco," said Alex.

AS WE branched off onto the federal highway in North Miami, I thought of Mr. Charles P. Rose, still fuming over his water bill behind one of those jalousie-windowed bungalows blinking out at us through the darkness. Had his water been cut off by now, or had he broken down and paid the additional $2.06?

Do you know who's driving by your house right now, sir?

Don't tell me, let me guess. Miss Grant, girl reporter. What's she sticking her nose into now?

She's driving two Cuban men to a private airfield in Fort Lauderdale; they're off to a training camp to take back their country. The elder half brother will teach flying, along with all the other pilots who have deserted Castro's air force, and the younger will fight however he can to help the cause.

Why can't they drive themselves to the airfield?

Who's going to take the car back to his mother?

Why couldn't his mother drive them, then?

Because she doesn't know the young one is going to the training camp. If she did, she'd stop him.

So how the hell is Miss Grant going to explain to the mother when she brings the car back?

The car will simply be parked outside in its usual place, with the keys under the mat and a note from the son to the mother.

And how will the girl reporter get home?

She lives in the same hotel as the mother, so all she has to do is slip in. The mother thinks she's been working late at the Star.

Now, look here, a lot of people can be fooled by deceitful wording, but some of us can't be shunted off so easily. You know what that mother is going to say to our cub reporter?

"Nobody could be that stupid!"

Damn right. You took the words right out of my mouth. If I was that Miss Grant— okay, Gant—I know what I'd be doing!

What, Mr. Rose?

I'd be looking for another hotel.

"EMMA, I left you some of my books. You will find them outside the door of your room in a box. Some Spanish poets and writers I know you will like. It makes me happy to think of you using them."

"Please, Alex, you sound like you're not coming back."

"Until I return is all I meant. Oh, and I included my Arden Shakespeare volumes, the footnotes are the best. There is *Hamlet* and *Macbeth* and, let's see, *A Midsummer's Night's Dream* and *The Tempest*. I had a funny thought when I was packing the *Hamlet*."

"What?" It was just sinking in what a large hole Alex was leaving in my life.

"Well, that Hamlet might still be alive if he had gone off to fight with those recruits of Fortinbras's. Maybe all he needed was to get away from Gertrude. Now, you'll want to take the first road on the left immediately after we pass the Dania Jai-Alai fronton."

"What is jai alai?"

"It's a Basque form of handball. The players throw a small hard ball and catch it with *cestas*, long curved baskets strapped on their arms. Besides horse racing, it's the only other way you can gamble legally in Florida. Back there was where we would have turned off to go to Bal

Harbour. I'll miss Nightingale's, but who knows, I may be back in Havana by the time it reopens in October."

I succeeded in keeping my mouth shut. What purpose would it serve for Alex to know Nightingale's went on the market this morning?

"YOU'LL HAVE to stop at that little hut by the gate, Emma, for Nestor to show some papers. Then you just drive right through the grass over to that red-and-white Beechcraft."

The man on duty in the hut spoke in Spanish with Nestor. After their animated conversation, all three men burst into uproarious laughter.

"Fill me in, please," I begged Alex as I angled the car in beside the de Costa family's plane.

"Well, Emma, if you want the precise translation, he said that a crop duster who took off earlier told him it only needed twenty pilots with balls to take back Cuba from Castro. Now Nestor and I will have to unload some dental equipment from the trunk, and then we'll get you on the road home."

"Did you say dental equipment?"

"That's your aunt Tess's word for it. We got our allotment from Dr. Rodriguez's office before we picked you up. Your aunt was there, too, helping out. Since the customs agents started cracking down in May, Hector is being cautious and sending out many small shipments, dividing them up. It is a federal offense to smuggle arms, you know. We are only carrying some crates of ammunition, the 'flosses and sample toothpastes.' The rifles and the automatics went out earlier with the crop duster. Your aunt calls them the 'toothbrushes.' The machine guns she calls 'dentist drills.' "

God, how blind and stupid could I be? When it was right under my nose!

"I'm going to miss you *muchísimo, señor* Bartleby."

"I'm going to miss you *extremely*, Deviled Egg. Listen, Emma, do you mind if I kiss you?"

23.

Truckload of Explosives Confiscated

Terrorist Suspects Captured in Cuba

HAVANA, Cuba (UPI) — An undisclosed number of suspected terrorists were captured aboard a dynamite-laden truck Monday in the beach resort of Guanabacoa. They will face execution by firing squad if convicted under drastic new antiterrorism laws.

The truck's cargo of explosives was believed intended for use in the manufacture of homemade bombs.

Police did not disclose how many were arrested, but said they will investigate the ramifications of the possible terrorist plot.

News of the detentions brought popular demonstrations against the prisoners.

Prime Minister Fidel Castro, meanwhile, told a mass meeting estimated at 100,000 persons in Santa Clara that "everyone" would have a chance to fight if the threats of invasion from abroad materialized.

"The enemies of the people have reason to tremble because the people of Cuba will defend their revolution unto death," Castro said.

He said he would like to see "war criminals" now in exile abroad land in Cuba. "The first thing we will do is to cut off their retreat so they cannot escape again.

"If war criminals decide to return to Cuba, they will be made to pay their debt with justice," Castro said.

"Emma, you look like you're going to take a bite out of that paper," said Rod Reynolds. "What is it you're reading?"

I passed it across to him.

"Hmmm, ha—oh, the 'terrorist suspects.' Isn't it funny how the other side are always the terrorists? Hey, this stuff is really getting to you, stuck over there in your hotel with all the exiles. How's your story on the old Cuban professor coming?"

I had to tell him Don Waldo was in Princeton and wasn't expected back until July.

"Too bad. I was gonna say, go ahead and leave early and interview him this afternoon. We could send a photographer and get a nice shot of him and his bride. Is she pretty?" My phone rang. "If it's one of your funeral homes," he went on, "tell 'em today's obits are already locked up."

"City desk, Emma Gant speaking."

"Hi, Emma. Lou Norbright here."

"Oh, *hi.*" Through the glass of the managing editor's office I could see the top part of him behind his desk, smiling into the receiver.

"Can you step over here for a minute?"

"HAVE A SEAT, Emma." Though Lucifer beamed on me his full gleaming attention as I entered, he didn't trouble himself to rise today. "How have things been going?"

"Well, I *think* they've been going pretty well."

"That's what we all think. You're a ferocious worker and you have a lot of potential."

"Thank you."

"Emma, as you know, Mr. Feeney is away until the middle of July, and I've made an executive decision concerning you. We have a shortage up in Broward. One of our staff there, Alma Olsen, has requested a leave of absence to take care of her mother, who's dying, and as Marge is so short-staffed, I'm going to take a gamble and let you skip a grade. New reporters normally spend three to six months in Miami before we assign them to a regular spot, but in a little more than a week you've shown yourself to be such a pressure cooker of industry and initiative that I'd like to send you up to Broward tomorrow."

"Tomorrow?"

"Tomorrow. Wednesday. Here's what I have in mind. Alma will drive down around midday tomorrow and pick you up herself. Alma's a nifty gal, you'll like her. She's offered you her car and her apartment while she's on leave. You'll be able to sock away some savings, because you're going to need a car soon. How does this sound to you, Emma?"

"How long is this for?"

The words came out sounding stupid because my mouth wasn't moving naturally. I felt like a snakebite victim once the venom starts inching through your system.

Though he continued to smile, Norbright conveyed that same aura of subliminal reservation that had shrunk me during our first meeting.

"Well, I haven't consulted Alma's mother," he replied cheerfully, "though I doubt even *she* knows when she's going to die. From what Alma tells me, I'd put it between two and three months. But if you prove yourself the way you have here, Emma, I see no reason why you can't stay on in Broward. As I said, everyone here thinks you have a lot of potential. Your leads are great and you have a knack for human-interest features. You're good at color. The next step is for you to learn how the world works in black-and-white so you can put together the big picture."

"The big picture," I gamely repeated, hardening my heart against the pity I felt for myself. If I cried now, I was finished.

"How municipalities are run; who the key players are; who stands to gain from what, who stands to lose; how justice is administered—or abused. What we call the hard news. The step beyond *that* is learning to sniff out what's going on behind the scenes, sharpening your nose for scandals and scams."

"Like your creep who sold religious relics through the mail."

At least this made his expression shift to frank amusement. "You've been reading my file, Emma. I did the same thing when I was new here; I checked out the competition. How much are you paid up in advance at your hotel?"

"The whole month. That was the deal for the special rate."

"Well, squeeze what refund you can get out of them. We'll pick up the difference. Meanwhile I've had them cut an early check for you since you won't be here for payday on Friday."

A FEW hours earlier, the thing I had been dreading most was encountering Lídia back at the Julia Tuttle. I had not seen her since my grand betrayal the night before. The Mercedes had been left in its spot, key under the mat, with no one the wiser. Alex's note in a Julia Tuttle envelope, addressed to his mother, I left, as instructed, on the seat.

Now the "Doña," wearing an ice blue linen sheath and looking cool as a mint, presided over the front desk, taking her fair turn with her rent-free vassals. I walked straight toward her, our gazes already locked. I was almost eager to hear her say her worst. She had no power over me now. By midday tomorrow I would be out of her orbit. But what a high price to pay for my freedom.

"Emma, you look exhausted. What have they been doing to you at that paper? You write extra stories for them late into the night and then, *además*, you put in a full workday. You have no mail or messages, I hope you were not expecting any."

"No, I haven't even had time to read my yesterday's letters yet."

"You have been *ess-TREME-ly* busy! Would you like some refreshments sent up? Maybe an aperitif and some savories to accompany your bath?"

"No, thank you. Listen, Lídia, I'm checking out of the Julia Tuttle tomorrow. I was wondering . . . I paid a month in advance . . . could I get some sort of refund?"

"Of course you will get a refund. We are not running a clip joint here." She hadn't missed a beat, but there was a new wariness, like a fox who's been chasing a chicken, only to realize it's being tracked itself by something bigger. "At what time would you like to have your bill ready—with your *refund*?"

"I have to check out at noon, if that's okay."

"Well, of *course* it's okay. Checkout time is not until two at the Julia Tuttle. But listen, *hija*, isn't this rather impulsive? Is there some fault you find with us, something we did not do right?"

"No, it's not that. They're sending me—" I had to turn away. *Mierda,* I was not going to cry in front of Lídia, of all people. "They're sending me up to the bureau in Lauderdale. One of their editors is taking a leave of absence. Her mother is dying of cancer and she wants to be with her."

"So you are going to be an editor yourself? That is fast work."

"Well, no. I'm to take over her women's features, but also I'll be broadening my scope, learning how municipalities are run, what they call the hard news. Apparently"—I laughed bitterly—"I've done so well with *color* stories that I'm being promoted to black-and-white for a while."

She was scrutinizing me. "Are you happy about this move, Emma?"

"Not particularly. I wasn't exactly given a choice."

"Ah, some of us aren't. You know, of course, that my Alejandro has gone off with Nestor?"

"I knew, yes."

"I thought you did. Let us keep straight lines between us, *chica*. Do you have plans for this evening? If not, I would like to take you to a five-star restaurant in Coral Gables."

"Thank you, that sounds lovely, but I'm having dinner with my aunt and a friend of hers."

"*Lo siento. Entonces,* you will want your bath. I am going to send up an aperitif and some little snacks—on the house, of course—and also a bar of my special soap I order from Spain. What a pity you must leave so quickly, *querida*. I would have liked to give you a send-off party."

"Well, I guess she is anxious to be by her mother's side."

"I know how it is, exactly! My mother—Alejandro's *abuelita*—also died of cancer. I was in Paris at the time with his favorite stepfather, but I will always regret not being by her side in Palm Beach."

I CAME down again at six, buzzing pleasantly from two small bottles of iced Cinzano, my hunger pangs appeased by roasted pecans and some great little cheese sticks, my skin exuding Lídia's trademark scent, which I had to admit I liked.

Tess, still in her white uniform, was deep in conversation with Lídia at the desk. As I had no idea who knew what, and who wasn't supposed to know what, about airport trips, "dentist drills," and so on, I chose from my personal arsenal the weapons of reserve and goal-oriented guile for the evening ahead. After all, getting to know Ginevra was my prime objective.

Tess, however, managed to offend me almost as soon as we were in the car—her Oldsmobile, not Hector's new Cadillac—by pointing out that this evening was to be a social one, "just among us girls," and so naturally I would understand that anything anybody said would be "off the record" as far as the *Star* was concerned.

"Well, of *course*, Tess," I said, stung to the quick.

For Pete's sake, who had unearthed Ginevra in the first place? Who had talked to her at the hospital, heard her recite the poem? Tess had never even spoken to her at the hairdresser's before I established the contact. Everything she knew about Ginevra had come secondhand from her old teacher, Edith Vine. And now Tess was acting as though they were old buddies and she had to protect Ginevra from the indiscreet reporter who might quote her in the *Star*. As though Ginevra hadn't already been quoted in the *Star*!

Had Lídia told Tess I was being shipped off to the boondocks ? Unless Tess brought it up, I would volunteer nothing. If Lídia *hadn't* told her, I would leave town tomorrow without telling her, either. That would be Tess's punishment for imposing such lofty standards of probity when she herself was up to her ears in subterfuges and counterplots.

"What do you hear from your mother?" Tess went on warmly, seemingly oblivious to her offense.

"Oh, there was a masterpiece of a long letter waiting for me when I arrived, and since then she's mailed me a few things, including my Spanish-English dictionary."

"You can certainly use that! Nancy is so gifted. I'll never forget the play she wrote for our class at Converse. I was sure she would be famous one day. Is she happy, do you think, Emma?"

"In many ways, I think so," I loyally replied. As we were already on South Bayshore Drive and would soon be turning off to Tess's houseboat, I decided to jettison my pique in favor of information. "But you were going to tell me how you arranged this date with Ginevra."

"Well, it was Saturday at Michel's. I was halfway through my two-color process when she came in and I saw her registering who I was, even though my head was in a swirl of foam. I can't even remember who spoke first, it was almost like we both said hello at the same time. And then she told Michel she wanted a new look, a really short, *short* haircut, but not one of those silly poodle cuts. And I said, 'Like Jean Seberg in *Saint Joan.*' And Michel said, 'That's going to be a big change,' and she said, 'That's exactly what I want, a big change.' So Michel put her in the chair and turned her this way and that way and then he said, 'Your bones would support a crew cut, Mrs. Brown.' And she laughed and said with that incredible Edith Vine diction, 'We needn't go *that* far, Michel, just Saint Joan will do.' And the three of us just kept on talking. By the time Michel finished transforming her, I still had more time to go on my color, and I asked if she'd be free to have dinner some night. I said you were quite taken with her, Emma, I hope you don't mind, and she said, 'Tuesday would be good because Edwin will be addressing a national psychiatrists' conference over on the Beach.' "

———

THE LAST time I'd boarded, the houseboat was in darkness and heavy rain, after Tess and I had unloaded the famous "dental equipment." Now early evening sunshine sparkled on the wavelets of the bay and bathed the assembly of male statues on the deck in a warm golden light. At first I thought there was a new statue among them, a boy in a tunic, reclining on a low bench between two potted plants. But then he moved and at the same time Tess cried, "Oh, dear, are we late?"

"No, I'm early," replied the figure in her thrilling contralto. "I've been looking forward to this smoke since noon."

Rising from the bench, Ginevra, locks sculpted almost as short as Paul's after his Saturday trim, took another drag on her cigarette, then extinguished it in the soil of a pot and carefully stored the remains in a silver case, which she dropped into a slim purse. She was absolutely dazzling in her white tunic dress—a cross between a goddess and a boy angel, on fire with the sultry golden evening light. Of course, up until now I had seen her in mere black-and-white newsprint or in washed-out color after having her stomach pumped.

"Well, Emma," she said, wending her way gracefully through the throng of statues to offer me her hand, "as you see, I took your advice and said hello to your aunt."

"Your haircut is spectacular," I could only say.

"Thank you. It was time for a change."

"Yes, isn't it a triumph?" said Tess. "Not many faces could bear up under a cut like that. Mine certainly couldn't, even when I was at my peak. Emma, while I freshen up, will you pour Ginevra and yourself daiquiris in the galley and show her around? The pitcher's in the fridge. I used limes this time; the peach was maybe a little too potent for us."

"Goodness, what a layout," said Ginevra, taking in the velvets and brocades, the bust of the Roman soldier with his lavender boa, the porcelain and the peacock feathers, the theater posters covering the walls.

"Not exactly what you'd expect of a seagoing interior," I said.

"To whom does all this belong?"

That refined "whom" again! Edith Vine had certainly left her imprint.

"He directs summer theater up in Connecticut."

"Ah, that figures."

"They've had this arrangement for years. Tess boat-sits in the summer and rents out her Coral Gables apartment for the extra income. Wait till you see the mirror collection in the bathroom, there's about a thousand and one of them. Lord, she's even frosted up the glasses. I hope you like daiquiris."

"As well as anything. I'm more of a social sipper than a drinker. Smoking is my vice. I started at twelve. My husband hates it, but I've managed to cut down to four a day and I no longer smoke inside the house or in the car. Thank you, that's plenty. And may I have a glass of water, too?"

"Coming up. Tall or short glass?"

"The taller the better. Thanks. How is the good old *Miami Star*? I read your delightful story about the old man and his dog. And Edwin and I were relieved at how little was said about my mishap. I don't know how you pulled it off, but we're grateful. Three times in a row is hard to live down."

"Oh, well." I took a hefty slurp of daiquiri. "It was deadline and I just called in the bare facts. I was sorry there wasn't time to do a real interview, but then the more I thought it over afterwards, the more I felt your story now belonged in another context."

"And what context would that be?"

She was sipping her water, the daiquiri so far untouched. Her wide-spaced smoky eyes were trained astutely on me. From a distance, with the cropped hair, she could have passed for a beautiful sixteen-year-old of either sex, but up close the eyes were too shrewd and the mouth, though as finely formed as the rest of her face, was a little hard.

"Less newspapery. More like a story behind a story." I fueled myself with more daiquiri to free up my powers of expression. "My first day on the *Star*, one of the older reporters took me to lunch and told me about the 'Queen of the Underworld' series. I went back to work and devoured your file. I felt Norbright had taken something that belonged to me, even though I was a sophomore in high school when the story broke. I felt this strange affinity with you."

"Yes, you said that at the hospital. I remembered it." She finally took a sip of the daiquiri, then went back to her water.

"Bisbee, that's the reporter who took me to lunch, said Norbright made you into a modern-day Persephone."

"Oh, yes, kidnapped by the Lord of the Underworld while picking flowers in a field. Only I was selling fruit behind a stand. Miss Edith always called her Proserpine. I didn't keep a scrapbook of the trial. After I'd been in therapy for a year with Edwin, he gave me his complete set of clippings and suggested I make up a ritual for myself and burn them. I did: I drove over to the beach one night and made a little bonfire."

"Did it make a difference?"

"It must have. Not long after that I was able to let Edwin persuade me I wouldn't destroy his life if we got married."

"Did—?"

"Yes?"

"Oh, nothing."

"I know what you were going to ask. I didn't destroy his, but I came close to destroying mine. Since I was old enough to stand on a crate and count money, I have held down a job, and I have always been good at my jobs. Whether I was selling oranges and peaches to tourists driving up and down the Sunshine Highway or coaching the Palm Island girls in deportment before a date, I was good at what I did. Even when Prince Charming's uncle was sending me to the Biscayne Academy, I worked for Miss Edith; I typed all her correspondence and cut all the mimeograph stencils. I'd learned touch-typing in high school. And then suddenly Dr. Brown made an honest woman of me and I lived in a nice house on Key Biscayne, with a maid who came twice a week to clean, and even the neighbors who remembered the trial were friendly. I was their exotic rescued neighborhood pet. Wives were always asking me to have lunch at the club, but after a while I begged off. I couldn't take those boozy lunches, they put me out for the rest of the day. Meanwhile Edwin's practice got bigger and bigger and I withdrew more and more into myself. Then I found I couldn't sleep, but I didn't want to stay awake, and that's when we got into the sleeping-potion habit. Sometimes I took it in the afternoon, when I could track down where he'd hidden it; I couldn't wait to conk out. It wasn't until my third trip to the emergency room last Wednesday that it finally dawned on me what I was missing—and you, showing up as you did, played an important part, Emma."

"I did?"

Of course Tess chose this moment to emerge from her freshening-up, changed into a low-necked blouse and slacks and sandals, and emanating Joy.

"If anyone needs to go to the head, please excuse the steamed-up mirrors from my shower. Oh, good, I see you've made a start on the daiquiris—at least you have, Emma, you need a freshener."

"I prepared her for the mirrors," I said, to deflect attention from Tess's refilling of my glass.

"Yes. They can be rather alarming if you're not prepared for them." Tess went into her amusing spiel about the mirrors for the benefit of her new guest. "I usually prefer to keep my eyes closed when I'm on the john, but some of them can be useful if you need a particular close-up of yourself." She poured herself a daiquiri. "Well, cheers, girls. It's so good to have you here, Ginevra. I'm sorry we didn't get acquainted sooner."

"So am I," replied Ginevra, clicking her glass to each of ours and taking another small sip, immediately followed by water.

A motorboat passed and the waters of the bay rocked Tess's floating summer home. Sarah Bernhardt as Hamlet, now carrying poignant associations with Alex's departure, presided over our "girls'" salon. Ginevra was only a year older than Alex.

Damn it, what had Ginevra been about to say about my playing an important part?

"I hope you don't mind," Tess was saying to Ginevra. "I gave a thought to clearing his dining table over there, but"—she waved helplessly at the Roman soldier and the peacock feathers and all the framed snapshots— "it was simply beyond me. However, I think we'll actually be cooler up here on our counter stools."

Out from the fridge came the orange Fiestaware platter. "Now, I'm not going to pretend I made all these cold salads from scratch. There's this wonderful deli on Miracle Mile. The only thing I did make, Emma, is your grandmother's seabreeze salad. I got up an hour early this morning to do it."

"That's really sweet of you, Tess." It would have been churlish to add, *It must have been hard, seeing you were up so late loading dental equipment.*

Now Tess was relating the story about Loney's seabreeze salad and how Loney had said to Tess, when Tess had come to lick her wounds with us in Mountain City, "Well, why shouldn't we be festive? *You're* here."

I was wondering whether the next story would be Tess being blown away in the hurricane of never-mind-what-year when Tess instead surprised me by comparing Loney with Edith Vine.

"They are both *gentlewomen* from a bygone era. Or, I regret to say, in Miss Edith's case, *was.* We won't see *their* stature again."

And here was Ginevra replying as if on cue (okay, Tess, so I underestimated your interviewing skills), "I'm sorry Miss Edith passed away before I got a chance to explain. I still dream about her. Sometimes we're sitting under her ficus trees and I'm telling her the whole thing, from beginning to end. I think she would have understood—Emma, how did you put it?—I think Miss Edith had enough wisdom and kindness to be able to hear the story behind the story. Once she said, 'Ginevra, let's you and me start another school.' "

"She said that to you?" Tess looked envious.

"Only in a dream, I meant." Ginevra uttered a sorrowful throaty laugh. "In real life, she would have said, 'Let's you and *I.*' "

Shared laughter. Then Tess said, "I have to tell you about the time she was trying to break an Alabama deb of her diphthongs. This was after I became Miss Miami Beach and hadn't found anyone I wanted to marry, so I was teaching at the academy . . . "

Out in the bay a larger craft zoomed by, and here came the high waves, sloshing against the deck, rocking the houseboat so violently I felt myself tipping sideways on the stool. The second of those two Cinzanos Lídia had sent up to my room probably had been one too many.

After a bleep of lost time, I heard myself saying in a woolly voice that I needed to visit the head.

"Oh, Emma, love, don't tell me I've gone and got you sozzled again."

"Oh, no, I'm perfectly fine. I just need to . . . say hello to those thousand and one mirrors behind the red door."

Managing not to fall off my stool, I got up and swayed off to the head.

Once inside, I splashed cold water on my face, then decided to help myself at Tess's cosmetics table. I slapped on some orange-smelling cold cream so rich it required a dozen tissues to wipe it off. I followed up with a toner "For Mature Skin," then experimented with a liquid foundation that felt like velvet.

After a brief toilet break, remembering to flush, I saluted all the mirrors—round, square, heart-shaped, Art Deco, framed in seashells, the masks of Comedy and Tragedy—with various snippets of my anatomy, and then curled up on the soft rug, still damp from Tess's shower, and took long, even breaths until things stopped spinning.

I could hear them laughing and talking on the other side of the door, the oft-repeated mantra of Miss Edith's name acting on my senses like a lullaby.

"OH MY Lord, Emma. You poor child. Your mother would kill me if she saw you wrapped around the toilet like that. What do you say to spending the night on board again? I can have you back first thing in the morning. I have to be at the office at seven."

"Unloading all those toothbrushes—"

"Oh, I can give you a toothbrush, and I can lend you a nightgown."

"No, I need to get back. I need to spend tonight at my hotel."

"I'll be glad to take her back," Ginevra said.

"Well, she's perfectly welcome to stay here again. But it's as you wish, Emma. Ginevra, the Julia Tuttle Hotel is right across from the Dupont Plaza."

"I know where it is. Edwin has his office suite at the Dupont Plaza."

———

"Where is this, Ginevra?"

"It's the beach. I thought you needed some air first."

"It's awfully dark for the beach. Where are the hotels?"

"This is Crandon Park Beach. Where I made a bonfire of those newspaper clippings."

"Where's Crandon Park?"

"Halfway across Rickenbacker Causeway. Farther on comes Key Biscayne, where Edwin and I live."

"Where is your famous Palm Island?"

"You'd want to take the next causeway, the MacArthur, for South Beach. The turnoff for Palm Island is halfway across."

"Have you ever gone back? I mean, just to look around."

"No, it doesn't interest me anymore. That was another time."

"It's very good of you to walk up and down with me like this. I feel a little better. At least I'm not seeing two of everything anymore."

"It was very good of you to show up when you did at the hospital. One good turn deserves another."

"What did you . . . ?"

"Yes, Emma?"

"I forgot what I was going to ask. These sweet alcohol drinks are just *poison*. I really must learn—"

"Yes. There were a couple of my girls I used to take on these night walks over on Palm Island. If I'd got to you earlier this evening, before you went to sleep in the john, I would have advised you to stick your finger down your throat, bring it all up, before it started circulating. Mind you, that's not a smart remedy for everyday use, but it does get the alcohol out. The best remedy of all is not to take the alcohol *in*."

"Your girls, the night walks . . . ?"

"They weren't supposed to drink on dates. There's nothing appealing about a woman who's had too much to drink. I should know. My mother was a drunk. Just order a single cocktail, I instructed them. And always ask for a glass of water on the side. For every sip of the cocktail, take three sips of water. But some of them disobeyed, especially the college girls. They thought they were immune. They considered themselves in a different class from the rest of us, they just thought it was cool to supplement their allowances this way. How are you feeling now, Emma? Have you remembered what you forgot to ask me?"

"It was something about . . . something you were going to say about my showing up at the hospital Wednesday night."

"Then I know what it was. Your appearing beside my gurney when you did, standing above me in your workday skirt and blouse, and your slightly awry French twist, your notebook all poised to capture my every utterance . . . You made me realize—I was still pretty groggy, but I said to myself, 'That's it, Ginevra! That young woman's got exactly what you've been dying for these past six years.' "

"Which was what?"

"A job, Emma, a *job.*"

Part Four

MARES

¡Siento que el barco mío
ha tropezado, allá en el fondo,
con algo grande!
¡Y nada
sucede! Nada . . . Quietud . . . Olas . . .

—¿Nada sucede; o es que ha sucedido todo,
y estamos ya, tranquilos, en lo nuevo?

OCEANS

I have a feeling that my boat
has blundered, down there in the deep,
against some tremendous thing!
And nothing
happens! Nothing . . . Stillness . . . Waves . . .

—Nothing happens? Or is it that everything
has happened
and we are here now, becalmed in the new?

—JUAN RAMÓN JIMÉNEZ

24.

W HAT DO YOU CALL those passages in a narrative where the hero is neither at the beginning nor even in the middle of his life's journey? When he's not yet setting forth in a new prologue or winding up a stage of his life in an epilogue?

Where was the word to describe . . . well . . . my life at the Broward bureau?

Even a word like "becalmed" was equivocal. Jiménez uses *"tranquilos"* in his poem to describe a hiatus after his boat has blundered into some tremendous thing. In English, "tranquil" can mean anything from peaceful to "not excitable; not preoccupied." Well, life at the Broward bureau was not excitable, and not peaceful, either, but I *was* preoccupied, much of the time, with how to profitably endure my exile there and how to prize (another equivocal word, but with that grace note of achievement) my way out.

I refused to think of myself as *stuck.* Being becalmed was not the same as being hellishly stuck, like the Ancient Mariner. Juan Ramón's boat might be arrested, but by the end of the poem it is sitting on an undercurrent of hopeful energy, and that is why I chose "becalmed" over "tranquil" in my translation. Quite possibly, I was "in the new," but just hadn't gotten my bearings yet.

Going back to Loney's magazine serials, where would I be?

The story so far: Emma has arrived in Fort Lauderdale, and . . .

Already, it was unsuitable. There was nothing remotely resembling a love interest in Fort Lauderdale. And the carryover love interest from Miami, Paul the married man from Miami Beach, wouldn't be allowed near Loney's magazines on the far end of a ten-foot pole. Paul was flying down next week, to finish emptying Stella's house on Espanola Way (a perfumer who had read my article was interested in buying Stella's business) and to attend the closing of P. Nightingale's, which had been bought by a Jewish foundation. We would have one of our good evenings together. I ardently anticipated a mutual refueling in the room he had reserved at the Diplomat.

Alex possibly could have made it into a Loney serial, had our farewell kiss been steamy, but it wasn't, even with the *Casablanca* background of whirring propellers on a nighttime airfield. I missed our conversations and worried about him.

Almost every day in the *Star* there were ominous news items. "Broward Deputies Prevent Takeoff" reported on a moonlit raid, in which undercover customs agents seized a cache of arms believed bound for Cuba at deserted airfield in Fort Lauderdale (*our* airfield!): thirty-five rifles with telescopic sights, fifteen Browning automatics, three Thompson light machine guns, eighty boxes of .30-caliber ammunition, and twenty boxes of Browning automatic ammo (aka "sample toothpastes and floss").

So far, Tess and Doctor Magnánimo had not made it into any illegal-export-of-arms headlines. Broward's political writer, Lance Moseley, a sweet middle-aged man with fur rather than hair on his scalp, covered this beat, along with police and crime.

My beats were:

the Port Authority commissioners meetings and anything to do with the Everglades (the Port Authority and Everglades person was on vacation);

the South Florida State Psychiatric Hospital (an Alma Olsen staple);

any women's stories that weren't about "society" (Broward's society editor, Candice McGee, an aging Southern belle, had the monopoly on those, always consulting her bible, the *Social Index*—she herself was in it—before starting a story).

Though I had inaugurated my Broward career with a splash of color ("A pair of flaming undershorts saved the life of Richard Mills, 47, who was lost for three nights in the Everglades" was my lead—the story made the front page of the Miami edition), I didn't need much empathy or much time to figure out that, to Kyle Breckinridge, our bureau chief, I was to be his vexation, his devilment, the daily hair in his soup.

Pausing beside my desk the first day while I rattled off a story, he took me in with a baffled incredulousness, and, after a moment, asked: "How can you type with those long fingernails?"

He and Alma Olsen were hand in glove. (Talk about fingernails, hers could have used a good nailbrush, for a start.) Both from Wisconsin, though they hadn't met until they came to the bureau, they were kind of a brother-and-sister team, midthirties-ish and complacently unkempt, with dirty-blond hair and plodding personalities. He was married, with "two and a half children," and she was single. In the three days she was "showing me the ropes" before flying off to her mother's bedside for an indefinite leave of absence, she and Kyle took frequent coffee breaks, and I could imagine the kinds of things they couldn't wait to say about me as they headed out the door.

ALMA AND I had gotten off to an unpropitious start on Wednesday when she came down from Broward to pick me up at the Julia Tuttle. Lídia, with her flair for an occasion and for self-dramatization, had gathered the entire staff, including Sunday's church recruits, to wave me off from the front steps. It was a scene out of a Victorian novel: "Farewell to the Young Mistress."

"You certainly have made a lot of friends in one week" was Alma's flat comment as she drove us away in her no-nonsense brown-and-tan Ford Fairlane.

"Actually, a week and three days," I corrected, flattered by Lídia's little send-off.

Long before we got to the city limits of Fort Lauderdale, I knew Alma had shut down her receptors to me. I was already the cuckoo in the sparrow's nest, the enemy to be carefully watched in order to be hindered and restrained.

I cannot tell myself why
You hold me back.
I do not know what the matter is.

—Juan Ramón Jiménez, "El Más Mío"

So that's where you got it, Bartleby. I found it in your volume of Jiménez.

THE LESS said about Alma's sparrow's nest, the better. Minimal set of Danish-modern furniture, brown fabric. Alma's weekend seashell collection marching across every surface. Writhing driftwood shapes blocking your way between rooms, snagging your clothes. No air conditioner, no TV—not that I had even once availed myself of the black-and-white set in Room 510 at the Julia Tuttle.

But now, on a certain weekday evening, Ingrid Bergman was going to be the governess in a TV production of *The Turn of the Screw.* The *Star* had run a laudatory piece about it that morning, and I was so desperate to see it that I considered—for about half a second, that is—throwing myself on the hospitality of the two unfriendly gents who rented the downstairs part of Alma's house. I knew they had a TV, because I heard it every night. They refinished and upholstered furniture, and were always loading and unloading their van, but for the entire month I had been here they had succeeded in avoiding me. One morning, as I clopped down the outside stairs on the way to work, they actually scurried back inside their apartment to keep from having to confront me.

It was starting. From below came Ingrid's rich voice with its distinctive cadences—I could hear only the tones, not the words. She was talking to a man. It must be the employer, the uncle in London who never wanted to be "bothered" about the children in the country.

I had purchased a ledger identical to Rod Reynolds's futures book and borrowed a glue pot and scissors from the office, and I was sitting on Alma's uncomfortable sofa, having dared to remove the seashells from the coffee table so I could lay my things out and proceed efficiently.

I first pasted in my Miami "appearances," except for the ones I had sent to Loney.

From below I heard the children's voices; the governess must have arrived at Bly. From somewhere else in my head I heard Lou Norbright saying, "You're good at color. The next step is for you to learn how the world works in black-and-white so you can put together the big picture."

For God's sake, Lucifer, give me a break. In one week and three days, I met a gangster walking a dog, sat behind his notorious boss at a funeral, became friends with the ex-madam who made your name, and helped two Cubans smuggle arms out of Florida. Shouldn't that count for something toward the big picture?

As I scissored my Broward stories, I felt close to Moira Parks. How many thousands of times her thumb and forefinger must have wielded those massive shears, slicing and separating the destinies, tucking each subject into its proper envelope, presiding over the patterns and the narratives—at least for those who *had* public narratives—right up until she clipped your final story.

I was alive and unhappy on all my cylinders, but I did not feel vanquished, not even in the dreary Broward office on its unshaded, dusty avenue, with its edgy, unglamorous staff—excepting maybe Candice McGee, who had a subversive streak and a wicked talent for mimicry. As long as I had this urge to keep track of myself and put my exile in perspective, I would not be vanquished.

"Saberse Transplantar." Know how to transplant yourself. That was one of the chapters in Don Waldo's little book of essays, *Pensamientos y Argumentos,* from Alex's box. It was not in an English translation, so I had been slogging through it with my dictionary, trying to finish before I drove down next week in Alma's car to interview him. (Rod Reynolds had let me keep this Miami assignment as a farewell present.)

"Know how to transplant yourself," Baltasar Gracián advises in Maxim 198 of his *Oráculo*, that canny handbook for getting on in life. "There are plants and persons who are esteemed only after transplanting themselves," the seventeenth-century Spanish Jesuit tells us. "Some who were scorned as fools in their own little corner attain worldly eminence in a foreign place."

But as every exile knows, the obverse must also be argued. Certain natures who flourished like the reigning bullfrog in their native bog might find their lordly song squelched or altogether extinguished (*apagado*) upon being relocated in a foreign pond.

Marisa had written one note on Julia Tuttle stationery. Lídia had thrown Luisa a birthday pool party, complete with balloons and piñata and exiled Cuban children like herself. "And just in case that *esbirro* Fidel isn't out by September, Enrique and I have enrolled Luisa in Assumption, a very good Catholic school on Brickell Avenue. However, Hortensia at the UN continues to hear promising rumors of the training camp—the CIA is involved now, they say! Don Waldo has accepted a professorship at the University of Miami, and he and Altagracia will continue to live in their suite at the Julia Tuttle. Lídia says she refuses to let them go."

BEHIND ALMA'S house was a chicken farm. Imagine the early mornings, when the sky grows light at six, and the heat and the smells press through the bedroom screens. After I had researched Baltasar Gracián, I was going to have to look up chickens. Unlike the birds I had grown up with—a peep here, a twitter there, rising into a dawn chorus—these chickens all seemed to start squawking at once.

My French twist was always wilting in the humidity—a far cry from Ginevra's affectionate description of it as "slightly awry." The Carolina-coed shoulder-length hair had to go.

I walked six doors down to the beauty shop on South Andrews Avenue and asked for a short haircut. Not as short as Ginevra's; I didn't have the facial scaffolding. I also treated myself to a manicure and bought a new platinum nail polish. "You are a sight for sore eyes in this office," said Candice McGee when I returned. "How would you like to come to Boca with me on Saturday for the fall fashion show? You'll be my guest at the Boca Raton Hotel for lunch."

ELSEWHERE IN the world, Marilyn Monroe, married to playwright Arthur Miller, went into a New York hospital to fix a "baby problem" so she could conceive; "Satchmo" was gravely ill with pneumonia in Spoleto (he "blew himself out"); Queen Elizabeth II of England was expecting her third baby; there were five thousand Castro-hating counterrevolutionaries training in the Dominican Republic; Princess Grace took a royal splash in the pool with the fifteen-month-old prince of Monaco; Hawaii became the fiftieth state; a thirteen-year-old mom was divorced in Columbia, Missouri; and Cuba had broken off diplomatic relations with the Dominican Republic.

Alex hadn't written, but what did I expect? A thick college-boy missive with one of those pennants stuck on the front of the envelope: *Anti-Castro U*? I had planned to know him for life. He would be that precious gift, an adoring male friend you could tell anything to. I tried to imagine him learning to load and shoot an assault weapon.

My Broward clippings were pasted up to date in my ledger. The Seminole twin papooses born in Dania; Broward's only woman plastic surgeon attending the International Plastic Surgeon Congress in London; Port Authority commissioners up for reelection commenting on how they got through election day; a hospital custodian fixing his hi-fi antenna electrocuted on his windy roof; the stowaway who begged the Port Everglades immigration officer who dug him out of a cruise ship's linen closet to put him in jail rather than send him back to Cuba.

On the Saturday morning I accompanied Candice McGee to the Boca Raton fashion show, I had left some dishes to soak in Alma's kitchen sink. During the hours of our happy outing (that day the society editor became the closest thing I had to a Broward collaborator), a dripping faucet did its worst. By early afternoon the men downstairs came home to find their ceiling leaking. Red-faced and furious, they were waiting for me when I got back.

"If we'd been ten minutes later, twelve yards of priceless silk brocade would have been ruined!" said one.

"Oh, Lord, I'm so sorry. I feel terrible. But at least the silk brocade wasn't ruined."

"No thanks to *you!*" snarled the other.

At last I had met my neighbors.

Two "Today's Chuckles" I had thought worth copying into my "Go, Tar Heels!" notebook:

"The measure of success is not whether you have a tough problem to deal with, but whether it's the same problem you had last year."

"Even if you are on the right track, you will get run over if you just sit there."

It looked as if the future of the Queen of the Underworld—if the Queen of the Underworld was to have a future—would be left up to me.

"Eavesdrop to your heart's content," Bisbee had said when I expressed my wish to overhear Ginevra telling her side of the story to the late Miss Edith. "Make it up . . . pursue your fascination while it's hot . . . just don't expect to have it run in the *Star.*" No word from Bisbee: maybe he was overwhelmed with his new responsibilities as Pompano bureau chief, or maybe he was embarrassed on my behalf by my abrupt exile to Broward. Or—who knows?—maybe he was finally getting his novel down on paper. Though I doubted it.

What if Ginevra were just suddenly to disappear? Walk out on her marriage, vanish? Where would she go? Perhaps it turned out that she had really loved the Mafia uncle all along and had gone to join him in Italy. I pictured him as something like Paul, only on the other side of the law. Or she might confide in the new friend she'd made, the young journalist: "You've made me realize I've got to get out or I'll die." And the young friend would pull out a card from her wallet—Major Erna Marjac. ("For many young women, we offer the only hope of independence.")

Could an ex-madam, even if she was still in her twenties, be accepted into the U.S. Army? I would have to research that. Maybe even consult Major Marjac.

Everyone would get new names, of course. Miss Edith was already Edna and Ginevra was Delfine. Maybe I would name the Mafia uncle Paolo. And what would Emma be called? It had to be a name that combined happily with a "-ness" suffix, as in "Emma-ness."

The one gift that boring Broward had vouchsafed me in spades was a glut of solitary time in which to assess my progress so far. And the more I thought of it, the more I prized my alliance with the Queen of the Underworld. Ever since Bisbee had related her story in his Walgreens Tutorial, even before my fortuitous meeting with her at the hospital, I had sensed she belonged to me. She was the worthy subject I had been waiting for, the opposite of the old maid who had died in her flyblown hamlet as my train passed without ever setting off on her own adventure. Norbright might have covered the notorious trial and given the Queen of the Underworld her name, but the rest of her was mine. She was my sister adventurer, another unique and untransferable self who had been places I hadn't and who had returned with just the sort of details I craved to imagine further.

MY MOST faithful correspondent was Mrs. Brown. Not that she was very eloquent or descriptive—she spoke much better than she wrote. That surprised me, but seeing her schoolgirl handwriting on an envelope addressed to me never failed to lift my Broward moods.

They were moving to Palo Alto. Dr. Brown had accepted a tenured teaching position in a department of psychiatry: "As long as he has a warm climate and can help people, Edwin doesn't care where he is.

"And I am going back to school. I still have some high school courses left to do, but they've got this thing for us 'oldies,' you just have to pass some exams. Edwin has already purchased some sample tests for me to practice on. I hardly dare to think what I may be doing one of these days!"

Because her letters were never more than a page, I didn't want to scare her off by sending epistles. So I restricted myself to one or two "bulletins" a week.

"Well, Ginevra, I didn't take touch-typing in high school, so you're ahead of the game there. At our Broward office you have to send your stories over the teletype machine, which has unmarked keys. I've been getting by with a keyboard I made for myself on a piece of cardboard that I balance on my lap while I'm 'sending to Miami,' but today the light finally dawned. After everyone left for the night, I took out my bottle of Platinum Frost nail polish and painted the numbers and letters and punctuation on the blank, black keys: 1, 2, 3, 4, 5, 6, 7, 8, 9, 0, Q, W, E, R, T, Y, U, I, O, P, etc., etc., etc.

"Now I am waiting for them to dry."

Acknowledgments

The author thanks Dan Starer for his rigorous and intuitive research. This is our seventh book together.

Robert Wyatt, once again, for vital early editorial guidance.

Nancy Miller, my editor at Random House, for her keenly sensitive fine-tuning of the manuscript.

The following books were of particular help:

Gustavo Pérez Firmat's *Next Year in Cuba*

Hugh Thomas's *Cuba, or The Pursuit of Freedom*

Howard Kleinberg's *Miami Beach: A History*

Harold Mehling's *The Most of Everything: The Story of Miami Beach*

Robert M. Neal's *News Gathering and News Writing*

Frank Luther Mott's *American Journalism*

Al Neuharth's *Confessions of an S.O.B.*

Queen of the Underworld

Gail Godwin

A Reader's Guide

An Afterword from Gail Godwin

Once upon a time, I found myself on the verge of being thirty, with not much to show for having lived to that symbolic age. I had traveled and worked abroad, plunged into many adventures, committed my share of wince-worthy mistakes, and chalked up some memorable failures. And now it was 1967 and I was back in the USA, working in Manhattan as a fact checker at the *Saturday Evening Post*. All around me are writers, but my humble job was only to check their facts, even in their fiction. If a cow in a short story had six udders, I had to phone the Farmers' Federation to make sure that number was correct.

Then an uncle in Texas died and left me a small legacy, just enough to pay for tuition and expenses at the Iowa Writers' Workshop (if I could get in), and I had sense enough to see this gift for what it was: a "soon or never" push to be the writer I'd wanted to be since age five. I was accepted by the workshop, on the basis of a story written in London several years earlier about a vicar who stumbles upon God on a rainy day, writes a book about it, goes on a transatlantic book tour, and loses his vision.

Off I flew to Iowa City, landing in a snowstorm. The airline lost my luggage: symbols abounding here. Then there I was, in Kurt Vonnegut's workshop—he had agreed to teach two sections in the spring of 1967, because so many people wanted to study with him. Under his benign tutelage I wrote the first draft of what would become my first published novel, *The Perfectionists* (1970).

The Chilean novelist José Donoso was a visiting lecturer in the workshop that spring, and I signed up for his Apprentice-Novel Seminar (also bulging at the seams to accommodate all those who wanted in.) Multilingual, passionate about literature, and with a sweeping knowledge of the history of the novel and its possibilities, José (or "Pepe," as his intimates called him) gave us a book list as rich as it was daunting. All were apprentice novels about artists: what literary handbooks call *künstlerromans,* or "artist-novels."

In artist-novels, the protagonists are struggling toward an understanding of how they will fulfill their creative missions. Donoso was particularly attracted to this topic because he himself had just written an apprentice novel, *Este Domingo,* or *This Sunday.*

Here is Donoso's reading list (in English translations, where necessary):

- Goethe's *Wilhelm Meister's Apprenticeship* (1795): the original apprentice novel; chronicles Wilhelm's progress from a naive, excitable youth to responsible manhood. He dreams of becoming a playwright and actor, but gradually comes to accept a more modest view of himself. (In a second novel, which we did not read, Wilhelm Meister travels, thinks, and ultimately becomes a surgeon.)
- Robert Musil's *Young Törless* (1906): an adolescent enclave of boys at a Bohemian military boarding school: a mystic, a future writer, a victim, and a bully. Törless, the future writer, searches for a bridge between rational, disciplined activity and destructive, forbidden impulses.
- Rainer Maria Rilke's, *The Notebooks of Malte Laurids Brigge* (1910; translated into English in 1930): written as a collection of diary entries by a budding young Danish poet, living alone in Paris.
- James Joyce's *Portrait of the Artist as a Young Man* (1916): revolves around experiences crucial to Stephen's growing awareness of his writer-vocation and his estrangement from his family, country, and religion.
- André Gide's *The Counterfeiters* (1926): the novelist Edouard keeps a journal of events in order to write a novel about the nature of reality. It's called *The Counterfeiters* and features two adolescent boys, Bernard

and Olivier, who leave home to find their true selves. They encounter many varieties of hypocrisy, wickedness, and self-deception.
(*The Counterfeiters* and *Malte* remain perennial favorites of mine.)
• Thomas Wolfe's *Look Homeward, Angel* (1929): Eugene Gant grows
up in Altamont, North Carolina, goes to the state university and to
Harvard, and at last sets out for Europe to fulfill his destiny as a
writer.

Donoso's seminar on the apprentice artist-novel was one of the high
points of my novelist education. How many ways you could present a
single theme! I loved listening to José's insight into the characters in the
novels and into the whole process of creating fiction. When I finally,
some thirty-eight years later, wrote my own apprentice artist-novel, I gave
his debonair cadences to Don Waldo Navarro, the Spanish man of letters, in *Queen of the Underworld*.

THAT THERE was not a single novel about a woman becoming an artist
on our reading list did not occur to me back in 1967. My failure to notice this wasn't really so amazing. After all, what "portrait of the artist as
a young woman" was out there at the time? Canada's Margaret Laurence
would not publish *The Diviners*, a complex, wide-ranging novel about a
woman writer in Manitoba approaching middle age and trying to come
to terms with past selves, until 1974. And it would be 1989 before her
countrywoman Margaret Atwood published *Cat's Eye*, about Elaine Ris-
ley, a controversial painter who has a retrospective in her old hometown
of Toronto and recalls the viciousness of the little-girl friendships that
were to influence the style and subject matter of her paintings. In 1981
Muriel Spark gave us *Loitering with Intent*, Fleur Talbot's memoir of her
young self as an apprentice-writer, who turns her secretarial job into
novel material, only to have the real people begin to act out scenes from
her manuscript.

The most helpful account of what it was like to be a writing woman
was Virginia Woolf's *A Writer's Diary* (1954), edited by Leonard Woolf,

who had selected entries dealing with his late wife's writing process from the personal diaries she had kept between 1918 and 1941. I remember lying on the Iowa River bank outside the English building, reading it like sacred text, underlining things like: "The test of a book (to a writer) is if it makes a space in which, quite naturally, you can say what you want to say. As this morning I could say what Rhoda said." Or this: "I am now in the thick of the mad scene in Regent's Park. I find I write it by clinging as tight to fact as I can, and write perhaps fifty words a morning. . . . I feel I can use up everything I've ever thought."

But where, in 1967, was a novel whose central focus was on a young woman feeling her way toward her writing vocation, while struggling with the usual woes and follies that accompany human development?

That I might write such a novel myself also did not occur to me back then. There were so many traps my protagonists were waiting in line to escape: the trap of family and society's expectations, of schools and workplaces, of loneliness and outsider-hood, of wrong marriages and wrong jobs; the traps of being born in a certain place and time and all the limits and restraints that go with that place and time—the traps that go with being born female.

My fourth novel, *Violet Clay* (1978), was about a painter, in her "soon or never" period. She's thirty-three, living in New York, illustrating Gothic romance novels and wondering why she hasn't become a real painter. I suppose *Violet Clay* could qualify for an apprentice-novel reading list, though its main focus is on the ghosts that keep her from risking her potential: her dead parents, her own "Gothic" upbringing in Charleston, South Carolina, and, finally, the suicide of her beloved uncle, Ambrose Clay, who published one novel and never completed another.

When I was writing *Queen of the Underworld*, I wanted to be totally inside the life of my twenty-two-year-old protagonist as she lived during her first ten days as a newspaper reporter in the Miami of 1959, sharing a hotel with the new Cuban exiles, who believed—as she did with them—that Castro would soon lay an egg and they would go home again.

I named her Emma Gant—the Gant after Thomas Wolfe's voraciously ambitious Eugene Gant; the Emma after Jane Austen's eponymous hero-ine, about whom Austen told a friend when beginning the novel: "I am going to take a heroine whom nobody but myself will much like."

Like Emma Woodhouse, my Emma Gant gets a crash course that takes her from self-delusion toward self-recognition. Notice I say "toward," not "to." Her self-discovery is only beginning at the novel's close, when she finds herself exiled, practically overnight, to the Broward Bureau. Both heroines also share a spunky self-regard, which often leads them to trample on the rights of others. However, Emma Woodhouse has a cor-rective mentor (and a future husband) in Mr. Knightley, while Emma Gant has neither.

I decided not to practice 20/20 hindsight by having a later, wiser Emma looking back on her apprenticeship. I also decided against dis-tancing myself from her foibles with authorial irony. Whatever my Emma thought and did, I would write, without smoothing over or pret-tifying. I let her be her complete, eager, resentful, vainglorious young self, determined to prevail as a writer. (Product Warning: If you would rather not remember your own youthful follies and overweening ambitions, this book may not entertain you.)

I also wanted to show Emma's emerging creative methods, what peo-ple and stories attracted her so much she couldn't stop spinning them forward in scenes of her own. And, conversely, how she recognized when a story idea was "not for her."

And I wanted to give her, even in her low moments, the certainty that I so love in young unpublished Fleur Talbot, the heroine of Spark's *Loitering with Intent*: "The thought came to me in a most articulate way: 'How won-derful it feels to be an artist and a woman in the twentieth century.' That I was a woman and living in the twentieth century were plain facts. That I was an artist was a conviction so strong that I never thought of doubting it then or since; and so, as I stood on the pathway in Hyde Park in that September of 1949, there were as good as three facts converging quite miraculously upon myself and I went on my way rejoicing."

———

346 A Reader's Guide

QUEEN OF the Underworld also has elements of the picaresque novel, the autobiographical narrative of a roguish character, usually young, moving through adventures and associating with people of all types, who serve as models or warnings, steppingstones or hindrances. The picaresque novel always rises out of a specific time and place, and depicts a society and an era in realistic detail. The first picaresque novel, *The Life of Lazarillo de Tormes and His Fortunes and Adversities*, published anonymously in 1554, was a mordant, satirical tale narrated by an orphan boy determined not to starve in scheming, church-haunted, poverty-ridden, mid-sixteenth-century Spain. He learns from, but is not defeated by, each of his mentors, or mentor/obstacles: from the shrewd blind man to the miserly priest to the proud but hungry squire to the mendicant friar to the greedy seller of indulgences. Lazarillo survives with his natural candor intact. He ends his career as Toledo's town crier (an early form of journalism!).

Though Emma Gant probably wouldn't classify herself as a rogue, she readily admits to her hard-earned stash of self-advancing "weaponry." After the dashing Major Erna Marjac, an Army recruiter, proudly confides to Emma on the train to Miami that "weaponry is opening up to women in an unprecedented way," Emma privately inventories her own "arsenal to date," the weapons she resorts to under duress: "guile, subterfuge, goal-oriented politeness, teeth-gritting staying power, and the ability, when necessary, to shut down my heart. Forces had been mobilizing inside me for the past eleven years to do battle with anything or anybody who might try to usurp me for their purposes again."

She also owns up to her inordinate ambition, which is not just about gaining her share of success, but avoiding the "usurpations" which would prevent her from taking full possession of her powers. She delights in the adventures of another picaroon, Felix Krull in Thomas Mann's *The Confessions of Felix Krull, Confidence Man: The Early Years*, written when Mann was in his late seventies. Emma finds similarities in their stories (both Felix and Emma know how to beguile, and both begin their careers by waiting tables) and she is crushed when she learns that Mann died before he could complete part two of *Felix*.

Reading Group Questions and Topics for Discussion

1. On page 117, Emma thinks it is "utterly spellbinding" that she is actually standing by the gurney of this former madam, "the Queen of the Underworld," she has been dying to meet. "How thankful I was that I'd headed straight for the hospital after the tornado. In a way, I realized, this amazing scene had been my creation." What does Emma mean by this? Can you cite other examples in the novel of Emma's resourcefulness?

2. This story takes place in 1959. Does the novel feel "historical" to you? How so? How not? How has the world changed since then?

3. Imagine Emma's story if it were unfolding today. How would this different era affect her chances to realize her ambitions? Would she have the same chances? Better? Worse?

4. On page 59, when Emma is in the newspaper morgue reading the news clips about Ginevra Snow, she thinks, "In some strange way I felt she offered an alternative version of myself. To follow her story would be to glimpse what I might have done had I been trapped in Waycross in her circumstances." Now go to page 335, where Emma again thinks of the Queen of the Underworld: "She was the worthy subject I had been waiting for, the opposite of the old maid who had died in her flyblown hamlet as my train passed without ever setting off on her own adventure. . . . She was my sister adventurer, another unique and untransferable self who

had been places I hadn't and who had returned with just the sort of details I craved to imagine further."

What are some "alternative versions" of yourself? Are there figures in your life, people you have glimpsed—or known—who embody some aspect of what you *don't* want to become (like Emma's imagined old maid)? And what about people who make you question what you would be like if you had been brought up in their history? And what about people who "have been places" you haven't and who "have returned with just the sort of details" you crave to imagine further?

5. *Queen of the Underworld* is dedicated "to the exiles, wherever you are now." Do you think the author refers to the Cuban exiles Emma meets in the summer of 1959, or does she mean it in a broader sense? Have you ever been an exile? From your homeland? From a life you felt was rightfully yours? How did your specific form of exile change your life?

6. The word "usurp," Emma tells us, has become her adversarial banner (page 9). She goes on to elaborate: "And the more I meditated on it, the more the 'usurp' word compounded in personal meanings. Not just kingdoms and crowns got usurped. A person's unique and untransferable self could, at any time, be diminished, annexed, or altogether extinguished by alien forces." What are your definitions of "usurpation"? What forms of it have you experienced?

7. Do you believe a person has a unique and untransferable self? Or not? Discuss how Emma's "story so far" might have been different if she had not believed in her unique and untransferable self.

8. *Queen of the Underworld* is a very populated book. How many of the characters can you recall? Which were your favorites? Which reminded you of someone you know—or of yourself? Which ones did you dislike? Which ones did you feel could have been left out? Which ones would you have liked to know more about?

9. Were there things about Emma that you disapproved of? If she had been a male character, would you have felt the same?

10. Were you surprised or disappointed by Ginevra's choices at the end of the book? Do you think Emma will ever write her novel inspired by "the Queen of the Underworld"? How might that novel be different from Ginevra Brown's story?

PHOTO: © JERRY BAUER

GAIL GODWIN is the three-time National Book Award finalist and the bestselling author of many critically acclaimed novels, including *A Mother and Two Daughters*, *Violet Clay*, *Father Melancholy's Daughter*, *Evensong*, *The Good Husband*, and *Evenings at Five*. She is also the author of *The Making of a Writer: Journals, 1961–1963*, the first of two volumes, edited by Rob Neufeld. She has received a Guggenheim Fellowship, a National Endowment for the Arts grant for both fiction and libretto writing, and the Award in Literature from the American Academy of Arts and Letters. She has written libretti for ten musical works with the composer Robert Starer. Visit the author's website at www.gailgodwin.com.

About the Type

This book was set in Centaur, a typeface designed by the American typographer Bruce Rogers in 1929. Centaur was a typeface that Rogers adapted from the fifteenth-century type of Nicolas Jenson and modified in 1948 for a cutting by the Monotype Corporation.

Join the Reader's Circle
to enhance your book club or
personal reading experience.

Our FREE monthly e-newsletter gives you:

- Sneak-peek excerpts from our newest titles

- Exclusive interviews with your favorite authors

- Fun ideas to spice up your book club meetings:
creative activities, outings, and discussion topics

- Opportunities to invite an author to your next
book club meeting

- Anecdotes and pearls of wisdom from other book group
members . . . and the opportunity to share your own!

- Special offers and promotions giving you access to
advance copies of books, our Reader's Circle catalog,
and much more

To sign up, visit our website at
www.thereaderscircle.com
or send a blank e-mail to
sub_rc@info.randomhouse.com

**When you see this seal on the outside,
there's a great book club read inside.**